# MANNHEIM REX

# MANNHEIM REX

## ROBERT POBI

THOMAS & MERCER

Text copyright © 2012 Robert Pobi

All rights reserved.

Printed in the United States of America.

No part of this book may be reproduced, or stored in a retrieval system, or transmitted in any form or by any means, electronic, mechanical, photocopying, recording, or otherwise, without express written permission of the publisher.

Published by Thomas & Mercer
P.O. Box 400818
Las Vegas, NV 89140

ISBN-13: 9781612184487
ISBN-10: 1612184480

## Author's Note

The New York Public Library has in its permanent collection a terrestrial globe known as the Hunt-Lenox Globe. Dating from 1510, it is the only known historical map with the inscription *HC SVNT DRACONES*—"hic sunt dracones," or "here are dragons"—over terra incognita. Less than fifty years later, the legend discussed in *Mannheim Rex* made its first printed appearance in Conrad Gesner's celebrated treatise *Historia animalium III*, of 1558. Although these are the oldest documented sources I was able to find, there is evidence that this legend dates as far back as 1230.

*After three-quarters of a millennium, there is still much in the way of terra incognita.*

◠ ROBERT POBI

*Now would I give a thousand furlongs of sea for an acre of barren ground.*

~ WILLIAM SHAKESPEARE, THE TEMPEST

Frank Knechtel slowed the boat and swiveled his head in the direction of the approaching storm. He took off the battered gold Ray-Bans and squinted into the ugly mass of clouds, trying to get a feel for her vitals; he had fished this lake long enough to know that when it came to weather, shit turned on a dime out here. The summer storms were the worst, screaming in from the north, washing out roads and downing trees like a malevolent force in a science-fiction movie.

As he turned, the thick rolls of stubbly flesh on the back of his neck squeezed out sweat, and a small part of him was happy that rain was coming—maybe it would cool things down a bit. Then he saw the ugly flash of lightning and his relief was short-circuited by the electrical charge he saw dancing in the clouds. It was going to be a bad one.

The slate thunderhead rolled in fast, devouring the land in great spasms of rain and wind and lightning. Behind the jagged cliff of stormcloud, brittle snaps of white pulsed in the dark body like the irregular firing of a vast volcanic heart. The cloud bank had flattened the horizon and the atmosphere was pregnant with the electricity beating in its chest. Ten miles off. Maybe less.

Frank slipped the throttle into neutral and pulled the big St. Croix musky rod out of the holder bolted to the oarlock. The cork handle was slick with warm beads of moisture, as if it too were sweating. While he worked, he kept glancing at the anvil head moving in, hoping that he wouldn't run out of time. A flash of lightning detonated and the lake went from blue to white for an instant. A few seconds later the sound wave screamed in and it pushed the oxygen from the air and he tasted the electrical charge in the atmosphere. He spit over the side, hoping to get rid of the metallic film that seemed welded to his teeth.

Frank pumped the handle of the reel and the big spool recovered line quickly. He felt the lure biting the water and the braid sung through the guides on the rod. There was another mortar round of thunder and the boat actually shook. He doubled his retrieval speed and spat again.

And then his lure snagged on something.

He yanked back on the heavy rod, the hundred-and-thirty-pound line twanging with each jolt he put into it, then checked the Lawrence fish finder with a precise pivot of his massive head. The bottom was fifty feet down. What the hell could he have hooked out here in the open water? Submerged log, maybe. If the storm hadn't been coming, Frank would have circled around and tried to work his lure free, but the wall of darkness had touched the far end of the lake, swallowing the dam, and he could see the glint of rain hammering down. Then he saw the rainbow shards of light dancing like sparks and realized that it wasn't rain at all; it was hail. Sonofabitch. If he didn't want to get stuck out in the middle of an electrical storm with bullets falling from the sky while waving his own personal lightning rod, he'd have to cut loose and head for shore right now. But at forty-five bucks he hated to let the big handcrafted lure go. Another jolt of electricity cracked the sky and made his mind up for him. He reached for his knife just as the snag started to move.

The bright slash of the line cut through the water and Frank yanked back, leaning into it. The rod tip bent, and he pulled with his shoulders, feeling the unmistakable throb of muscle at the other end of the line, telegraphing out to him. It was massive, sinuous, sure.

A wave sloshed over the gunwale as the wind set in. The line zagged back, then pulled taut, and his reel screamed against the strain on the drag.

Frank had spent four years stationed at Subic Naval Base in the Philippines and he'd eyeballed everything from giant bluefin to Mark 48 torpedoes slicing through the water, and nothing he'd ever seen had moved this fast. Not even close. He pulled back again and the whine of his reel rose above the howl of the wind that had started to wail.

The boat swung like a compass needle, pulled by the force he had hooked. He couldn't stop it. Hell, he couldn't even slow it down. The motor was gurgling in the irregular swells, coughing blue smoke thick with the smell of oil. The pulse of the sky at the edge of his vision caught his attention once again and he glanced up.

The wall of hail was thrashing across the surface of the lake, bearing down on him. There was another shot of lightning and the world lit up in eerie blues and the air ripped open with the roar of thunder. He had to cut loose and head for one of the shallow bays to wait out the storm or he'd get chewed up out here. Whatever the lightning didn't fry, the hail would smash to bits.

He slashed at the line with the big Buck knife.

The world went supernova again as Mother Nature slammed a billion volts into the lake. The shock wave hammered him back over the bench, and he tripped. He reached out to steady himself. Line wrapped around his wrist and for a second he felt a pinch. There was another violent surge from the lake itself and the line dug into his arm. Then the tension let go and he stumbled back. There was a splash.

He felt a stinging in his fingers and looked at his hand. It was gone. Neatly. Cleanly. Gone.

The braided line had garroted his hand.

A piss-rope of blood drooled out. Thick drops splattered his boots and turned the water sloshing around the bottom of the boat pink at first. Then quickly black.

Then the sky opened up. The staccato clatter of hail bouncing off the boat almost drowned out his single, girlish scream.

Frank fumbled with his belt. Managed to get it off. Pulled it tight around his arm to slow the bleeding. Pain hit. He howled again. Grit his teeth. Then saw the shadow moving just below the surface of the lake. The hail was pounding the water, distorting it, but it was huge. Massive. Something about the way it behaved transmitted more than its shape could. There was purpose in the way it moved. It wanted something.

Frank scrambled back against the transom, his eyes never leaving the nightmare that surged through the water, skirting his field of vision. He tripped on the bench and almost went sprawling backward, over the gunwale. He stood at the transom, crying, staring into the water. It wasn't going away. It was getting closer, circling in.

There was no longer the sensation of blood drooling out of his wrist or of the hail clattering down; his universe had been reduced to the black shape that wanted him. He knew it wanted him. He could feel it.

What was it?

Why was it doing this?

But he knew. It was here to feed.

Somewhere above him there was a flash of lightning and the air cracked with the pressure. Frank stumbled. His thigh hit the throttle and engaged the propeller. The boat lurched forward with a jolt.

There was a split second as he teetered on the edge of his balance. Then he fell, screaming, into the water.

His boat! He needed to get to—

The boat chugged steadily off into the haze of the storm and was soon gone, leaving him alone. With *it*.

He spun, searching.

It found him first.

He heard his humerus break before he felt it and the thing pulled him down into the black, toward the center of the earth. His body seesawed with the pulse of its muscles as it pulled him away from the world.

*Please stop. Oh God, it hurts. STOP! Please. Please, please, pleasepleasepleaseplee—*

Stars filled with phosphorescent blisters of pain burst behind his eyes. His lungs screamed for air. Something else broke deep inside him and fear replaced all the things he had ever hoped for.

He tried to free himself. Each movement to get away brought him a jolting slap of hurt. He punched at the snout. Connected with bone and slime and teeth. His palm ripped open. Hit it again. And again. Suddenly he was free. Floating. Knechtel kicked his legs and his life vest brought him up.

He broke into the mist and sucked in greedily, filling his lungs. Water splashed into his mouth and down his throat. He coughed. And screamed. *What the fuck is it?* was all he could think.

Get to shore. He looked around and could see it at the edge of the haze. Three hundred yards. Maybe less.

The first stroke was awkward and he faltered over onto his side. He tried again and the same thing happened. The bad arm was not working. He reached over and felt the denuded bone and slimy tendrils of tendon sticking out of his shoulder. There was no arm. It was *gone*. And that was when the pain went supernova. Bucketloads that spilled through his body and set his mind on fire.

There was the swish of something in the water in front of him and he felt the pulse of a wave as it moved by.

Then it came back and grabbed him.

It clamped down onto his remaining arm. Yanked him under. All the fuses in Knechtel's mind exploded in a flash of fear. He felt his body pulling to the surface, the buoyant life vest doing what it was designed to. But the freight train driving him down just kept going. There was nothing he could do, not against the force taking him into the earth. He felt a sharp snap as his eardrums imploded and white noise of static filled what few corners of his mind weren't packed with agony. Blackness started creeping in and he started to lose consciousness. Then, for some reason, it let go.

The life vest pulled him toward the white world above. The fuses in his mind that were not yet blown kept him holding on to consciousness. For the second time he bobbed to the surface.

The first breath burned down his throat. He coughed and vomited, bile splattering out his nose in red strings. The world spun dizzily and he saw the distant outline of the shore flash by. He spun in a whirlpool created by whatever it was circling him.

He had to make it to shore. To get away from it. Far away.

Knechtel tried to swim and nothing happened. It took a second for him to realize that he wasn't moving because he had no arms. They were both gone. *No*, a voice somewhere back there at the edge of consciousness said, *not gone—bitten off.* He kicked his legs and he spun in place, amid the widening pool of blood.

There was a surge of pressure as it hit him from below and he knew he had shit himself. For an instant the pain was brain blinding. And then it...wasn't. He hardly felt anything at all except disbelief. But he heard it. The sound was intimate. And with some disconnection he realized that his body was being torn apart. Chewed. Crunched. Consumed.

Below the foaming surface of Lake Caldasac, Frank Knechtel's head slowly swirled toward the bottom. His mouth instinctively sucked for air that, had it come, would have done no good whatsoever because he no longer had a body to process oxygen. It spiraled down into the cold water, blood billowing out as it sank.

The last message his brain received before the electrical impulses stopped firing had been sent from his eyes.

Madness was coming for him.

Frank Knechtel's face, although no longer technically alive, had time to involuntarily wince before it was torn from his skull.

**2**

*That's my last duchess painted on the wall, Looking as if she were alive.*

⌒ ROBERT BROWNING, MY LAST DUCHESS

NEW YORK CITY

LATE JUNE

He sat in the big oak Morris chair watching the first marmalade hues of morning grudgingly bleed into the sky. An untouched day-old cup of coffee sat on one dark waxed arm of the chair and a stainless-steel pistol lay in his lap. On the rug, half under a table, lay an open whiskey bottle, the contents reduced to a shallow crescent of brown against the clear glass.

Across the street the Museum of Natural History was still, the walkway on Eighty-First barren of life. It was early, not yet five thirty, and traffic was just starting to work its way onto the streets, identifiable by the rumble of delivery trucks and the sharp slingshot of cabs in a rush. In another hour the asphalt arteries would start to bog down, the metal cholesterol of traffic clogging up the blood flow of the city. An hour after that the heat would start, quickly pushing New York to the brink of cardiac failure. But Gavin Corlie thought of none of this. He stared out the window trying to build up enough courage to kill himself—a desire that three months of drinking hadn't been able to convert into any form of action. *Pussy*, he thought, and stood up.

Gavin stretched, pushing the rigor mortis caused by the hours of catatonic inactivity out of his muscles with a labored groan. He felt old and very tired. He picked up the coffee and the jelled surface moved slightly, tight lines pulling across its skin. Christ, he thought, even coffee forms scar tissue. And it hit him. Again. Chelsea was dead. He closed his eyes.

What felt like a long time later he opened them and found himself staring at the bottle of Royal Lachnagar sitting on the blood-red rug beside the chair. Another drink suddenly seemed like a good idea. He picked up the bottle and held it up to the window, the centrifugal force swirling the last ounce around in the bottle, and he grunted in satisfaction. Small mercies. He swallowed the last of the scotch, dropped the empty bottle to the carpeted floor with a thud, and turned away from the new day rising over the city.

He padded across the warm expanse of the big Persian. As he passed the coffee table, his knee sideswiped a pillar of condolence cards and they scattered like a flock of pastel birds. Shannon, his assistant, took care of the bills and groceries, but she had insisted on leaving these with him. They were personal, she had said. Sure they were. What could be more personal than a saccharine pseudohaiku offering condolence that your wife had been crushed beyond recognition, incinerated, and placed in a decorative receptacle for safekeeping. Safekeeping from what? Getting old? He let the Easter-egg-colored envelopes avalanche over onto the floor and kicked most of them under one of the silk velvet sofas that flanked the big fireplace. Fuck it, he thought. Most of the letters were from fans and industry people he didn't even know. Then he had an idea.

He put the cold coffee down on the table and shuffled the cards into a pile in a halfhearted attempt at order, going so far as getting down on his hands and knees and pawing under the sofa for the ones he had kicked into the shadows. If he was going to do something, he was going to do it right. When they were stacked pretty much like they had been before he knocked them over, he picked the pile up with both hands and threw it into the fireplace. He stood back, pressed the button on the remote, and watched the big gas grate flicker to life. It didn't take long for the pile of paper to start burning in earnest. Ashes to ashes. Thank you. And good night.

He walked down the hall, past the twenty-seven dust jackets displayed in black metal frames that lined the marble passage, heading for the kitchen. He brushed against one and it tilted over on its hook. He didn't look up, but turned the corner to the kitchen on autopilot, fifteen years of living in the apartment having hammered in the coordinates.

The lights in the kitchen were on, the dishes had been done, and there was a cold roast chicken on the counter along with utensils. Gavin made a mental note to thank Maria—besides Shannon, she was the only other person looking after him right now. He had to stop yelling at her. A raise probably wouldn't hurt the situation, either. Especially in light of his surly behavior. It would be her third in as many months. *Great*, he thought, *just great. I'm paying the maid to take abuse. Evidently I am doing just fine.*

As he entered the kitchen he absentmindedly ran his hand along Ernie's spine. Ernie was an ancient ten-foot-long taxidermied Nile crocodile that Chelsea had bought him as an anniversary present after his second book had gone bestseller. The crocodile had come from an antique shop downtown and she had brought him home strapped to the roof of the cab like some great white hunter with a prized kill. It had been one of those little ways she had pinched herself, back when they were still worried that someone was going to take it all away and yell, *Surprise! We were just kidding! You have to give it all back!* So Ernie had moved in, a bizarre addition that their decorator had hated but Gavin had insisted go on top of an antique sideboard that took up one whole wall of the kitchen. The hide on top of Ernie's ancient head was worn smooth and shiny from Gavin's habitual petting whenever he came in. He no longer noticed—or felt he could stop—doing it.

His hand touched Ernie's head and his eyes froze on the marble urn sitting in the middle of the table. Dust and ashes and maybe a little chunk of bone that hadn't been pulverized, amounting to nothing that even remotely resembled the woman he had spent almost half of his life with. He had seen it there every day for weeks, something about it comforting, maybe even welcoming. But this morning, after endless nights of no sleep and too much booze, he suddenly felt a little more alone and a lot more out of place in his own life.

He felt his hand tighten around Ernie's upper jaw and his fingers found purchase between the yellow teeth. There was no forethought in his action—it was the kind of stupid nonsensical outburst that he had never given in to. Until now.

He ran at the window, Ernie clasped in his arms like a battering ram out of a psychotic's dream. The crocodile's ancient tobacco-colored snout connected with the glass and for a brief instant the glass actually bent. The window and the reptile put Newton's law to the test. Then the double-pane exploded and Ernie was catapulted out into the great wide open.

Silence disappeared as the wail of the alarm cut the air into high-pitched shards that spun around his head. Gavin leaned out the opening and watched the creature drop thirteen floors, a spinning Messerschmitt of hide and teeth screaming toward the asphalt at terminal velocity. Ernie's tail trailed out behind him like a dark oil fire.

Ernie hit the middle of Eighty-First Street in a spectacular explosion of whatever it was they used to fill taxidermied crocodiles with in the nineteenth century. There was a heavy screech of rubber and a bone-crunching crack as a delivery truck barreling down Eighty-First finished whatever damage the fall hadn't inflicted on poor old Ernie and he relinquished his hold on this world in one final cloud of leathery dust. His jaws bounced up on the sidewalk like a novelty-store gag. The driver of the truck skidded to a halt, got out, and looked up.

Gavin turned back to the kitchen, slid down the wall until he was sitting in the pile of glass, and started to weep with the shrill wail of the alarm screaming around him.

**3**

From somewhere in the comfort of sleep, Shannon Leibowicz heard the sound. At first it was distant and faint, like the chirping of birds, and she almost let it slip away. But it grew. Louder. Nearer. The noise solidified, tumbling into something recognizable, familiar even. It sounded like a bell. Then her girlfriend's voice woke her up.

"Get the phone." Amy let out a groan and buried her face in her pillow. "I bet it's him again."

Shannon reached over. Pulled the phone off the stand. Managed to press the Answer button.

"Hmpmp?" was all that came out.

"Shannon, it's me. I know it's your day off and—"

"Um, Gavin?" She was awake now, her CPU had kicked in. For the most part, anyway.

"I know—"

"No, Gavin, I don't think you do. Is everything all right?"

"I can't stay here anymore. I want to leave the city. I *have* to leave the city. Bring the real estate listings we talked about the other day."

Shannon looked over at the clock. It was almost seven a.m. She had squeezed in an extra hour of sleep—not bad for her day off. "I'll be there in about an hour. Put on some coffee."

"Thanks, Shannon." There was a pause and she thought she heard him crying, then he continued, "Thank Amy too. I appreciate this."

All she could think to say was, "I'll bring bagels."

But he had already hung up.

# 4

The elevator stopped and Shannon stepped into the plush apartment. The roses on the center table were long stemmed and deep red; Gavin had a fresh bouquet brought up every third morning—Chelsea had loved roses. For a second she stared at them, noting their lush beauty in the dark atmosphere of what had once been a happy home. The contrast was not lost on her.

Then she saw a thick yellow extension cord that snaked off down the hall. Shannon followed it to where it wound into the kitchen. There were two men in coveralls replacing the big kitchen window. Against the doorjamb, standing with his arms crossed, was Marty Shriver, the building's superintendent. When Shannon stopped in the doorway Marty nodded a curt greeting and came over.

"What happened?" she asked Marty.

"Apparently Mr. Corlie had some sort of an accident. His lizard went through the window. Smashed into the street." Shriver's tone told her that he didn't believe that this was any sort of an accident.

"Anyone hurt?" Subtext: *Do I need to call a lawyer?*

"Only Mr. Corlie and the lizard. Cut his feet up pretty bad—Mr. Corlie, that is. Lizard's got no feet left. Well, maybe one." Shriver shrugged. "Mr. Corlie's off in the apartment somewhere." Shriver glanced down at his shoes, then back at

Shannon. "I don't mean to step out of line here, but maybe he shouldn't be spending all this time alone."

Marty had always been reliable, especially during the media frenzy after Chelsea's death. Shannon knew he was speaking out of concern. "I appreciate you taking care of this. I'm going to go find Gavin. You need anything, you call me, okay? How 'bout some Knicks tickets?"

Marty's face spread out into a grin. "That's not necessary."

"Oh yes it is." She turned to leave the kitchen, then paused. "Marty?"

Shriver's face still hadn't recovered from the Knicks tickets.

"Can you—?"

"Nobody has to know, Miss Leibowicz."

Shannon sighed in relief; Marty had been here as long as she could remember for a reason. "I appreciate it."

"For Knicks tickets, I'll help you bury bodies." Marty smiled, completely won over. "Besides, Mr. Corlie's a good guy. He didn't deserve what happened."

"No one does," she said, and went to find Gavin.

In the hall, one of Gavin's dust jackets hung lopsided in its frame, the color image of the author grinning at the camera with boyish charisma. Before. Way back when.

He was in the living room, sitting in the big oak seat by the window with his wounded feet scabbed to the floor and his hands gripping the chair arms, looking very much like a man in an electric chair.

She dumped her coat, laptop, and paper sack of bagels on the dark buffet against the wall and pulled a big ottoman over in front of his chair. She sat down quietly.

The scotch bottle on the floor was empty and out of the corner of her eye she saw a crystal tumbler that had rolled under an end table, the morning light glinting off its wheel-cut surface. There was a yellow crust on the rim. A stainless-steel pistol sat in his lap. Right now she knew that she had to say something smart.

Shannon took in his features, trying to discern what was going on behind his eyes. You didn't have to be a psychiatrist to see that Gavin Corlie was sad.

His face was lean—it had *always* been lean—but now it looked hollow, deserted, as if he no longer lived in himself. He hadn't shaved in days and a dark shadow of stubble had set in, almost a beard now, peppered with gray. As long as she had known him, he had looked older, but now he looked ancient, used up. In a little over two months he would be turning forty.

Gavin's long hair fell onto his face and wide streaks of silver had come out. The intense brown eyes were the color of old pennies and rimmed with red, as if copper oxidation was working its way out from the pupils. He was dressed in a pair of black jeans and a black shirt, this one velvet, open to the middle of his chest out of neglect, not an attempt at style. On the naked expanse of his arm, she could see the beginning of the tattoo that she knew snaked up, covering the flesh from his wrist to his shoulder and wrapping around onto his back. He wore no socks and it made his bloody feet all the more poignant.

For the most part his feet had stopped bleeding, the blood caked and cracked around his soles. But they needed to be cleaned up. Probably by a doctor. If he was lucky, he wouldn't need stitches. And there was the floor to deal with.

"Gav? How can I help?" It wasn't much but it was all she had to offer.

"I think that I'm losing my mind." His mouth barely moved. "I could have hurt somebody with that stunt."

Shannon turned her head to look out at the city. What was there to say? She had found him by following bloody footprints. There wasn't a lot of subtlety at work here. "But you didn't. You're not crazy, Gav—you're unhappy. There's a difference."

"I'm through with this place."

"Before I call the movers we need to get you cleaned up. I'm going to get Dr. Stephenson. You look like a fire walker."

"Fire walkers don't get hurt."

"A *failed* fire walker, okay? And the floor is a mess."

Gavin kept his eyes focused on the monolithic structure of the museum across the street. "I didn't walk on the carpet."

Shannon looked around. "See? You're thinking clearly."

She reached over, lifted the heavy revolver, and gently slipped it into her jacket pocket. She knew him better than almost anyone, knew how his mind worked, and it wasn't what he let out that frightened her—the stories that scared people on seven continents—no, what scared Shannon was what was on the inside. Gavin Corlie was wired differently than most people; the episode with that stalker had been a perfect example of how he thought out of the box. "I'm going to call Stephenson. Wait here."

"It hurts too much to walk and I'm too sober to crawl."

"That's a start."

\*\*\*

Later, Gavin stood in the bathroom, the shower belting steam behind him. He stared at his ghostly outline in the mirror, wondering when he was going to start feeling like he hadn't died along with his marriage. But he knew, just like when he knew that a story was going to work, that he was never going to be okay again.

But he might be able to heal a little. It wasn't much in the way of comfort but it was better than sucking up a round from his .357. *Change your thinking*, Shannon had said. *Start by taking a shower.* So he had.

Gavin put his hand out and wiped away the steam on the mirror, examining the face staring back at him. "Gavin, my boy, you look like shit." And it was true. "So, where do you begin?"

A shave was all that came to mind.

And that's what he had to look forward to. A shave.

Maybe even a haircut.

When he met Shannon back in the living room, he looked like a new man. Or, if he thought about it, a less shitty version of the old one.

Shannon stood up and smiled, her mouth looking like it had more teeth than it did. "What did you do to your hair?" She circled him.

"Cut it."

"Yourself?"

He nodded. Smiled weakly. He felt good. Better anyway. "Stood in the shower with some scissors and lopped off everything that I thought should go. Thanks for not taking all the pointy objects away from me."

"Gav, we've been paying two hundred bucks an appointment down at La Cirque for the past five years and Jean never did a job like this."

He smiled again. "Not bad?"

"Are you kidding?" She had never seen him with short hair—the long dark mane had been as much his trademark as the tattoo and the black clothes he wore, an anomaly in an industry marked by the clean-cut novelists that dominated the media as America's pop writers. The boy had grown into a man. "Gav, I can get you an Absolut ad if you want. Maybe even American Express."

"If they'll give me free booze, go with the vodka people." He wore black jeans and a black linen shirt, moccasins on his feet. Shannon could see the edge of a Band-Aid peeking up out of one shoe. "I felt a little like Geldof's Pink in *The Wall*. Wasn't sure it would fly."

"It beats the hell out of bloody footprints all over the apartment."

They sat down on the sofa facing the fireplace. He tucked his feet up under himself, the new bandages winding up out of his moccasins, a heavy mug of coffee cradled in his hands. Shannon waited patiently for him to start talking.

Gavin stared intently at the fire. "I need to leave for a while." He took a sip of the coffee, his eyes off on the flames.

Shannon followed his gaze and saw the charred corners of envelopes around the perimeter of the hearth. She recognized them and smiled. "London?" He had a flat in South Kensington and had always liked spending the autumn there.

Gavin shook his head. "Somewhere new. Somewhere I won't see Chelsea." He remembered the Café Nero, across from Christie's on Old Brompton Road, Chelsea sitting in one of the leather booths and dumping five sugars into the strong Italian coffee that she drank because she thought it made her look less American even though she preferred hot chocolate. He remembered her green eyes smiling over the rim of the cup. Back before they had been pulverized by a man named Mole Roper who had fallen asleep behind the wheel of his Lincoln Continental.

"Gav?" Shannon's voice melted the image.

"Sorry, I was…never mind." Gavin blinked and the photo in his head faded. But it would be back; grief, the gift that kept on giving. "I have to go somewhere I won't be reminded of her," he repeated.

"Greenberg said that you shouldn't make any decisions for a full six months." But the tone in her voice said that she understood.

"Arthur's my accountant—he keeps track of my money, not my life." He took a sip of the coffee, swirled it around in his mouth, then continued. "I'm not selling this place, I couldn't—Chelsea loved it here. But I need someplace new.

Someplace I can think. Someplace I can write. I mean fuck, why do I have all this goddamned money if it's not going to help me?"

"You want to work again?"

"Sure I want to. Can I?" He shrugged. "I don't know. I don't have any ideas. At least not any new ideas and I don't want to work with old ones. Not now. I need something that doesn't come with any baggage. I feel like some fat fucker in a flat-top crawled out from under the bed and twisted my head off." His voice dropped to a whisper. "I do know that I need to do something and I need to do it now. If I don't, you're going to get a call from some cop telling you that I followed old Ernie out the window."

She opened up her briefcase and pulled out a pile of manila folders. "I've short-listed it to nine properties. There are a few that stand out."

He took the papers from her hand, the happy pink paper-clip incongruous in these surroundings.

The first two fit the bill mechanically; they had all the qualities that should have made them right, but something was missing. The first was too close to the neighbors. It flew into the fireplace. The second had been renovated and what had been a charming late-nineteenth century cottage had been Holly-Hobbied into a parallel dimension. Chintz, phony French fabrics, and junk masquerading as shabby chic furniture lent a saccharine malignancy to the space. Fireplace again with a "What the fuck is wrong with people?" to answer any questions Shannon had about whether or not he liked the place.

He opened the next file folder to a color print of a country home from the classic period of American Federal architecture: stone facade, three big chimneys growing out through the roof, Palladian window. Beyond the big oaks he could see a stone boathouse, a wide planked dock. The black expanse of a lake.

21

"This is it." He picked up the photograph and put his nose close to the paper, trying to see beyond the pixelated image into the soul of the building: the wide stairs he knew were there; the oak-beamed ceilings; the stone hearths, blackened by two hundred years of fireside meals, drinks, after-dinner humor, and late nights spent waiting for a baby to be born or a fever to break; the worn-down spots on the floor in front of the master bedroom door where the dogs had slept; and the cellar, where children had played Blind Man's Bluff, maybe had their first kiss, their first clumsy lovemaking. This house was alive, he could feel it, and it was speaking to him. "Where is it?"

"Five hours upstate. Near a town called New Mannheim." She dropped her vision to a yellow legal page decorated in her neat writing. "I spoke to McFee." Roger McFee was an advisor that Gavin worked with at the FBI. The relationship was 100 percent public-information only; McFee had helped Gavin flesh out a lot of work over the years. "On paper the place looks great. Except for maybe one detail. Total population five thousand, two hundred and one individuals as of 1994; no significant population growth suspected since last census—plus or minus fifty—FBI rhetoric, *not mine*."

"Why do I hear a *but* coming here?" Gavin asked.

Shannon scanned the file. "There have been a lot of fatalities on the local highway—at least in the past. This year things have been pretty quiet—only one vehicular death. Four drownings so far, which is about the same as every year. It's on the fringe of the tourist area. Very few break-ins. Suicide rate is higher than the national average by twenty-one points but homicide is well under the national average.

"One bar. It's been there since the turn of the century. General store, sporting-goods store, local haberdasher, hardware store. Massena is half an hour away, has everything you need. Groceries and a Walmart." She stopped, looked up, winked at him. "Walmart. Remember those days?"

Gavin's eyes crinkled up at the edges, like an aerial photograph of river tributaries. "Never thought I'd be able to afford the new clothes at Walmart. Man." He shook his head, wondering how he had got to here and now. "What's the name of the lake?"

"You're gonna love this." Shannon looked up from the page. "Lake Caldasac. It was given to the English by the Algonquin, who got it from the French."

Gavin raised an eyebrow, impressed that she had bothered to look. "It's phonetic French. Caldasac. Cul-de-sac. Dead end." His mouth moved into a line that looked like it might smile. "Five hours?" As things stood, his office was precisely thirty-eight steps from his bedroom—forty-nine if he went around the far side of the coffee table. Five hours was far enough.

"Buy it," he said.

# 5

*If we no longer insist on our notions of how Nature ought to behave but instead stand before Nature with an open and receptive mind, we find that common sense often doesn't work.*

~ CARL SAGAN, THE DEMON-HAUNTED WORLD

## LAKE CALDASAC, NEW YORK.

Finn Horn pushed the big red sombrero off his head so it hung on his back like Eli Wallach's in *The Good, the Bad and the Ugly*. He pulled the quick-release lever and the right arm of the wheelchair slid back and clicked home. With a routine gone through more times than he could count, he tightened the strap around his thighs, picked up the deadweight of his legs, and swung them around so that they hung over the wheel. Reaching up, he grabbed hold of the monkey bars his mom and Mr. Hecht from next door had installed for him—good old-fashioned cast-iron piping from the big Home Hardware over in Massena—and lifted his weight out of the chair. The piping was rough, rusty, but provided good grip. Hand over hand, he negotiated the metal contraption, finally stopping his swinging body over the seat. Using two vertical bars, with a motion that his mother called *milking the cow*, he dropped into the seat at the back of the eighteen-foot skiff with the homemade Jolly Roger hanging proudly at the bow.

"All right," he said to no one. "Done." For the first month after the bars had been installed, his mother had insisted on being there every time he had used them, her body flexing to jump every time he missed a hold, swung too far out, or grunted with the effort. But there had been no accidents and she had, in the way that mothers do, learned to trust him. Besides, the lake had become his unofficial babysitter since she had to work all the time. Out here he was happy. And safe.

Three years ago, a week shy of his tenth birthday, Finn's spine had collapsed. There had been no forewarning, no signs, no symptoms to let anyone know that cancer had leached the density from his bones. He had been at the table with his mother, entertaining her with a joke that involved a mouthful of macaroni and cheese and a snort, when he let out a white-hot howl and slumped forward onto the table. At first she thought it was all part of the joke. Then he coughed and macaroni and cheese and blood puked out of his nose.

An orthopedic surgeon in Albany had done the work, shaving off the anterior portion of six vertebrae, bolting titanium caps on in their stead. The metal supports had replaced the decayed sections of bone, giving his back the strength it needed to support his upper body. Dr. Rasan had said that he was lucky that his spinal cord hadn't been severed, or Finn would have died. After that Finn considered Dr. Rasan to be a pretty miserable guy. His mother had been informed that he'd have a permanent hunch, as if he were an old man trapped in a little kid's body. Physiotherapy had begun.

Three months later, he had been rolled out of the hospital, never to walk again. Good news was, they had gotten all the cancer. Probably. Then again, if it ever came back there were lots of options. Chemotherapy, radiation, more surgery. If nothing else, the hospital had taught Finn to fear doctors.

Finn pulled the sombrero back on, slipped the strap tight around his chin, and adjusted his life vest, making sure all the belts were tight—at almost forty dollars, it was an expensive item, but his mom had insisted. She was always saying things like she didn't want to lose him. At least she didn't walk around crying anymore.

Finn strapped himself into the seat and took one last look at the sky. A late-summer fog had descended during the night, blanketing the lake in a dense low-pressure system that promised little in the way of rain and wind but lots in the way of lousy visibility; there was no blue, only a vast expanse of white that gave him neither clouds nor horizon. Experience told him that even though this would help the fishing it would make navigation difficult. Someday he'd save up enough money for a GPS, but until then he had to rely on his old compass and the homemade map.

He pulled the cord on the ancient Johnson. It started first try and Finn smiled with pride. He had seen the motors they sold down at Izzy's: two thousand dollars for a ten-horse Mercury and the thing took three yanks to start. The little Johnson, left over from when his dad was still alive, had been sitting in the shed for years. After the hospital, with nothing to do but read his fishing books or watch his mother cry, Finn had asked to have the motor brought inside. There, at his dad's old worktable in the furnace room, under the plywood shelves of tobacco tins filled with odd nails and half-used cans of paint, Finn had taken it apart and cleaned it, learning how it worked in the process. He could fix that little engine in the dark now. And it worked just fine.

He eased the boat away from the lopsided old dock. With the monkey bars and wheelchair ramp it looked odd and out of place amid the trees on this side of Lake Caldasac. Then again, at the end of the day the monkey bars made it easy to spot his house. One of those silver linings he was always hearing about. He had grown up on the lake and loved it more than anything else in the world except his mom.

The morning was crisp and Finn was glad that he had worn his plastic rain pants—not that he could feel anything in his bum, but he knew from experience that sitting on a wet cushion all day would give him a rash. His mother always got worried about stuff like that. He wanted to get himself a pair of Gore-Tex pants from Bass Pro Shops—they breathed and he wouldn't sweat like crazy in them—but even when they went on sale they were sixty dollars and Finn didn't want to ask his mom for the money. Maybe by next spring, if he saved his allowances. After he got the GPS of course.

When he was well away from the dock, Finn cranked the throttle up to full and headed out across the lake. His big sombrero provided little in the way of aerodynamics but lots in the way of wind resistance and he had to continually adjust his head to keep the hat from being pulled off. Today he was going to fish near the haunted place. The ancient steel fence that had been strung across the mouth of the bay had been wiped away by a storm not that long ago and the fishing in there would be cherry. The enclosed body of water was deep and protected by a lot of shade so the water was always cold, the perfect environment for suckers. Late-summer black suckers, between one and two pounds, were the best bait for muskies and Finn wanted to break the state record this year. Guides in the Adirondacks mostly fished the old-fashioned way, dragging lures along the weed banks, day in, day out. But Finn had read an article about big pike fishing in Scotland in one of his books. Over there, they used live and dead bait—no lures. Besides, to catch a sucker it took eleven cents' worth of hook and some patience. In a good morning, if you found where they were hitting, you could pull in two or three dozen. As far as he was concerned, that was two or three dozen lures. Finn figured he knew enough about fish to realize that a natural bait like a sucker had to taste better than a piece of plastic. Cheaper too.

Worst-case scenario, he would probably find some great perch fishing in the bay, and perch were like gold back in town; Finn caught and cleaned hundreds of perch each year and his mom froze them into blocks in milk cartons. The blocks were then sold to Black Eyed Susie's, a local restaurant/bar, for three bucks a piece—supplementing his allowance by a good fifteen dollars a week. Not bad work if you could get it.

Thinking of a deep-fried perch fillet suddenly made Finn hungry. He fished an O'Henry out of his pocket and opened it up, humming happily as he bit into it, the chocolate hard from being in the freezer all night.

Finn was small for his age, and the hunched back didn't help his stature. He was thin, even slight, but very strong in his upper body now that it was doing all the work in getting him around. His hair was jet black—like his dad's used to be, everyone always said—and always shaggy, whether he combed it after a bath or not. Once, for his school picture, he had tried to get it to stay down with some cooking oil.

Today he wore his yellow rain suit and red-and-black Billy boots that his mom had bought for him at Walmart—as always, the pants were a little too big, purchased in the empty hope that his little body would soon fill them out. Beside him, lying lengthwise across the seats and fastened down with a rubber clip he had designed, was his fishing rig. The reel he had wanted for months, a Shimano Stradic in the 6000 size—but it was something he had to save up for. He had kept the flyer up in his small room all last fall, hoping that they would go on sale at Izzy's. But like so many things, the sale at Izzy's had never materialized and the hope of owning it had frozen up with the first snowfall of winter. Then Mom had given it to him for Christmas along with the big Shakespeare Ugly Stik—the best rod they carried at Walmart. No-name twenty-pound monofilament line at two dollars a spool, some hooks that he had bought at a garage sale two summers ago, and he had a setup he was proud of. Finn hunkered down, his natural stoop making him less of a target for the cool wind, and settled in for the twenty-five-minute trek across the fog-shrouded lake.

Finn worked on his O'Henry candy bar and negotiated the small boat across the expanse of water with a big smile. He loved it out here by himself and was glad that more people didn't fish the lake.

Without a GPS he had to navigate Lake Caldasac with an old compass and his Frankensteined map. He knew this long, jagged slice of water by heart and, had someone put him in the middle of the lake, blindfolded him, and spun him around, he could have pointed out all the features he needed to navigate back home. But he always carried his map with him—a dog-eared pastiche of four photocopied pages he had made at the library and folded into a Wonder Bread bag in order to keep it dry. This map was his prized possession. Every musky he had landed or hooked was clearly indicated in red pen. And for the last two years, from the beginning of the season in late April to the close in early December, Finn spent every spare minute out on the lake. His map had dozens of battle scars to prove it, red Xs dotting the blue expanse like chicken pox.

There were quite a few guys who would pay big bucks for Finn's map, but it wasn't for sale and he would never show it to anyone. He knew that a lot of fishermen didn't believe in catch and release. Finn didn't want any strangers fishing what he thought of as *his lake*. Almost no one from town fished the lake, unless it was for some weekend derby that basically meant everyone would get drunk, someone would get a bloody nose, and no one would go out on the water. It was as if they were all scared of the lake or something. Sometimes strangers fished the lake. But not often. New Mannheim was a used-to-be-going-someplace-but-never-got-there town, his mother said. But Finn couldn't have loved the place more.

There used to be one other steady fisherman on the lake. His name had been Frank Knechtel. Unlike most guys, who never ate musky, Frank said they were great. Fished them for food. Finn had never personally tasted one (although he had read that they were supposed to be good eating) because they were the world's premier game fish and he'd rather get to catch one twice than eat one once. Old Frank used to mount the heads and sell them to whatever few tourists happened through town in a season. Apparently the fence outside his house was decorated with the things, hundreds of dried grinning fish skulls. Finn had never been there but he had heard lots of stories from guys who knew guys who had. One night after Frank had died, Finn had talked his mom into driving him out to old Frank's place, just to see if there was any truth to the stories.

When they had arrived Finn's mother had gasped. Literally gasped. The fence, front of the house, and yard were strung with hundreds of musky heads. At first Finn was disgusted. Then the disgust boiled over into anger. These fish, especially the trophy-sized ones, were getting harder and harder to find. Why would someone kill them? Especially so many of them? Finn knew muskies, knew that catching them made you love them more than anything in the whole world when you hoisted one aboard. It was impossible to kill one. But Frank's fish-head ornaments were proof positive that some people hated this fish.

Finn had taken a few pictures, then they had driven home in silence. Now, two months later, his anger had slowly cooled to a numb sadness. It still felt like a shame, though.

But Frank was dead now, drowned in a freak accident. Probably didn't have his life jacket on, Finn's mom had told him. Of course, they never found his body.

Like an image slowly coming to life in a developing tank, a green smudge of forest grew out of the mist. Finn sighted the shoreline to get his bearings. Not a bad crossing in the fog. Maybe two hundred yards northwest of a perfectly straight line. Not bad at all.

With skills like that, who needed a GPS? Out here, all alone, he was as safe as at home.

Safer, maybe.

# 6

Gavin sat on the hood of the brand-new four-by-four, a travel mug of coffee beside him. He watched the white wisps of fog that were manipulating his vision with the vengeance of an acid trip; some close trees were all but invisible, yet a fence post at the edge of his property stuck out as if it were painted over the fog—then the whole thing would shift around. No wonder sailors hated the stuff; it could really play with your head.

He adjusted his position and was surprised that the expanse of hood was so comfortable. Gavin had hated the Hummer as soon as he saw it but Shannon had insisted that it was the best there was. "What about all the dead dinosaurs it would take to run the thing?" he had asked. He worked at home, the only time he'd need it being when he went into town for groceries, or was taking 87 back to New York for a visit. Small carbon footprint. Argument over.

The handyman that Shannon had located through the local realtor had worked out well. Mr. Johannus, as Gavin had learned to call the solid Finnish contractor, had done an exemplary job of getting the place ready so far. The change had been monumental: the front yard had been cleared—the grass wasn't pretty, but the small thickets of evergreens and the overgrown patches of small scrub had been chopped back to the old tree line; the wrought-iron fence had been sandblasted and painted; the fountain, although still broken, had been cleaned out and scrubbed with acid.

Mr. Johannus had been surprised when he and Gavin had discussed what was expected in the way of interior renovations. Gavin had wanted a bare-bones modernization. After all, he knew that most people attempting to "restore" their homes usually ended up hopelessly destroying any charm that the house had originally possessed. Besides, how can you historically restore an eighteenth-century home and at the same time incorporate indoor plumbing, electricity, insulation, bathrooms, and central heating? Let alone satellite television and wireless Internet? What Gavin wanted was a home repaired, not restored. He had been specific. Even the kitchen was to be left pretty much as he had purchased it even though it had been "updated" sometime in the 1920s.

Since the house had been abandoned for the better part of seventy years, there was a lot of catching up to do. The ceilings had suffered water damage—albeit truncated since the original slate roof had held up remarkably well. The windows had to be reglazed, especially the ones that faced the lake, almost a hundred years of storms having finally taken their toll on the eighteenth-century sashes. The big oil furnace, although not original to the structure by a hundred and fifty years, was shot and had to be changed before winter set in.

The inside was well on its way to being a home. It would still be months—Mr. Johannus had said that Gavin was looking at Christmas—until everything was done; 90 percent of work was in the last 10 percent of the details. But he had made excellent headway. Out of necessity, the floors had been redone on the second floor—the ground floor was stone and, therefore, had only needed a stringent cleaning with wire brushes and an acid solution. The wiring was another story—

the old wiring had oxidized and corroded and Gavin had brought in an electrician who had rewired the whole house. After the electrician finished making Gavin's walls look like they had been used for target practice at howitzer camp, Mr. Johannus had attacked the plasterwork. Many of the rooms had already been sanded and primed and were just waiting for Gavin to pick out colors. But he had decided to wait. Like a novel, he felt that the house was a work in progress and he wanted to live with the blank slate for a while—the basic painter's white reminding him of empty pages waiting for a story. He liked to walk around the house, taking it in, sipping a coffee. To him, the action was like working on a book, and he liked thinking about writing again, even if it was in the abstract.

On one of these little inspections he had found the paw print—left two hundred years ago by a cat with too many toes and not enough sense to stay away from wet mortar. Something told Gavin that the impression was meant to be there because it was on the wall. Whoever had built this house had pressed his cat's footprint into the mortar as if to say, *We were here*. Like cave paintings signed with handprints, the man who had built this house had left his mark for future generations to see, as if to say, *Don't forget me*.

The first thing he had ordered was a replacement weather-vane. A local craftsman had built him a bright shiny torpedo-like fish swimming defiantly into the wind. In a few years, he said, it would develop the verdigris that would give it a sense of character. Or for eighty bucks more, he could patinate it with a solution. It stayed shiny, a fitting, albeit unusual sub-stitute for the original copper cockerel that had long since vanished and probably found its way into an upscale folk-art auction, the realtor had said.

Gavin was staring up at the weathervane when he heard the distant crunch of tires on gravel. He took a sip of the almost cold coffee and turned toward the forest where the drive opened up onto the front lawn. Shannon's BMW came out of the trees.

Shannon parked behind the Hummer and got out of the car, grinning. "Well, look at you—sitting outside with a cup of coffee and smiling. Who'd have thunk it?"

"I'm having a good day," he said matter-of-factly. He was excited that the movers would be here soon and he would not be spending any more time at the Luau Hideaway Motel in town. He'd had enough of tiki torches and plastic hula skirts to last him for a while, although the cheeseburgers at the roach coach across the road from the motel had been nothing short of addictive—the best part was biting into them and feeling the grease ooze out and drip down his arm.

Amy got out of the passenger's side. Gavin nodded a hello and gave her a smile. Amy was a tax attorney for one of the city's larger firms, and she looked every bit the part. Hair pulled back into a tight bun, black pants and matching jacket that did a lot to hide her figure, which, Gavin knew, was voluptuous to the point of being distracting. She was tallish, maybe five nine, with a small waist that accentuated the fact that she was both bottom- and top-heavy. The harsh man's suit was a departure from the usual business skirt-suit she usually sported; normally, she wasn't so butch.

"Ah, Amy, I see you've dressed for the country. Will you be chopping any wood this evening?" Gavin went over and kissed both women hello.

Amy punched him lightly in the shoulder as she pushed by. "Is the bathroom ready?"

"Plumber's coming back at three. Until then it's—" Gavin jerked a thumb at the forest. "Just keep your eyes peeled for Mr. Johannus. One look at you squatting in the woods and he'll never go back to his wife."

Amy gave Gavin the finger and headed off into the woods. "What do I use to wipe myself?"

"The old snake skins you see lying around do a pretty good job."

Amy mumbled a string of obscenities and stomped off into the underbrush, snapping twigs as she went.

Gavin turned to Shannon. "Thanks for coming."

She looked up at the house. "Place looks great. This Danish guy seems to be working out."

"He's Finnish," Gavin corrected. "He's got to be sixty-five. Carries four slabs of Sheetrock all by himself. Unbelievable." Almost on cue, Mr. Johannus walked out of the house, blue work pants, a white T-shirt with a dark triangle of sweat across the front, and big suspenders marked off like a tape measure making up his standard work uniform. He had dirty-blond hair and a mustache that curled down at the corners of his mouth, dropping to his chin, giving him the look of someone who frowned a lot. He was squarely built, of medium height, and whistled the same seven bars of some forgotten Finnish folk song as he moved.

"Hello, Mr. Gavin," Mr. Johannus said. He was typically Scandinavian and his foreign sense of humor blocked Gavin's usually innate ability to read people.

Mr. Johannus went to the side of the house and opened the double back doors of the big blue Econoline parked in the shade. "Those yoists are yunk!" he said to no one in particular. "Fuckin' hemlock's no good for nothing. Goddamned shit!"

Shannon raised her eyebrows.

Gavin smiled, offering, "And he swears a lot too."

"Well then, you two should get along famously, Mr. Tourette's."

A thin bumblebee hum needled into the morning air. "What the hell is that?"

"A boat, Mr. Gavin," Mr. Johannus said as he passed by, a battle-scarred reciprocating saw propped up on his beefy shoulder like some Viking weapon. "Out in the bay."

"Thanks, Mr. Johannus," Gavin said flatly, feeling like an idiot.

"Anytime, Mr. Gavin." Mr. Johannus stepped into the building, no doubt to attack one of the yunky yoists. "You have a lot to learn about this place."

# 7

Nestled in the northernmost flange of the Adirondacks, New Mannheim was one of the few towns in the area that never learned to live off of the lake it bordered. Lake Caldasac occupied eighteen thousand hectares and by definition was not a large body of water—certainly not in the way of Saint Francis or the other big lakes that made up the mass of the Saint Lawrence Seaway a mere twenty miles north. From the time it had been born, scooped out by the frozen hands of the receding glaciers of the last ice age, until the end of the first quarter of the twentieth century, Lake Caldasac had been small, totaling roughly eleven thousand hectares. But its spring-fed body was very deep and very cold and created enough of a current that when the New York Energy Commission, under the umbrella of Hoover's first job-creation program of the early 1930s, studied the lake, it was found to be the perfect site for a new hydroelectric dam. The ribbon was cut on December 9, 1932. True to government form, the project was underplanned and poorly executed, and what could have been a colossal and innovative milestone in supplying power to the tristate area turned out to be just another midlevel disaster that no one really took the time to notice.

The trickle of power that did come off the dam was sold, very cheaply, to Vermont. The only mitigating factor that had helped the local population warm to the dam was the newly created seventy-one miles of waterfront property now available. But *mitigating* was the most colorful word you could apply to the real estate. Lake Caldasac, being stuck where it was, was a rural farming community that had little use for waterfront. A few houses were built by local speculators who thought they'd be the first to rake in big bucks from the out-of-towners eager to spend money. Only thing was, New York was too far away to attract a crowd of weekend homeowners. The few men who had built homes either moved into them or abandoned them, the latter being the most obvious choice since in reality no one wanted to live out on the lake, not even the men who had hoped to make a mint on selling other people that very same idea.

Etymological research into the origins of *Caldasac* would show that it had started out as *Lac Cul De Sac*, meaning *Dead-End Lake*, a moniker bestowed by the French trappers who had worked the area during the early part of the seventeenth century. From the French, the name had been passed on to the British via the Algonquin. The British, in their usual snobbery against all things non-English, spelled the lake's name phonetically, consciously avoiding a nod to the French. Initially, the lake's name had been derived from its most obvious topographical feature: it terminated in a series of boulder-strewn rapids at an abrupt slate wall that grew a hundred feet into the sky, the topmost edge trimmed with forest. Indian lore had it that anyone trying to leave through the rapids would be devoured by an angry serpent. The residents of twentieth-century New Mannheim had forgotten most of this, including that the dam was meant to have been a blessing.

Through the throes of the Great Depression, a world war, a medium-sized war, one police action that was never called a war, and fifteen presidents, New Mannheim was a place that lots of folks passed through or passed by altogether. Like the rest of postwar America, the population bulged, but New Mannheim grew east, away from the lake, as if it were poisoned, and it stayed pretty much uninhabited through most of the twentieth century. The birth rate eventually passed the death rate, and the town, though far from swelling to capacity, grew a little more. But there was plenty of land for everyone and no one seemed inclined to either move *to* New Mannheim or move *away* from it either. Its stasis, therefore, continued long after it should have expired.

The town of New Mannheim was eventually pulled, kicking and screaming, into the modern age when physical isolation finally succumbed to the natural laws of economics. Property values finally climbed, albeit ever so slightly. This weak short boom, which was really little more than a blip, blossomed in the late 1970s, and the trickle of money that seeped into the area was hardly the economic boost that New Mannheim had been waiting for most of its life.

For the rest of the Adirondacks, the Thirteenth Winter Olympics at Lake Placid supplied a positive influx of much-needed money, which, almost magically, seemed to elude the haven of New Mannheim. Soon after all the hoopla was over, the town nestled back into sour-grapes mode while the rest of the nearby townships flourished under the weight of their burgeoning tourist industries. But New Mannheim's luck held and the population explosion never even threatened to happen. No one else came here. Or thought about it.

Now, ten years into the twenty-first century, Lake Caldasac was still a dusty time capsule from an almost forgotten America.

*** 

Finn shifted the ancient Johnson into neutral. The bow dropped and the boat drifted toward shore on its momentum. He scanned the tree line. On the right he could see where the bush thinned and Lake Road was visible. To the left of that, Finn knew that there was a cutoff that went to the old place with the three chimneys; he had heard stories about that house since forever and the thought of the place scared him. But the bay in there hadn't been fished in what? Seventy-five years maybe. The chance to fish virgin water bolstered him with courage.

The wind and current pushed the little skiff and the bow swung to the left, toward the old stone house, as if the boat knew where it was going. With a fluid motion of his arm and elbow he pushed the throttle into forward and headed toward shore at a forty-five-degree cant.

As he eased into the silent black bay he was overcome by the same awe he felt whenever his mom had managed to coax him into going to church—it was a place where you felt like you had to be quiet not because anyone told you to but because you *knew* it was the thing to do. No talking. No whispering. No farting. And no falling asleep. He rotated his wrist back and the engine's pitch decreased, dropping from an insect's whine down to a throaty whisper.

Time seemed to stop inside the bay. Nothing moved, not even wind. The only sound was the bow splitting the water, swishing as it washed along the hull. Even with great concentration all he heard were the sounds he generated as his little skiff putted into the bay where he was going to be the first one to fish in a very long time. Overhead the white sky shone through the overhanging trees with jagged spears of light that somehow managed to penetrate the darkness just enough to let him know that it was daylight. He felt like Humphrey Bogart in *The African Queen*. He looked up and saw the house for the first time.

The clean lines of the building stood out among the dark shadows of the forest. Big limestone blocks made up the body of the beast, and the three trademark chimneys grew from the roof. A large window faced the dock and water, its surface rippled and unclear due to the many panes that made up its surface. A small red door was sliced into the middle of the wall, and another window, this one smaller, had been built into the opposite side. Something about the house made it seem as if it were winking at Finn.

Down by the water was the boathouse, an old stone structure that years of sitting on the soft bank had tilted to one side, as if it were falling asleep. The peeling red door looked cancerous, like the mouth of a monster. As his boat crawled nearer the little building, the grimy windows blinked back, letting him know that they were watching him. There was probably excellent perch fishing under the collapsing building but Finn couldn't bring himself to go near it. Not in a million years.

The dilapidated dock was beside the boathouse. The back of the structure had failed and the joists were bowed and crumbling, much like his own little body. Planks were broken and missing, and one of the corner posts had separated from the frame and was reaching out into the bay, letting Finn know that it would eventually fall into the water. Finn stopped the little boat, killed the engine, and listened. Dead quiet. He heard the urine bag strapped to his calf fill up. He couldn't feel the warmth, but wished he could.

Being as quiet as he could, he unclipped his rod, jammed it in between his legs, and reached into the small Styrofoam cooler filled with the pencil-thick night crawlers he had cultivated in the garage over the winter. Finding a nice juicy one near the top, he threaded it onto the 2/0 hook with the skill of a tailor. Brown wet paste bubbled out onto his fingers. He opened the bail on his reel, dropped the worm and the lead over the side into the water with a loud plop, rinsed the worm guts off his hands, and settled back into the seat as much as the straps holding him upright would allow. The worm seemed to drop for hours, finally settling on the bottom when about thirty-five yards of line was off his spool. Deep water.

In the sheltered bay the little craft swirled lazily in the almost imperceptible eddies, rotating slowly. Finn's concentration was on the rod, on the feel of the line, his hands picking up the slight vibration as the slow drift of the boat dragged the worm over the bottom. When a fish hit, he would know. He waited with the patience of a stone and quickly forgot about the house, about the silent forest where it stood, about being afraid. All he thought about was the feel of the line against his index finger.

He eyed his spool suspiciously. He had never seen water this deep so close to shore. Finn snapped on the ancient sonar that he had bought at Mr. Kingsbury's garage sale last summer. The dial powered up and the green LED waves settled out at almost a hundred feet. Finn reset it and the lines bounced back to the hundred-foot mark. How could a little bay like this be that deep? Dark and cold; the spring-fed depths were frigid all year round. Great sucker water. Of course the drawback was that the ice melted later than the other mountain lakes and froze up earlier. But it kept the fishing world-class.

Finn concentrated on the tip of his rod—the bait was being moved, but not by the current; a fish was nosing the worm around the bottom. There were slight, tentative pokes. Finn tensed the muscles in his arms and shoulders for the big upsweep of the rod when the fish finally took it.

The bow was slipping back toward shore with the soft current. Finn kept his fingers locked around the handle of the rod, waiting for the line to tell him that it was time to set the hook. Suddenly the line nudged away, just enough to let him know that the fish was trying to move off. Finn yanked up hard. The rod tip dipped once, then bounced back as the fish shot upward, trying to shake the hook. Finn reeled, remembering what he had heard Randy Ketchum repeat on his show, time and time again—*maintain contact.*

He cranked the handle of his reel and pulled the rod tip up.

"Hey, kid!" a voice called from the forest.

Finn dropped his rod and yanked the cord on the Johnson. It started. He cycled the throttle up to full and the boat shot out, away from the dock. His rod twitched and he caught it just before it was dragged over the side. As the boat lurched out into the lake, the rod tip bent back under the weight of the fish still on. There was a moment where either line or rod would break under the force. Then the line snapped, and zinged back, snapping Finn in the cheek.

He kept the little boat pointed across the lake. Toward home. The man was still screaming when his boat burst out into the big water. He didn't look back. Never look back. Everyone always said that.

And he didn't.

# 8

Gavin had negotiated his way down the hand-hewn steps, staggering on the uneven stones as if he were drunk. The big blocks of granite were crooked and slanted, like a mouth full of bad teeth, three-quarters of a century of neglect reducing the trek to an ankle-breaking stunt.

The retaining wall at the water's edge had fared no better than the steps; scrub, ferns, and full-sized trees had poked up through the spots where the mortar had rotted away. Gavin pulled back the branch of a tree and stuck his head out.

The bay was a perfect oval, with only a narrow pass out into the big water. A vertical granite wall encircled the isolated piece of water as if it had been scooped out of the earth by an Olympian shovel. Just below his vantage point a boy was fishing.

Contrary to popular perception, as a writer Gavin rarely observed the world with a conscious effort; when he sat down to write, it was usually through the eye of memory that he was able to pull up details that gave his work the vividness he was known for. But this time he had found himself actually recording the scene in his mind's eye.

The boy was maybe twelve and had the wiry build of a child. He wore a yellow rain suit, black and red rain boots, and an oversize sombrero replete with fake jewels and shiny gold braid that spelled out the word *GRINGO* in cowboy script across the rim. He was strapped into an aluminum chair that was bolted to the boat and Gavin realized that he was handicapped in some way. Even though he knew absolutely nothing about boats, he could see that the boy's craft was ancient, the scratched hull showing at least three different paint colors and patched all over with riveted plates of varying sizes and shapes. The streamlined cover of the engine harkened back to the 1950s and there was a little homemade Jolly Roger hanging limply off the bow in the breezeless air. But it wasn't the boy's appearance that captivated Gavin, it was the concentration he exercised over what he was doing.

The boy plucked a thick brown worm from a Styrofoam box and threaded it onto the hook. When the worm was secured he fiddled with his reel, dropped the worm into the depths of the bay, and rinsed his hand in the water. But he looked edgy, frightened even. The boy kept glancing nervously over his shoulder. Why? Maybe he thought that he wasn't allowed to fish in the bay. Maybe he subscribed to the hokum that the house on the hill was haunted. *Christ*, Gavin thought, *the kid has enough to worry about without being scared about fishing in my bay*.

Gavin pulled the branch back and stepped out onto the rim of the wall to tell the boy that he was allowed to fish there whenever he wanted. Suddenly, the boy's rod jerked up. He had a fish on.

"Hey, kid!"

The boy's reactions would have made a kung fu master proud. Without a split second of hesitation he had the motor started and was roaring out of the bay at full steam.

"It's okay. You can fish here whenever you—" But he let it die out because the noise of the boy's engine drowned out his yelling. In less than ten seconds, what had once been a boy fishing within feet of him was little more than an S-shaped wake that pulsed on the surface of the water and lapped up against the primordial stone walls that rose out of the dark water.

"Great," Gavin said aloud. "Just great. I scared a handi-capped kid."

\*\*\*

"You okay?" Shannon asked.

"Some kid in a boat wearing a three-foot red sombrero. He was fishing and I went down to say hello. He looked up, saw me, and took off." Gavin shook his head in disbelief. "I was just going to tell him that he can fish here anytime he wants." The sound of the outboard motor was now a distant whisper.

Shannon smiled, swatted an imaginary insect away. "It's your winning personality."

"Thanks." Gavin took in a deep breath. Country air. Clean. Strange. Having spent his entire life in New York, with the occasional sybaritic retreat to his flat in London, the country was an entirely new experience to him. "It smells different up here," he observed.

Shannon smiled. "Uh, yeah, Gav, it's the country. It's sup-posed to smell better. Trees, grass, manure. Nature's little Chanel Number Five."

He nodded appreciatively, breathing in theatrically.

Amy came around from the side of the house, walked by the shiny Hummer, hitching up her pants. "Well, that's a first."

"What?" Gavin was staring out at the lake. The view was milky but bright, the sun hidden behind a film of clouds. There was no horizon, just space.

"I've never taken a pee with wild animals watching me. That was exhilarating." Amy smiled.

"Wild animals?" Shannon asked and moved closer to Gavin. "What wild animals?"

Amy shrugged. "This cat was staring at me."

Gavin thought back to the too-many-toed footprint in the mortar by the side of the house. "You see his feet?" he asked.

"Yeah, Gavin, I saw his feet. There were four of them." She shielded her eyes from the hazy bright sky and stared at his new home. "Great house, Gavin." Her eyes moved up to the weathervane. "What's with the fish? Isn't it supposed to be a cock?"

"Traditionally it's a cockerel, yes. But the craftsman and I had a talk about a befitting replacement. Before the dam was opened back in '32, this house looked out over a field and a small pond that was remote from the large lake. After the dam went operational, and the reservoir swallowed all the low land, including my pond, the whole backyard became lakeside property."

"What kind of fish is it?" she asked.

"Musky," Mr. Johannus said as he came back outside, a five-foot length of lead drain slung over his shoulder. "About the size of a forty-pounder."

"You fish, Mr. Johannus?" Gavin had a hard time imagining the man out in a boat without a hammer in his hand.

"Used to fish for musky. Gave it up years ago." The old man held up his forearm, exposing a patch of yellow scar tissue roughly the size of a dollar bill. "They're mean."

Shannon's face screwed up in awe. "Is this really a fish? What kind of name is musky anyway?"

Gavin narrated from memory. "*Esox masquinongy*. Muskellunge. Northern musky. Sometimes spelled with a *y*, sometimes with an *ie*. Largest member of the Esox family, the most widely distributed freshwater fish family in the world. The musky is renowned for its sporting qualities. World record was caught by Louie Spray in the Chippewa Flowage in 1969, weighed in at sixty-nine pounds, eleven ounces. Specimens over a hundred pounds have been netted. Etymological history is unclear but some people think that the word has its origins in Canadian French, coming from *mask allonge*, meaning 'long snout.'"

He had no practical knowledge of fishing but years of research had developed a very good recall of factoids, sound bites, and definitions read in the dictionary. Once Gavin had looked up a word, it was in his memory banks—verbatim—for good. It was a neat bar trick that had won him his share of free booze back when he couldn't afford to drink past happy hour.

"You need to get out more," Amy said through a look that was half awe, half pity.

They all heard it at the same time, the unmistakable sound of a big diesel downshifting. The screech of tree branches scraping along the truck body accompanied the popping of the tires over the stone road as the truck pulled into the private drive.

"Looks like your stuff's here."

But Gavin's mind was back on the little boy he had scared into the arms of Caldasac.

# 9

The creature barely moved. Except for the signals sent to its organs from the primitive brain, and the slow pulse of its gill plates and finely sculpted jaws, it was motionless. It lay in the deep water, sixty feet down, its muscular scaled body hovering within the boundaries of the weed bed, the long snout opening and closing slightly with the throb of the current washing by. It had no memory, no sense of time, but it had age. Millions of years of evolution and the happenstance of selective breeding had made it a king of its kind, an apex predator that knew no enemies. This was its home and it was comfortable. But a new sensation had crept into its existence lately. The small brain had no logic, no deductive reasoning, only the ability to function on instinct and experience, and this minimal computing mechanism understood that something within the closed system of its world was wrong. It was having trouble finding food.

The beast had no sense of self, no personal awareness, just synaptic impulses that fired in its misshapen head and delivered the most rudimentary of messages. The concept of survival meant nothing to it. All that it understood was that it felt hunger. It had to feed. It was what it was made for.

The small sphere of its senses detected motion. The lateral sensory system, common to many creatures of the water, picked up the vibrations of distress in the black depths of the lake. At sixty feet the visibility, in human terms, was nil. But this being could not be described in human terms. And it did not hunt with its eyes, it hunted with a sense of feel, and now it felt food in its vicinity. Something large.

With a pulse of its muscles it surged forward, scattering a school of yellow perch that had set up by the edge of the weed bed where the creature had lain. Perch were not big enough to consider food, not anymore; the beast had grown too large for them decades ago. It needed something more.

Surging along the bottom, it negotiated by feel, the elongated snout sensing pressure changes as it approached underwater structure. In this way it moved quickly, without impedance, toward prey.

It reached the epicenter of the vibrations and knew that food was above it. It angled sharply up, amazingly agile for its enormous bulk, and thrust for the surface.

Toward food.

***

Finn was having a hard time breathing and it took a concerted effort to get the steroid puffer out of his pocket. He didn't have asthma, but the permanent bend in his frame put pressure on his lungs, and he often needed the inhaler to clear the vessels and open up his breathing passage. Especially when he was agitated.

He clamped his teeth around the plastic nozzle, pressed down on the aluminum canister, and sucked in greedily. He felt better instantly.

The boy slowed the motor.

***

It was above. The vibrations coming off of it were erratic and panicked. The creature turned into its path, picked up speed, and headed for the prey.

Now it was visible, struggling; the water around it rippled with its efforts. It was a shadow against the brightness of above. The creature didn't recognize it as prey by sight, only by its movement. It was in the water. It moved. It was, therefore, food.

There was heat in its system as the lactic acid filled its muscles and it felt the rush of power. It moved in on its prey.

The shadow on the surface was now growing rapidly as the beast closed in.

\*\*\*

*Okay*, Finn told himself, *that guy was mad. Angrier than heck.* He sucked in the damp late-summer air. *Why was he*—and the thought died as he saw it.

A few feet ahead, just under the surface, a shadow was coming. Straight for his boat.

It hit.

The bow rose out of the water and Finn felt himself tilt back. There was nothing he could do but hope the boat wouldn't capsize. He was strapped to his chair—there was no jumping overboard for him. An adrenaline ball of fear flooded his stomach.

Then the boat passed over whatever it was, and there was a moment when the prop made a sickening noise and it *thud-thud-thudded* into something hard and meaty. Then the boat was on its way again, seesawing back and forth.

Finn circled around to see what he had hit. Out here in the deep water it could only be one thing—a submerged log. But logs didn't move. There was nothing else that it could be—it had to be a log. And Finn knew that it was his responsibility to mark it off so that no one else would hit it. He kept an empty bleach bottle in the boat for just such an occasion—hand-painted with a big orange smiley-face and ten feet of yellow Dacron rope to tie it off.

As the bow swung around, Finn saw the black slick, an inky cloud in the water. Was that blood?

\*\*\*

The beast was puzzled. The prey did not feel as it should. It had not been soft.

And the tiny brain relayed another message, a more urgent one. Its system was not right. Something was not as it was supposed to be. It did not understand that it was injured, but it knew that its own body was not reacting as it should. And there was pain.

But it still had to feed.

Its senses switched from its own system to the panicked fluttering above. The rhythm had changed again and the beast's brain came to the same conclusion it had before; the thing above was acting like food so it must be. It turned back to the surface.

\*\*\*

Finn saw the shadow close on him. This time he braced for the impact.

It hit the boat and the bow jumped out of the water again and he had to grab his rod to prevent it from going over the side. As the boat tilted back and up, the wind pulled off his sombrero and it rolled over the side and disappeared. It hit the boat again. And again. And again.

The gunwale dipped under the cold surface and a thick surge of water rushed in. For a second the boat bobbed up, and then there was another loud *crack!* as the hull caved in. More water flowed in. Finn's legs had no feeling, but the sensation of cold washing over his whole body filled every corner of his brain.

And the little boy began to scream.

## 10

Sheriff Xavier Pope snapped two Benzedrine into his mouth, washed them down with a mouthful of vodka, and got out of his cruiser trying to look like he gave a shit.

Truth be told, he hated being here; he hadn't seen Chuck Horn's widow in an easy ten years. Of course Finn Horn was a regular fixture around town and everyone seemed to like the kid. But Pope found the boy unsettling, creepy even. If he had drowned, who would really give a shit? Maybe the fishing was good and the kid hadn't felt like coming home to a lunch of weenies, shitty potato salad, and welfare cola. Sonofabitch, Pope thought, I do *not* want to be here. Then he got annoyed with himself for letting a little crippled kid get under his skin.

As Pope's foot hit the wheelchair ramp that grew out of the walkway, his cerebral cortex got the first jolt of Benzedrine-fueled static as the cockroaches came out to play, filling his mind with white noise. He listened to them tuning up, getting their orchestra in line. He rang the bell and felt an electric jolt travel from his finger through his hand, crawl up his arm, and needle into his brain. It set off the music, and his mind was filled with the crooning of thousands of insects. It felt *good*.

Mary Horn opened the door immediately. The sheriff hadn't seen her in years, not since the funeral, and he noted that she was still good-looking in a never-seen-makeup kind of way. She had grown a little plump in the ass and he guessed that she was probably not bad in the sack when you got her juiced up with a couple of brewskies. He focused on her eyes and stayed there, staring intently. The Bennies were starting to light up his head. "Mary, how are you?"

She waved Pope in with a chubby arm. "Finn's gone. He was supposed to be back hours ago. He always comes back. I'm worried he drowned. I hope he didn't drown. Could he have drowned? I didn't want—"

Pope lifted his big hand, directing traffic to stop. "Calm down. I have to ask a few questions first and then you can fill me in."

She stepped back and put her hand to her mouth. "I'm sorry, Xavier, I'm really worried about him."

Pope continued. "Can we sit down?"

"Of course."

Pope stepped into the small living room and was instantly grateful that the place didn't smell like piss; for some reason, he had expected it to. Mary Horn led the big sheriff through the orange shag and plastic-paneled living room. The second-nature cop habit of scanning his surroundings had the sheriff take in the details of the people who lived there. Of course, there was a photo of Chuck on top of the TV. And pictures of the kid everywhere. Pope had never been in the house, not even when he had worked with Chuck Horn, but being here now unleashed that creepy feeling that had been skittering around the edge of his mind in the driveway, even if the place smelled okay.

The furniture was in pretty good shape but nowhere near new. There was an old television—the vacuum-tube variety—and there was a Cold War–era top-loading VCR. No DVD player. One of the walls was covered with bookshelves made of plywood and bricks that were filled with books on fishing—from old taped-together hardcovers to glossy new magazines; someone liked to read about fishing.

No stereo. One plaid and maple sofa, the kind that had been out of style when it was in style. A La-Z-Boy. And a worn spot on the rug where he guessed the kid parked his chair when he either read his books or watched the shitty old TV.

As they entered the kitchen, Pope turned his eyes back to the woman's ass. Sure, it was a little big, but bent over the front of his cruiser, lathered with a little butter, it would probably taste pretty fucking good. The cockroaches did a little samba timed to the shake of her rump and Pope found himself hypnotized by her hips.

They sat down in the kitchen and Pope continued the mental inventory. The place was clean and tidy, but you could tell that these folks didn't spend a whole lot of time at the mall; the fridge was baby blue and the stove avocado green; none of the dishes in the rack by the sink matched; and there wasn't much in the way of clutter on the countertops. The walls were a little beat up at about the two-foot mark and there were worn spots on the floor that made it look like someone spent a lot of time dragging stuff around. Pope could see the scars across the edge of the table where Finn was parked for meals. Pope was amazed at the beautiful view of Lake Caldasac out of the big picture window that felt like it wrapped around the table.

"How old is Finn?" the sheriff asked before he lost his tenuous interest in why he was there. Not that the Benzedrine made concentrating a difficulty—if anything it added a certain edge to his focus. No, he was afraid of losing interest because he wasn't starting this conversation with a whole lot to begin with.

"Thirteen. Finn is thirteen."

Pope pulled a black Moleskine notebook from his pocket, snapped his pen to life with a theatrical flick of his thumb, and started his notes. "Thirteen. When was the last time you saw him?"

"This morning. Seven."

"Where did he go?" Pope wanted to slap the bitch. The fucking kid was crippled. He should have been locked up in the house. Give him a TV, a peanut butter sandwich, and a clean colostomy bag and he'd be fine. Shit, a box of crayons should keep a kid like that happy for days as long as you made sure he didn't eat them.

"He goes out all the time by himself. This—"

Pope's big hand came up again and this time he resisted the temptation to let it fly and take out a few of her teeth. "Please, let me finish." How had Chuck put up with this broad's machine-gun chatter as long as he had? Getting killed had been a big old stroke of lottery luck for Chuck Horn. "What was he wearing?"

Mary Horn's eyes rolled up and she focused on a corner of the room. Pope fought the temptation to follow her eyes because he knew that the corner of the room would be a hell of a lot more interesting than the load of crap coming out of her mouth. He tuned back into Cockroach FM and that band was doing a nice little zydeco rendition of Johnny Cash and June Carter's "Jackson," and the female vocalist could have nailed old June's ass to the floor with her little insect pipes.

"His yellow rain suit, Billy boots, and a red sombrero."

The cockroaches faded out. "Sombrero? Oh, yeah. A hat."

"He likes it. Says it keeps the sun off. His dad brought it back from our honeymoon and Finn kind of adopted it."

Pope nodded and jotted down the details. His eyes kept skipping to the dock, to the strange pipe structure rising above it. The thing reminded Pope of a television show he had once seen about a family in Texas who had constructed an antenna out of thousands of vacuum cleaner hoses. They passed their days sitting around an old television set that didn't have a picture—only sound—listening to the cosmos for messages from Jesus. "What does his boat look like?"

She went to the fridge and removed one of a dozen photos haphazardly taped to the door. As her hand came away, the images fluttered on their tape hinges and it looked like the old refrigerator actually took a breath. The cockroaches gasped at the beauty of it.

She handed the photograph to Pope. "That was last fall."

Pope examined the glossy print. Eighteen-foot aluminum boat, three-seater, modified with some sort of railing that ran around the gunwale. He examined the shitty Johnson outboard clamped on the back, the patchy green paint, Finn sitting inside, clamped into the seat with straps and buckles, his face spread into a grin that said he was either very happy or very stupid. When the cucarachas saw the big red sombrero the boy was wearing they started up with a little mariachi number and Pope's brain got another jolt of the pills. He looked at the little boy and his face lifted off of the page, features becoming clearer, pores on his skin standing out. The kid looked sick, really sick, and he wondered if this woman was sane letting him out of bed, let alone out on the lake. He might have been cute except for the sunken head on shoulders that looked too big for his body. Beside him, on a little chrome flagpole, was a Jolly Roger in midflap, the skull grinning back at Pope. The sheriff couldn't help noticing that the grinning skull did not look dissimilar to the grinning child. He had to concentrate to pull his eyes away from the photo. When he did, all the cockroaches screamed in protest. They wanted more of the kid.

"Look, Mary, I don't want to say that your son's not fine, but this engine looks, well, old. He ever have engine trouble out on the lake?" Pope couldn't stop looking at the flag smiling back at him. Christ, did it ever look like the boy.

"Nope. Never. He cleans that engine all the time."

"*He* cleans it?" Pope imagined the kid on the floor, drool coming out of his mouth, banging on the old chipped engine with a wrench. What was wrong with this woman? She needed someone to fill in the blanks for her. "Are you telling me that you let your thirteen-year-old crippled—"

"Handicapped," she interrupted.

Pope tried not to roll his eyes. He had been forced to take the state's course on how to be more sympathetic and *politically correct*. Taking the word *nigger* out of the job made sense, people didn't know how to use that one—it took a certain *skill*. But *handicapped*? The kid wasn't handicapped, he was fucking *crippled*. "Sorry—your thirteen-year-old *handicapped* son out on the lake, by himself, with an engine that was an antique thirty years ago, that he maintains himself, in the fog, *alone*?" It was the last word he wanted her to hear. That kid should not have been going anywhere by himself. Not even the shitter. Period. Even the cockroaches agreed.

"Look, Xavier, I don't expect you to understand." Her words carried some of the old animosity in them. "You're right, Finn's handicapped. The motor he uses is old. It was foggy. What am I supposed to do? My son spent ninety-one days on the water last year. Ninety-one," she repeated proudly. "All winter long he reads his fishing books and counts the days until he can go out again. Rain, snow, freezing cold—don't matter to him. Out there he's independent. He's free. Out there he's a happy little boy, not a sick kid." Her eyes misted over, and she stared at Pope, angry.

The big cop swallowed hard and once again fought back the urge to knock her fucking teeth out with a solid backhand. Instead he nodded like he understood; the courses on civilian interaction had taught him about body language too. "Was he ever late before?" he asked, making a concerted effort to be polite.

"Never. One every day on the dot for lunch then back on the lake by two until dark."

"Any clue as to where your son likes to fish?" But this broad didn't have a clue about anything. Probably thought the kid was going to be a figure skater one day.

"I know that he spends a lot of time near the islands at the south side of the lake—he says that the biggest muskies are in that pass—and he goes across to the old German place too. I heard him talk about it lots."

"The old haunted place?" Pope asked, smiling. His smile wasn't reflected in Mary Horn's face. *Some people have no sense of humor.* "Okay, Mary, I'll get some people out on the water." Pope pointed at the old rotary phone hanging across the room on the kitchen cabinet. "Mind if I use your phone?"

She nodded absentmindedly. "Go ahead."

By the time Pope had dialed the station number, his head was lit up like a pinball machine with the cockroach mosh pit surging through his skull. Kathy Gorsky answered the phone in one ring. Finally! thought Pope, someone who is *up to speed.* "Yeah, Kath, this is Pope. I'm out at the Horn place— I think we've got a floater."

Kathy's voice dropped down into the somber zone. "The handicapped boy we got the call about?"

*Crippled!* the cockroaches screamed in unison. "Uh, yeah, the handicapped boy." Pope leaned back, closed his eyes, and enjoyed the waves of music rinsing through his gray matter. "Look, can you ring up Uncle Charlie, ask him to get out on the lake? With the fog like it is, I doubt I'll be able to get *any-one* out on that lake but Uncle Charlie could use the pay right now and that might help. Tell him that a kid's gone this time. We'll pay for the gas—he'll get a town credit for fifteen gallons for every hour he's out there. Try Tom Stockman too— same deal. If the kid's got into any real trouble, I want some guys who know what they're doing out there. Maybe the kid's just a little lost. I don't know. I'll be in the car." Pope hung up and turned to nod a good-bye to Mary.

The woman stood there with her mouth open. What the fu—? Then he realized that the word *floater* probably hadn't been politically correct, either. *Shit.* "As soon as we have a boat on the lake, I'll let you know."

Pope let himself out, leaving Mary Horn crying in the kitchen.

# 11

Uncle Charlie had been on the lake for two hours and his eyes felt like they belonged on an owl. The fog had visibility down to maybe twenty feet and he was running as slow as he could without stalling the engine. And he was in no mood to be looking for a dead kid. Pretty straightforward when he thought about it.

It wasn't that Charlie hadn't seen his share of dead people and horror stories out here. Hell, if anything, he had seen too much. Not too long ago he had been the guy to find Frank Knechtel's boat floating empty like something out of a movie. One oar gone and no sign of Frank except for one rubber boot with a wool sock inside sitting on one of the seats. And about five years back, Uncle Charlie had found that kid that had been attacked by a bear. Charlie had found him near the dam, tangled in a patch of weeds that were floating in the current. The medical examiner never figured out how the body had gone from the campground where the kid had gone missing to the dam, six miles down the lake, in just under an hour. Body had been a mess, legs gone, stringy swollen tendons sticking out where they used to be attached. So, no, Charlie, was no stranger to bad things out here. But today it was a little too foggy to be out by himself. It was more than creepy, it was damn near scary.

Charlie checked the GPS for the thousandth time in the last hour. He had covered quite a bit of water considering how slow he was going, but there was still a shitload of space out there. Caldasac looked deceptively small, but even when you took away all the little hidden bays and points that dotted the shore, the body of water was plenty big to lose one little kid in. Even though people considered it to be a small lake, it still chewed up almost sixty-one square miles—more space than San Francisco took up, people said. And at twenty-foot visibility, it was going to take a month of Sundays to see the whole lake.

Tom Stockman was out there too, patrolling near the dam. If the kid had got sucked into one of the floodgates it would be better for the mother if they *never* found the body. Charlie had seen a moose that had gone through one of the big turbines before they had installed the guard net; thing looked like God had smashed the shit out of it with a hammer the size of a dump truck. Only thing that told you it was a moose was the nose. Other than that, it was one huge hairy flapjack with splintered antlers.

Uncle Charlie traced his finger over the LCD screen, taking the path that was most likely the route the boy had used. Up until now, he had been searching under the premise that something had happened to the kid on the way to the old German place. But what if the kid had made it there, fished, then had a problem on the way back? Charlie had circled both Kintner and Gardner's Island several times in ever widening concentric circles. He looked at the GPS, then out at the fog, then at the GPS again. If the kid was still alive—a big IF according to Sheriff Pope—he needed to be found before nightfall. Combined with the already cold temperature of the water in Caldasac, nightfall was promising to bring weather in the low forties and a sick little kid wouldn't make it through the night. Not out here. Not on this lake. And dark was only a little while off—an hour tops. He pushed the throttle into forward, revved up the big twin Mercs, and swung the wheel around, heading off for the German place.

The old man lit a Lucky Strike off his USMC Zippo and sucked in a good lungful of smoke. Besides himself, little Finn Horn was one of the few people who fished Caldasac. Charlie had seen Finn almost every time he had gone out on the water, which, truth be told, was getting to be a rare thing for him these days. Seemed like a nice little kid. Wearing that big weird sombrero, his little Johnson coughing blue smoke, the thin arm saying hello in the universal gesture of seamen passing one another on the water. Uncle Charlie had never talked to the kid, but he always waved back, hollered, "Howdy, young feller!" and Finn would smile broadly, tip his sombrero as if he were at the helm of a million-dollar yacht, and continue on his way. If something had happened to the little boy, it wouldn't be fair.

But Lake Caldasac didn't believe in fair.

It never had.

# 12

The movers had been gone for two hours and he had managed to open one box—the one with the booze in it. The rest were piled up in the entryway, like the ruins of an ancient church, irregular-sized blocks of cardboard with "GV" scrawled across the surfaces in Shannon's broad, efficient script. In reality, there weren't that many, maybe forty in total. He would get to them tomorrow. Or the next day. It really didn't matter.

He moved into the kitchen and eyed a few boxes that Shannon had asked the movers to put in an accessible spot. She had marked them as ESSENTIALS and the movers had left them on an old pine table that had come with the house. Gavin examined them, wondering what they contained. Shannon had handled all the packing—selectively going through his apartment and shipping all the things that she thought he would need in the country to get by for a little while. Most of his office had been packed up. Probably all of his LPs; there were an easy two dozen record-sized boxes carefully piled in the corner of the living room. Clothes. A new stereo, television, two iMacs, and two MacBooks, all still in their boxes. In the way of furniture, the movers had brought one Georgian linen press, a Georgian chest of drawers, a William IV dining table, ten chairs, a library table, and a pedestal desk, all in mahogany, all purchased over the phone from the only antique dealer in Manhattan whom Gavin trusted. The bed, mattress, three sofas, two armchairs, coffee table, and assorted other "comfort pieces" had come from an hour-long tour of ABC Decorating on Broadway. ABC had also supplied all the new towels, bedding, linens, and dishware. There was still a lot of space to fill but that would come in time. He had seen a little antique shop in town, maybe he'd even find something there. As long as he could make it past the next month without painting the new headboard with his gray matter. It was all about goals.

Gavin looked into the box he had opened, the broad word BOOZE bleeding across the top flap in red felt marker. A few bottles were neatly nestled inside, conscientiously wrapped in paper and looking like mortar rounds. He pulled out the first one that came to hand, stripped the paper away, and twisted off the cap without looking at the label. The Scottish single malt went down like lava and he realized that it had all started to taste like shit to him—good scotch, bad whiskey, it didn't matter. He swallowed audibly and the sound smacked of echo in the empty room. Unpacking was the perfect way to fill the hollowness of his new home. And the alcohol helped in the feeling less department, and that's what counted. Ignorance and bliss, the secrets to a happy life.

"Amen," he said aloud, and put another mouthful into the furnace.

For its size, Gavin was amazed at how much the first box marked ESSENTIALS held. Portable CD player, two dozen CDs to keep him going until he got the big vinyl engine set up, toilet paper, six bottles of water, a crystal tumbler, paper towels, Windex, two empty notebooks and a box of Rollerballs, some candles, matches, a flashlight, a bag of Snickers bars, some beef jerky, a bag of Doritos, a coffee maker, a bag of ground coffee, a Victoria's Secret catalogue, a digital camera, and a Ziploc containing three joints. Gavin stood back and smiled. Shannon, in her not-so-subtle way, was telling him to get back on track. The notebooks were telling him to start working, the grass was telling him to relax, and the lingerie catalog was telling him to smile.

There was only one item in the second box, an auto-graphed black-and-white photograph of Adolph Hitler, sitting in his study at Obersalzberg, reading a book, a German shepherd curled up contentedly at his feet. When Gavin's first book, *Ironmonger*, had gone best-seller, his publisher had asked Mickey Spillane to write a blurb for the cover of the mass-market paperback. Spillane had loved the book, acknowledging Gavin as the first true voice to come out of American publishing in ten years. As a gesture in welcoming Gavin to the inner circle of great American writers, Spillane had sent him the autographed photo of the Führer. Spillane, notorious for never signing photos of himself, had inscribed the bottom of the photo with the line: *Monsters do not always appear monstrous—Mickey Spillane*. Of all the awards and accolades that *Ironmonger* had garnered, that photograph meant the most.

Gavin held the portrait at arm's length and examined the figure in the overstuffed antique wing chair. All the twisted images and horrors that his mind could conjure paled in comparison to the meek little man with the Chaplin mustache who had systematically cooked thirteen million human beings and burned his way through most of Europe in a handful of years. One thing you had to give old Adolph, he was the real deal—history's one true bad apple. Gavin slipped the portrait under his arm and decided it was time to find a place for Mr. Hitler.

After a cursory glance around the old kitchen, he realized that there simply weren't any walls. Period. Cabinets and a big window that spilled out onto the patio and garden where three old iron chairs were trying to outdo each other in a race to rust beyond recognition. Nope, it would have to be another room.

In the dining room he studied his new table, a big English affair that looked like a mahogany runway on tapered legs. Even though it eclipsed his needs, Gavin liked the table with its two hundred years of patina that gave it the depth of old leather. A part of him wondered why the fuck he needed this thing. He was alone out here in the country and for the foreseeable future he'd be eating by himself. He and Chelsea used to have parties a few times a year, mostly Christmastime and in the summer. They didn't have a lot of friends; the people they met all seemed so phony, mostly hangers-on. All their old friends had somehow slipped away. But they had managed to scrape together half a dozen acquaintances whose company they enjoyed. Chelsea had been the one to get him out, to pull him away from the self-imposed schedule of his writing and force him to socialize. She had enjoyed having people over. Chelsea had enjoyed a lot of things. Had. Past tense. She was dead.

Gavin thought of her beautiful black hair, matted down with blood and liquid and brains. "Stop it," he said aloud. But it didn't help much.

Whatever tenuous grasp he had on finding a spot for Adolph had slipped away. He was no longer interested. So the portrait ended up on the mantel beside the large mahogany table where it would stay for the rest of the season.

Music. He needed some music. And the joints suddenly made a lot of sense.

Five minutes later he was sitting out on the patio, on the top of the steps that led down to the boathouse and the lake. Gavin was resting his elbow on one knee, his chin in his hand, a joint in his free hand, the rise and drop of the ember slow and relaxed in the foggy afternoon. The patio doors were wide open and the thunderous roar of the Guns

N' Roses opus "Paradise City" was belting out into the yard and across the lake. He wore black leather jeans and a gray T-shirt with *The New York Dolls* printed across the chest in cracked letters the hue of old bone. His tattoo crawled out of his sleeve and wound down his arm, the flesh colored with myriad pigments. Except for the intermittent swing of his arm bringing the joint to his lips, he was motionless, staring at the lake through a gossamer haze of marijuana smoke.

The rough feeling of the cool stone on his bare feet fought the warmth of the alcohol firing his belly. The sensation was not unpleasant. He smiled and took another hit of the grass.

Gavin thought about the hunched little boy in the sombrero he had seen fishing in the bay. Man, had he scared the shit out of that kid. When he thought about it, it made sense. The house had been deserted for what? Three-quarters of a century. Maybe the kid fished here every day, never saw a soul. Hell, even the real estate agent had called the place "the haunted house." Everyone in town probably did. Gavin had walked down the stone steps to check out the little boat with the Jolly Roger hanging off the bow. When he saw it was a kid, he thought that maybe it would be nice to say hi, to meet someone from here. Let the kid know that it was okay to fish here anytime he wanted. Gavin had spoken and the boy vanished. Maybe he hadn't really been there at all.

Bullshit, Gavin thought, that's the grass. The kid had been here. And he had been scared shitless. When he thought about it, it was actually quite funny. The laugh started as a smile, grew into a grin, and exploded in a laugh. It felt good. He had forgotten how good. Christ, when was the last time he had laughed? Before Chelsea had died. And the image of her smashed skull flashed across the television inside his head and the laugh dried in his throat.

Well, better to have laughed and lost than to never have laughed at all. Sure. Like love. Chelsea was dead. This was all going to take a while. He took another drag on the joint and held it in. He hadn't smoked dope in years. It had never made sense to him because it interfered with his work. He'd smoke pot and his writing would go to shit. *If* he wrote at all. And no writing, no paycheck. But the writing had never been about the money, not even when Chelsea had been clipping coupons and waiting for mac and cheese to go on sale for seventeen cents at the Price Chopper over on Morgan Avenue. Back a million years ago in Brooklyn on the dark side of the moon.

The writing had always been about the work. About getting it done because it was the one thing he was good at. Maybe even talented at. And Chelsea had been his biggest fan, sending out stories, queries, and manuscripts to every publisher in the *Writer's Market*, alphabetically, as their budget would allow. Three bucks, ninety-one cents postage for one of his novels, seventy-seven cents media rate for a short story in a manila envelope, standard postage for a query letter. Always with a note saying that they would be happy to pay return postage for a rejected submission because the postage cost less than having the work photocopied down at Samuel's Printing. He worked every day, up at five a.m., breakfast with Chelsea when she got up at seven, back to work at eight, pounding away at the keyboard until five in the afternoon.

He did his work on a big IBM Selectric, the first true electric typewriter. Then, for their first Christmas together, Chelsea had bought him an old laptop—a Toshiba T-100XE, loaded with a bootleg copy of WordPerfect 5.1. It had taken him a few days to get used to both the newfound freedom as well as the constraints of the computer. But the program stuck and, for years afterward, all he would use was WordPerfect 5.1 because it had always done the job. Three months after Chelsea had given him that first laptop, he handed her the first draft of *Ironmonger* and left the apartment.

When he had come back that night, she had been sitting on the sofa, crying. She loved the book. Completely loved it. After Gavin pounded out a rewrite, she had sent it off to Mike Remington, an editor at Blacktree Books who had been encouraging in his personal replies to Gavin's last two submissions even though he had turned the work down. Five mornings after the book had been slipped over the counter at the Brooklyn Post Office, Remington had called. About a book deal—a three-book deal. His first contract.

Gavin felt the heat of the joint reach the V in his fingers and he was back to the now. Back to the patio, the fog-shrouded lake, and to being alone. He let the tail end of the grass drop to the stone step where he crushed it out with the heel of his bare foot and stood up. When he was vertical he teetered for a second, smiled weakly, and started down to the dock. The harmonic opening riff to "Sweet Child O' Mine" started up, the echo of the primal recording fluttering through the forest on a swarm of wings.

He stood on the dilapidated dock, the old timbers gray and porous with dry rot. Standing as near as he could to the edge, he stared out into the small bay. The fog was still thick but it was dimmer now as the Egyptian sun god, Ra, finished the final leg of the day's journey—the bright white of an hour ago had faded to a muted gray and the russet shards of sunset were gone. Gavin swayed with the alcohol and drugs floating around in his system and tried to focus on the lake, to see if there was anything to see. Maybe the little kid in the boat would be back.

Off in the distance, somewhere at the edge of where the fog and the water melted together, Gavin saw a ripple. The ripple drew out, elongated, and grew into a hump. It zigged slowly to one side, then lazily zagged back. The writer stood, mesmerized, watching its progress across the small bay. He couldn't tell how far it was from him. Or how big it was. But it looked too big to be a fish—*any* fish. There was a quick flutter behind the hump, the water erupted, and it was gone, leaving a widening circle of rings undulating across the mercury still of the bay.

Gavin was still staring at the epicenter when a wave sloshed up against one of the pilings, the first in a series that hit with a metronomic rhythm that went on for a while. He watched the little bay until it was once again silent and still and he suddenly realized that he was very drunk and very stoned.

# 13

Tom Stockman's eyes were about to give out. Like Uncle Charlie, he had been out here for hours, scouring the area for any signs of Finn Horn's boat. Off to starboard he heard the loud rumble of water pounding through the turbines of Caldasac Dam. Stockman was less of an optimist than Charlie; he had reached the point of just wanting to get the call that they were shutting down for the night. Anywhere else, they'd stay out all night. But not on Caldasac. You never went out on this lake at night. That's just the way it was. And Stockman wanted to go home, pop the cap off a Lucky Lager, drop down in front of the tube, and develop a nice combination of slurred speech and square eyes so he wouldn't have to think of this goddamned shitty piece of water for another night.

Stockman adjusted the rudder to bring the boat to port a few degrees. The continual rumble from the dam gates coupled with the constant pressure he had to put on the rudder to keep his course were reminders of just how close he was to the big dam. The current here was relentless, and a minute of inattention could end up in the boat being sucked through one of the floodgates. He couldn't see it, but out there, a hundred yards to his port side, the dam rose out of the water like the face of a mountain. Stockman had a healthy respect for the dam—three people had been chewed through the grinders and he did not want to add his name to the list. As long as he stayed in the boat, there was little chance of that. There was a swatch of fence that ran across the feed for the dam, but it only extended ten feet into the depths (maybe less when the water level was low) and he knew that the suction from the dam could pull someone under the barrier in less time than it took to shit your pants. So he kept the dam in the back of his mind and three hundred feet off his starboard side. But it was a good place to be; the kid had been wearing a life jacket and would therefore float, and if he floated, the dam would suck him this way. If he hadn't already disappeared forever.

Stockman revved the engine again, and the Skeeter bass boat tacked to port by about thirty feet. On the GPS screen he saw the zigzag pattern of his past two hours, an irregular heartbeat. He checked the gas gauge—running out of fuel next to a monolithic meat grinder was not high on his list of to-dos today. Over half a tank. Plenty.

Stockman rubbed the bridge of his nose to stave off the headache he felt coming on. At least that asshole had stopped playing rock music, the strains of which Stockman could hear even through the rumbling power of the dam. He closed his eyes for a second, clamped them down to clear out the tension building up. When he opened them he saw it.

It was coming in quick and looked to be moving faster than the current, a big red sombrero spinning on the water. It belonged to Finn Horn. The kid *always* wore that thing. Stockman peered into the fog and called out the boy's name. "Finn!"

Silence.

"Finn!" he called once more, his voice bouncing with crisp echo.

Stockman stared into the vast expanse of white that was dimming with the sunset. There was no sign of the boy other than the big hat moving toward him. He was going to let it slip by, get sucked through one of the flood gates, but it was coming close enough that reaching it wasn't much of an effort. It spun in close and glanced off the prow of Stockman's boat then angled back and slid aft. Stockman reached over the side to pull it in. He missed the hat but grabbed the leather lanyard.

A snout erupted from the water, long and sleek and deadly. Stockman jerked. Stumbled back. Teeth clamped down on his arm and in one quick jerk tore him overboard.

He never felt it hit his body. Or the rush of water into his throat and lungs as it carried him under.

But he did feel the pain of the beast eating him. All of it. Intimately.

It lasted for the rest of his life.

# 14

Three miles upstream from Caldasac Dam, Uncle Charlie saw Finn Horn's boat materialize out of the fog, growing from an indistinct shadow to a pewter patch of geometry against the black background of water. He squinted into the haze and the boat took shape. It was half-submerged and abandoned, sunk to within a few inches of the gunwale, dead in the water. Caldasac had taken someone else.

He eased the deep-V hull up to Finn's little skiff and dropped the engine revs so there would be no wake; he didn't want to risk sinking the boat, as it would be needed for evidence.

What the hell had happened? The side was almost smashed in, the aluminum buckled as if a car had hit it. When he killed his engine the sound of water sloshing around inside the little boat sounded bizarre and out of place and it struck him as odd that out here, in the middle of a lake, the sound of water would be foreign.

"Jesus Christ," Uncle Charlie muttered. The little crippled boy had probably been thrown out of the boat and drowned. Charlie shook his head sadly. They'd never find him now. Not on this lake.

As he came alongside, something yellow flashed in the little boat. Pants. Yellow pants. And a jacket. A kid's rain suit. Then he saw the boots and the almost blue face rising from the flooded interior of the boat. The goddamned kid was inside! Uncle Charlie looked at the little form, laid out, blue lips and pale skin, floating like he probably did at home in the bathtub. His hand clenched his fishing rod. The rod was vibrating, the tip shaking from the shock waves traveling up the fiberglass blank. The kid was alive!

"Finn!" Uncle Charlie hollered, and almost jumped into the sinking craft.

The boy's eyes fluttered open and he smiled weakly. "Please don't let it get me," was all he said. Then he closed his eyes.

# 15

Sheriff Pope pulled into the drive on autopilot. His mind was in fine form, and he couldn't stop smiling. Not because they had found the little gimp—Pope really couldn't have cared less on that one; another burden on society as far as he was concerned. And not because he had managed to fuck that new flat-chested waitress up the ass in the bathroom of the Dunkin' Donuts over on State Road 47E. Nope. Today Pope was just high on life. And the 150 milligrams of Benzedrine he had fed into his boiler ten minutes ago.

And the scratchy-scratch insect symphony that was creaking away in his brain.

Pope looked up and shook his head. The change in the house was amazing. In just a few weeks the new owner had transformed a ramshackle pile of shit into a not-bad-looking place. Like almost everyone in New Mannheim, Pope had been here at least once in his life. Everyone knew the house. Just as everyone was afraid of it. He had been hearing stories since he had been a kid. Not that he believed any of the bullshit, but he had paid attention.

The sign at the mouth of the drive was new and clean; the words PRIVATE—NO TRESSPASSING so bold that a retard with glaucoma couldn't miss it. The closed-in, feral feeling of the double canopy forest was still there but the trees had been cut back and there were no branches scraping against the doors of his cruiser. The ruts had been filled in with gravel and the road graded.

After a few minutes of slowly negotiating the dark tunnel, the trees opened up and Pope found himself in the circular drive. The change was even more eye-jarring than the road down. Pulled up beside the house, the sheriff saw Mr. Johannus's blue Econoline and a new black Hummer. The sheriff shook his head at the big-city asshole vehicle.

He parked the cruiser, got out, and walked slowly to the door, taking in the changes to the house. Off on the property he heard the unmistakable clang of a hammer connecting with wood. From inside the house the stringy sound of some faggy classical music was whining away.

He paused at the door and took a deep breath that filled his chest with air. His lungs took the air, transformed it into oxygen for his blood, and sent it whirling off into his system as an electric charge. Yep, today he was high on life. The sheriff rang the bell.

And the cockroaches started up with an old number by Zeppelin.

***

Gavin was on the floor in the living room listening to Vivaldi and fingering the hammer on the stainless-steel .357. The handgun had been a gift from his agent after the stalker incident—said a handgun would make less of a mess the next time. Agents. Hilarious bunch of guys.

There had been no paperwork with the pistol and Gavin had no idea where it had come from. But he knew how to use it. At least at close range. And you couldn't get any closer than sticking the barrel into your mouth and blowing your brains all over the ceiling. There was no way to fuck this up as long as the gun was pointed well behind his eyes. He had seen photographs of a suicide gone bad—the barrel pointed too far forward. The slug took off the top half of the guy's face and once the doctors were done saving him, all that was left was an eyeless, noseless head that looked like a clenched fist that had been stitched together with butcher's twine. No, if he did this, he was going to do it properly.

He took another swig out of one of the tumblers that Shannon had so thoughtfully packed for him and squeezed the rubber combat grip. It was sweaty in his hand and the gun shifted in his palm. Outside he heard Mr. Johannus's hammer thwacking away at the boathouse roof, banging framing nails home with the precision of a machine. There was a man who worked with pride. Mr. Johannus liked what he did and it showed. *Like I used to be with the writing*, he thought morosely, feeling like he was thinking about someone else. Someone who cared. Fuck it, he thought, and dropped his head back, connecting with the mahogany paneling with a thud.

The doorbell rang.

Gavin squeezed his eyes shut and hoped whoever it was would go away.

They rang again.

He stood up and walked to the door, the pistol hanging loosely in his hand.

Once in the entryway, he realized that answering the door with a gun in his hand was bad manners, even in the country. He stuck it in his waistband and the cold steel made him realize that that was not much of a solution, either. It would probably slip down his pant leg, fall out his cuff, and blow a hole in his foot. He unceremoniously dropped it into a planter beside the staircase.

Gavin opened the door and stepped back, away from the bright morning sunshine, squinting. His eyes took a second to adjust to the bright flash of the sun. For an instant the shadow of a man was all he saw. Then the image slowly took form into a sheriff, hand on his pistol, Stetson low over his eyes doing a very good job of making him look like a stereotype.

He was a big man, maybe six four, all solid, even the thick deposit of fat around his middle that stretched the buttons on his khaki shirt. He had a face that seemed a little loose for the intense eyes that it held. The broad, flat nose of a boxer and a mouth that looked like it didn't know how to smile finished off the central casting features of the man.

"Mr. Corlie?" the figure asked.

Gavin nodded. He had no idea why the cops were here and didn't much care as long as they weren't asking for money.

The cop was taking him in, going over him in one long look. Gavin still wore the leather jeans from the night before but had left his shirt on the bed upstairs. The cop stared at the bright ink that stretched from his chest around his shoulder and down his arm. "G. Corlie?"

"Yeah."

"What do your friends call you?" The cop's expression told Gavin that he wasn't impressed by what he saw.

"You'll never know."

The cop took a breath and approached the question from another angle. Evidently, he didn't know Gavin's first name. "What does the G stand for?"

"Gavin." And he waited. Everyone said the same thing.

The cop was no different. "Like the horror writer?"

Gavin nodded. "Yeah, like the horror writer."

The sheriff smiled his best smile to let Gavin know what a swell guy he was. Gavin was surprised that the cop knew how to smile. "Mr. Corlie, I'm Sheriff Xavier Pope. A little boy had an accident on the lake yesterday. I'd like to ask you a few questions." He spoke with the clipped diction of his type. Halfway through the dialogue his hand shifted on his gun in a not-so-subtle way to let Gavin know that he was expecting cooperation.

Gavin fought the urge to tell the cop to go fuck himself and slam the door. He was not in the mood to be coerced by some jerkoff who thought that a gun strapped to his hip gave him the right to bully people. Gavin had grown up with people like this back in the neighborhood, only their uniform had been track suits, clean trainers, and last names ending in "ini." Then the image of the kid with the sombrero popped into his head and he wondered if anything had happened to the boy.

"Yeah, sure," he said, and walked away from the door, leaving the sheriff to come in.

He picked up a white T-shirt from one of the open boxes and stretched it over his frame.

Pope crossed the threshold and stepped into character, slowly looking around and taking in the place. He looked at the antique furniture, the stereo boxes piled up, the bottle of booze sitting on the newel post. "What you listening to?"

*Music, asshole.* "Vivaldi. *The Four Seasons.*" Gavin paused for a second, listened. "'Winter.'" In truth, Gavin knew very little about classical music; it just so happened that Vivaldi was the only classical album he owned.

Pope nodded like he really didn't care.

Gavin's back was to Pope and he rolled his eyes. "You want a cup of coffee?" This had not started well and Gavin wanted to get it on track.

"Sure. Black. No sugar."

*That's what black means.* Gavin washed his hands at the sink, opened the rolled paper bag of coffee that Shannon had packed for him, and got to work with a spoon. While he was putting the filter in the machine, Pope swept his arm through the air in a general way, indicating the house.

"Place looks great. Must have set you back some."

Gavin nodded. "A bit."

"I see. Must be fun, making stuff up and getting paid for it."

Gavin thought about that for a second; Pope wasn't all wrong. "At times, yes."

Pope nodded again, this time with even less enthusiasm. The big sheriff looked around the kitchen like the place had suddenly become very interesting. As Pope's eyes crawled over the walls, the conversation drifted off into an uncommunicative silence that was marred only by the gurgling of the coffee maker.

There was something unsettling about the big cop that took a conscious effort to figure out. It took a few seconds for it to come to him—there was no rustle of fabric when the man moved, his boot soles didn't scrape the floor, his leather holster didn't creak as he shifted his weight. He was completely and utterly silent.

"So, what happened on the lake yesterday?" Gavin asked.

Pope seemed to snap awake. "Yeah. Yesterday. Little kid from town. Crippled. Hit something with his boat and almost drowned. He's in the hospital over in Malone. Said that he was out here by the haunted house—which is *this* house— and saw something that spooked him. Doesn't remember what happened." Pope shifted his gun belt. "*You* remember what happened, Mr. Corlie?"

The coffee maker was wheezing its way through the first cup. "I was here with my assistant and another friend. We were waiting for the movers to show up and I heard a boat out behind the house. Went down to see who was there. I saw a kid fishing under the dock. Thought it would be nice to say hello. Said hi and he got scared and took off. Disappeared like a shot." Gavin paused for a second, remembering the terrified look on the boy's face. "That's it." The boy had run his boat into something and almost drowned. Swell. Maybe Gavin's luck was getting contagious. "Is he all right?"

"He's fine. Someone that went out to find him didn't do so well. Local man by the name of Tom Stockman was searching for the cri—uh...*handicapped* boy. We found Stockman's boat near the dam."

"And Stockman?"

Pope shook his head. "Drowned probably. No body."

"Without a body, how can you be sure?" Gavin saw a lot missing in the deductive reasoning department.

Pope rolled his eyes as if he was dealing with a small child. "Caldasac is a spring-fed lake, cold and deep. Body gets water-logged and sinks to the bottom. In a warmer lake, the gasses form quickly and a body will rise after a day or so. In Caldasac, the cold temperatures keep the gasses from forming for a long time and a body stays submerged for weeks. Of course in a stretch like that, all the little creatures that live in the water have time to pick away at the body and it's eaten before it has time to rise to the surface and get found." Pope dictated from memory, giving Gavin the speech that Duncan Parks, the medical examiner, had once given him. "It's rare we find a body on Caldasac. People just go missing." Pope's eyes narrowed in the universal expression of mistrust. "What did you say to the boy?"

Gavin looked into Pope's fidgety green eyes. "I told you, *nothing*. I wanted to say hi but the kid took off. That's the story. Period."

"And you were here with your assistant?"

Gavin nodded.

"Your assistant, he got a name?"

"This has nothing to do with my assistant."

"So you don't want to give me your assistant's name?"

Gavin took a deep breath. There was a definite gap in the communication process here. "No, I don't want to give you my assistant's name. You can speak to my lawyer. Harold Lexman. Lexman, Grizwacz, and Steiner, 191 Park Avenue, Suite 1106."

Pope nodded like he had expected this. "Know your lawyer's address by heart, huh?"

Gavin smiled sourly. "Get the fuck out of my house right now."

Pope stepped back. "Excuse me?"

"No, I won't. I answered your questions. Now we're done. Get the fuck out." Gavin pointed at the door.

"Have it your way." Pope backed out, his hand on the grip of his pistol. His eyes told Gavin that he wanted something to happen.

After Pope's car had disappeared through the trees, Gavin poured himself a cup of coffee. What the fuck had that been about? That guy gave new meaning to the word *intense*. Welcome to the country. Drops of coffee hit the hot surface of the burner and skidded around. He put the pot back and walked outside, leaving the machine to hiss away.

He went out onto the patio with his hands wrapped around the warm mug. Down on the dock, Mr. Johannus was finishing up with the yoists on the new boathouse roof. The old one had been peeled away early in the morning and the carpenter had piled it up at the edge of the yard, near his van. At the end of the day he'd load it up and take it off to the dump. Gavin smiled and shook his head, wondering where the man got his energy.

He watched the carpenter for a few minutes but his eye kept being drawn out, past the man swinging the hammer, to the lake. He couldn't push the image of the little boy in the red sombrero out of his mind. He had scared the kid and he had an accident. And someone else was missing. In a not too abstract way, these accidents were his fault. But there were no accidents. Everyone said that.

And he remembered Chelsea's broken, bloody body.

People were wrong. There were plenty of accidents. Enough to go around.

# 16

He was awake. Instantly and completely. The full moon was bouncing light off the lake, and shadows floated across the wall in jagged spears. Gavin sat up in bed and wondered what the time was. The night was silent, and the first glow of morning was nowhere in sight; it had to be early. He fumbled around on the night table for his watch. The luminous hands read 3:10 a.m. Not bad. Almost two solid hours of sleep. Things were getting better. He suddenly wished that he had cows to milk. Or a tractor to start. After thinking about it for a few seconds he decided that he'd settle on a book to write.

He got out of bed and the cool night air washed over his naked body, bringing out an involuntary shiver. He looked out through the big Palladian window at the dark surface of the lake, dancing with flashes of moonlight. The fog had lifted and the view was once again beautiful, almost serene. A pair of birds, black ellipses trailing thin wakes, slowly toured the bay. They looked to be in no great hurry to go anywhere.

He had never understood the attraction of living on the water. Not unless you were a muskrat. But the past two days had changed him. There was something calming about the water that he had never experienced. In some small way he was starting to understand why people went boating. There was something primal, almost elemental, about the lake. And it felt natural to look at it. And why not? The biomechanical connection between humans and water was undeniable; the human body was almost 80 percent pure unfiltered H-Two-Oh, a leftover attachment to the primordial puddle where our distant ancestors were first spawned. All this assuming that you subscribed to Darwin, Leakey, and the rest of the heretics that had fathered modern anthropology. The other option was believing in the Bible. But even there you had the flood myth. Water as a punishment. Water to cleanse. Holy water in the original form, pre-dating Jesus and the biblical vision of the world. And you couldn't ignore its physical presence/manifestation on the planet. Two-thirds of the earth is water. The moon is responsible for the tides. A lunar cycle is comprised of 29.5 days. As is a woman's menstrual cycle, which is a cleansing. You could go in circles.

He stood in front of the window, staring at the lake, trying to decide what to do. He had two options—go back to sleep or get up and do something. Sleep was ixnayed out of the gate. He knew himself, knew how his body worked, and sleep was not an option. Time to get up. Get up and do what? In the old days the answer would have been simple: *Write, asshole!* He slid on a pair of jeans and a hoodie, slipped his feet into a pair of moccasins, and headed downstairs in the dark.

He heard the pulse of crickets as he descended the old oak staircase. The chirp of the insects was interrupted by the long wail of a loon and he instantly recognized it for what it was. *Crazy as a loon. Birds of a feather stick together. Fuck, I start thinking like this and I'm never going to write a decent story ever again.* But it made him smile.

He walked into the kitchen, flipped on the light, and started a pot of coffee. Out of the corner of his eye he thought he saw the silhouette of a cat slink by the window but when he turned, the pane was empty. He wondered if he had really seen it and, if he had, if it was the cat that Amy had seen the other day. By extension, he wondered if it was related to the Michelangelo cat that had left his paw print in the mortar on the house two hundred years ago. He turned away from the window and concentrated on the pot of coffee, hoping that focusing on it would make the coffee magically appear faster. The machine slowly got up to speed, coughing out the first—or last, depending how you looked at it—pot of the day. The loon let loose again, this one somehow longer and more mournful. Gavin leaned back against the counter and watched the dark brown liquid fill up the glass pot. The smell was wonderful. It was one of his favorite smells. Chelsea had loved it too.

The thought froze him where he stood. Chelsea had *loved* something. She was never going *to love* something. Past tense. Good night, New York.

Gavin walked down to the lake in his slippers. The mason Mr. Johannus had found had started repointing the steps, and the awkward lopsided stones of a week ago were solid and sure—or at least the first third were—and it was nice to make the trek without having to worry about breaking his neck. The dark form of the boathouse was outlined against the silver surface of the water. Mr. Johannus had made progress with the roof, and the uncompleted timber skeleton stood out against the sky like a rib cage. Gavin had to hand it to the old Finnish carpenter, the man didn't fuck around. Arrived every morning by seven, sat in his truck until seven thirty reading Boob Palace and sipping coffee from a dented travel mug. Started work at seven thirty sharp and worked through until ten a.m. when he stopped for his fifteen-minute coffee break, taken back in the van, this time with a piece of cake. Then he would work until noon, take a twenty-minute break for lunch, then work straight through until five. Never wore a watch and was never more than a minute off his schedule either way. Gavin was very happy that he had found someone who was helping him turn the house into a home.

The beauty of the house was that it hadn't been occupied for the better part of the twentieth century, and therefore had not succumbed to any well-intentioned but fundamentally ill-conceived attempts at modernization. Gavin was the first owner since the summer of 1938, when the last owner had died. What little Gavin knew he had learned from the agent. The former proprietor, one Maximillian Koestler, had drowned and the house had been taken over by the town of New Mannheim after a probationary period of five years. It had not been sold or occupied since, and Gavin was the first to show even moderate interest in the place.

He saw the pair of loons silhouetted out in the bay. They were moving about in their own lazy way, twenty yards apart. They were supposed to taste like shit—totally inedible even if you were starving. Something akin to rotting fish. But good luck. He had read that somewhere. What the fuck, he could use a little luck right about now. Maybe things were going to work out after all.

The breakwater was an old stone affair that ran about a hundred and fifty feet across the waterfront. The stones grew up out of the lake and wrapped around the ledge, rolling back ten feet to the lawn, providing a deck. The boathouse sat at the far end of this deck, and the steps from the house joined it at the other.

Gavin dropped into a new unpainted Adirondack chair that Mr. Johannus had built for him as a gift. The scent of freshly cut wood and pine sap was foreign to him and he added it to his list of favorite smells right under coffee. Mr. Johannus had not painted the chair on purpose, he had pointed out, stating that the old weathered look was the way a real man would want it. Gavin didn't have an opinion one way or the other so he followed the handyman's words, figuring that he knew what he was talking about. The surface was cool and rough and smelled wonderful. Gavin was surprised at how comfortable it was considering the lack of cushions. Old-time thinking—keep things simple, low-tech. Gavin smiled at that one and thought about how he still did most of his writing with a fountain pen and a pile of Mead composition notebooks. Pen and paper, keep it simple. Like the loons. Which is what he was trying to do. He thought about the John Prine song, "Spanish Pipedream." And it all made sense. Then again, that was what made Prine the voice he was—*that* and a bout with a squamous cell carcinoma. Gavin leaned back into the chair and began to sing.

He was in the middle of a very bad impression of a dreadnought guitar being plucked by a West Kentucky farm boy when something exploded out in the bay. He snapped his head down, mouth still open from singing, and peered out into the dark water. He saw the tail end of something *large* reenter the water. Or at least he thought he had. He stood up and stared at the ever-widening circle of waves spreading out into the bay. One of the loons was gone. Its partner at the edge of the bay began its run and was airborne before Gavin's last note had died out.

Gavin stared at the waves rolling out. *Yeah, sure, loons are lucky. Luckiest little fuckers around. Can't get luckier than that.* Gavin shook his head. *Apparently they didn't taste too bad, either.* He had to stop believing everything he read. Fucking writers, all they do is lie.

# 17

Gavin rolled into the parking lot and found a good spot immediately. He looked around and realized that there were a lot of good spots. He smiled. Welcome to the country, Shannon had said.

The Malone hospital was a rectangular stone affair dating from the turn of the century, built with function, not aesthetics, in mind. He got out of the big unwieldy vehicle and grimaced. He hated the beast—it was loud, sucked gas like a German Panzer, and turned heads in a way that only a banker would understand. Gavin slammed the door and the heavy portal thudded home and hermetically sealed the black tank. He decided that one of these days he was going to throw some mud on the thing to tone it down. He really felt like an idiot driving it around.

He looked around the lot and smiled when he saw that parking was free, because back in the city there was no such thing. Nothing had been free in New York, especially parking, because cars, like real estate, took up space and on an island they weren't building any more land. He had never been a car buff but when *Ironmonger* had gone best-seller, and the paperback rights had sold for a then record, he had gone out and bought himself a used Porsche. It had been the first car he had ever owned and it was the last car he had purchased— the new Hummer Shannon had talked him into now voiding that claim. The vintage 911 now sat in the garage back in the city, forty years old and living under a tarp like the furniture in his apartment.

The parking lot was full of four-by-fours and pickups, all purchased out of necessity, not an urge to keep up with the Joneses. The morning was warm and the unmistakable scent of a barbecue not too far away was mouth-watering. But who the hell barbecued at this hour? He chalked it up to another quirk of living in the country. He wove between the parked cars toward the building.

There had been two stories about the lake in the local paper that morning. The first was about Finn Horn, the handicapped boy who had almost died of hypothermia after hitting what a nameless official had described as a *water hazard*. The second story was bogged down with the somber prose of a small-town newspaperman who didn't have enough tragedy to keep himself happy—all topped off with too many exclamation points. One of the men who had been involved in the rescue had somehow fallen overboard and drowned. The body had yet to be found and, in the tradition of Caldasac, it was doubted that it ever would be. Local authorities were looking into the accident but it seemed straightforward. Gavin thought about Sheriff Pope and decided that there wouldn't be that much looking into the incident regardless of what the official line was.

Gavin had called the reporter after reading the article on Finn. The story had been pretty clear that the little boy had lost his boat and that his mother, a waitress in a local diner, was not going to be able to replace it. Evidently, the family was not that well off. Gavin couldn't shake the feeling that he was somehow responsible for the whole mess. It took a little finagling but Gavin finally convinced the reporter to get the boy's mother to call him. Ten minutes later the phone rang.

Ms. Horn was a no-nonsense woman who sounded tired and worried and kind and Gavin just came out and asked if it was all right for him to go and visit Finn. At first Ms. Horn had sounded unsure, but after tentative first-impression-type questions she slowly eased into the idea. He explained the responsibility that he felt and simply wanted to make good on what he considered to be a karma debt. After a little *I-don't-know*-ing she had given in. It was pretty clear that Finn didn't have a lot of friends and was spending a lot of his time alone and maybe a visitor would do him some good. Then we have a lot in common, Gavin had thought, and hung up the phone.

The information board was a square backlit console bolted to the floor in the middle of the battleship-gray lobby, which had elements of *Star Trek* about it that for some odd reason seemed aesthetically appropriate for the building. *Pediatrics, Fourth Floor*. There was one elevator, a small cubicle that looked as if it was smaller than when it had first been built due to three hundred coats of lead-based paint, various shades of yellow, white, and lavender, that had been system-atically scabbed onto the walls. As the small car ascended the core of the building, Gavin read some graffiti scrawled onto the door. *Nurse Groucho has a dik.* Gavin rode up the four floors wondering who Nurse Groucho was and how the barely literate but cinematically versed vandal had come by this very personal information.

Gavin got off on the pediatrics ward and went to the desk. A large nurse with short, mannish hair and a mustache covering most of her upper lip came over from an antique green-screened desktop computer. Gavin tried not to look at the mustache. This had to be Nurse Groucho. He wondered if she really *did* have a dick.

"May I help you?" she asked.

"I'm here to visit somebody." He tried to focus on her eyes. It wasn't easy. "Finn Horn."

The nurse nodded curtly. "Room four fourteen."

Gavin stared at the mustache then at her eyes, then back at the mustache, then down at her hands where he saw a wedding ring, then back at the mustache. *Why doesn't she get that thing waxed? She's got to see it. Hell, it's got to tickle her husband's cock, for fuck's sake.* "Um, thanks. Four fourteen. Appreciated."

She smiled again, snapped the binder closed, and went back to her work, apparently unaware that she had a distracting mustache growing out of her face. Gavin turned away, wondering if she'd ever seen the graffiti in the elevator. If so, did she know it was about her? If not, she had to wonder just who the fuck Nurse Groucho was, especially if there was a dick involved, didn't she? After all, she did work in the hospital and, due to its size, would know the entire nursing staff, correct? Regardless of the graffiti, Gavin presumed that she owned a mirror. The logic of *If I shave, it will only grow back* couldn't apply. Frequent shaving *had* to be better than looking like Alberta Einstein. He walked on down the hall with his train of thought rambling over the mustache track.

Finn Horn was sitting upright in bed reading a tattered copy of *Musky Hunter Magazine*. He looked very much like Pinocchio, lying there quietly reading his magazine, his small frame accentuated by the slack sheets that hung over his legs, his too-big head resting on the pillow. His pure black hair was haloed by the sun coming in through the window and, coupled with his pale complexion, lent him an ethereal quality. Finn turned to see Gavin.

"What room you looking for?" the little boy asked.

"Four fourteen."

The boy looked puzzled and his face scrunched up. "*This* is four fourteen. Who you looking for?"

"Finn Horn."

Finn eyed the gift-wrapped box under Gavin's arm, then Gavin's face, then the gift again. "Who are you?"

*Beware of strangers bearing gifts.* Smart kid. "I'm Gavin Corlie," he said, wondering if Finn would recognize the name.

Finn eyed Gavin suspiciously. "The horror writer?"

Gavin was surprised not to hear *like* precede the question. But kids were like that. Perceptive. "Yeah, the horror writer."

Finn folded up his magazine, reverently placed it on the chipped metal nightstand as if it were a religious tome, and turned to Gavin. He folded his hands on his lap, his face serious. "Are you here about the monster?"

# 18

Sheriff Pope grunted and leaned back in his chair. He propped his size 13 boots up on the linoleum-topped steel desk, closed his eyes, and concentrated on not puking. He had a headache directly proportional to the amount of Wild Turkey shooters he had knocked back at Black Eyed Susie's last night, and the ratio was considerable. He had crawled out of the bar at about three a.m., driven home, and fallen asleep while fucking his wife. He didn't remember the falling asleep part but she had reminded him this morning over his breakfast of vulcanized eggs, cinder toast, and shitty potatoes. For the rest of the week he would be eating three squares a day at Black Eyed Susie's just to be sure that Doris wasn't slipping any arsenic into his food. Unless he managed to stay awake through the horror of sticking his cock in the water buffalo who used to be his wife. Which required a lot of booze. And that put him back at square one. *Aw, fuck it*, he thought. *Eat at the diner. Less painful.*

A meal was the last thing he wanted to think about at this particular juncture in time. He closed his eyes and tried to clear his mind. He was listing to one side, nodding off into the soft haze of a nap, when the phone jolted him awake.

"Yeah, Sheriff Pope here?" It came out as a question, as if he wasn't sure who he was.

"Sheriff Pope, this is Dr. Laurel over in Malone. You said that I should call when we had definitive news on Finn Horn's condition."

Pope grunted and tried to listen. It wasn't easy. The little men with the castanets were dancing away inside his skull, trying to knock a few of the floorboards loose. He just hoped that they wouldn't rouse the cockroaches—they got ugly real fast when you woke them with no reason. He fumbled around in his desk drawer without opening his eyes and was rewarded with a bottle of aspirin.

"I just thought you'd like to know that he's going to be fine." Dr. Laurel's voice had started to echo and Pope had to concentrate.

"Hmm," Pope mumbled. He popped the cap off the aspirin and tilted the bottle back into his mouth. The pills were bitter and chalky. "Mokay." He opened one eye, saw the coffee cup with yesterday's bitter offerings, and reached over for it. He tried to swallow a mouthful. The combination of the old coffee and the powdery tablets brought a gag to his throat that he was barely able to fight back. The pills went down in one acidic surge.

There was a pause at the other end of the line. "Sheriff Pope?"

"Um, yeah, sorry. Just looking for a pen." *Shit!* Pope tried to bring up an image of Dr. Laurel and was pleasantly rewarded by what he saw. Beautiful big brown eyes set deep in a face that looked like it came off a fairy out of a children's book. Short black hair. And a smile that would look good wrapped around his cock.

Dr. Laurel continued. "He's had a good scare and I want to keep him for another day."

"Thanks, Doc. Look, the reason I wanted you to keep me informed is that we still don't know what happened out on that lake. The boy say anything else?"

"Not to me."

Pope thought about that one for a second.

"What, exactly, are you looking for?" she asked.

"A man died out there. I'm not a big believer in coincidences."

"You think that Finn Horn had something to do with the drowning?" Laurel asked.

"Let's just say that I'm curious by nature."

"I'll talk to him myself, see what he has to say." Laurel sounded like she honestly cared. "Are you going to come down and speak to him before he's released?"

Pope thought about the boy's house, about the cheap carpet with the tire ruts and the plastic-paneled living room. Last place he wanted to be was back there, talking to the idiot mother. "Yeah. I'll come by later. He ain't going anywhere on his own, huh?" Pope liked that one.

Dr. Laurel didn't sound impressed. "I'll be here until seven p.m. Come talk to me first. Nurse Scott will be on the floor, tell her that I want to speak to you."

"She the one with the mustache?" he asked.

"She's the one with the name tag that says *Nurse Scott* on it." And the line went dead.

Pope dropped the phone on its cradle and leaned back. What was wrong with people? The broad *did* have a mustache. Had a dick too, from what he had heard. Probably one of them hermaphrodites. Tits and a dong. Shit, not a bad way to be born when you thought about it. Kept things interesting in the sack. Except she had one of those faces that all the scotch in the world wouldn't help to make any better. Then Pope's mind drifted back to last night. And all the whiskey shooters he had put away. And Doris, pissed off and burning his eggs into little Frisbees. That did it.

Pope bent over and puked in the garbage can.

# 19

Dr. Laurel slammed the phone down. She toyed around with a few medical terms for Sheriff Pope and finally settled for the old catchall: *asshole*. Why would anyone give an ignorant man like him a gun? Unless he was suicidal. That would make sense. But the world didn't work like that. Then she got irritated with herself for letting the sheriff make her angry. At least he had seemed honestly concerned about Finn, and that was something. He couldn't be *all* bad, could he?

As the head of pediatrics she deserved more space than she had but knew that square footage in the hospital was at a premium. Her office was small and cramped and most of the room was taken up by her desk. The few square feet that were left over held a guest chair and three filing cabinets. There were no photos on the walls, and the top of her desk was simply an extension of the filing cabinets, piles of folders and paper that looked ready to avalanche at the slightest noise. This was a place where work was done.

Dr. Laurel filed Finn Horn's folder deep within her paper mountain range. The boy had come in two days ago just after dark. His boat had hit something and he had spent the better part of the day in water that was hovering in the low fifties. He had displayed all the classic symptoms of hypothermia when they had wheeled him into the ER. His skin was bluish, and that combined with slurred speech led to a pretty straightforward diagnosis of cyanosis. The boy's pupils were dilated to their limits and his heart rate and respiration had dropped into the basement. His muscles were rigid but the ER doctor had noted that full tests were deemed too risky due to Finn's spinal condition. Laurel nodded her head; whoever had been on duty had done a good job.

In the whole file, only one little detail was troubling her—one word at the bottom of the page. The word was *monster*. Loss of perceptual contact with one's environment and hallucinations were capstones in the hypothermia diagnosis. But sometimes delirium brought out buried truths in a patient's world. What could this monster be? Or who?

# 20

Gavin stood at the foot of the bed and stared at the boy.

Finn's face was clenched into a knot. "You don't believe me." It was a statement, not a question.

Finn had *sounded* sincere. The story was improbable. Not very possible. But convincing. And Gavin understood that. It was what he did. Convinced people that spiders lived in their minds; that the little old lady who lived in the house at the corner wore a necklace of tongues under her human skin bustier; that the Sunday school teacher was addicted to heroin and cut parts of her body off every night in front of a webcam. He convinced people that what wasn't actually *was*. By definition, he was a professional liar. "I believe that you think you saw something."

Finn smiled sadly and shook his head, as if Gavin had a problem. "I'm not dopey. I'm not retarded. Something sure smashed the heck out of my boat and it wasn't me."

Gavin smiled.

"What's so funny?" Finn asked, more hurt than upset.

"I haven't heard the word *heck* since I left PS Ninety-Two."

"What's a PS Ninety-Two?" Finn asked blankly.

"PS. Public School. Brooklyn. Lot of swearing back in those days. Come to think of it, I didn't hear a lot of *heck*s there, either." Gavin saw the urine bag hanging at the foot of the bed, lopsided and half full, and he grew serious again.

"Yeah, I saw *West Side Story*," Finn said. "You guys dance around with switchblades and goofy sneakers?"

"Not quite." He thought about the time he saw Bobby Iannantuono stick a knife into Vincent Pasalipo and his breakfast eggs spilled down the front of his pants and onto the sidewalk, all slick and looking like snot.

"My mom don't like it when I swear."

"I know."

"How would you know?" The kid squared his shoulders against the pillow. It helped him look less sick. Not much, but a little.

"I talked to her on the phone. Nice lady, your mom. Didn't swear once during the whole conversation. And believe me, having you locked up in the hospital is a good reason to swear."

"You swear?"

"I accidentally put a screwdriver under my fingernail once. I swore then."

Finn winced and whistled in through his teeth. "You're not supposed to do stuff like that!"

Gavin smiled. "Thanks for the advice. I'll know better next time."

"Do stuff like what?" Dr. Laurel asked as she walked into the room.

Gavin looked at the little boy, held his finger to his lips in a half-secretive way. Finn laughed. "Put screwdrivers under your fingernails."

She nodded in approval. "As a doctor, I can say that your lack of medical training has in no way impaired your good sense."

Gavin looked over and studied her features. Small woman, maybe five three, and compact. She wore high heels, which looked out of place in the hospital, and black wool slacks with a big Navajo belt buckle. Her hair was jet black and cut very short, which forced you to fall back on her natural beauty for an impression. She had brown eyes, deep-set, and a smile a foot wide. "As a doctor you must have a long list of stupid things people have done to themselves," he said.

"Oh, I've seen some pretty dumb things in my career." Her face lit up. "Things that would make you sick."

"Sick? Really?" Finn asked. "Like what? Come on! You gotta tell me something cool!"

She seemed to seriously consider the option for a second, then her smile came back on. "First introduce me to your friend, Finn. I'm Dr. Laurel."

Gavin reached out and shook her hand. It was surprisingly firm. "Gavin Corlie."

Her eyebrow arched and Gavin tried not to look too annoyed. Here it comes—*Like the horror writer?*

"The writer?"

He smiled and nodded.

"What's so amusing?"

"Sorry, it's just that most people call me *the horror writer*. It's nice to just be called a writer." Gavin turned to Finn. "I like her."

Finn grinned. "Me too."

Gavin suddenly realized that he had been doing a lot of smiling today.

Dr. Laurel rolled the blood pressure monitor over from the door. "So, Finn," she said, her smile playing around on her mouth. "How do you know Mr. Corlie?"

"Forget him," the boy said, waving Gavin away with his arm. "I wanna hear the stories about the stupid stuff people do to themselves. Come on, just one." Finn held his arm out half in cooperation, half as a bribe for more information. "Come on!"

She acquiesced. "When I was working at the Shriners burn hospital in Boston they brought this mechanic in—the man worked in a foundry repairing iron-melting machin-ery. Big blast furnaces. Molten metal buckets. That kind of stuff. Anyhow, he was repairing something over a vat of mol-ten metal that was running somewhere around twenty-four hundred degrees. He dropped his wrench into the vat. Guess what he did?" she asked.

"He went and got a new wrench?" The unmistakable tim-bre of hope was in Finn's voice.

"Good guess but no. He reached into the molten metal right up to his elbow."

Finn made a face that was somewhere between the Tas-manian devil and Munch's *The Scream*. "Ouch!"

"Yeah. Ouch." Dr. Laurel turned to Gavin. "Right up there with putting a screwdriver under your fingernail. What were you doing at the time?"

"Stealing a car."

It was Dr. Laurel's turn to smile again and she did a great job of it. "Divine retribution is a bitch."

"I am having a hard time believing that you're a little country doctor," Gavin said defensively.

"I have that effect on people." She scanned Finn's file. "What are you doing in Malone, Mr. Corlie?"

"It's Gavin. I'm local now."

Dr. Laurel shook her head. "Oh no, you're not! Buying a place out here doesn't make you a local. I've been here for four years and they still follow me through Mickey's Grocer-ies to make sure I don't steal any potatoes."

"I look more trustworthy than you do."

"Why the move? Seems a little lost." She looked Gavin over as if to add, *city boy*.

An image of Chelsea's pulverized face reared up in his mind. "Just needed to get out of the city. Try the country life. Make some new friends."

"And how do you two know each other?"

"Finn and I had a little run-in two days ago and I thought I'd come by to see if the only person I know in town was doing all right. No one likes being in the hospital, so I thought..." He let the sentence trail off, realizing that he didn't really have a concrete plan.

Dr. Laurel looked down at the gift-wrapped box resting on the floor at the foot of the bed, beside the urine bag. "Don't you want to see what's in the box?" she asked Finn.

Finn beamed. "It beats the heck out of hearing about guys melting their arms off."

"You asked, kiddo." Dr. Laurel wrapped the rubber and Velcro pad around the boy's arm and reset the monitor. The machine started with a long, protracted farting sound. Dr. Laurel waited until the boy's blood pressure came up on the digital monitor. "One-twenty over sixty-five." She noted the readout on his chart. "You're doing good, Finn." She nodded to Gavin. "He can open his present while I take his temperature."

Gavin handed the big box over to Finn. It took a few seconds for Finn to find a chink in the tough cellophane wrapping with his mouth gaping open. When the plastic-sleeved probe was finally inserted under his tongue, he went at the paper with a vengeance.

"Ohmygod! Ohmygod! Ohmygod!" The thermometer fell out of his mouth.

Dr. Laurel picked up the probe and looked over at Gavin. "I guess he likes, um, whatever that stuff is."

Finn held up the small plastic cylinder that was hooked up to a valve and tank. "CO2 activated life vest—I've read about these. You wear 'em under your coat when you go out on the lake and they aren't bulky like the big Styrofoam suckers—it's easy to fish wearing one of these. You go into the drink and all you have to do is yank this string," Finn indicated the plastic pull. "And *boop*—you pop to the surface.

And this," he said, holding up a large red bait-casting reel, "is an Abu Garcia Ambassadeur 7000. The best musky reel in the world. Louis Spray used one of these."

"I take it that Louis Spray was a fisherman."

Finn looked up at Dr. Laurel like she was from another planet. "They just thaw you out?" he asked seriously. "Louis Spray was not just *a* fisherman. He was *the* fisherman. Landed more muskies than anyone. Got the world record, I don't care what those forensic idiots keep squawking about. He's dead now. I'm going to beat his record. Hopefully."

"Why hopefully?"

"I could die tomorrow." There was an awkward silence that Finn expertly filled up with, "Oh, man, and this," he said, holding up a reel that looked like a medieval torture device, "is a Fin-Nor Ahab." Finn snapped back the bail and slowly turned the handle, his fingers in tune with the instrument in his hand. He went through the process with the patience of a safe cracker, nodding appreciatively as he listened to the mechanism. "Solid brass gearing. Instant antireverse. Strong bail return," the grizzled veteran of countless fishing battles said. "This is the best."

"What's that?" Dr. Laurel asked. She held up her stethoscope with intent, then draped it over her neck. The kid's heart rate would be through the roof. She pointed at a small electronic device.

"I think it's a GPS," Finn said. "Is that right?"

Gavin nodded. "This way you can navigate in the dark or fog. No matter what, this thing contacts at least three—and up to seven—military satellites. Pinpoints your location within three feet. It floats too."

Finn's eyes widened. "No crap?"

Gavin smiled. "I hate to admit this, but I bought all this stuff at Izzy's Hunting and Fishing in New Mannheim—the old guy there picked everything out. I know shit about fishing. Even less about military satellites."

Dr. Laurel watched the two males going through their ritual. "Well, that's about it for me." Dr. Laurel turned to Finn. "I'll be back in a few hours for a few more tests." Then, as an obvious afterthought, added, "Finn, I spoke with Sheriff Pope a little while ago. Wanted me to ask you if you had seen anything out on the lake that was unusual." She thought about the file tucked away in her office. *Monster.* "Something that might help him figure out what had happened to the man who drowned."

"I hit something and the next thing I know I'm in the hospital having my temperature taken by a nurse with a mustache."

Gavin smiled and turned away. Dr. Laurel just rolled her eyes. "I'll let him know." She turned to Gavin. "And it was nice to meet you, Mr. Corlie. Good luck making friends."

"It's Gavin."

"Okay, Gavin."

Then, for no reason apparent to himself, he added. "If you're ever in my neighborhood, drop by. I mix a mean whiskey sour."

Dr. Laurel smiled. "My weakness." She gestured at the little boy. "That was a nice thing to do."

"I did it for me, not for him."

"It was still a nice thing to do." She pivoted and left the room, her heels tap-tap-tapping as she walked on down the hall.

# 21

Night was a gray smudge on the horizon. It was warm out, pushing into the seventies, and the lake was calm and flat, lifeless on the surface. The last hatch of mayflies of the year came in on the warm easterly wind, the misnomer of their birth month another mystery to be added to the list right after the luck of the loon. Gavin watched the insects flutter in the air like snow. Their oversize translucent wings caught light from the setting sun, and if he squinted, it really did look like winter. It was a nice night to be out.

He was propped up in the chair Mr. Johannus had made for him. A tray piled with a jury-rigged version of supper sat on the table beside him: a jar of anchovies, a banana, a half loaf of olive bread, a few knockwursts, a jar of Coleman's hot mustard, some chocolate chip cookies, spray cheese in a can, a bottle of whiskey and another of homemade sour mix (the different densities of lemon, soda, and sugar separated by definitive lines of demarcation), and a cold apple pie. On the arm of the Adirondack chair sat a half-eaten knockwurst, a line of mustard across its surface like an Andy Warhol zipper. Thirty feet away, at the edge of the forest, he had placed a few anchovies on a plate in the hope that he would entice the mystery cat out of hiding; he had seen it several times out of the corner of his eye and was hoping to let it know that he wanted to be friends. Free anchovies seemed like a good place to start.

The drink was cool and sour and fresh and made his mouth pucker with each sip. But it was good and he nodded with satisfaction after it washed over his tongue. Somewhere off in the distance a loon howled. The mournful echo bounced around the lake for a few seconds then died out. Gavin thought about the other night and winced. Yeah, sure, luckiest bird in the world. That and the dodo. He took another sip just as the bird cried again and wondered if it was the same one that had lost a mate in the bay to whatever the hell had swallowed it. Maybe it was calling for its partner—maybe that's what the cry was. Like dolphins in pods, their continual sonar pings nothing more than simple long-distance hand-holding. He had to get a book on birds. At least Google it.

The bay that opened onto Caldasac was a small lake in its own right. It had to be a half mile wide and just as long, the body closing up to a narrow passage that measured maybe a hundred feet across before opening onto the big water. The bay itself was a geological amphitheater that looked like a giant thumb print pressed into the rolling terrain where his house sat, the trees and rocks that surrounded the bay creating a natural enclosure. When he thought about it, anyone who fell into the water would have a hard time finding a way out other than the dock and boathouse; the rocks were steep and there were no low points to get a handhold, almost as if they had been removed on purpose. His real estate agent had told him that this bay used to be a pond on the farm's property, but when the big dam at the end of the lake had gone operational, it had swallowed all the low ground and connected his pond with the big water.

At the mouth of the bay there were iron posts on each end of the passage that he assumed had been some sort of property markers before time and decay had chewed them to rusty pickets. But the natural protection of the bay offered almost continually calm water, which was maybe why the loons had liked it here. Had. Before. He wondered if his luck had started to rub off on the world around him. Now he was killing birds too. The soft tread of footfalls on the stone steps interrupted Gavin's ornithological musings.

He turned and was surprised to see Dr. Laurel coming down to the water's edge. She was dressed in a pair of jeans and an oversize black sweater, her high heels from the hospital traded in for a pair of well-worn moccasins. The only jewelry she wore was an antique silver and turquoise squash-blossom necklace. She carried a bottle wrapped in a brown paper bag.

"Good evening, Doc," Gavin said and stood up.

"Mr. Corlie." She nodded a greeting and held up the bottle. "A little welcome-to-the-neighborhood."

"Look out for the anchovies."

"Anchovies?" she asked, and stopped on the last step.

"There," he said, pointing at the little plate on the stones. "Don't step on them."

"Booby-trapped?" she asked, and came off the last step with a smile.

"There's a cat in the neighborhood and I was hoping that we could meet."

"You better hope you don't attract any bears."

"Bears like anchovies? Great."

Dr. Laurel handed over the bottle and smiled up at him.

He peeled back the paper to find a bottle of Jack Daniel's. "Good taste."

"You too," she said, indicating the view. "Nobody thought that this place would ever sell."

Gavin laughed. "Yeah, I know. It's haunted."

"No, it's *expensive*." Her face lit up with her big smile. "Gotcha."

"Okay, lady, you win. I really do refuse to believe that you're a country doctor."

"As in *what's a nice girl like you doing in a place like this?*"

"Something like that, yeah." He looked around and realized that there was only one chair. "Um, would you like to sit down?"

"On the ground?"

Gavin had met his share of doctors and had found them to be a singularly boring and uninteresting bunch. This one was different. "I'll get a chair from the house. Take this one."

When he returned a few minutes later she was comfortably installed in the big pine chair that Mr. Johannus had built for him. The design of the chair made rigid posture an impossibility and she was stretched out and relaxed looking. He placed one of his Georgian carvers beside the Adirondack, and put an old wooden toolbox that was doing double duty as a bar cart down on the ground. In a few seconds he had mixed up a fresh whiskey sour and handed it over with a flourish.

Laurel took a sip. "Much better than mine. They always taste like formaldehyde."

"Being a doctor, I trust you have the culinary experience." Now that the drinks were served he suddenly realized that he had no idea what she was doing here.

Almost on cue, she started. "I wanted to thank you for what you did for Finn Horn." She paused, as if there were more to say but she didn't know how to say it. "He's a very bright little boy. He has a lot of gifts. He has a mother who loves him and a spirit that you couldn't crush with a steamroller." Her eyes grew distant for a second. "But he is going to die. Soon. Maybe in six months, maybe in a year. But before he grows up."

Gavin swilled the ice and dregs of his drink around in the tumbler for a few seconds. He didn't want to hear this. He held up his hand. "Look, Doc, I don't need to know this. I don't *want* to know this. It's none of my business." He finished the drink and sucked an ice cube into his mouth that clacked around his teeth when he spoke. "Will money help?"

Laurel shook her head. "His checkups are handled by the head of oncology at Cornell; Harvard and Mass General are handling the lab work. Martin Meany at the American Cancer and Leukemia Association in Las Vegas coordinates between the different labs. The treatments are recommended by a panel at the CLGB."

"CLGB?"

"Cancer and Leukemia Group B."

"Is there a Group A?"

Laurel thought about it. "I don't think so." She paused. "Hey, we're doctors, not geniuses!"

"And how is Finn getting all this very costly treatment?"

"I wasn't always a little country doctor, you know." Laurel took a sip of her drink and sighed. "I used to be a city girl. Big lab, lots of assistants."

"Why the move out here?"

"I was working on a procedure for epidermal replication in burn victims. I was using porcine cells in my research and I got tired of the PETA people calling at three in the morning and threatening to torch my house with me in it. I decided that if I couldn't do the work I needed to do in peace, I'd move somewhere they couldn't afford someone like me and make a difference to people who really needed it."

"Finn's lucky to have you, Doc."

"No. He's lucky to have *you.*"

"I gave him a couple of things because he lost them in the lake. That's it."

"You bought the boy a new boat, Mr. Corlie, you didn't *just give him a few things*! You gave that boy a real gift."

Gavin rolled his eyes. How had she found out about the boat? Small town, that's how. "Look, I scared him the other day. He was out there in the fog, trying to get away, and he cracked up his boat. Back in the real world his mother would have sued me and, with the right lawyer, would have won. I was just making amends." He took another sip. "Let's talk about something else."

Laurel looked at him for a minute. "Okay, Mr. Corlie." She took a sip of the drink and turned away. "I just want you to know that what you did was an important thing. Maybe not to you, but to Finn."

"Do me a favor, Doc?"

"What?"

"Call me Gavin. I hate the *Mr. Corlie* thing."

"Only if you stop calling me *Doc*."

"Deal. But I have one question."

"Which is?"

"What's your name?"

"Jennifer, but everyone calls me by my last name."

"Laurel it is." There, subject changed.

Laurel brushed a mayfly off her sleeve. "Where are you from?"

Gavin thought about New York. The people. The cars. Chelsea's destroyed body on the slab in the morgue. He fought back the temptation to walk up to the house. "New York City."

"Why here?"

What could he say? "Last spring my wife was killed. I spent a lot of time feeling bad, and that turned into feeling sorry for myself, and I got to the point where I needed to get out of the city."

She froze, unsure what to say. "Oh—I—I'm sorry—I—had no idea. I didn't mean—it's just that—"

Gavin waved it away. "It's okay. You asked. I can't spend the rest of my life hiding from it. It was either get away from all the things that reminded me of her—or kill myself." There was no melodrama in his voice. No pressure. Just flat truth.

Gavin played his thumb over the rim of the heavy tumbler. "I've always wanted to live in the country. Always had reasons—or excuses that I disguised as reasons—not to make the move. So life stepped in and kicked the chair out from under me." He thought about the pistol up in the house, still in the planter by the front door. There was one bullet in the cylinder. Just one. "I told my assistant that I wanted a place on the water. This," he waved his hand like a game-show model showing off a new set of golf clubs, "is what she came up with."

They sat quietly for a few minutes, staring out at the now dark lake. The mayflies were still flitting about, the light from the house up on the hill bouncing off their wings, and now they looked like sparks in the night.

It was Laurel who finally broke the silence. "You've done a lot of work on the place." It sounded weak but it was probably all she had. What else could you say to a man who had just told you his wife had died?

Gavin snapped back to the conversation. "A ton of work," he agreed. "I've got this great handyman—Mr. Johannus. Finnish Viking. Guy can do anything. Apparently all of my yoists are yunk."

"Penicillin should clear that up." She laughed into her glass. "I can write you a script."

"No, seriously, Mr. Johannus has informed me that all of my yoists are yunk. It's a real problem. I just wish I knew what yoists were."

Her eyes were smiling at him over the rim of her glass and he suddenly realized that she was a very beautiful woman. "You like it here?" she asked.

It was a good question. "I think so."

Laurel nodded at the edge of the forest. "Your mystery cat appears," she whispered.

Gavin slowly turned his head and saw the cat. "Think he's interested in the anchovies?"

"He's not here for the whiskey."

The cat eyed them skeptically for a few minutes before the scent of the anchovies overrode any doubts it had and the creature stepped out of the undergrowth. It was huge, at least thirty pounds, and had the slow, cautious gait of a hunter. It approached the saucer of anchovies, keeping an eye on the two humans.

From the moment the cat stepped out of the woods, Gavin could see the enormous, oversize feet, splayed with too many toes. Striped like a tiger, alternating between a dark charcoal and a medium brown. Gavin didn't know much about cats in general, and even less about specific breeds, but this one was beautiful. It sat down in front of the fish and went to work, keeping its eyes on the two humans.

"He's gorgeous," Laurel whispered.

"Christ, I didn't know that they made cats that big." Gavin was awed.

"I think he's a Maine coon. They're a big breed. If he's not pure, he's a good two-thirds."

They watched the animal feed in silence and when it was done it stood up, licked its whiskers, and turned away slowly, moseying silently back to the undergrowth where it disappeared, not even leaving a quivering leaf in his wake.

"Step one in establishing new friends? Anchovies. Can't have too many anchovies. Friendships are like books, there's an order to everything."

"You writing anything?" she asked.

"Not right now."

"Writer's block?"

Gavin shook his head, watched the mayflies. "Writer's block is for amateurs. It doesn't exist. You write or you don't. That's all there is to it. And when you do, sometimes nothing but shit comes out. Sometimes a whole novel's worth. But it's still writing. Is it good writing? If bad writing was considered writer's block, half the *New York Times* best-selling authors have a lifelong case." It was the most he had thought about writing in a long time.

"So?" she prodded.

"So I don't feel like writing." He took a sip of his drink and his lips puckered. "I've stopped."

"For good?"

Another good question. "I hope not."

She shifted in her seat and her necklace clinked against the arm. "If I'm being too nosy, just let me know."

"You're being too nosy."

"Oh." There was silence for a second. "Sorry."

Gavin smiled into the dark and hoped that she couldn't see it. "No, I'm sorry. This is called conversation. I've forgotten it existed." He looked down at his glass. "You want some food? I've worked out a nice little treat with this spray cheese and the chocolate chip cookies. Good combination. Or I can offer you some anchovies and a banana. The knockwurst might be the most obvious choice." He held up the tray.

"Step one to establishing a friendship?" She was smiling again. "I think I'll go with the sausages."

"They're *knockwurst*," he corrected.

"Then I'll go with the knockwurst."

"I'd go for the olive bread too."

She reached over and made herself a little sandwich out of the offered ingredients. He had carried no plates down, so she balanced the finished snack on her knee, using a napkin.

"I can see you're a high-maintenance girl."

Laurel bit into the sandwich. "No one's called me a girl in a long time." She nodded in approval. "Good mustard."

"Clears your sinuses."

She breathed in through her mouth. "This stuff would clear a room. Whew!" She slurped down a mouthful of her whiskey sour. "What is that stuff?"

Gavin laughed and popped half a chocolate chip cookie into his mouth. "Thanks for coming by tonight. It's nice to meet a person."

"I've gone from girl to person in three sentences. Not bad. Evidently you've never met a person before."

"Funny. No. I just haven't met anyone from here. Except for Mr. Johannus and a cop that came by the other day. I wouldn't want to sit here swapping martini recipes with them."

"I don't know any martini recipes."

"Gin or vodka and ice. Maybe throw in an olive or three. Boom. You're done. It's a figure of speech. It's just nice to make friends."

Laurel laughed. "Wow. From girl to person to friend. I like the way this is going. What's next, *pal*?"

"Actually, when I think about it, not a chance. You show up, drink my welcome present, make fun of me, steal the comfortable chair, then proceed to eat all my food. I've seen people like you before. They're called in-laws." For some reason the conversation had just got a whole lot easier.

"Thanks," she said through a mouthful of food.

"For what?"

"Not running me off your place with a shotgun. Not a literal one, anyway. I did kind of interrupt your little party here. Not that I would consider bacon-flavored cheese in a can much of a party. But the olive loaf and the kryptonite mustard do give it a little class. And now I know that you mix a mean cocktail. And that you hate most of the writers in the western world. Important to know."

"Whoa—back up. I did *not* say that I hated most of the writers in the western world. I said that if bad writing could be considered writer's block, then half of the best-selling writers on the *New York Times* list would be categorized as having a lifelong case. Half. Not most. Don't misquote me." Gavin pointed his finger at her. "Big difference, lady. There are a lot of great writers out there."

"Who?"

"Herman Melville, Bram Stoker, William Faulkner, Ernest Heming—"

"Gavin?"

"—way, Trevanian, Seth Morgan—"

"*Gavin*?"

"Yes?"

"What about living writers? Compos mentis, at the least."

"Besides Jimmy Breslin?" He smiled, then laughed. "There's a lot of great work out there, but to paraphrase John Milner, writing has been going downhill since Mark Twain died. I'll excuse you based on the fact that you know nothing about writing. But sure, this country's got a lot of great fiction writers. Every single word a guy like Thomas Harris has put down is poetry. It's just that—" The dark was scraped open by the wail of the loon and it pulled his attention. "You know anything about loons?" he immediately asked, his voice hushed as if telling a secret.

"I know you can't eat them." She thought about it for a minute. "And they're supposed to be good luck too. That's about it."

Gavin stared off into the darkness. She didn't know shit about loons either. "I'll try to remember that."

# 22

Laurel opened her eyes and smiled. The big bed was soft and enveloping and the down comforter was warm and cozy. She wanted to lie there all day. She shifted her weight over onto her hip and the linen sheets felt good against her bare skin. Her eyes focused on the ceiling, an expanse of white cross-hatched by big, hand-hewn beams. Sunlight filtered in through the window, bursts of white dancing across the walls and furniture as a breeze tickled the trees outside. Somewhere nearby music hummed in low tones. She smiled, yawned, and suddenly realized that she wasn't at home. And she was in her bra and panties in a room she had never seen before. In a bed she didn't remember climbing into. She bolted upright.

The room was large and informal. She was in the middle of a huge four-poster mahogany bed that made her feel very tiny. The old plaster walls were white and patchy and hadn't been painted in a long time. The floor was made of twelve-inch-wide oak planks, scarred and beaten, and the big bed sat in the middle of a thick hand-woven Persian rug.

She sat on the edge of the bed and tentatively reached down and touched the carpet with her toe, making sure that it—and she—was actually there. Besides the bed, the room contained a Georgian chest of drawers, a linen press, a cheval mirror in one corner, and an eight-foot Gothic bench that stood at the foot of the bed. The bench was piled high with books and her clothes were hung—neatly folded—over the back.

The only window in the room was an enormous Palladian that was individually paned. Laurel stood up and slowly walked over to the window, the view of trees undulating across the rippled eighteenth-century glass. The bright day blinded her and she had to squint for a moment. The view gradually developed from raw whites into deep greens and blues and she saw the lawn that rolled down to the stone embankment and the lake beyond. It was a beautiful day, bright and crisp. The lone Adirondack chair was sitting by the water's edge and the boathouse that had been little more than a silhouette against the sky last night was vivid and three-dimensional. She remembered coming here. And the conversation by the lake. The big cat that ate anchovies. Drinking the first whiskey sour. And the second. Part of the third. Had there been a fourth?

That was it.

A mental dead end.

Laurel concentrated, trying to bring up the memories that were buried in her brain under a thick layer of hangover. What had happened? She was standing in the window, her arms holding the frame, when the lone figure of Mr. Johannus waved from the yard. She almost waved back, then realized that she was standing there in white underwear, facing a bright morning sun. She did the only thing she could think of—she dropped to the floor. She was on all fours, under the sill of the window, when it struck her that maybe she was being a little paranoid. Her underwear could be misinterpreted as a bathing suit. She crawled away from the window and stood up.

She paused in front of the cheval, examined her body. For fifty-six she was pleased with the almost nude reflection she saw staring back at her. She was smallish, just under five two, and had the supple body and movements of a natural athlete, which the five miles she ran every morning helped to heighten. In a general sense, she viewed food as fuel, not as a reward, and it had helped her keep fat off her body. She had a washboard stomach and when she moved her arms, thick veins bulged in the compact biceps. She had a small chest and could see the ribs crossing her lithe frame under the silk camisole. Besides the dark tangle of short hair, the only other contrasts against her pale skin were her deep-set eyes and the black triangle visible under her white panties. No, it didn't look like a bathing suit. Too much bush. At least she had made the handyman's day.

What the hell had happened last night? The evening had been wonderful in that it had been beautiful out and the conversation hadn't been strained in the usual battle-of-the-sexes combat-talk that made up the bulk of her dates. *Date?* No, it hadn't been a *date.* The man's wife had just died how long ago? She had come here as a non-woman, and Gavin, with his own basket of grief, was not supposed to be remotely interested in trying to get her into the sack. The dynamics had been unthreatening and relaxed once they had got past the initial handshakes. She remembered Gavin going back to the house for another egg and some sugar for the sour mix. They had talked about loons. He had juiced some lemons by hand. They had shared stories. For hours, it seemed. How much booze had she put away?

One thing was a certainty: she had no memory of her clothes coming off. The big squash-blossom necklace hung off one of the mahogany posts of the bed. She tried to reach it and had to stand on the mattress itself to pull it down—and she had certainly been too drunk to have climbed up there last night. Besides, it wasn't the type of thing she'd do—she'd have tucked it into her shoe. There was only one explanation: Gavin had put it there for her. Logic dictated that he had therefore undressed her. But deductive reasoning wasn't always right. Not when it came to men and sex and the rest of the funhouse dynamics that went along with that particular combination. Had he done more than undress her? Had they had sex? It wouldn't have been the first time in her life she had done something like this, but it didn't seem like the kind of thing that she was likely to do now, regardless of ingesting a gallon of sour mash whiskey. She was a grown-up now. Wasn't she?

Then she started to think of him in terms of sexuality. He *was* handsome. He *was* single. They *had* had a nice evening. What did it really add up to? A fling? A one-night stand? A fuck? Only one way to find out. She started to put on her clothes.

Laurel found Gavin sitting on the stone porch off the back of the house, facing the lake. Halfway down the lawn the big cat from last night was lying in the sun, examining the human that had moved in. Gavin had dragged a dining room chair outside and was perched in it, wearing a pair of jeans and a white cotton shirt with his initials monogrammed on the cuff. He was sipping a coffee and listening to choral music that was filtering out from the big stereo he had set up in the living room. He sat motionless.

Laurel eased up beside him and stopped. She would let his actions tell her what had happened. If he kissed her, they had slept together. If not, they hadn't.

Gavin turned to her, smiled up. "I'm telling you, the anchovies did it. He's moved about twenty feet closer in the past ten minutes."

Laurel was momentarily disoriented by the pleasure Gavin was having in the friendship game with the cat, and the awkward way she had felt a few minutes before softened.

"Coffee?" he offered.

She smiled. "Sounds good."

"You want some aspirin with that?" Gavin got up and moved toward the back door. Fifty feet down the hill, the cat eyed his every movement, not sure whether to bolt or stick it out.

She nodded. "Please."

While Gavin was gone, she watched the cat rolling in the grass, enjoying the morning. She wondered if he knew what had happened last night. If he did, he wasn't saying.

Gavin came back with a second chair and a dark green mug. "Here," he said, and sat down.

She sipped tentatively and tried to look casual. Gavin was smiling at nothing in particular and seemed easy with himself. Was it postcoital glow? Postcoital smugness?

He took a bottle of aspirin out of his pocket and the noise was jarring to her. "Last night was fun," he said.

She closed her eyes and thought she was going to be sick. She liked him. But she hadn't wanted to sleep with him. First of all, he was too young for her. What was he? Thirty-eight? Forty, tops? And he was not on an emotionally solid footing right now. And she didn't want to look like she was an easy lay. If they had gone to bed, the friendship was doomed from here on out. There would be no turning back. "Um, I thought so too…It's just…"

Gavin's smile broadened. "You don't remember a thing, do you?"

She sipped her coffee, looked out at the lake. She was too old to feel like this. This was for teenagers. "Sure I do. We were down at the lake, drinking thermonuclear whiskey sours, and I—"

"Did we go to bed?" Gavin asked.

She looked down and almost whispered, "I was hoping that you would tell me."

Gavin laughed.

Then she began to laugh too.

"You're a great W. C. Fields. You were too drunk to drive and I gave you my room. Hell, you were too drunk to walk. You stepped out of your jeans on the steps and almost cartwheeled through the front window. I got you upstairs, helped you get the rest of your clothes off, and tucked you in."

"That's all?"

"You sound disappointed."

She realized that she was. A little. "No. No. I just thought that, well, I know I didn't undress myself. I just assumed—you're a man—I'm a woman."

"Yeah, I know. And as Woody Allen says, that's what those kinds of people do," he said. "But we didn't."

She laughed, more at herself than at the situation. The high tinkle of her voice carried down the hill and the cat's ears snapped back, unsure of what it was hearing—laughter a foreign sound.

Laurel shook her head and took a long swallow of coffee. After all this time she should have been able to read people better. Gavin seemed like an honestly nice guy. Maybe there were still a few out there.

Gavin turned to her. "You tried to, though."

Her mouth dropped open and she had to close it quickly before she lost a few drops of coffee.

"When I was taking off your sweater you winked at me and said, 'Not bad, huh?'" Gavin turned away. "Shocking." He was enjoying the upper hand and he played it out. "Take two aspirin. Writer's orders."

They sat in silence for a few minutes with only the soft rustling of wind and the sound of Hildegard von Bingen's choral strains filling the empty space that their conversation had occupied so effortlessly the night before. The cat seemed happy too and worked his way slowly up the hill.

"What time is it?" Laurel finally asked.

Gavin lifted his arm and for the first time Laurel saw the bearded figure of Poseidon wrestling with the green and purple sea monster that wound down his arm. The vivid tattoo was in sharp contrast to his white shirt. "It's ten fifteen. I called the hospital and you don't start until two today."

Laurel smiled. He *was* a considerate man. "Thank you."

"Hell, any woman that happy about me taking her clothes off deserves to hang out as much as she wants to."

"Does she get breakfast?"

"Yeah," he said and got up. "She gets breakfast." The sleeve of his shirt dropped down and covered the purple tail of the sea monster fanning out onto his wrist. She had never liked tattoos, but for some reason, it looked good on him. Maybe there were surprises left for her.

He disappeared into the house.

# 23

They were saying good-bye on the front steps. Off to the side, close to the trees, the cat watched them.

"Thanks for last night," Laurel said.

"For the gourmet supper or for respecting your chastity?"

"Both." Her face scrunched up and she thought about it. "I guess." She reached up and straightened his collar. "I had no idea that knackwurst and olive bread was such a winning combination."

"You should have tried the anchovies. Maybe next time I can do us a real meal. Steaks or something. I've always wanted to have a barbecue."

Laurel's mouth dropped open. "Just exactly what kind of a guy are you? Every man I know loves to cook raw meat over an open flame with a beer in his hand."

"Beer is a country thing. At least for me. In the city it's real booze. And there aren't any barbecues in the city." She was standing in front of him, on the limestone step, and the gentle breeze was blowing scents of her perfume up to him. For a second it was beautiful, then something jarred open in his mind and he stepped back. "Maybe I'll pick one up."

"Oh nonononono." She shook her head. "If you've never barbecued before you need someone who knows what they're doing to give you pointers. Otherwise you end up with filet of shoe-sole. Noooooo waaaay!"

Gavin nodded in deference to her advice. "Okay. When I go for a barbecue, I'll call you."

"Deal."

They were staring at each other when the low-pitched growl of a car coming down the drive interrupted the moment. The cat disappeared into the forest.

Shannon's blue BMW emerged from the trees. The top was down and she looked like an Edith Head creation—all that was missing was the Henry Mancini soundtrack.

"Girlfriend?" Laurel asked.

Gavin noted that she sounded just a little bit jealous. He found the image amusing and he couldn't suppress the smile that stretched over his mouth. "Not quite. No."

The car rolled to a stop in front of the steps and Shannon got out. She walked over and threw her arms around Gavin. "You look *great.*" She kissed him and, without being introduced, turned to Laurel. "I'm Shannon Leibowicz, Gavin's assistant."

Laurel extended her hand. "Jennifer Laurel. Pleasure."

"*Doctor* Jennifer Laurel," Gavin added immediately.

"Doctor?" Shannon gave him a cursory once-over. "Everything okay, Gav?"

He nodded in an *of course* kind of way. "Dr. Laurel works at the Malone hospital. She's taking care of Finn Horn."

Shannon's smile came back on. "I see," she said. "I just assumed that, um, well…"

"That I got liquored up, took a golf club, and Elvised the television."

"Um, yeah, something like that."

Laurel turned to Gavin. "Well, Elvis, I'm off. Last night was—" She paused, looking for the appropriate word. "Fun."

"Thanks for bringing the Jack Daniel's. Maybe next time you'll let me have some."

Laurel's foot-wide smile opened up and she blushed. "Really? I get a next time?" She kissed him tentatively on the cheek. "I promise not to peel off my pants."

"Thanks, Doc. Thanks a lot."

Gavin opened the door to her late-model Mercedes wagon and she slid in behind the wheel. She waved good-bye and drove off, the sound of her stereo getting louder as the sunroof on the old car slid open. In a few seconds she was swallowed by the trees.

When she was gone, Gavin turned to see Shannon staring up at him with her mouth open.

"Mr. Corlie! Were you involved in a pants-peeling incident last night?"

"It's not what you think."

"What I think is that it's about time you made some friends."

Mr. Johannus was walking by, a big four-by-four balanced on his muscular shoulder. "Me too. I saw her upstairs in the window. Fine-looking lady. A little small in the boobs. But pretty." He winked and walked on by.

For a second Gavin stared after him, wondering if he had really spoken. He turned to Shannon to complain but she was smiling up at him. "What is this, a conspiracy?" he asked.

"Only the paranoid know for sure. Speaking of which, I saw the sheriff parked at the top of your drive. She his wife?"

"Hardly." Gavin thought about the sour meeting the other day and it made him wince. He and Pope were never going to be real close after that one. But there was no use regretting it now. Past tense. Move forward. "You want coffee?"

Shannon was still smiling. "Yeah. Coffee. Sure. Whatever you say."

There, subject changed. Coffee.

"But I'm keeping my pants *on*," she said, and squeezed by him.

"That's not fair. You don't even know what happened!" He wondered if that had sounded as defensive to her as it had to him.

"You're right, I don't. But what I *think* happened is that she came by for a visit to say thanks for what you did for Finn Horn. Brought you a bottle of Jack Daniel's. You two hit it off and the combination of her having no one to get home to as well as having the best drinking buddy in the world culminated with her swallowing half a gallon of cheap whiskey disguised in one of your mind-melting whiskey sours. She's pretty, but you probably didn't see that. She couldn't drive and you, being the perfect gentleman that you are, probably put her in your bed, undressing her in the process; you figured that she wouldn't be too shy about the whole thing since she was a doctor. This morning she was probably a little embarrassed, couldn't remember what happened. You made her breakfast, probably poached eggs on tomato and garlic toast, and she was off to work." Shannon patted him on the arm condescendingly. "But that's just what I *think*." She walked off into the house.

"You're wrong!" Gavin called after her. "The eggs were scrambled!"

\*\*\*

Twenty minutes later they were spread out on the sofa, the coffee table covered with papers, mostly translation rights forwarded by his agent. For some reason he always had a stack every spring and fall—it just worked out that way. His agent had already gone over everything. It was simply a matter of John Hancocking all the spaces indicated with little colored Post-its. He didn't bother reading a single one.

After filing the last of the contracts away in her Hermès briefcase, Shannon leaned back into the sofa and looked around. "Place is looking nice, Gav. Starting to look like a home." She looked out the window and saw the big cat sitting on the porch. "You've got friends coming out of the wood-work," she said.

Gavin looked over at the cat. "It's the anchovies."

"What a monster! Which model is that?"

"It's *breed*, not *model*. It's a cat, not a car."

"The only pussy I know anything about—"

"Yeah, yeah, save it for your sailor friends, lady." Gavin cut her off. "It's a Maine coon. Apparently they're all this size."

"Handsome fellow." Her eyes were drawn out past the cat, to the lake. "Do you like living here?"

He thought about Finn Horn and his monster and Lau-rel. "So far, yeah."

She lifted her head, looked around. "I see you have Adolph on the mantel." Outside the cat stretched. "How have you been spending your time?" Meaning, *Are you writing?*

"I'll show you." Gavin stood up and crossed the room to the floor-to-ceiling French doors. He turned the antique bronze handles and swung the two heavy doors in. The cat bolted away. The light in the room doubled and Shannon squinted involuntarily. She fumbled around in her brief-case, produced a pair of sunglasses, and followed Gavin outside.

They slowly descended the stone steps in the bright morning light. The walk down from the house to the stone terrace that flanked the water was about a hundred yards, the stone steps snaking down in a gentle flex. Mr. Johannus was sitting in the rafters of the boathouse, furiously whack-ing away with his hammer. The roof would be going on soon.

As they reached the water's edge, Gavin called up. "Every-thing going all right, Mr. Johannus?"

"Other than these yunky yoists, it's like butter up a dog's ass!"

Gavin nodded. "Nice analogy," he said through his teeth. "Keep it up. Looks great! Could you do me a favor?"

"Sure," Mr. Johannus stopped and dropped his hammer into the ring on his tool belt. "Anything you want, Mr. Gavin."

"Can you build me another one of these chairs?" Gavin asked, pointing at the chair by the water.

"The Adirondack chair?"

"What?"

"They're called Adirondack chairs."

"Okay, can you build me another one?"

"Sure." Mr. Johannus smiled broadly, his mustache curling up at the sides of his mouth. "For the woman with the little boobies?"

Shannon suppressed a laugh.

Gavin groaned. "You married, Mr. Johannus?"

The carpenter nodded proudly. "Twenty-eight years."

"Would your wife like being described like that?"

Mr. Johannus shook his head. "Not one bit. She has very *big* boobies." The carpenter tipped his hat to Shannon. "No offense, Ms. Shannon."

Shannon stepped back. "Keep me out of this."

Gavin was getting irritated. "Just build the Catskill chair, okay?"

"Adirondack," Mr. Johannus corrected.

"Whatever." Gavin turned back to Shannon.

"Gav?" she started. "You like this doctor?"

Gavin thought about it for a moment. "What's not to like? But we're not fucking dating. Chelsea just died—"

"Before that you and Chelsea weren't—"

"Don't. Not now. Not ever." He thought about the last time they had said good-bye. She was going out to get flowers at the shop on the corner of Eightieth and Columbus beside the Starbucks. The last image he had of her alive was her smile as the bronze elevator doors slid shut. It had been a sad little smile that disappeared as the doors closed on her. The next time he saw her she was a pulpy wreck that had nothing to do with the beautiful woman he had loved. Mole Roper had taken all that away. Not just her life. But her beauty too.

"Gavin?" Shannon's voice brought him back.

"Sorry."

"No, I'm sorry. I had no right to start up with that. This isn't about me. It's about you." Shannon sat down on the stone ledge and dangled her feet over the water. Gavin sat down beside her. "You doing any work?"

He could tell she was making a real effort not to sound accusatory. He looked out at the water. The sun was bright and bounced off the waves and suddenly the lake looked more beautiful than he had ever seen it. Then his mind turned to Finn Horn and the story he had told him. "I've got an idea I've been playing around with."

The cat came out of nowhere and sat down beside them, maybe three feet away. Gavin wanted to reach out and touch it, to see if it was real, but something told him that if he did, the animal would dissolve. So he just let it sit there, watching the water with them. "It's got good bones." He focused on the water. "I'll see."

"Want to tell me about it?"

The question was more for something to say than an actual inquiry. Gavin rarely spoke about what he was working on until the first draft got up off the operating table, usually around the four-month mark.

What could he say? That Finn Horn said he had been attacked by a monster? The thing had wrecked his boat and tried to eat him? That Finn believed that divine providence or karma or whatever other system of belief the boy held had sent Gavin here for the purpose of validating his story? That maybe he saw a new book in all of this? No, it didn't sound quite right. When he thought about it, it sounded a little silly.

It also felt real. And Gavin knew that's what counted. The nutty part he could work with as long as it felt true at its core.

"I'm not making promises to anyone." The cat came over, rubbed against his side, and sat down. "Least of all to myself," he said.

# 24

The best things in life are free. At least that's what those English assholes yodeled on the radio. But back in the real world everything cost a shitload of money. What wasn't burned up on taxes was immediately stolen by the bank for the mortgage, Mutual of Omaha for insurance, and the Dodge dealership for the set of wheels in the garage. After the automatic withdrawals were done speed-dancing the zeroes out of your bank account, you were really fucking lucky if what was left somehow managed to pay for Budweiser and Tampax at Price Chopper. Maybe bowling for the wife, kibble for the dog, and a new bass rod every season. That was *it*. If you were nine-to-fiving it, life had you by the short and curlies with an iron hand that was colder than a mother-in-law's love.

Unless you were some New York writer who made crap up and sold it by the truckload to bored morons who probably couldn't afford it in the first place.

Sheriff Xavier Pope sat in his cruiser under the dark overhang of trees and watched Gavin's drive with the cold anger of a man who was able to hate simply because he had decided to. Sitting there, balancing a beer on his knee, he had little to do but fuel the finance merry-go-round with one angry thought after another. If that Corlie fucker had been nice the other day when he'd visited, maybe he would have liked the guy. Probably not. But you never could tell. The world had a way of keeping you guessing. Corlie's big mistake had been the smug entitlement that came along with having a bunch of dollar signs attached to his name. Pope shook his head in disgust and swallowed another mouthful of Bud. Hell, give him ten minutes in a room with that rich cocksucker and then see who's smiling. No uniform. No gun. Just the two of them and the ten longest minutes of City Boy's life. How long would that *I'm loaded and can buy myself out of trouble* attitude last? A lot less than ten minutes. *Guaran-fucking-teed*. Pope had run up against the same kind of untouchableness before. Back in the old days when it had still been easy to have a little fun.

It had been a hot July night, sixteen years back. Pope had voluntarily drawn night shift all that summer so he wouldn't have to see so much of Doris. Sleep all day and watch the radar all night. It was a nice balance and he had enjoyed the three months that it had lasted. The best part had been the endless hours of ticketing the out-of-towners who thought that the stretch of country highway through the mountains was the perfect place to open up the engine. Pope loved explaining the rules to them. Just fucking *because*.

He had been parked in the brush beside State Road 47E, the long white snout of his cruiser pointing uphill, the radar locked in ON. It was about one thirty in the a.m. and he was happily humming away to some oldie on the FM radio. Frank and the Nitwits were doing a nice little number about getting Mrs. Brown's permission to fuck her daughter (although they had worded it differently, the meaning was clear as day to anyone who had ever seen a horny kid) when a car crested the hill in front of him pulling almost a hundred and ten miles an hour. The radar lit up and Pope opened the double cherries and pulled out after the car in an arc of smoking rubber. Much to his disappointment, the driver pulled over before he got up to speed.

The cop unfolded himself from the big Cutlass and unclipped the heavy Smith in the tooled leather holster. He moved slowly up on the car, the sound of the gravel sliding along his leather soles traveling up his spine to his brain, where the cockroach cage was vibrating.

He had never seen a Bentley in real life before and the car impressed him. The rims alone probably cost as much as his cruiser. New York plates in a Manhattan dealership frame. He flashed the Maglite inside and there was only one occupant— a man. Pope knocked on the window with his flashlight and it rolled open. *Even the windows sound expensive*, he thought. A blast of air-conditioned interior hit him in the face.

The driver turned into the beam of the flashlight and Pope couldn't decide whether the guy's shirt or complexion won the *which-is-whiter?* contest. "Is there a problem, officer?" His voice had an annoyed timbre to it.

"License and registration, please." Pope spoke the last word with a tired sigh attached to it as if he had been doing this all day.

"I don't understand, did I do something wrong?"

Pope examined the face staring up at him. Thick lips that hung slightly slack, droopy eyes. And that waxy skin. This guy needed to see some sun. "Well, mister, unless my radar's broken, yeah, you did something wrong." Pope leaned back and placed his hand on the heavy handle of his revolver. "Now can I see your license and registration, please?"

The guy huffed like this was all a big inconvenience and pulled out a thick black crocodile wallet. Under the watchful eye of the flashlight, the driver flipped through the folds of hide as Pope watched the light bounce off his gold medic-alert bracelet. When he stopped at the clear plastic window where his license was, Pope saw the photo.

Pretty blonde in a little black dress and a pearl necklace smiling on a yacht somewhere looking all happy and rich and carefree. Big smile. Big tits. And at least twenty years this guy's junior. Pope watched the hand with the big gold Rolex hold out the identification.

Pope scanned the license: Mr. Seymour White. Park Avenue address. Pope smiled. Nice name. Appropriate too.

"I'd like to see the radar tape," Mr. White said.

"What?"

"I'd like to see the radar tape. I have been accused of speeding and I have the right to see the tape."

One of the cockroaches giggled. It was a lonely echo-filled snicker in the empty auditorium in his skull. "Get out of the car," he hissed, and pulled the heavy revolver out of the holster.

"Excuse me?" Mr. White asked.

Pope had to give the guy credit in the balls department.

"I said get out of the car. I have a gun and I have the right to tell you to do whatever the fuck I want." Pope let it all come out slowly so there would be no misunderstanding here. After all, he didn't want the guy to think that he was angry. "*Get. Out. Of. The. Fucking. Car.*"

First doubt, then indecision crossed Mr. White's face.

The cockroaches started clambering into the theater. It was general admission and they fought and pushed and elbowed one another for the good seats. There was nothing they loved more than a surprise screening. "I am going to tell you this one more time. There won't be a third. Get out of the car." The tone in Pope's voice had a convincing steadiness to it. Mr. White obeyed.

"Do you know who I am?" Mr. White slammed the door and snarled at Pope. "You ever hear of Jimmy Burtelli? I'm the guy that got him off! I make one phone call and you are a dead man. You hear me?"

Blinded by the beam of Pope's flashlight, he didn't see the big hand come out of the dark. The butt of the revolver hit him in the cheek and his head snapped back. For a second he hung there as if his body hadn't figured out that he was unconscious. The cockroaches applauded as White crashed to the warm asphalt.

"Yeah, Toots, I heard you." Pope holstered his pistol and glanced up the road to make sure he didn't see any headlights coming.

The sheriff barely had to move White's body. He grabbed the ankles and swung them out away from the car and the lawyer's head pivoted under the frame, just behind the driver's front tire. Pope got into the big car. The Bentley felt even more expensive from the inside and smelled of leather and cologne. He turned the key in the ignition and stepped on the brake, then shifted the heavy leather knob into neutral. The car rocked forward a few inches.

The car was already facing downhill so Pope didn't have to do much to get it moving. He pushed against the back bumper and the car started a gentle roll. From that instant on, whenever Pope heard the crunch of gravel under a tire, he remembered Seymour White's face being rolled over by his own car—the image never failed to bring a smile to his face. The incline was slight and the heavy English vehicle moved slowly. White's face got wedged between the asphalt and the tire for a second. The car paused, White's skull acting as a natural chock. Pope heard something crack loudly, probably the guy's jawbone. The cockroaches giggled, clapped. And then it got good because Mr. White woke up.

Screamed.

And started to thrash.

But couldn't move because his face was pinned against the ground by nearly fourteen hundred pounds of pressure from the tire.

He clawed at the wheel that had already flattened his jawbone and was rolling forward over on his face. For a full half minute the man flopped around under the car, ripping his fingernails out in his efforts to extricate himself. He clawed at the tire, finger-painting the rubber with his bloody stubs. He gurgled. And whimpered. And screamed something awful. His legs thrashed and one of his Gucci loafers flopped off and bounced into the middle of the road, landing on its side like a dead turtle. Pope let him writhe there for a bit. After all, you didn't get to see something this cool every day. Not anymore.

When Pope finally got a little bored of watching White trying to push the car off his head, he took a deep breath and leaned on the bumper with his steel-toed boot. The car inched forward a bit and Pope didn't think that White had it in him but he shrieked louder, a horrible sound of agony that Pope felt at the base of his skull. It was beautiful. Poetic. The audience of bugs sucked in a communal breath and some loudmouth at the back yelled out, *That's gonna leave a mark, asshole!* and the whole theater howled with laughter.

There was a hard crunch followed by a heavy liquid splash as the car rolled over White's skull and sprayed the road with brains.

"Make your call," Pope said and slowly walked back to his cruiser.

The accident report stated that Seymour White had stopped on a stretch of deserted road, probably to relieve himself (the subject's fly had been open, his penis out), and had collapsed, possibly fainted (he was a diabetic—his medic-alert bracelet was on him at the time), and his car, which he had just received as a gift and was unused to operating, had rolled over his head because he had parked on an incline and had left the transmission in neutral. He had been found by Sheriff Xavier Pope.

Sitting at City Boy's drive, Pope took another swig of the beer and a few drops spilled out of the corner of his mouth. He wiped the back of his hand across his chin before the beer had time to drip onto his chest. It wouldn't be too wise to go back to the station smelling like beer. And after a day like today he deserved a beer. Hell, he *deserved* a blow job. But a beer was better than nothing. And it helped the time tick by a little faster.

His shitty day had started with his trip to the hospital. The Horn kid had seemed normal enough—you know, *considering*—but he was lying about something. Pope had been a cop too long to miss the signs.

What was the deal between Corlie and the kid? The kid said he had never met Corlie before. If some rich asshole was helping out some poor kid there was a reason—a motive, they called it. And the motive was never something pretty. Not by a long shot. Greed. Sex. Hate. Jealousy. Control. All top-tenners in the motive department. You don't go out and buy some kid you claimed to have never met a new fucking boat. You just didn't do shit like that. Never. Period. No matter how much money you had sitting around, gathering dust. No fucking way.

So, first off, Pope knew that the kid was lying. They *did* know each other. They *had* to know each other. Which meant that they were probably lying to him about what had happened out on the lake. If this had been the good old days, way back when he had first started, it would have been easy. Roll the cruiser up to the Horn house, kick in the front door, and smack Ms. Horn around the living room in a good old-fashioned game of Truth or Dare. *Dare* to lie to me, and I'll kick the fucking *Truth* out of you. By the time the bitch had a ruptured eardrum and a few bicuspids on the floor, the crippled little fucker would be more than happy to play the game.

But it wasn't the old days. Now there were *rules*. But you could bend rules. Just a little. If that didn't work, they could be gotten around. There was always a way to disco; all you needed was a little creative thinking.

Pope knew his cruiser wasn't invisible under the canopy of big pine trees. He was just a country cop keeping his eye on things. Protecting his citizens. Serving the community. Sipping a beer, surfing on Benzedrine, and waiting for some way to fuck this rich asshole to the floor.

A blue convertible BMW came crawling down the gravel road—city person, driving slowly to avoid scratching up their fancy paint job. As it got closer, Pope saw that it was driven by a woman wearing big sunglasses and a goofy-looking hat on her head. Even from the distance, she smelled rich. And pretty. Pope could just imagine the perfume, the pearl necklace, expensive lace panties, and he felt himself getting hard. The pills riding his system scraped the walls of his arteries, and he shivered and thought that his cock was going to explode. And it nearly did.

The blue convertible paused in front of Corlie's driveway. The plates were New York but the car wasn't from New Mannheim. Big-city car being driven by a big-city broad coming down to suck Corlie's rich big-city cock. Pope watched the car disappear into the shrouded drive and eased back into the seat, begrudgingly enjoying the rush of blood to his crotch.

What felt like hours later to Pope's speeded-up brain, Dr. Laurel's beige late-model Mercedes station wagon came out of the drive. Ah, he thought, the one with the small titties who didn't like him calling the nurse with a mustache *the nurse with a mustache*. What was she doing at Corlie's? Pope had been there since he started his shift, just after six a.m., and she had not gone in. So she had gone in last night. And stayed. And she had promised to talk to the Horn kid to see if he had anything new to add to his story. And she hadn't called back because she had been at Corlie's all night.

Pope realized that there were a lot of people who claimed to not know each other suddenly appearing at all the same places at all the same times. Someone was lying. Maybe all of them were lying. And if there was anything Pope hated more than criminals, it was liars. But you dealt with both of them the same way.

*It's disco time!* the paperclip-thin voices of the cockroaches roared inside his head.

And with that Pope decided that now was as good a time as any to put on his dancing shoes.

# 25

She was beautiful in the morning sun, naked and freshly scrubbed from the shower. Patches stood out on her pale skin, red and raw, where she had washed with pumice soap. She stood motionless, leaning her forehead against the window, humming softly as she looked out at the world beyond their bedroom. Her ass, heart shaped and still wet, moved back and forth with her humming. It was impossible not to see that she was happy.

"You look like a beautiful vampire." Gavin was on his stomach, naked. His chin was propped up on a pillow and his tattooed arm hung down off the edge of the bed, a bright splash of living color against the inanimate white of the sheets.

Chelsea turned her head and the sun silhouetted her long black hair, cut straight across the back and bangs, and the corners of her mouth curled up in a deep red smile. She blew him a kiss. "You just say that because I've stolen all of your fluids."

Gavin nodded and sunk his face into the pillow. "I ache. My groin actually aches."

Chelsea turned and came back to the bed. "Yeah, well, it's not just my groin that aches, buster." She flopped down beside him, her face buried in the feather duvet. "My ass won't speak to me for a few hours."

"Don't blame me, it was your idea."

"Mmm." She faded out and for a moment they were silent and breathing in unison. It was Gavin who broke the quiet.

"And it was a good one." He rolled over onto her and enveloped her with his body.

"Oh no you don't. No no no!" She wriggled and tried to get away but her heart wasn't in it. He kissed her neck, her shoulder, and her body started to move with his, her bum pushing up to meet him. She lifted her head and turned, and his tongue slipped into her mouth. They kissed. Her hips pushed up, lifting herself to a convenient angle for him. And then he was inside and the warmth was almost overwhelming. He closed his eyes. He wanted to enjoy it, to feel it, to let it go. But he also wanted it to last forever.

"Oh, God," she whispered from her throat, "don't stop!"

Gavin opened his eyes and the ceiling was staring down at him, the hand-hewn beams in sharp contrast to where his mind had just been. He was hard and out of breath. And alone. Totally alone.

He got up from the bed, ran to the bathroom, and was sick.

He lay on the cool white tiles for an hour, trying to put his mind back together. Images of Chelsea kept fading in and out of his head. In all of them she was smiling. Happy. Alive. But there was no putting it back together. A line had been crossed and everything on the other side had been erased— irrevocably obliterated—and there was nothing left of that time. It had slipped away. He thought of the bad times, and there *had* been bad times. Plenty of them. Especially at the end. But he had hoped they would get over it. After all, everybody had bad times. Not forever, not always, but they were there. The cross that relationships had to bear. Good, bad, better, worse, thick, thin, sickness, health, as long as you both shall live. Amen.

Only *as long as you both shall live* didn't come with any sort of guarantee. Not even an implied guarantee. It was take *what* you can *when* you can because it could all be wiped out tomorrow. So, when he thought about it, *as long as you both shall live* was a crock of shit. *As long as one of you ain't dead* made a lot more sense. At least that way you knew it could come down on you: murder, heart disease, bad shellfish, forest fire, tidal wave, banana peel on the sidewalk, earthquake, bubonic plague, killer bees, airplane crash, Mole Roper in a Lincoln Continental. Christ, there were a million things that could get you. A better way to put it would be: *as long as you both have the miraculous fortune not to be destroyed by some random act of finality.*

Now he was getting somewhere.

That somewhere was the bathroom floor. Alone. And Chelsea was completely, not-ever-coming-back dead. No more kissing. No more hand-holding. No more fighting or fucking or grocery shopping. It was all gone. Really gone. Old-love-story kind of gone.

Gavin rolled over on his back and lay there, staring up at the plaster ceiling, trying to come up with one good reason not to kill himself. Not an average reason and not a great reason—just a *good* reason. The kind that would make him stop, shake his head, and say, *Man, this is crazy!*

He.

Couldn't.

Come.

Up.

With.

One.

He suddenly felt better. There was nothing keeping him here. Not anymore. Who the fuck would miss him? His folks were both dead. Chelsea's folks lived in Australia and had never liked him anyway. Shannon? She had her own life. His fans? His back-catalog sales would go through the roof for a few weeks and eventually someone would talk Shannon into giving up his letters and they would be published in a big hardcover tome with a foreword by one of his peers— some hack writer Gavin had never liked. The book would go best-seller, and everyone would realize that he had been crying out for years. All the death and anguish he wrote about would suddenly have *meaning*. Meaning with a capital *M*. It had been therapeutic, they would say. But he hadn't been able to exorcise his demons. Not really. And his suicide had been inevitable.

But he thought of Chelsea. What would she say? Chelsea was dead. She had nothing to say. And if she could, she would understand. She always had. Everything about him. She would know that he missed her. That he wanted her back. That he wanted their marriage back. That the pain was worse than being dead.

He curled into a ball.

And wept.

***

Dr. Laurel paused her wagon at the mouth of Gavin's driveway. Everything had made sense until about ten seconds ago. What had been a perfectly logical and well-planned maneuver suddenly seemed ill advised and unbalanced. The guy was not ready for a woman in his life—that much was obvious. And her courage—courage she had spent the last three days building up—was on shaky legs. She didn't know what to do. She had bought him a barbecue, steaks, and a bottle of wine. Was she being selfish? She knew what she wanted for her. But what did she want for him? Supper was the only thing she could say with any certainty. And she had supper. Not a lot in the way of answers. But supper she could do. Supper wasn't complicated.

She turned into the drive.

\*\*\*

Gavin was staring at the subway tile when he heard the bell. He felt no need for action. It was as if the wind had whistled or the furnace had started. The bell had rung and that was all there was to it. No need to do anything except lie on the floor and stare at the wall.

It rang again.

\*\*\*

Laurel stood on the stone step and pressed the button a third time. He was home—he had to be. The big black four-by-four was in the driveway and there wasn't anything within walking distance. Maybe he was down at the lake again.

Around back she saw Mr. Johannus working on a project that was starting to resemble a chair. She quickly did an about-face but Johannus had already seen her and was in the middle of a wave. She turned back and converted the move into a little dance step as if she was singing some song. What else could she do? Say, "Sorry, Mr. Johannus, I'm a little shy since you saw my bush up in the window the other morning"? No, that didn't quite work. It was face-the-carpenter time.

"Good morning," she said as she moved by the side of the house.

"Good morning, you-self!" Mr. Johannus winked jovially, his eyes traveling over her body. The big Maine coon sat off to the side, watching the two humans with feline indifference.

For a minute Laurel thought that maybe he didn't remember seeing her in her underwear. But she was dealing with a man and if life had taught her anything, it had taught her that men required a different type of thinking. Less left brain, more right brain. No, seeing a triangular patch of hair would definitely make him a little friendlier—it always did.

"Mr. Corlie around the house today?" she asked.

Mr. Johannus smiled broadly. "Yep. I saw him earlier. He's inside."

"I rang the bell. Maybe he doesn't want to see me." She hoped that it wasn't true but you could never tell. After all, what had the other night amounted to? Woman shows up, gets drunk, and steals his bed, all the while making lascivious comments. Sure, he would be dying to see her again.

"Who knows?" Mr. Johannus leaned in close. "He keeps very strange hours. I've never caught him sleeping. When I get here in the morning, he's been up for hours, down at the water or sitting in the living room listening to music and drinking. I don't think he sleeps all that much."

"Maybe he's working," she tried. And it was true. He was a writer, and writers write. He had explained it himself. How could you schedule something like that? "Thanks, I'll try the bell again."

"Just go in and holler." He gave her the once-over, his eyes resting a little too long on her chest. "He won't mind."

Laurel crossed her arms. "Thanks. Thanks a lot. I will." She turned and walked back to the house, realizing that every time Mr. Johannus saw her, he'd be remembering her bush popping out.

\*\*\*

The doorbell had stopped and Gavin had drifted back into himself. Then a door opened somewhere in the house. He heard the soft tread of feet, the steps barely audible in the quiet house. He lifted his head off the tile and wondered who the fuck was inside. Mr. Johannus would never come in without hollering. Besides, he wore those boots. Mr. Johannus never used the bathroom—Gavin had seen him peeing all over the place outside. Unless it was Number Two calling his name. Maybe taking a shit in the woods was beyond where he felt comfortable. But there was a bathroom downstairs. He wouldn't come upstairs. The cop? You'd never hear that guy coming. Gavin put his head back on the cool tiles.

Whoever was in the house started up the stairs. They took three steps, then called out, half whispering, "Gavin?"

For a second he thought it was Chelsea. And he almost believed it. The voice was different than Chelsea's. But still familiar. Then he got it.

Gavin groaned and sat up, pushed himself against the wall. His hips hurt and there were needles in his left leg from lying on the floor. What the fuck was she doing in the house?

"Gavin?" she called out again.

Gavin dropped his head back against the tiled wall. "I'm in the bathroom. Upstairs," he called out. He heard her pace pick up and she was there, in the doorway. She froze at the threshold.

"Everything all right?"

*Yeah, sure. I was trying to come up with one single reason not to kill myself. Apparently there aren't any.* "I'm swell." He closed his eyes. "What are you doing here?"

Laurel stepped back. "I'm sorry. I thought—I'm sorry—maybe I should have called."

"You think?"

"I rang the bell. Mr. Johannus said that I should come in and—"

"It's not his house. It's mine. I don't have to answer the fucking door if I don't feel like it."

"I see." Dr. Laurel nodded. "You're right."

Gavin looked up and the doorway was empty and he was left with the sound of her feet racing down the stairs. The front door slammed.

And he was alone again.

# 26

Finn Horn sat in his wheelchair on the dock in front of his house looking out at the lake. The sky was cloudless and blue and he could see for miles, clear across to the other side, which was some kind of rarity in itself. Even in the midst of clear winter weather, the opposite shore was blocked out here and there by patches of mist and humidity. Today he saw pretty much the whole thing. He figured that if he was at the right spot, he would be able to see clear down to Caldasac Dam where Tom Stockman had been killed while out looking for him. The paper said he had drowned, but Finn knew better.

Finn felt strange about the whole thing. Weird, even. Maybe the word was *responsible*. Until he thought about what had happened to him. Then he realized that he was just a boy who didn't always know what was going on in the world.

Heck, he didn't even know what was going on in his own lake.

Something out there had tried to get him. That was the only way he could put it—*get*. It had probably wanted to eat him. Kill him at the very least. But *get* made the most sense. Like the bogeyman—look out or the bogeyman will *get* you. What he did after the *getting* was never specified. But the *getting* was. The *getting* was the whole point. Once he got you, the rest of the stuff you could make up no longer mattered.

You were already *got*. End of story. Picture-on-a-milk-carton time.

Part of Finn was afraid. Afraid of what had happened. Afraid of what might happen if he got back on the water. Something was out there. Something big and dangerous and fast and strong as heck. Finn thought about hitting it with his boat. He had run over the thing and when he circled back and saw the cloud of black in the water it hadn't made sense. Not then. But it did now. And the end result was always the same: if it bled, it could be killed. You could *get* it. And have your picture in the paper. Be famous.

All it took was a little luck.

# 27

"Hey, little man," Gavin called, startling the kid.

Finn swung the wheelchair around.

"Gavin! I was just thinking about you."

Gavin gave Finn's wheelchair a quick once-over. "Great chair, kiddo. You do the work?" Every square inch of the aluminum tubing was covered with stickers and paint and he had swapped out the regular rims for red resin off-road wheels. It was impossible not to see the endless hours that had gone into the process.

"Yeah, thanks! I saw a show on TV where these guys take some old piece of crap car and pour tons of money and time into it and thought that I could do that with my chair. Cost me thirteen bucks altogether," he said proudly.

Gavin smiled and looked out past the boy. "You can see the whole lake from here. From my place I just get the bay and a slice of the big water through the trees." He walked over, put his hand on Finn's shoulder. "You look good."

"For what? A sick kid?" Finn didn't like being treated like he was ill. As far as he was concerned, he had it pretty good. He couldn't understand all the kids at school who spent their time inside slumped in front of the computer chatting with friends that lived down the street when they had two perfectly good legs that would carry them out the door and down the street in about six seconds flat. Lazy bunch of knuckleheads as far as he was concerned.

"No, for a kid who almost froze to death a week ago." Gavin shook his head. "You're going to have to learn to relax a bit."

Finn slapped his knee. "No time. Too many things to do." His jeans looked baggy and huge over his shrunken legs.

Gavin turned away from the little boy in the sick body, focused on the lake. "I know what you mean. Your boat come yet?"

Finn deflated. "Not yet. Izzy is having the chair adapted for me—putting in some kind of a rail so that I can steer from the console then slide back to the trolling motor without ever having to get up. Smart guy, Izzy." Finn looked up at Gavin and his face turned serious. "I wanted to say thanks. I don't know why you did what you did. You don't know me. If you did, maybe you wouldn't even like me; people feel, I don't know, uneasy I guess, around me—but it was a really, really great thing you did. My mom's been walking around crying for days. I don't cry. But I know how to say thanks." He reached out with his hand. "So thanks."

Gavin shook Finn's hand. "My pleasure, Finn. It looks like I have a shot at a new friend. Maybe the second in a week if I can get Dr. Laurel to forgive me. The third if I can get the cat to hang around more."

"Dr. Laurel mad at you? Buy her flowers. Blow her a smooch." He snapped his fingers. "They forget their own names."

"I think it'll be harder than that."

Finn looked at Gavin and shook his head. "Trust me."

"Since you're the one who brought it up, I wanted to talk to you about what you said at the hospital."

Finn's eyes hardened. "I wasn't making it up."

"That's why I'm here." Gavin stared out at the lake like it held the answer to some great cosmic secret. "I believe you."

Finn rolled back a foot and the wheels bumped up against the four-by-four lip that ran around the dock. "But?"

"No *but*s. At first I was a little unsure. I did a little research on hypothermia. One of the most common side effects is the onset of hallucinations. But it's momentary. Afterward, people doubt what they claimed to have seen while they were in shock. But you—" Gavin squatted down on his haunches. "You didn't doubt what you saw. Not for a second. And that says a lot."

"It could be saying that I'm a nut." Finn made a goofy face—the kind only a thirteen-year-old can.

"Yeah, I thought about that. But you're not." Gavin felt like he already understood the boy. This wasn't the kind of child to make things up. For Finn, there would be no point. His was a world of doing. His legs were worthless, yet every free day he got out in the world and *did* something. Maybe he knew that he didn't have a lot of time left and had decided to live his life. He certainly didn't deserve the big Fuck You that life had given him.

"I know what you're thinking," Finn said.

"Which is?"

"That I'm old for my age." His face was serious, stern even. "I've been old since I was born. Everyone says so."

"That you are, Finn." Gavin thought about the little boy alone out in the water, and wondered what really had happened out there. "I wanted to talk to you about the accident. You tell anyone else about what you saw?"

"You mean the monster?" Finn shook his head. "No one would believe me. Crazy little freak kid—cancer finally got to his brain. More meds. More doctors. More poking and prodding. No, thank you."

Some thirteen-year-old, Gavin thought. "Why tell me?"

"I thought that was why you had come to the hospital. You write about monsters. It all made sense."

"Didn't you wonder how I had *known* if you hadn't *told anyone*?"

Finn thought about the question and pursed his lips. "Not really. It just—I don't know—made sense. You showed up because you were supposed to."

Gavin thought about that one for a bit. Kids had always amazed him. No flurry of doubts. No *whys*, *wheres*, *whens*, *hows*. Just thinking it was so. If it was supposed to happen, it would. Period. *Next question, please.* "It was a coincidence. An accident. Luck. Call it whatever you want."

"No, *you* call it whatever *you* want. It happened."

Gavin was intrigued by this boy in the wheelchair. Life hadn't had a chance to beat the shit out of him. Not yet anyway. "*Why* did it happen?"

"I need help," Finn said flatly.

"With what?"

"With getting this thing."

Gavin averted his gaze, focusing on the far side of the lake. The water was glistening with scattered light and the sun was bright in the sky. And out there, somewhere, Finn Horn said there was a monster. And they were going to catch it. *Gavin, my boy*, he said to himself, *weirder shit has happened to you in your life*. And that little voice at the back of his skull, the one that always came up with the logic, spoke up. All it asked was: *When?* "You don't need me for that."

"Yes, I do. You believe in monsters."

"Whoa. Whoa. No. Wrong. I don't."

Finn looked Gavin up and down, as if he had suddenly grown purple skin. "But you write about them."

"That doesn't mean they exist, at least not in the form you're thinking of. There is no Loch Ness Monster, no Bigfoot, no Yeti. If you want to take it a step further, there are no aliens in flying saucers, no ghosts, no faith healing, no talking to the spirit world, and no religious visions."

"But you write about monsters and aliens and psychic kids that can make people's bones turn to jelly."

Gavin smiled, sat down on the worn wooden deck. "Doesn't mean that I believe in any of it. It's not a matter of belief, it's a matter of proof."

"But I saw a show on Discovery that said—"

"The world's round, Finn. Science has proven that much. Yet there are people out there who still think it's flat because that's what they *want to believe*."

"But how can you write about them if they don't exist?"

Good question. He looked at the boy. "A few years before I was born, a man named Roger Patterson took a shaky little sixteen-millimeter film of Bigfoot. Nine hundred and fifty-three frames that lasted for about fifty-two seconds. That film mesmerized me. Hell, it still does. I *want* that film to be real more than you can imagine. People still talk about it. Look it up on the web, and you'll find hundreds of sources where people swear that it's real. The experts they cite are usually nobodies. Real science dismissed that film years ago. People want to believe, so they do. People don't care. How many people have you met in the hospital who went to see a doctor too late? They had symptoms for months and they hoped it would go away. They refused to look at the *proof* of the blood in their urine or the lump in their breast and instead focused on what they *wanted to believe*, that they were doing just as swell as could be. Well, guess what? Belief and truth have nothing to do with one another."

"So you don't believe in monsters?"

"I may not believe in monsters, but I need something to believe in right now and I've chosen to believe in you." Gavin scanned the water. He could see the gray mass of a thundercloud forming at the far end of the lake. He watched the dark body swirl and pulse and wondered what, exactly, had happened to Finn out there. "I have to talk to your mom first. We'll tell her that you're going to teach me how to fish or something."

The boy's mouth split open in a grin that looked like a bucket of bathroom tiles, all white and shiny.

"What are you grinning at?" Gavin asked.

"I'm practicing for the newspapers."

# 28

Dr. Laurel pulled up to her home. Bought with the money she had left after her divorce, the old converted carriage house sat at the edge of property owned by the area's largest law firm. It was technically deemed a condominium as part of the bigger property, but the lawyers left her alone and she left them alone. They were happy with the way she had fixed up the old stone building and she was happy with the way they never asked her to let them approve plans for her ongoing renovations. All in all, it was a textbook example of a symbiotic relationship.

She found her driveway blocked by Gavin's Hummer; she hated that overpriced Tonka toy. Gavin sat on the hood, looking like he was either sorry or depressed. Probably both, Laurel guessed as she pulled up.

As she shifted into Park, Gavin came over, his hands in his pockets. She got out and nodded a greeting. "Hello, Gavin."

Gavin smiled uncomfortably. "I came to say I'm sorry."

Laurel shook her head. She had seen people in pain before, she knew what it was like, but she didn't always know how to deal with it. Medical school had prepared her for the biomechanical aspect of human beings, but psychology was a science that, as far as she was concerned, was still rooted in the Dark Ages. "You don't owe me a thing."

"Yes." Gavin looked into her eyes. "Yes, I do."

He looked like he honestly felt bad about what had happened. She wasn't used to men who made themselves emotionally available and she was momentarily uncomfortable about it. Then she remembered how he had treated her back at his house. When she thought about it, she realized that he did owe her an apology. "Okay. You do."

"I've been living in a vacuum for a while. And it's been my vacuum. No people. Just me. And it hasn't been healthy. When you came over this morning—"

She remembered him sitting on the bathroom floor, the distant look in his eyes.

"—I had been in the bathroom for hours. Feeling sorry for myself."

"You're doing a lot of that—the feeling sorry thing. Sorry for how you acted. Sorry for how you felt. Sorry all around." She wasn't going to give him an in, not just yet. He had to dig himself out.

"Look, I don't expect you to understand. I really don't. I had a great time the other night. And I rarely have a great time. Ever. And not just since Chelsea died. I've always been on the edge of things—on the edge of conversation, on the edge of a group of friends, on the edge of a crowd. Maybe that's why I write—I observe, I don't participate." Gavin stepped back and spread his arms. "I don't have a lot of friends, and I don't want to push away any new ones." There, that was it.

Laurel bit her lip and tried to fight off the tears that misted her eyes. "Not a bad apology," she said. "Now what?"

"Now I take you out to dinner."

Laurel shook her head. "Can't."

"Why?"

"I've got steaks in the fridge. Bought them for us." She smiled and her face lit up. "And I bought you a barbecue. It's in the back of my car."

"You bought me a barbecue?" He shook his head and laughed. "Doc, you're the best."

The sun was dropping behind the horizon and the long shadows of dusk stretched across the driveway and building. "I bet you say that to all the girls who buy you barbecues."

\*\*\*

They sat across from one another at the old wicker table in the courtyard. The space was small, maybe twenty feet squared, and enclosed by a low fence that she had constructed out of salvaged brick. English ivy clung to the uneven surface and last spring's shoots were already starting to wane, their death starting to pepper the green twigs with specks of gray. In another month the autumn courtyard would look like a tangle of dead sticks. There was one small shrub in a corner and a perfect little willow tree in the center of the yard, its branches sparkling with thousands of small clear Christmas lights that she had spent two evenings and three bottles of wine getting just right. The wicker table was Victorian, salvaged from the only antique shop in town, and the two chairs were from the hardware store. Three candles flickered and danced in the dark, illuminating the empty plates and half-empty wineglasses. The only sounds in the air were the chirp of the late-summer crickets and the echo of Laurel's laughter.

"Not true!" she giggled.

"Sorry, but I have to call you on this one. She may be a great nurse, but the mustache *has* to go. *Has* to. End of story."

Every time Laurel laughed, her head would cock to one side and her left eye would close. The reaction was growing on Gavin and he found himself trying to make her laugh just to see the eye close.

"Stop it," she said. "I have to work with Joyce. I won't be able to if you keep this up." She was shaking her head and her big smile was lit up in the almost light of the candles. For the second time since meeting her, Gavin realized that she was a truly beautiful woman.

"So—" Laurel changed the subject. "Have you seen Finn?"

Gavin nodded as he swallowed a mouthful of the California red. "This afternoon. Dropped by his place on the way over. Interesting kid. More like a miniature man, really."

Laurel nodded. "It happens to sick children all the time. It's like they know that they don't have a lot of time and they end up filling out their souls faster than they should. You should see some of the kids I've met. You're talking to a nine-year-old about how they feel and the next thing you know, *they're* giving *you* advice on life."

"Can I ask about Finn?"

Laurel's voice turned hard, brittle, the doctor in her coming out. "I'm technically not allowed to discuss a patient's file, but Finn—and his mother—have given me the okay when it comes to you. I think that you've caught them a little off guard. Cancer in his spine was cleaned out to the best of the osteopath's ability. But it's not a quantifiable thing. It's probably traveling in his body either through his lymphatic system or through his bloodstream. If it comes back and goes for his bones, his spinal column could just collapse and his spinal cord might sever. Or the cancer moves into his lungs—it's a very common route for spinal cancer. That happens and it's a matter of a few weeks for a boy in his health. Then there are his legs. They're shot—completely—and thrombosis is an issue for him. Blood clot forms, breaks away, travels, ends up in his lung. The result is a pulmonary embolism, and a PE kills instantly."

"Okay!" Gavin held up his hand. "I get it. Fuck, what is it with you doctors?" He shook his head.

"Sorry, Gavin. I just want you to know that he doesn't have a lot of time. There are no miracles on this one. It's not going to go away."

*And why would it?* Gavin asked himself. As long as you both shall live. Amen. If you lived long enough to get married. Or long enough to hit puberty. No, life had one grand sense of humor. "Yeah, sure. Sorry. Me too." He felt very sober now. Painfully so.

"What did you two talk about? I'm not trying to pry. I'm trying to understand."

Gavin thought about the question. What could he tell her? Finn wanted to find a monster in the lake? What would she say to that? "Finn has promised to teach me how to fish." What the fuck, it was close to the truth.

Laurel smiled over the rim of her glass again, and her eyes looked like they were on fire. "Fishing? For some reason I'm having a hard time picturing you skewering a worm with a hook."

"Me too," he said.

# 29

The road was a tunnel of blue, and the stitched yellow line blinked intermittently and disappeared under the chrome edge of the hood. It was late, almost two thirty a.m., and he tasted wine and smelled her perfume on him. They had hugged good-bye at the gate to her garden and the gentle scents of whatever she was wearing clung to him, and every now and then he would smell her. Gavin shook his head and cranked up the volume and Noel Gallagher's haunting "Cigarettes in Hell" filled the air.

There was no boy-girl formula in this. He wasn't ready. She probably thought he was too young for her anyway. So there were safeties at work here. A few of them. There was nothing to worry about.

But his mind kept drifting back to her smile. And that perfume.

He wasn't ready to let someone back into his life. And certainly not the first woman he met. Things like that never worked out. Not for him. Right now he needed something to work out. Anything would do. But no more accidents. No more fuckups. He couldn't take that.

Besides, what she was expressing was just a general enthusiasm for life. Not a specific enthusiasm for him. She was like that—positive, funny, vivacious. She was alive. *Alive.* The word rang in his head for a while.

Forget it.

Leave it alone.

He focused on the road, on the blue world ahead. The music was vivid and vibrant. He opened the windows. The interior exploded with a cold blast of air and his hair whipped around. Noel Gallagher sang about working and shopping.

The cool night air felt good. Pure. He pushed down on the accelerator. The big V8 growled and the truck lurched forward, pushing its mass up to nearly ninety miles an hour. He was a few miles from the turnoff to Lake Road and he could still afford a little speed.

There was a brilliant moment of light, and the blue of the road was washed away in a supernova flash of white so bright that he felt it heat his skin. The truck jolted to the right, and he felt it lose its footing. Instinctively, he jerked the wheel to the left. But he could no longer see.

The truck began to slide to the left. He hit the brake, but the vehicle kept moving. He was pinned back in his seat. The truck shook as it rattled across the shoulder. Then the rattling stopped and he was airborne.

A man with a Manchester accent told him that he didn't mind not going to heaven.

The Humvee hung in the air for an eternity. A split-second eternity.

Then sight started to come back. He saw the ground come rushing up at him and he realized he was upside-down. He braced his body as the truck impacted with the earth.

Glass and dirt and trees exploded through the wind-shield. There was the bone-jarring smash of the engine instantaneously stopping.

Gavin screamed.

Dirt sprayed into the car. Rocks. Glass. Branches. A stump rushed out of the dark, came at his head.

There was a metal-rending squeal.

The car shuddered, rolled. There was a *whump* as the roof disappeared, torn away by the stump. Another shriek as his door ripped away. Somewhere out of the corner of his eye he saw a tire careen off into the dark.

The air was above him. But only for an instant. It flashed by and was gone. Then the ground came swinging up again.

The singing had stopped and he had time to wonder if they had cigarettes in hell.

Impact.

There was the sound of a horn blowing. Slowly it began to fade. And then there was nothing. Nothing at all. Not even silence.

# 30

Her ass, lathered with suds, was pushed up against the glass shower door like ripe Greek olives against the side of a jar. She moved and the wet globes left a trail of milky suds and water on the smooth surface. She turned her head and smiled over her shoulder, bright and white in the candlelight womb of the bathroom. She knew that he was watching her, and she knew what it was doing to him. She reached down and back, lathered with more creamy soap, and bent over, pushing her behind up against the glass. As she bent forward, the moist oyster of her vulva winked out at him. Again her head turned, this time beside her knee, and she smiled once again, inviting him inside.

Gavin dropped his white linen pajama pants and opened the door. He stepped over the threshold and thick steam licked over his body, heating his skin. The tiles were warm against the soles of his feet and he moved slowly forward, toward her.

"Can you hear me?" she asked. Her voice was far away. Tinny.

He didn't respond. He just kept moving toward her. He didn't want to talk. He couldn't talk.

But her voice came back. "Gavin, can you hear me?" The sharp echo made it sound like she was calling him from outer space.

He shook his head. *Shut up. Don't talk.* Or this will go away. "Gavin?"

She faded.

Dissolved.

And was gone.

Then she started to come back. Her face melting into the white clouds above him. No, not clouds—ceiling tiles. First her silhouette formed, then her features. Eyes followed by the line of a mouth. But it wasn't Chelsea. It was Shannon. She was standing over him, looking down. Looking sad. He noticed that her eyes looked smaller without makeup.

"Hey," she said, wobbly, as if her speaker was broken.

Gavin tried to speak but nothing came out. His mouth was dry and he had the unusual sensation of his breath coming from some other place. *What other place?*

"Don't talk." She paused and the tears came back in earnest. "You were in an accident, Gavin. No...no...you're fine." She paused. "Mostly." The words sounded like an old-time trans-Atlantic phone call.

He forced his eyebrows up in a question mark and the pain dug through his scalp. It took all of his energy and he wanted to sleep after it was done. But he had to hear her answer.

"You went off the road. The truck is gone. Totaled."

*Good,* he wanted to say. *I hated that thing.* Then he realized that he had no idea where he was. He swung his eyes left and right. It was a large room and he could see other beds filled with patients, none of whom looked too healthy. All the computerized monitors told him that he was in someplace serious. It looked like there were enough technical gizmos to launch the space shuttle in here. He figured it out. NASA, that's where he was, hence the space talk.

Then his eyes found her, at the back, leaning against a door with a lost expression on her face. She was dressed as a doctor now, and the image pushed away the thought of her curling up in his bed the other night, drunk. Now she was a professional. There were tears in her eyes too. His mind started to race. What had happened? Was he paralyzed? How badly was he hurt?

Shannon brushed his hair back. "Your pal Dr. Laurel will fill you in on what happened."

Gavin tried to move all of his parts. He felt his right arm slide under the sheets. He thought he felt his legs move, but he wasn't sure. The left arm felt gone. Just not there. Panic started to set in. *Just tell me what the fuck happened!* he wanted to scream. All that came out was a Darth Vader rasp.

Now Laurel was beside his bed. She took his hand and her little fingers felt cold. "Hey, Gav. You're fine. Really. Everything's still there and whatever doesn't work now, will in a few days. You're in the surgical ICU. You went off the road four days ago, the night you left my house. You remember that?"

*Great*, Gavin thought, *dummy talk. They think I'm a vegetable.* He nodded slowly and the room throbbed.

"Good. That's good." She took a breath. "First off, you suffered a head trauma. All your signs are clear and there's no evidence of an aneurism—which was my biggest fear. You feel anything besides a headache?"

Gavin shook his head and the room started to spin. He closed his eyes to fight off the nausea he felt coming on. Bad idea. He opened them and everything equalized. *Okay, remember that one—don't shake your head.*

"So your head's good. Your eyebrow was pretty banged up—we stitched it back together but you're going to have a scar. Other than that and a few cuts and contusions, your face will be fine. You broke your left arm—it's probably a little numb right now, if you can feel it at all—"

Gavin thought about shaking his head then remembered the little men with the puke buckets running around in his skull and decided it could wait.

"Your humerus went through your bicep and we had to have an orthopod put it back together. Again, you'll have a little scarring, but the doctor was kind enough to do the work within the lines of your tattoo, so besides a little rough patch where the bone went through, your tattoo will be fine."

Gavin tried to laugh. Darth Vader made a comeback and he decided against laughing too. Who gave a shit about the tattoo?

"You've got a few bruised ribs but the airbag and seatbelt saved your life. You will be here for about another week. You might need a little physiotherapy for the arm, but all in all, I'd say you were pretty lucky. When the paramedics arrived on the scene you weren't breathing. They gave you a tracheotomy, and that's how you're breathing now. Until we take it out tomorrow, it's pad and pencil communication. Or sign language."

Gavin raised his right arm and forced his middle finger up.

Laurel laughed. "Exactly." She leaned in close, put her hand on his cheek. "I'm glad you're still here. I had a nice time with you."

Gavin smiled back at her. *Me too*, he wanted to say.

"Don't worry about the cat. I'll keep him in anchovies." She smiled down on him and he felt tears welling up in his eyes for no reason other than the fact that he wanted to say thank you.

She continued, the doctor in her back on the job. "We took a blood test and your alcohol level was fine. You must have nodded off at the wheel."

*Mole Roper had nodded off at the wheel. Not me*, he thought. Then he remembered the magnesium flash and the accident. He shook his head. And the room started to spin and he thought he was going to throw up again.

"It's the only explanation, Gavin," Laurel said.

Gavin raised his hand and made a scribbling gesture in the air.

"Sure." Laurel pulled a pad and pen out from her pocket. Gavin saw that she was wearing the squash-blossom necklace from the first night she had slept over. She put the pen in his hand and held the pad for him. It took a few minutes to get it out.

Laurel looked at the pad and tried to read the writing.

Shannon stepped forward. "I can read his writing—it's always like that." She picked up the pad, scanned the words, then looked down at Gavin. "You certain, Gav?"

He had never been so sure of anything in his life. He nodded. No easier than shaking his head. Thanks a bunch. *Try to remember that.*

Shannon turned to Laurel. "He was run off the road."

Laurel's face darkened. "Run off the road?"

Gavin nodded again. He wanted her to know that he was lucid, serious.

"Who would—?"

He drifted back into the dark again. This time there was no shower, only the grainy image of a man leaning over him, ear to his chest.

The image grumbled, "It's disco time, fuckface."

Then dissolved.

# 31

"Wake up!" The voice was tinny and persistent. "Gavin!" His name was followed by a knocking. Also tinny. And as persistent as the voice.

He opened his eyes.

When Gavin's eyes fluttered open, Finn stopped banging on the chrome bed rail and smiled. The boy was in his wheelchair and Gavin was on his level. He started to talk and that weird sucking rasp filled his ears. He reached up with his good arm and felt the corrugated plastic tube sticking out of his throat.

"Fun place, huh?" Finn asked. "You get all kinds of free stuff, mostly needles and infections. I spend more time here than at home. You're lucky, you were put in a private room." Finn looked around and nodded approvingly. "I was stuck with Russel Sprouts. His real name was Russel Wozniak but everyone called him Russel Sprouts, even his mom. Guy was in worse shape than me. No guts or something. Farted and pooped all the time. I mean *all the time*." Finn waved his hand in front of his face to fend off the imaginary farts. "It smelled like a backed-up septic tank in that room. Especially on chili night. Wednesday's chili night here. Don't worry," Finn held up his hand protectively. "I'll make sure you don't get any chili. I'm friends with Frank—the guy who takes care of the meals. I'll tell him that you're allergic to crappy food. You'll get a bologna sandwich and a bag of Cheetos. Can't go wrong with bologna. When you get better we can go up to the third floor and play with the bald kids, they're pretty cool."

Finn was smiling and talking a million miles an hour and Gavin realized that all things considered, he felt pretty good. And he also realized that a few days ago—how many now? Five? Ten? He'd have to ask the date—he had been ready to kill himself. Not completely committed. But frighteningly close. He didn't realize that he was smiling until Finn stopped talking and asked, "What's so funny?"

Gavin waved it away as nothing.

"Heck, when I'm in here I don't look this bad. You look like a distributor cap." Finn's face broke open in his own special version of a grin. "But you ain't dead."

Gavin smiled back at the kid and gave him a thumbs-up. The back of the boy's T-shirt sat unevenly on his body, as if one of his shoulders was jacked up by a few inches. Gavin reached over and tapped Finn on the shoulder and the T-shirt deflated.

"No. No. Don't touch it!" Finn slapped Gavin's hand away. "I like to hang my T-shirt on the doorknob at night. I like the weird little hump it leaves—takes people's eyes off the rest of me." He grinned through a big white smile and winked. "Always keep them off guard."

Gavin tried to laugh and the sound was not a pleasant one.

"Okay, you're getting out of here in a few days. Next week, we start looking for the Creature."

Gavin raised an eyebrow. After the laugh he realized that all communication would work out better if he kept it limited to facial expressions.

Finn leaned in close, conspiratorially, and whispered, "We're calling it the Creature. No one will know what we're talking about."

Gavin nodded and winked and tried not to laugh. The kid watched too much TV.

"This is what we are going to do. This afternoon they're taking that tube out of your throat. I'll be back here with a pad and paper to discuss our plan."

Gavin raised an eyebrow again in a *let's hear it* expression.

Finn's thin voice dropped down another notch. "I've been thinking about this a lot. Whatever the Creature is, it wasn't scared of my boat. Eighteen-footer with a six-six coming didn't scare it away. Either I hit it and it got mad, or it was hungry and tried to turn me into its lunchtime nachos and peanut butter."

Gavin flinched.

"You ever try nachos and peanut butter?" the kid snapped. "Then don't knock it!" Finn rolled his wheelchair as close to Gavin's bed as possible, and leaned in. "So either way, this thing ain't scared of boats or people. But it lives in the lake. It bleeds. And it sure as heck eats. Anything that size eats. A lot every day. And if there's one thing I know how to do, it's catch stuff that lives in the water. It's all a question of bait. We are going to get ourselves some animals— dead ones—relax, Jesus, you think I'm nuts? We're gonna sucker-rig them."

Gavin gave Finn an *I don't understand* expression.

"To catch a musky—you know what a musky is?"

Gavin nodded.

"Well, to catch a musky, most guys go out and spend eighteen bucks on a fancy balsa or plastic lure. Then they troll it around all day like gas is free until they're lucky enough to put it right in the strike zone of some fish that's too lazy to go hunt down its own dinner. The way I work—and all the big European pike pros do, too—is with a sucker. Live or dead. Black sucker is a bottom-feeding fish. And it's the prime baitfish for muskies. Any musky fisherman will tell you that they've cut open muskies and found suckers in them. All the good lures—the Jitterbug or the Creek Chub Pikie—work best in black because it imitates the musky's favorite snack choice—the sucker. You seeing a pattern here? It's like nachos and…okay…okay…how about cranberry and Cheez Whiz? Sheesh, what *do* you eat?

"So, I catch suckers, wrap them in steel cable with three big treble hooks at various lengths, so that they resemble a big piece of Velcro. Musky can't resist the natural smell of a skewered fish. Even a tired fish that ain't hungry will hit a sucker. With a balsa or plastic lure, if the hook doesn't set immediately, the fish will turn and run—plastic and wood don't taste natural. But you rig up a big juicy sucker and it's like Krispy Kremes and yogurt to these guys."

Gavin made a face again.

Finn waved his culinary skepticism away. "And that's how we catch the Creature," he said, and winked, letting Gavin know that they were speaking in code. "Only we don't use suckers. We use something big. Something tasty. Something that will look like food to it. I wish we could go down to the cemetery and dig up a body, drag it behind the boat. Man, that'd be great!"

Gavin shook his head. The little men with the hammers didn't start up and he felt a rush of relief. His head was getting back to normal.

Finn's eyes rolled in their sockets. "I'm exaggerating. To make a point. You're a writer. You ever exaggerate?"

Gavin smiled and nodded.

"I'm trying to be creative. All I'm saying is that we need something big. BIG. Bigger than suckers. We can make special harnesses out of leader wire and big saltwater treble hooks." The little boy pounded his fist into the palm of his hand and the sound echoed. "If there's one thing I know, it's how to fish. When I'm not fishing, I'm reading about fishing.

I've read every book that there is on fishing. If anyone can catch this thing, it's me!"

Gavin wanted to ask *What then?* But Finn answered it for him.

"You own a gun?" Finn asked through a big shit-eating grin.

Sure he had a gun. A beautiful little stainless-steel Colt Python with a round in the cylinder that would go through a cinder block. What the fuck, maybe now he'd get to use it. He gave Finn the thumbs-up.

Finn's face did its own special version of a grin once again that he punctuated with, "We'll need *lots* of bullets."

## 32

Shannon had gone home to the city. Evidently everyone concerned was satisfied that having survived both the crash and a medical system that Finn told him would do everything within its extensive power to help him expire prematurely, he could be left on his own. *More or less*, she had added before leaving. Shannon had mothered him for two days, then abruptly left when he had unceremoniously told her to. No *please*. Just a curt *Leave* and she was gone. And he was back to being alone on the lake. Well, alone when it came to human company. The cat was there—the big scruffy Maine coon that still didn't have a name even though he had moved into the house (only when he felt like it, of course). Gavin didn't want to cramp his style and, evidently, the cat didn't want to cramp his. Maybe it would be the perfect marriage. As long as the anchovies kept coming. Every relationship had its price— this one happened to cost a dozen tins of fish a week.

Gavin had seen lots of Finn and Dr. Laurel in the hospital. At the end of the night, when her shift was over, Laurel would come by the room and usually find Finn there, his incessant chatter still on overdrive. She would ease into a chair with her coffee and the three of them would play Yahtzee with antique dice that Finn's grandfather had bought in a Vegas casino back in the 1950s. More often than not, when one of them threw a hand, a dot popped off. As the light dimmed and one side of the dice became indiscernible from another, they would have to improvise a shot at Braille. Finn had quickly dubbed their game Ray Charles Yahtzee and for some reason, he always won by at least a hundred points.

Now Gavin was home, back in the world. Back in the *now*. Back with Mr. Cat. And by extension, Laurel and Finn. Not a family. Something different. Something new. What could he call them? He mulled it over for a few minutes. They were called friends. *Friends.* A good solid word, he told himself.

And he realized something else. That maybe—just maybe—Chelsea had been right. Maybe they should have had kids. Maybe he would have been a good father. At least not a bad one. And it had taken coming out here to get him to even consider it. Sonofabitch.

Gavin moved down the stone steps to the lake. It was evening and the sun was setting; the orange and purple sky hung over the black lake. It was warm but he wore a big shirt over his T-shirt. The cast on his left arm was bulky and awkward and his bruised ribs still felt like exposed electrical conduits under his skin. But he wasn't dead. Or broken. Merely damaged. Strange part was, he was glad. To be around. To be *not* dead.

Mr. Johannus had finished the second Adirondack chair and it sat beside the first, facing the lake. There was something different about the new one. Then Gavin realized that it was smaller. He smiled and slowly eased into the larger one. With this came another realization; he wished that Laurel were there.

So, what's on the agenda? he asked himself. First off, there was Finn and his monster out there. Kid wanted to rig a dead Saint Bernard with hooks and drag it through the lake. It sounded nutty. But Finn was convinced.

Gavin was about to give himself the *there has to be a logical explanation for this* talk. He felt it coming. But why bother? He had been writing about this stuff for years. Writing about things that no one believed were out there. Writing about monsters. Maybe that's what this really was. Something that went bump in the night. Something that had tried to eat Finn.

He wanted to forget it, to dismiss it. It would be easy. *Sorry, Finn, I can't. Too much to do. Go on. Good luck*. But he wouldn't. He couldn't. Why? Because he *wanted* to believe in this for the simple reason that it sounded like a whole lot of fun.

There was the other problem lurking out there, though. A very real problem. Someone had taken him off the road. Deliberately. Sheriff Pope had investigated and found nothing suspicious. The sheriff was sure that Gavin had fallen asleep. He'd seen it a thousand times before. On the way home, tired, close your eyes for a minute. BAM! Impact with a telephone pole and you had a free pass to the coroner's table.

But the grainy image of a figure listening to his chest in search of a heartbeat, then grumbling, *It's disco time, fuckface*, was too real to dismiss.

And Pope was wrong. He had been awake. He remembered everything about the accident. He had opened the window to Noel Gallagher's "Cigarettes in Hell" and forty seconds into the song something had blinded him. The big ugly truck had gone off the road. He even remembered the stump ripping through the roof. No, he hadn't fallen asleep. Not a chance.

The next big question then was, Why? The answers, when he really thought about it, were endless on that one: some drunk asshole pissed off at the world, decides it would be fun to put the next car coming down the road into the ditch; some save-the-whales dickhead disapproves of your gas-guzzling bitch the size of an airliner and hates the fact that you don't recycle your Heineken cans. You could make yourself crazy guessing at the possibilities. Only this hadn't been random. It had been deliberate and it was supposed to have killed him. Problem being that he was still alive. Would they be back?

And beyond it all was Chelsea. Beautiful, dead Chelsea. Invading his dreams. Reminding him every time he closed his eyes just how much she was gone. Just how much their marriage was over. Gavin shifted in the seat and winced as the arm of the chair pushed into his ribs. The pain was physical, intimate. A reminder that he was alive.

What was with the dreams? Every time he closed his eyes, she was there, tormenting him. They had started immediately after her death. At first they had been innocent enough—little visions of her dressing in the morning, or getting out of a cab. A few weeks later, they had grown more intimate, more personal. She'd blow him a kiss, wink, maybe wave. It hadn't taken long for the lid to be blown off whatever restraint his mind had been exercising. His latest dreams had crossed the line from the erotic to pornographic, and they were starting to feel unhealthy. Maybe it was just biomechanical; he hadn't had sex in months and his body had a need to dispose of the surplus semen. But it wasn't as if he had no release; he wasn't the first person to rely on masturbation in a pinch. So what did filthy dreams about his dead wife mean? Christ, when he thought about it in those terms, he sounded like a Freudian jackpot.

Mr. Johannus came down to the ledge, his tool belt slung over his shoulder. He was sticky with sweat and peppered with sawdust. "I'm finished with the ramp. The little boy should have no trouble getting into the house or down to the lake." The big cat was by his side, still looking as disheveled as ever, his plus-sized paws goofy looking.

"Thanks, Mr. Johannus. I appreciate it."

"No need to thank me, that's what you pay me for. The ramp from the house down to the lake can be taken up in the winter." The old man paused. "You'll get more years out of the plywood that way."

*You mean why bother when Finn's not going to be around to use it, huh?* "No, it's fine. We can leave it there for the winter." Gavin turned and examined the long plywood runway that snaked down the hillside from the house, each eight-foot section ending at a landing where the chair would have space to turn to take the next section down. It looked like it had always been there.

"Nice job, Mr. Johannus. It looks great."

"You want it painted to match the house? I could do it the same color as the window trim. It would look less—" The carpenter took off his hat and ran a big hand through his thinning blond hair, and the muscles in his arm rippled. The cat lay down beside him, stretching out in the sun.

"Conspicuous? No, it's fine. You got a name for that cat, Mr. Johannus?" he asked, changing the subject. Someone else coming up with the name seemed like the solution, since he didn't seem to be able to make the commitment himself.

Mr. Johannus looked down at the cat and shook his head. "I just call him Cat—it seems to work."

Gavin dropped his head in defeat—the poor creature was still nameless.

Mr. Johannus continued. "Well, that's it for me today. Going to go home and take a sauna."

"Sauna?"

"It's Wednesday. Always take a sauna on Wednesday. *Puhas pillu paiva ilta,*" he said, ending in his native Finnish.

Gavin cocked his head. "Which means what, exactly?"

Mr. Johannus translated in his head for a second. "Exactly?" Mr. Johannus's mustache curled up in an honest smile. "It doesn't translate."

Gavin smiled, then laughed. "If nothing else, you are consistent."

"I do my best, Mr. Gavin."

"You beat yourself with the sticks in there?"

"They're birch branches. And yes, I whip myself with them. Sometimes I whip my wife. Sometimes she whips me. It's tradition. You should try it."

Gavin shook his head. "Getting into an oven is an involuntary act on my part."

"With a good beer it can be life's second-best experience."

"The first is?"

Mr. Johannus smiled broadly again. "If you don't know by now—"

Gavin wondered what Mr. Johannus would think about the dirty dreams he was having about his dead wife. He'd probably get a kick out of it. "I see."

Their conversation was interrupted by the sight of Laurel coming down the steps. "Ah, the lovely doctor with the tiny boobies," Mr. Johannus whispered.

Gavin was about to protest when he realized that the man was right in a very factual kind of way. She *was* lovely. And she *did* have small boobies. "Keep it to yourself," he said, and stood up.

Laurel was wearing a pink sequined tank top pulled tight over a pink Lycra shirt, brown suede jeans, and pink and brown Puma trainers. She looked very metropolitan. And pretty.

"Hey, Doc."

"I brought supper." Laurel smiled mischievously. "And a new barbecue!"

Gavin nodded down at his arm. "I can't do a thing."

Laurel came over, gave him a big, enthusiastic hug, and a kiss on the cheek. "That's okay. We have Mr. Johannus to help." She smiled over at the Finnish carpenter. "Don't we, Mr. Johannus?"

Mr. Johannus looked her over, his eyes stopping a little too long on her chest. "I can help for a few minutes."

Laurel took a breath and held it, accentuating her nipples through the thin shirts she wore. "Then let's get cracking."

Mr. Johannus nodded obediently and followed her up the steps, leaving Gavin to stare, slack-jawed, after them. The cat followed close behind, interested in what was going on.

"Try to come up with a name for the cat while you're at it," he called after them.

# 33

The fire snickered in the hearth, the soft crackles and pops of the burning wood in sharp contrast with the soft voice of Julie London meowing "Blue Moon." Gavin hobbled back and forth between the open boxes of LPs on the carpet and the new built-ins, organizing his records. His bad arm slowed him down, and after Lou Reed's *Transformer* rolled out of the sleeve and shattered on the floor like a clay pigeon, he began moving them one LP at a time. Finn was in his chair in front of the coffee table, his face deeply accentuated by the harsh chiaroscuro the firelight etched into his features, his attention focused on the large plastic-laminated hydrographic map of Lake Caldasac held down by cans of Coke. The cat—still nameless and uncombed—slept on his back in front of the fireplace on the floor, his feet poking up into the air.

Outside the weather had taken a classic Caldasac turn for the worse, and a late-summer thunderstorm hammered the countryside. Every now and again lightning lit up the walls with a bright flash of electricity that screamed into the ground. Whenever a bolt would let go, Finn would hold up his hand and count out loud. *Just to see how far away it is*, he had said. Gavin found the action amusing and somewhat magical in a Middle Ages alchemist kind of way. No one did things like that back in the city—except maybe the nut down on Mott Street who stood on his milk crate screaming about the future. The harsh pelting of rain and the grumble of intermittent thunder accentuated the warm crackling of the fire and the smooth singing.

Gavin slid an LP into the mass of colored record spines that now occupied most of the wall. "We've got to do some research," he said to Finn.

"Research? What kind of research?" Finn slurped down the last drops of Coke and crushed the can in his compact hand. The cat twitched with the noise, then went back to imitating an overstuffed beanbag.

*Stronger than he looks*, Gavin thought. "Has it occurred to you that we don't have a clue as to what we're doing?"

Finn's brow creased. "What does knowing what you're doing have to do with anything? The *Titanic* was built by the best shipbuilding and special-effects guy in Hollywood. And what did it get them? A bunch of frozen wet dead people in a *really* crappy movie."

"Look, Finn, if you have any expectations of success here, you have to arm yourself with as much information as you can. You said that you saw a big shadow before you hit it, right?"

Finn put the compacted can down on the coffee table and leaned back in his chair. "I *think* so. *Think*. Don't *know*." He shook his head. "It all happened so fast. But even if I didn't see it, something smashed up my boat." Finn's eyes unfocused and he went back to that day on the lake. "I remember the bow getting hit and the way the boat plowed sideways. I remember seeing the gunwale buckle and water spill into the boat. I remember being hit again. And losing my favorite freakin' hat. I can remember the boat almost flipping over. And lying in that freezing water, petrified to move. I remember thinking: *If I move, it will hear me; if it hears me, it will come back.* I didn't want it to come back. So I didn't make any noise. I didn't even shiver. At least not for a while. Then when my teeth started chattering, I couldn't hear nothing. For the whole time I was there. Days, felt like. Nothing in that lake can cave in a reinforced aluminum hull like that. Nothing but the flood gate on the dam."

"Can you guesstimate the size?"

Finn shrugged and the emotion started his head nodding like it was on springs. "Had to be huge. Bigger than you and me put together."

"And something that size has to eat. Has to feed. All the time, right?"

Finn kept nodding.

"So someone else has to have seen it, or been attacked by it, maybe even been eaten by it." Gavin picked up an old copy of *Why Can't We Be Friends?* and flipped it over, reading the track listing.

"And?" Finn asked.

Gavin looked up from the record. "And that means we can find out about it. Gather some information. Information is power. I'm not going out there without knowing what my options are."

There was a bright flash and the sky lit up in a phosphorescent flash—a giant television tube overloading. Finn held up his hand and counted out time like a bandleader. "One… two…three—" The count was ended by a loud *snap!* that sounded like it had come from all the windows exploding at once. Once again the cat twitched, then went limp. Finn's mouth slid into a grin. "Man, that was close! My teeth rattled with that one. Quarter a mile off. You probably lost a tree."

Gavin shifted uneasily. "What happens if we get hit by lightning?"

"Usually you die." Finn was smiling.

"I mean *the house*. What if the house gets hit? What happens to us?"

"In here? Nothing. Unless the windows are open. Or if you're in the shower. Then it could be bad. I saw your lightning rod on the roof—is it grounded?"

Gavin thought about the questions. "What's a lightning rod?" *By which I mean I have no fucking idea if it's grounded*, he thought. "Shannon had the house inspected before I bought it. I suppose that's something they would have checked for, right?"

"How the heck would I know? I'm thirteen. I guess. Sure." Finn looked over at Gavin. "All I know is I got rubber tires and you're in bare feet. I'm probably safe."

Gavin glanced at his feet, then went back to scanning the album cover.

"Can I ask you a question?" Finn asked.

"Ask away."

"What the heck are these things?" Finn swept his arm over the cemetery of LP boxes.

Gavin looked up. "You're kidding, right?"

"Yeah, I'm kidding. I've seen millions of these things. They're everywhere. Walmart. Nascar shows. Heck, they even make sandwiches out of them. I'm just asking because I have nothing else to do with my time." For a thirteen-year-old, Finn was a master of sarcasm.

"They're records," Gavin offered matter-of-factly.

"Records? Of what?"

Gavin looked up from the LP in his hand. "What the fuck do you mean, *records of what*? Music."

Finn nodded. "I see." But it was clear that he didn't.

"Haven't you seen an album before?" Gavin fumbled the inner sleeve out of the jacket and held up the twelve-inch vinyl disk. "One of these?"

Finn scrutinized the album. "What does that thing do?"

Gavin dropped his head in defeat. "I'm getting old."

"Me too. What does that thing do?" Finn repeated, reaching for the record.

"No. No. No. You never touch the surface with your hands." He turned off the CD they had been listening to and placed the album on the platter. After a few adjustments and machinations, he lowered the needle onto the vinyl. Then he stood back to wait.

The cowbell came on. Followed by the simultaneous fade-in of the congas and dug-down bass. Finn cocked his head to one side, interested in what he was hearing.

"What is this song?"

Gavin held up the album cover. "'Low Rider' by War. Pretty cool, huh?"

"Cool? This is freakin' awesome!"

The vocals slid into the mix.

"Man, this is the best!" Finn's head was bopping to the thirty-year-old song that had summed up the street culture of fast cars and pretty women in the barrios of Los Angeles.

Finn started dancing in his wheelchair, moving the wheels back and forth to the heavy groove of the song, his head keeping time.

Every time the words *low rider* were sung, Finn pumped his arm to the beat and hollered, "That's me! That's me!"

He was boogieing in earnest now.

Finn stopped spinning his chair and started air-drumming the beat, improvising for a few bars. He was absorbed by the music and for a moment he was just a little boy again.

"Whoo-whoo! That's me!" Finn shouted, still drumming away. "Hey, I don't drive too fast either! Whoo-whoo!"

Gavin danced slowly beside the boy, smiling, trying to remember the last time he had danced.

As the music wound down, Finn was beaming. "Man," he said, winded from his performance, "that was cool as heck." He ceremoniously wiped a forearm across his brow, more for show than necessity. "Too bad you can't get that stuff on CD."

"You can," Gavin responded.

Finn's face screwed up into a question mark. "So what's the point?" He surveyed the records piled on the shelving, strewn about the floor, and leaning against the wall. "Look how much space these record things take up! I got more music on my iPod, and it ain't even a real one, it's some crappy free-at-the-gas-station thing that someone left behind at my mom's restaurant that she brought home for me." He shook his head. "They like Star Wars collectibles? Are they expensive or something?"

Gavin thought about it. "I pay about a buck a piece at flea markets. Sometimes two. I think the most expensive album in the whole lot cost me ten—but that was something I *really* wanted."

"So you can buy eight or nine for the price of a CD? Saving money I can understand."

Gavin was about to tell Finn that the stylus on his turntable cost almost three grand then thought better of it. The boy made sense in that no-nonsense way kids often have. "And I like flipping through the covers. You can't do that with a CD or an MP3."

Finn nodded. "That makes sense. I love my *Musky Hunter Magazine* covers! Still, you've got a load of these record things." The walls flashed brilliant and Finn counted off. Two miles. Too far for any fun.

Gavin awkwardly lifted the disk from the turntable and closed the Plexiglas cover.

"What's it like to be rich?"

Gavin stared back at the kid. In a way it was an inevitable question. But it was something that he no longer thought about. When he had been younger, when he and Chelsea had been living in that shithole apartment in Brooklyn, his vision of success had been the fantasy of going into a grocery store and not having to look at the prices. That had come with *Iron-monger*'s first royalty check. Since then, money had just been there. He had a few investments and two homes, three now with the house on the lake, but otherwise it was all just sitting in the bank, mostly in useless tax shelters and various funds he didn't even know he owned. He had enough now that even if it stopped cold he'd never be able to spend it all unless he went crazy, buying mansions and Learjets for everyone he knew. When he bought something, he bought the thing he wanted; sometimes it was the most expensive one, more often than not it wasn't. "I don't know, Finn. I never think about it. I remember *not* having money more than I feel like I have money now."

Finn looked around the room, his eyes locking on the sound system. "How much was that?" he asked.

"I don't know. Thirty grand." When he said it, he realized how ridiculous it was. Thirty thousand dollars for a stereo. And by the standards of an audiophile, it was cheap, poor even. He knew that some people spent a hundred grand for their turntable alone.

Finn's face contorted in confusion. "Thirty thousand dollars? For a radio?"

In the way of defense, Gavin said, "It's handmade. McIntosh. Tube driven. Very pure sound."

Finn looked at Gavin. "It's a radio," was all the boy said.

Gavin felt embarrassed. What could he say to that? "Yeah."

"You feel bad having all this money. You know—guilty?"

That was a very good question, too. The kid would make a great journalist. "I used to. What the hell have I done? Written a few books. That's it. Is what I do that important? Not in a real sense. I'm not curing any diseases. I'm not making the world a better place. I entertain people. And I don't feel guilty about that."

Finn's eyes narrowed slightly. "So what *do* you feel guilty about?"

*About not stopping Chelsea from getting into the elevator. About arguing with her that day. About saying the things I said. About almost anything you can think of.* "I used to feel guilty that I wrote horror novels for a living, like I was wasting my talent. People would ask me, 'When are you going to write something serious?' and I would smile and *aw-shucks* them, and stare at my shoes and feel like I was just faking it until I grew up. But you know what? I walked into your hospital room and you knew who I was. I have affected people. I have affected you. There's something to be said for that. So, no, I don't feel guilty anymore. I used to. I sit down at my desk with my hands and my mind and I create. And out of that creating, I give a lot of people something to enjoy. And I get paid for it, too. Is what I do worth all the money they throw at me? Hey, is *any* guy that hits a little white ball four hundred yards worth thirty million bucks a year? No fucking way. The president of the United States—the guy that runs this country—makes three percent a year of what I do when I'm on a roll. Three percent! And his job is a lot tougher than mine is."

"You'd probably be better at it than he is, though," Finn said in that matter-of-fact way that Gavin was getting accustomed to.

Gavin searched his head for an example. "Who's the most famous fisherman around? In magazines and on TV?"

"Randy Ketchum."

"What does Randy Ketchum make a year?"

Finn shrugged his shoulders. "I don't know."

"If he has a TV show, signature series gear, public appearances, articles, and the franchise rights to his own face, I'd say it's north of a mil. Could be two if he controls any of his products. And that's if he has a *bad* PR guy."

Finn's eyes lit up. "A million bucks? For fishing?"

Gavin nodded. "That's my point. How many days you fish last year?"

"Ninety-one," Finn said.

"That's a quarter of a year you spent working. I bet you Ketchum spent most of his time in shopping malls, at boat shows, and touring chain stores. No way he spent that much time on the water. No way. So, why does he get two million a year and you don't?"

Gavin could actually see the wheels turning in the boy's head. There was only one answer to the question. And it was an answer that had taken Gavin years to figure out. "Luck?" Finn asked.

The kid was smart. "Mostly," he confirmed. "The world gives some people a break. That's just the way it is. There are better writers than me out there. Lots of them. Some of them are working at McDonalds; some are antique dealers; some just got married and have to choose between being a writer or being a father and provider. All because they haven't met the right agent. You've heard of right-place-right-time? Some people never get their shot. I was lucky. John Kennedy Toole wrote one of the most important American novels of all time. His editor didn't see the point in the book, so he dropped him, and Toole committed suicide. Ten years after his death, his mother put it in the right hands and it won the highest prize for fiction that this country has."

"You ever win it?" Finn asked.

"No." Gavin smiled. "They don't hand out Pulitzers for the kind of stuff I write."

"Then why do you write it?"

Another good question. "Because I have to." It was the truth. "It's how my brain works. I think about serial killers and evolutionary mechanics and monsters."

"Like the one that lives in our lake?"

"Like the one that lives in our lake." Gavin sunk back into the sofa and took a third off his Coke. "So where do we start with this thing?"

Finn thought about the way the hull of his boat had folded in. "We get a PT boat and depth charges." He was smiling but something in his eyes told Gavin that he was only half joking. The lightning struck again and this time the cat didn't raise an eyebrow. Finn went through his ritual of counting off the seconds, this time making it to eleven. "Two miles and a smidge."

"Can you find this thing?"

"I found it once when I wasn't looking for it. Nobody knows that water like I do." He pointed at the lake, invisible through the rain. "This is *my* lake. Only the next time, it ain't gonna be me that gets the crap-kicking." The kid was serious.

Gavin suppressed a smile. "But we don't know what it is."

"Hey, it's in the water, I can catch it. The brainwork is up to you."

"The way I look at it is, the more we know about it, the more chance we have of finding it. Someone out there has had *contact*." Gavin took a long pull on the Coke and smacked his lips. "This thing has made an appearance before. Someone out there knows something. There is no way you are the first person to have come across whatever is out there. No way. Statistically impossible on a lake this size."

"But no one fishes out there. Not regular like me, anyhow."

That seemed odd to Gavin. "What do you mean?"

"What do you mean, what do I mean? I mean that no one fishes out there. Just me."

"Why?"

Finn shrugged. "Dunno. Even Izzy thinks I'm a dumbass fishing Caldasac. Everyone fishes the Saranac over at the edge of the county. Izzy told me that this lake's bad water.

No fish." Finn threw his arms up in the air. "Frank Knechtel caught plenty of muskies out there. I've caught plenty of fish out there, pal. Those guys are idiots."

"That still doesn't tell us what's out there."

"Maybe it's like the Loch Ness Monster."

Gavin's stare flattened out. "You're kidding, right?"

"It's been around for years. And no one's caught it. Tons of pictures. Tons of people seen it. Movies about it. They even got Time–Life books on it. Research hasn't helped no one."

Gavin nodded. "Good point." He didn't have the heart to tell the kid that Nessie was an out-and-out lie dreamed up by a hotel owner to bring in business. Instead, he dredged some facts from his memory banks. "We're not talking about some bottomless Scottish lake here, Finn. Loch Ness averages four hundred and fifty feet in depth and bottoms out at seven hundred and fifty feet. Caldasac is what, seven miles long? Eight? Two and a half, maybe three across at the widest point? No deeper than…?"

Finn rolled over to the coffee table and drilled his finger into the laminated map of the lake. Almost on cue the walls sparked bright white as another bolt of lightning connected with the earth. Finn didn't bother counting, he was too busy studying the map. "Hundred-and-ten-foot hole across from Kintner Island right here." He tapped his finger. "And I think that your bay is deeper than that. But Caldasac is less than thirty on average."

Lightning cracked and the sound wave came in low and hard, rattling the windows.

"Loch Ness is twenty-three miles long; Caldasac isn't Loch Ness, not by a long shot. We're going to need more than a little luck and a lot of hard work. We're going to have to think. We'll examine the county records for boating accidents, fatalities, and injuries around this lake."

"The library," Finn offered.

"Only if they have back issues of the local papers. The best bet would be the medical examiner. Maybe police records." Gavin thought about Sheriff Pope and realized that the police probably wouldn't be all that eager to help. "Forget the cops."

"What about the Department of Fish and Wildlife?" Finn asked.

"What exactly do they do?"

"They manage the fish and animals. They've got a local office."

The corners of Gavin's mouth turned down. "If they knew about this thing, they'd already be after it. What we need is access to reports where people have been hurt, attacked, killed, or had an unusual happening of some sort. All this stuff would be filed under accidents or a cause of death other than *monster*. Medical examiner is our best shot."

Finn broke out laughing. "We sound like a couple of retards. Monsters? If you'd have told me a month ago that I'd be hunting down a monster, I'd have told you to cut down on the Flinstones vitamins." He shook his head.

What could Gavin say? A month ago he was considering throwing himself out of an eleventh-story window. In more ways than one, hunting down the monster made at least a little sense. "I've made my living by writing about monsters, Finn. The ones we can see and the ones we can't see. I've sold millions of books. Millions. I can't even begin to wrap my brain around those numbers. Anyone who's bought one of my books— except the Hardcore Creepies, as my agent calls them—will tell you the same thing: *There's no such thing as monsters.* Then why do they buy my books? Because there *are* monsters, Finn. That man over there on the mantel in the dining room was a monster. The Bloodman was a monster. Mole Roper was a monster. They're out there, kid, and they fuck up lives all the time."

"I never thought about it like that." Finn's face grew serious and his eyes narrowed. "You think cancer is a monster?"

There was no pretending that it wasn't there. Not with a boy whose body was going to shut down on him before he learned to make love. "I guess it is, Finn."

"And before I die, I'm going to do something important. Something big. BIG!" Finn smacked his fist into the palm of his hand. "Like get this thing!"

"I still want to know what *this thing* is."

The only sound in the room was the crackling of the fire, offset by the heavy thunk of raindrops on the windows and the slate roof. Gavin got up from the sofa, went to the hearth, and tossed a log onto the grate. The fire hissed and cried as the new bark burned off. Mr. Cat, stirred by the noise, expressed his pissed-offedness by snapping his ears back. After a few seconds of lazily eyeing the sizzling log, he jumped up onto Finn's lap.

Finn snapped his fingers. "Maybe there was a nuclear spill and a lizard mutated and it's big and scary and has superhuman intelligence and laser-beam eyeballs!" Finn put his fingers out in front of his eyes, imitating what he figured laser beams would look like, complete with lots of sound effects.

Gavin rolled his eyes. "Would you cut that shit out? I'm trying to be serious here. Nuclear waste does not produce giant animals with laser beams for eyes. Never gonna happen. Doesn't work that way. Forget comic books, forget Hollywood, forget schlock writers. Creatures *can* mutate, but the mutation—regardless of how benign it appears to be—is so traumatic to the being's genetic code that the body rejects it and death steps in. Mutations are incompatible with life. That's the rule."

"Like cancer cells," Finn added.

"Fuck. Finn, don't do that to me. You know what counts? I mean *really* counts? You are fine right now. Right now. Right here. This second. That's as much as you could ask for. My wife had her *right now*. Then some fucker riding the heroin highway in a Lincoln Continental decided to use her as a crash test dummy. All any of us get are the *right nows*. That's it, Finn. Yes, you are going to die. But you know what? So am I. So yes, life can be really crappy at times. But you have to stop this. It's not fair when you're here, drinking Coke, making bad jokes, and letting Mr. Cat sleep in your lap." Gavin immediately regretted his outburst.

Finn changed the subject for him. "You gonna come up with a name for this cat?"

"Haven't thought about it," Gavin lied.

"For a writer, you sure have a lousy imagination sometimes."

"So *you* come up with a name for the cat. Just no Mittens or Cuddles or Whiskers or any such saccharine bullshit."

"How about Foots?"

Gavin laughed. "Foots isn't even a word."

"Look at his feet! They're so big that we need a new word for them. I like Foots." Finn kneaded the cat's big paw in his hand, the nails coming out when he put pressure on the ball of the foot. The cat purred, arched his back, and stretched. "See? He likes it, too."

Gavin waved his hand. What the hell, it was better than Mr. Cat. "Okay. Foots the cat. I guess it beats Snuggles."

"How come he's so huge?"

"It's the breed. He's a Maine coon. They're big cats."

The cat rolled over in Finn's lap and the boy instantly made a face. "Jesus, what is this thing eating? His farts are poisonous."

"Anchovies."

"Buy him some cat food, it may save my life." Finn pulled the neck of his T-shirt up around his face so that only his eyes were visible. "Yours too."

"I've been meaning to."

Lightning flashed again and the whole room flickered blue and clear in three solid bursts. Then the thunder rolled in and the lights blinked out. "Blew a transformer," Finn said with authority. Foots, newly named, got up and headed off into the house, probably looking for someplace less noisy.

A few minutes later, Finn spoke again. "I'm sorry about your wife, Gavin. I bet she was a nice lady."

"Yeah, Finn, she was pretty good for the most part. She wasn't out to hurt anyone." He thought back to the blasting he had given the kid. "I didn't mean to blow up at you before. I just don't want you to be negative."

"Hey, I'm the most positive guy you know."

"And when it comes to fishing, you're the Original Bad Motherfucker."

"OBM? Me? Really?" Finn's face was radiant with the compliment.

Gavin smiled at the acronym—*dumbass* was the cutting edge of Finn's expletive lexicon.

"So, what now?" Finn was spinning his wheelchair in tight circles on the Persian rug.

"Well, the way I see it, we find out what we can about this thing. See if it's actually hurt anyone. Not that it makes that much of a difference. But if we learn that someone had a tractor eaten off of their lawn last summer, we're gonna need a bigger boat."

As if cued by the special-effects department, the wind picked up and the rain thrummed into the windows, echoing loudly. "It's raining something biblical out there," Gavin said more to himself than Finn. He had never seen storms like this in the city.

"I bet the fishing is great."

"In weather like this?" Gavin had to raise his voice to be heard over the din of the cloudburst. Nothing seemed like a worse idea in the world to him right then, sitting by the fire all warm and dry.

"Best musky weather there is. The nastier, the better. Mean fish, the musky. Whitecaps, freezing water, wind—nothing that fish likes more."

The windows lit up in another white flash that was followed by a sound wave that hit the house. The building shivered.

"Okay, so we start with the medical examiner."

Finn turned his wheelchair away from the big picture window, a gray rectangle against the paneled walls. Visibility was almost nil and nothing seemed to exist beyond the small stone terrace with the two rusted chairs save for a black hole of wind and rain.

"Do I have time to finish my Coke?" the boy asked.

# 34

Chief Medical Examiner Duncan Parks looked puzzled. And more than a little uncomfortable. "I'm not sure I understand exactly what you are looking for, Mr. Corlie?"

Gavin leaned back in the vinyl-upholstered chair that had traveled from the sixties to the new millennium without so much as a scratch in the orange pseudoleather. "Accidents in the area, specifically on Lake Caldasac. Anything that you would consider to be unusual. Out of the ordinary. Not necessarily violent accidents but not necessarily nonviolent, either. Anomalies within your experience."

Parks crossed his arms across his big breasts and stared into Gavin's eyes. "I'm not trying to be difficult, Mr. Corlie, but why are you interested in this? I mean, you aren't here in any sort of a professional capacity, are you?" The question said that he had dealt with plenty of policemen in his time and the man sitting in front of him was anything but official.

Gavin smiled and shook his head. "Sorry, Dr. Parks, I should have been more clear. I'm a writer. I'm doing some research for a book that I'm work—"

Parks sat straight up and his face switched to friendly mode. "Gavin Corlie? As in the horror writer Gavin Corlie?"

Gavin smiled his best PR smile and nodded. "That's me." The rare occasion when he actually found his unusual celebrity to be useful was in interviews. If you got past the introduction, some people loved opening up to a writer, helping with the work.

Parks stuck out his hand. "I am a huge fan of your work, Mr. Corlie. I loved *Bloodletting*."

Gavin shook the big hand that Parks offered. It was the size of a ham, and for a split second, Gavin wondered how the hell he navigated within the human body with those things. Then he realized that the patient wasn't going to file any malpractice claims. "That means a lot coming from you." The research in *Bloodletting* had been checked by Becky Strong, the chief medical examiner for Manhattan. Anyone in Parks's position would have been impressed with the details. "Whenever someone in your profession compliments me on that book I can't help but smile. It means I did my homework." He was being honest.

Parks nodded vigorously. "I read that book cover to cover in two days. The dissection scene in the Piggly Wiggly still comes to me when I'm grocery shopping. Every time I see someone buying ham hocks I wince. And believe you me, it takes a *lot* to make me wince."

Gavin realized that he was suddenly enjoying this conversation. After all, the writing was about the reading. When his fourth novel, *Drainpipe*, had come out, Blacktree Books had received a court order from the Department of Defense demanding to know his source for the details pertaining to "infrastructure and architecture not available to the general public" in reference to Area 51. True to government form, they had refused to specify exactly which details they wanted to know about and the case was eventually dismissed. "I can't take all the credit for *Bloodletting*. Becky Strong, the chief ME for New York, had a lot to do with that novel. If it wasn't for her, the book would not have turned out like it did."

"And now you're writing a novel about Caldasac?" Parks was hooked. It was in his eyes.

Gavin thought about lying; it would be easy enough. He decided on the least damaging version of the truth. "I live on Caldasac. Bought a place there."

Parks smiled but his eyes didn't seem to be part of it. "Caldasac, huh? Why the move?"

Gavin thought about another lie. But the truth was easier. Sort of. "My wife was killed. I needed a change."

With the word *killed*, Parks shifted in his chair and his body language softened. "I'm sorry. I didn't know," he said with the awkward stutter of a doctor who was not used to dealing with live patients.

Gavin ignored the fumbling. "I needed to start a new life somewhere. I thought that being my own fish out of water would be the way to go. A house on a lake seemed like a good idea. The place on Caldasac came to my attention and the next thing I know, I find myself talking to you."

Parks seemed happy to grab the new turn in conversation. "Where on the lake?" Then quickly added: "I'm not prying here. You don't have to worry about me showing up for dinner. I'm not a stalker. Unless you count my love of a medium chocolate dip at the Dairy Queen," he added as comic relief, patting his not-insignificant belly.

Why was it that everyone knew about the stalker? Even people who had never read any of his books knew about it. *The price of celebrity.* "I bought the old German house on the hill."

"Interesting that a horror writer bought *that* house. I guess it all fits. And now you're writing about Caldasac." The last sentence was a statement, not a question.

"Not exactly *about* Caldasac. But I'd be lying if I said that the place had failed to affect my thinking. I've been here a while now and I've got a few ideas floating around in my head. Like all my stories, a lot of it will be loosely based on the physical aspects of a specific place—the people, the geography—where I got my inspiration."

"I don't want to pry—and don't worry about me stealing any industry secrets—but where *do* you get your ideas? No," Parks shook his head, doing a mental backing up. "Not your ideas. *Everyone* has ideas. How do you develop a fifteen-second idea into a hundred-thousand-word novel? Where does all the meat come from?"

Gavin liked the question. If he had a dollar for all the times strangers had approached him at parties, in cabs, at the Starbucks across the street from the apartment, and offered to tell him their great idea in exchange for his writing it and a 50 percent split of the profits, he'd never have to write again. Gavin's usual response was a curtly delivered: "I'll tell you what? *I'll* give *you* a ten-second idea, then *you* can spend five months of *your* life writing the novel and *if* you sell it and *if* the money eventually comes rolling in, *you* can split the profits with *me!*" That usually shut them up. Not as fast as he would have liked. But it more or less did the job.

"I can't explain it—and I have tried in interviews and the writers' workshops that I do. But it usually starts out as a little idea. Something like"—he reached into the black space of his mind—"cool serial killer story. I think about all the serial killers that I've read about. Then I go off and research those. Which inevitably leads me to other sources. Before you know it I'm a newfound expert on the subject. Then I approach it from an angle that I feel like only I've seen. I try to bring something to the mix that is new. Different. Unexpected. Then I work on that in my head for a bit, let it cook. I usually come up with a main character I like, then I try to figure out how to put him or her in a situation that will bring out the qualities that draw me to that character and that's where I begin. All I have to do is put them somewhere—a car wash, an apartment, a waiting room, then I introduce the unknown element that will turn the story on. Then I do nothing but sit back and follow them. If I'm not having any fun watching them progress, neither will the reader. I scrub the book and start something new.

"When I sit down, it's not so much inventing as remembering for me. Time's my problem, not inspiration. Call it divine channeling, stealing from ancestral memory—whatever you want to—it just comes to me."

"You ever have a dry spell? A time when you couldn't come up with any ideas?"

Gavin thought about it. "Only since my wife died, and even that's softening up. Three months in twenty-one years of writing six days a week, time off only on my birthday and Christmas, isn't such a bad spell. My gray matter is pumping again, and I've got a new notebook started that's already full of characters, dialogue, and descriptive." It was a lie, but a small one. Or maybe not so small. "If I don't write, I die. That's it. Writing keeps me sane. Keeps me from going Charles Joseph Whitman somewhere. I guess that's what makes me lucky in what I do. I produce three first drafts a year. And I usually polish off two of them and get them to print. Some guys take eight years between books. Either they're not working or they're working slower than plate tectonics. I'd shoot myself if I had to stay away from my keyboard for that long or if it took me that long to finish a book. You sit down and write all day, there's no way that it takes eight years to write a book. Unless you should be doing something else, which most writers should." Gavin never really liked talking about writing in interviews or to groups, but with people who had read his work, and liked what he did, he always enjoyed himself, even if it felt a little narcissistic.

"Life throws material at me every day. You know that disclaimer at the front of every piece of fiction that states: *any resemblance to persons either living or dead is purely coincidental—* a lie dreamed up by lawyers to protect profits. Keith Richards writes a song called 'Sister Morphine' and everyone nods their head knowingly and says: *Of course! He knows what he's talking about. Keef's lived it, man!* And that little disclaimer has contributed to the erroneous assumption that a writer just pulls his work from outer space when it's really a combination. Which is why I am here. I need truth to pad out my fiction.

"I'm working on a story set on a lake in the mountains. So I wanted to ask around to see if I could find anything that would push my brain in one direction or the other. First port of call was your office. You would get full credit for any help, and anything that you wanted to say off the record would be held in the strictest of confidence." Gavin could tell that Parks was still interested. "I would like to know about any mysterious deaths or accidents over the past ten years. Even typical deaths that had any—and I mean *any*—atypical earmarks. Especially cases involving victims who died in, or were found in, the water. I'm looking for drowning victims that haven't been found. Or campers that went missing. If there is anything like that, I'm curious. It's the little details that make a story real, kind of like the right perfume on a beautiful woman; it should be a nothing detail, but when you get up close, the payoff's worth the extra effort."

For a second Parks looked away. Then his eyes came back to Gavin. "Can you give me some specifics? It might make my end a little easier."

Gavin shook his head and smiled. "I never discuss the details of a work-in-progress. I'm kind of noted for it."

"Which is why I asked," Parks said with a grin. "I've got a few cases that I can think of off the top of my head. I've been at this for three-plus decades, so there's bound to be *something*. I'll see what I can dig up. Give me a few days."

Gavin stood up and extended the hand that wasn't bound up in the shoulder-to-wrist cast. "Thank you, Dr. Parks. I really appreciate your help."

"Forget the appreciation," Parks said as he shook Gavin's hand. "Just write another great novel."

Gavin nodded. "I'll do my best."

"Mornings are best for me. Ten o'clock-ish?"

"I'm up by five every day. Ten's good. I can drop by the Piggly Wiggly for my morning ham hocks before coming here."

Parks's face turned a little sour. "Yeah. Sure."

# 35

After Gavin left the subterranean lab of the ME, Parks found himself sitting in his vinyl office chair staring at the bank of ancient oak filing cabinets that took up the wall. He was thinking of ham hocks while staring at one of the drawers, wondering if it was finally going to open up and bite him in the ass.

Like all small towns, the secrets of the dead lived down here, in the underworld library of ghosts. The worst secrets of New Mannheim were nestled snugly in that drawer. The drawer had been passed over to him by his predecessor and mentor, Dr. Gregory Steiner, as his predecessor had done to him, and probably the man who held the office before that, going back almost a hundred years. The faded hand-scripted blue ink on the yellowed label read *Pending Cases*; in reality it was the final resting place for the autopsy protocols that no one could quite figure out. A law-enforcement agency would have labeled the contents of the drawer as *Unsolved*. Under Park's watch, now coming up on its twenty-ninth year, three cases had been added to the drawer. This brought the population of the unexplained dead to an uneven thirty-one. Of course, in the way of small-town politics, each and every file in the drawer had been declared officially closed, but this was simply a balm for the public's sense of well-being. After all, town officials couldn't use unsolved deaths to get reelected any more than basing their platform on raising taxes, cutting services, and making hunting illegal.

The first case dated back to June 1933 when four-year-old Hadley Schmidt had disappeared while swimming. A single pencil-scrawled line in the margin of page 3 of the report stated that her mother swore that the little girl had been "torn from my arms by *something* in the water." Other than that one single disassociated entry, the file was otherwise a cut-and-dried drowning. Parks, having the benefit of hindsight on his side, knew that drowning wasn't the cause of death at all. After little Miss Schmidt had disappeared, the contents of the drawer had steadily grown, like a child with bad eating habits. Deaths, for the most part, were usually years, sometimes decades, apart. The biggest binge—an anomaly in the history of the area—had been the summer and fall of 1962, when three people had expired in grisly fashions mere weeks apart. Normally, this would have garnered some attention in a small town like New Mannheim, but these deaths coincided with the nuclear stalemate of the Cuban Missile Crisis and the town's attention was focused on Walter Cronkite rather than local goings-on. The then medical examiner, Dr. Steiner—under urging from the town sheriff—had managed to close the three cases with more than a flourish of fiction, writing off one death to a boating mishap, one to a bear attack, and the last one, perhaps too creatively, to a hunting accident. The only statement on record for any of the deaths had been given by Joseph Reinhardt, a sometimes fisherman and full-time drunk who had witnessed the death that had been labeled a boating accident. Mr. Reinhardt said that the victim had been fishing a hundred yards offshore when out of the blue the victim had screamed and been pulled out of his boat by *something*. Mr. Reinhardt's statement had, for reasons of obvious unreliability, been dismissed.

So New Mannheim had, for lack of a better explanation, a specter living in the shadows. A specter that tore children away from their mothers, pulled men out of boats, and had killed almost three dozen people in the past nine decades. It had been quiet for years now; the last case Parks had dealt with had been in the summer of 1983 when an Italian tourist named Massimo Tataglia had gone out in his kayak one morning and not come back. Within hours (it was not good to let things like this linger, lest the newspapers find out) his little craft was discovered a mile upstream from where he had left, the fiberglass hull pockmarked with what could only be described as teeth marks; but nothing on earth had the teeth necessary to do that kind of damage. Once again, the death had been written off as a hunting accident, the holes in the kayak denoted as buckshot damage. Xavier Pope had burned the kayak and no one had bothered to complain, the fact that the tourist had been Italian probably adding to the community's indifference. After all, they didn't like outsiders hanging around New Mannheim, especially if they weren't American.

The citizens of New Mannheim knew that something was not quite right out on the lake. There is no place where secrets are kept quite as badly as a small town. But these people were of strong Germanic stock and refused to acknowledge that anything was wrong. Parks knew that it wasn't stoicism that held their feet to the floor. It was fear.

Like most of the residents of New Mannheim, Dr. Parks knew the history of the town. But his knowledge blossomed where most of the townspeople knew little or nothing other than rumors or half-forgotten stories. Parks knew that something *was* out there. And now it looked like someone else did, too. An internationally best-selling author. Not good. Not good at all.

Gavin Corlie had been living on the lake for what, a month? Five weeks? What had he seen? Did writers really have the ability to look at their surroundings with X-ray glasses? Did he possess some preternatural ability to zero in on the unusual, the macabre, the horrifying? Is that what made him so good at what he did? No matter how Parks flipped it over in his head, the fact was that Gavin Corlie had seen *something*. And that had been enough.

Parks was still staring at the scarred oak drawer when the phone rang. He snapped his usual Pavlovian response into the phone, "Parks."

"Yeah, Doc, this is Reggie. I just got a call from Pete McGibbon. He's found half a body. I'm on the way over with the meat wagon right now." Reggie Hogarth had been Parks's assistant for the better part of a decade. Although not much of a go-getter in an aggressive sense, Hogarth was a good Man Friday and his fuckups were always of the manageable variety.

"What do you mean, *half* a body?"

"McGibbon wouldn't say. Just said that I'd need a Rubbermaid box. Sheriff's office already sent someone over, probably Pope."

The question came out of his mouth before he had even thought about it. "Where did McGibbon say this body is?" he asked.

Hogarth's voice was distant and disembodied with cellphone echo but there was no mistaking the words. "Lake Caldasac."

Parks's eyes crawled back to the pending cases drawer.

Thirty-two now.

# 36

The morning was warm and the humidity of yesterday's storm hung in the air. Puddles dappled the south side of the main street where the sun had yet to touch the pavement. If he moved too quickly his footfalls jarred his ribs, so he moved slowly, using the time to take in New Mannheim. Up until now he had been limited to his stay at the Luau Hideaway Motel on the edge of town, two visits to the real estate agent's office, his time at the house by the lake, the hospital, and a few nocturnal forays to the all-night grocery-mart/gas station off State Route 47E. As a writer, he was comfortable spending time alone and until today had never really felt much of an urge to explore New Mannheim. Now, walking the main street, he realized that had been an oversight—it was a pretty little place. With the exception of the FedEx drop-off station, the town looked like it had been shielded from the last five decades of progress and remained in the 1960s.

The downtown core of New Mannheim was two blocks of Victorian red-brick and limestone buildings built with function, not complicated architecture, in mind. The town faded out a few blocks from the commercial core, the heavy brick buildings giving way to the rambling ugliness of once-wealthy Victorian homes that had been chopped up into rooming houses, real estate offices, and multifamily dwellings.

At the edge of town, sitting lopsided in a patch of unten-ded wild flowers and a tangle of brush, sat the sun-beaten skeleton of an ancient Dodge Challenger, its engine lost to hot-rod cannibals years ago. The town had towed it out here from the wrecking yard, painted it black and white, and stuck a broken red light on top. It was a small-town trick to slow down nonresidents when the speed limit went from fifty-five to thirty-five as they rolled in. In the better towns, they would mow around these derelict cruisers but they wouldn't weed-whack. In the wealthy ones they would mow *and* weed-whack. New Mannheim's ancient car sat amid bramble bushes and evergreens, unpainted in twenty-five years and a thick choking garden of weeds growing up through the floor and upholstery. A tree sprouted through the back window. Finn had given him the car's history and Gavin found it an interesting welcome.

The unmistakable scent of lost prosperity was palpable from one end of town to the other. But for all its has-been traits, the little town possessed a lived-in feeling for Gavin, as if he had known this place all his life, and in a way he did. Movies, American novels, and *Saturday Evening Post* covers had made him feel like this was a place he understood. Was it a viable assumption? Who the fuck knew? Peyton Place and Stepford, two valid visions of the American small town. The idea was to give it a shot. To try. And a good place to start trying was anywhere they had coffee. Gavin searched for a coffee shop.

The ubiquitous small-town department store, different from thousands of others across the country in name only, took up an entire half block, the corner facing two transepts of the main intersection. The windows showed sun-bleached mannequins in the latest fashions of a decade ago, their vulcanized fiber bodies frozen in the rigor mortis poses of judo experts. Stapled to the painted plywood imitation shoji screen behind them was a faded *Weekend at Bernie's* poster. The big Art Deco sign bolted to the red-brick building hadn't been repainted since before the introduction of the eight-track player to the world of hi-fidelity. *Morton's*, it read, an establishing shot out of *American Graffitti.*

Sharing the rest of the block with the once-grand retailer were a pharmacy, a plumbing supply store, a florist, and a repair shop with a sign that read: *We repair everything but a broken heart.*

The opposing block was home to Izzy's Sporting Goods, an auto supply store, a jewelry store, and, at the end of the block, a general store that had a sign in the window advertising hot coffee and fresh doughnuts. Gavin crossed the street.

As he stepped down onto the puddle-scattered pavement, his eye caught sight of the snout of a police cruiser hanging back in the street's single alley. Only the grill was visible, the chrome and resin clean and shiny. The rest of the car was in shadow and as he moved across the pavement, Gavin thought he saw a silhouette shift behind the wheel. Sheriff Pope? Were there any other cops in New Mannheim? And what was he doing parked in an alley in the center of town where the chances of him doing any protecting and serving were at their slimmest? Locals wouldn't speed through town and tourists (if there were any) would be put off by the ancient Challenger parked in the weeds. What was he doing here? As the strong smell of coffee filled his brain, the thought of Pope slipped back and away, melting into the memory banks. He opened the heavy oak and glass door and stepped into the store.

The woman behind the cash was anywhere from seventy-five to ninety-five and had on a pair of glasses that made her eyes look like they had been salvaged from the front end of a 1928 Ford. She nodded a friendly hello to Gavin when he walked in. "Mornin," she said.

Gavin nodded back. "Good morning." He looked around the old shop.

The floors were well-worn wide oak planks and the shelving was from the turn of the century, constructed of painted wood with brass hardware, the white powder-coated metal and chrome fittings of modern grocery store shelving conspicuously absent. Most of the store was packed with bright modern packaging that was at odds with the turn-of-the-century decor. There was a big walk-in fridge with a heavy oak door that had a panic bar in the middle, through the small window of which Gavin saw hanging sides of meat. Large beer cooler, and one aisle of household necessities that didn't fall under the heading of food; things like lightbulbs, duct tape, playing cards, and fishing line were neatly arranged and individually priced.

"Coffee fresh?" he asked, scanning the magazine rack. Under *Musky Hunter Magazine*, *Guns and Ammo*, and a few copies of *People* magazine there were a few dog-eared paperback novels that a lopsided Scotch tape–repaired sign denoted as a poor man's lending library with the words: *Books—Free. Pleaz bring em back*. The first under the sign was a mass-market copy of *Ironmonger*.

"Not ten minutes into the pot," she responded cheerily. "Want a cup?"

"You bet." He smiled down on the book that felt like it had been written a thousand lifetimes ago. When was the last time he had read it? Ten years ago? Twelve? He picked it up and leafed through. "A doughnut would be great. Plain if you've got." He scanned a page and unconsciously shook his head. That passage could have been done a little differently, he thought. Someone had once said that a novel was never truly finished, merely abandoned at the most opportune time— Gavin couldn't remember who.

Assuming he was shaking his head at the story as opposed to the mechanics of the writing, the woman said, "I read that one. Scared the bejeesus out of me. Couldn't go into a hardware store for a month after I read it."

Gavin looked up and smiled. "Then the writer did his job."

She screwed her face up. "I guess that's one way to look at it." Behind her, neatly wrapped in brown paper and grocer's twine, were a half-dozen packages with names scrawled in pencil across their surfaces.

"You deliver?"

The old woman shook her head. "Not me. Too old to drive. But my grandson, Early, he delivers. Little dim-witted but likes the truck. Beeps the horn like crazy. If you close your eyes it's kinda like driving in one of them clown cars in the circus that's honking all the time."

Gavin smiled at the colorful imagery. "How do I set up an account?" He put the dog-eared novel back into the rack and took the coffee she offered over the glass baker's counter. Outside the police cruiser eased by, the driver's face shielded by the brim of his Stetson and a big pair of aviator sunglasses. The car was moving slow, too slow, and Gavin had to tell himself to stop being paranoid.

He was brought back to the here and now by the old woman's voice. "You the guy what bought the old German place?" The doughnut came on a red-and-white-checkered napkin that was already starting to go transparent with leached grease.

Gavin nodded. "Small town, huh?" The doughnut was delicious as only something that is truly detrimental to your health can be.

She looked him over. "I guess. For new accounts you got to leave a deposit. After we get to know you we go on faith, until then it's strictly a cash basis."

Gavin took a sip of the coffee. "Good coffee." He put it on the counter and wrestled his wallet out of his back pocket. "Can I leave you a check?"

"Sure."

Gavin took a pen out of a jar by the cash register. As he awkwardly wrote out the check, she added, "Make it out to Mickey's Mercantile. I'm Mickey."

"Can I e-mail orders in?"

"You can *call in* orders. Deliveries are three dollars to cover gas; can't wait until them Iraqis stop raising the price," she said, pronouncing it Eye-Rackies. "We do same-day deliveries if you call by two. No Saturday deliveries—too busy." She waved her hand through the air as if illustrating her point. Gavin looked around the empty store and realized that it *was* Saturday. "Today we may make an exception."

He pushed the check across the counter and she examined it with the myopic scrutiny of mistrust. "This is for a thousand dollars," she said flatly.

"When I use it up, please let me know. And put ten dollars on each bill for your grandson. I appreciate the service."

"You ain't seen him drive," she joked, some of her mistrust melting back to the friendly little old lady she had been when he had walked in. "We pick up booze from the liquor store as a service but you have to order at least ten dollars of supplies from us. We got every kind of beer here, including Guinness," she said, pronouncing it Gwinn-ess. "What we bring in for that antique guy around the corner. But you gotta order it special, 'cause he buys everything we get. Drinks it too, I s'pose. We've got fresh meat all the time. Anything you want in steaks. In the fall we get moose, too—usually lasts through to the end of February. Fresh fish all year."

Gavin's eyes wandered back to the tattered copy of *Iron-monger*.

"Take the book," Mickey said. "It'll scare the crap out of you. Especially living out there all by yourself."

"Not much scares the crap out of me."

"That book will. It'll keep you up nights. Makes me wonder what kind of a nut wrote it."

"Maybe a talented one," Gavin offered as he turned to leave.

Mickey seemed to consider the statement for a few seconds. "Why would someone with talent waste his time writing that kind of stuff? He ain't no Hemingway."

"But he scared you."

"Hell, my grandson's driving scares me. That don't take no skill."

"Thanks," Gavin replied. "I'll remember that."

# 37

Reggie Hogarth backed the white Econoline into a clearing between the trees that lined the water's edge. Sheriff Xavier Pope's cruiser was already there. So was McGibbon's county four-by-four. Hogarth hated officials in any capacity, particularly cops, and specifically Pope. The big sheriff was all attitude and a wonderful example of how too much power and possession of a firearm could rot someone's brain. Hogarth kept his eyes locked on the mirror as the van beep-beep-beeped through the scrub. He wished he had smoked a joint a few minutes ago to help get him through this meeting of the minds.

Hogarth liked smoking a little grass, eating a little pussy, and watching a little TV, all in that order with the occasional bag of M&Ms thrown in for variety. Unless *Star Trek* was on. For Spock the whole fucking world could stand still as far as Hogarth was concerned. Spock had it down. Spock was the iceman cometh. Spock was everything that Hogarth wished he was. Cool, unaffected, and not afraid of a fucking thing, man. And outside the system in a *you can't scare me* kind of way.

Pete McGibbon of the New York Department of Fish and Wildlife stood at the tree line and directed Hogarth's white van with the arm signals of an airport runway traffic coordinator. Hogarth and McGibbon went way back, and it was McGibbon's old-school polished-boots-and-standard-issue-.45 law-enforcement mentality that freaked Hogarth out. McGibbon was a smart enough man, but man, he was as inflexible as a government employee could get.

The backup indicator pinged for the last time and the white reverse lights cut out as Hogarth switched the engine off. He grabbed a pair of orange plastic sunglasses—left over from a DUI fatality he had cleaned up last month—and bounced out of the van. He always wore sunglasses around other people to hide his red eyes.

"Hey, Mac, how's it hanging?" Hogarth asked cheerily.

McGibbon rested his hand on his holster and nodded a greeting. "Not bad unless you're the person down by the river. I have seen some shit in my time," he said melodramatically, and Hogarth was glad McGibbon couldn't see him roll his eyes behind the cheap mirrored lenses. "But this is freaky-fucking-deaky."

Hogarth opened the back door and started taking out the stretcher. "Male or female?"

"Yes."

"It's usually easy to tell them apart if you look at the plumbing. Outsy—boy. Insy—girl."

McGibbon winced. "That's just it. There ain't no parts."

Hogarth shrugged. It was all the same to him. He snapped on a pair of latex gloves. "The fuzz down with the body?" Hogarth had seen every violation that the human body could go through and fancied himself above being affected by the sight of the dead. But compared to the sheriff, he was a lightweight. That guy could chow down on buffalo wings dipped in ranch while cleaning a kid out of the grill of a car with a Q-tip and tweezers.

McGibbon nodded, his expression making it look like he might finish the gesture by puking in the shrubbery. "Sheriff Pope is down there with one of his men. They're almost done taking pictures." His voice wobbled a little.

Hogarth snapped a piece of gum in his mouth and the noise echoed in the empty little clearing. "Bear attack?"

McGibbon looked away. "More like a chain saw."

Hogarth stopped chewing his gum.

"Could be a wood chipper. Or a bucksaw. There's a body—actually it's *half of a body*—down on the water's edge. Some kids looking for a place to party found it. They thought it was a drowning but drownings don't rip themselves in half, right? We got a pair of legs. That's it. That's all. End of story. Legs. Two of them. Connected by a few strands of flesh, tendon, skin, and whatever else the fuck holds a body together."

"You wanna tell me what's going on?" Hogarth hated admitting it but he found a certain sense of satisfaction in McGibbon's discomfort. One of those *Fuck-you, man!* moments. He smiled behind the mirrored lenses of his dime-store glasses.

"I already did. There's part of someone down by the lake. No crotch. No body. No arms. No head. Just a pair of white waxy legs that look like they've been sawed off some poor fucker who probably had a grocery list taped to the fridge at home. Had on yellow rain pants and big ol' Billy boots—size nine. Height? Who the hell knows. Weight? Beefy thighs is all I know. Sex? No goddamned idea. So, you wanna know what's going on, you go down to the goddamned water's edge, ask the county cops real nice if you can pretty please take a look at the legs, and then you won't have to ask me any more stupid-ass goddamned fucking idiot questions. We clear?"

Hogarth stared at the guy for a second, wondering if he should tell McGibbon about the time that Pope had called him out to 47 after he had found that hitchhiker painted along the yellow line for nearly three miles in a greasy red-black smear. Someone had tied him to their back bumper and dragged him from Third Concession right past the Millers' barn at about a hundred and ten. All that was left were his arms and head—the rest had been sanded off by the asphalt. What would McGibbon say about that? Probably chuck his cookies. At least he'd stop being a dick. "You stay here," he said with authority, and headed off through the trees for the water's edge.

Fifty feet from where the trail broke out on the shore he started to hear voices; two men were talking. One was speaking in the hushed tones of fear mixed with respect for the dead. The other voice was jovial and relaxed—that motherfucker Pope.

Hogarth walked out onto the shoreline, a broken patch of dirt and grass held together by rocks and roots of the nearby trees. The sheriff and another deputy Hogarth recognized from league night over in Massena were squatting down on their haunches, leaning over something. Hogarth slowly advanced on the two men and tried to get a peek over their shoulders. When he was almost on top of them, he saw it. Or them. Or him. Or maybe even her. The victim. *The legs.*

Pope nodded a terse greeting and stood up to give Hogarth a view of the scene. Hogarth, who was no stranger to death, squinted a little to take the edge off of what he saw. Two legs lay on the shore, the soles of the rubber boots facing the trees, the tops of the thighs almost in the water. Hogarth leaned over the tops of the thighs and saw the socket ball of both femurs. He leaned in close and examined the swollen purple and black flesh. There were no saw marks, no scrapings on the bones, no symmetrical tears in the flesh. This person hadn't been sawed up. They had just…come apart.

Pope's silent shadow slid over the legs, his hat a dark disk. "Whacha think?" Pope asked. Unlike McGibbon's tense body language up at the van, Pope could have been at Mickey's Mercantile, picking out socks with little happy faces on them. The legs on the ground didn't seem to ruffle the guy too much, and Hogarth realized that all the times that he had met the sheriff in a professional capacity, the big cop always seemed to be in a good mood around the dead. Happy, even.

"This guy wasn't sawed up. No signs of a blade—of any sort—in the flesh *or* bones. No cuts or scrapes on the femur. No signs of teeth marks in the skin or flesh or remnants of clothing. Nothing to signify mechanical intervention of any sort." Now Hogarth *really* wished he had smoked a joint on the way in—would have made this whole thing a little more bearable. Not much, but a little.

"So." Pope pushed his big Stetson back on his forehead and locked eyes with Hogarth. "The big question is what happened to this guy."

"Or girl," Hogarth offered.

"Yeah, or girl." Pope leaned in close and examined the femoral head neatly exposed at the end of the thick thigh, white and shiny and clean as a cue ball.

Hogarth thought about it for a second. "If I had to make an educated guess, I'd say that this guy's legs were taken off in one clean yank." Hogarth looked back at the two limbs. "And I'd say that it was done while he was alive."

# 38

Gavin was down by the water, enjoying the restorative rays of the sun. He wasn't thinking about cancer or harmful ultraviolet light or cracked skin. No, he was concentrating on the wonderful feeling of the sun. Akhenaton and his clan of heliophiles had it right—worshiping the sun made a lot more sense than worshiping the dead. Gavin had lived that one and knew where it could lead.

Gavin thought about the bust of Nefertiti that Chelsea had bought in London a few years back. There had been something magical about her features. The big almond eyes, the gentle slope of her nose, the regal chin—a timeless beauty. Like Chelsea. Beautiful, happy, dead Chelsea. Only she hadn't been so happy before she had died, had she, Gavin? No. Not by a long shot. She had been unhappy for months. Ever since you had said no to a baby, remember that? And the morning she was killed she had asked for a divorce. Then she had stepped into the elevator and smiled that last sad smile that you are going to remember for the rest of your life. Your wife wanted a divorce, went out to get away from you, and was obliterated from the planet. Thank you. Good night.

Not now, he told himself. Not now. Later. Think of something. Anything. The sun. The wind.

So he concentrated on the whisper of wind through the trees, the sweat of the cold bottle in his hand, the sound of footfalls creeping down the stone steps—

He opened his eyes and turned as much as his bruised ribs would allow. Laurel was coming down to the water. "Afternoon," he said, holding up his beer. Beside him, sunning on the flagstone terrace, Foots the cat raised his head as if to say hello.

"Afternoon, yourself," she said through that now-familiar big smile. "And you're not supposed to have alcohol." Laurel was dressed in a pair of jeans and a man's white cotton shirt, obviously tailored to her frame. In the way of shoes she sported a pair of well-worn English brogues. The look was not unappealing.

Gavin deflated, sunk back into the Adirondack chair. "Foots drank most of it. I'm just helping him finish off the rest." He took a swig of the ice-cold beer. "Doctors could take the fun out of anything." He had no idea of the brand, he had picked it up at the minimart on the way back from town. He couldn't remember ever having a better drink.

"We try."

Gavin shook his head and downed another swallow. "Want one?" He gestured lazily to the tin washbasin filled with ice and bottles.

Laurel nodded approvingly at the empties jammed upside-down in the ice. "Apparently you and the cat have been at this a little while." She pulled a frosted bottle from the tub, popped the cap in one fluid twist, and sat down. Foots rolled over and flexed, pushing his toes out in too many directions.

Gavin raised his bottle appreciatively. "Nice work with that cap, Doc. You've done this before."

Laurel flexed her muscular arm. "Strong like bull," she said in a pretty good rendition of an East European accent. She knocked back half the beer in one long go.

"Something tells me that if I knew more about you, I'd get scared."

Laurel nodded in affirmative. "That you would, my boy."

"As in?"

Laurel nestled into the pine chair and got comfortable. "As in, I'll never tell unless you get me drunk."

Gavin sized her up. "Let's see, five three, maybe five four. Hundred and fifteen pounds with your boots on. Drinking cheap beer before lunch. I'd say four, five tops, and you're in the bag. Probably start taking your pants off right here."

Laurel threw her head back and laughed. Gavin peeked over and watched her eye close in that little motion that he loved so much. "That's not fair!" she said between spasms of laughter. "Not fair at all. I was drunk."

"*In vino veritas.*"

"Oh, I get it. You think that it's impossible for a woman not to be attracted to you. Wrong. You're not my type. Hell, I doubt that you're anyone's type. Good looks and charm and a sense of humor. Pleeeaaaaase!"

"You left out the tattoos," he offered.

"No, the tattoos I like." A smile played across her lips as she stared out at the water. "I actually like the tattoos a lot." There was genuine surprise in her voice.

They sat quietly for a few minutes, absorbing the sun and the common comfortable silence. The only sound was the baritone purr of the big cat stretched out between them.

"I stopped the painkillers," he offered in way of explanation for the alcohol he was drinking.

"You don't owe me any sort of an explanation." Her eyes were closed, her face pointed up at the warmth of the sun.

"Yeah, I do. I stopped the painkillers because they were making me sleep all the time. I'd rather have a little pain every time I turn my back than not know where the hell I am. And the beers are the first in over a week. Nice summer day and it seemed like a fun thing to do. The hard part was getting the ice down here a pitcherful at a time. Thank God the cat was here to help."

Laurel laughed again. "It's all in the priorities."

"You seeing anyone?" The question came out of nowhere and as soon as it was out, he regretted saying it.

"Nope." She seemed unflustered. "Although there is this writer character that I seem to be taking a fancy to."

Gavin didn't say anything for a minute. Then he realized that his silence was probably making her uneasy. "I like you, too." What the hell, it was the truth. It was also good. And he had gone without both for too long.

They were sitting on the deck and the waves were washing in with a slow easiness. Every now and then there was a breeze that caressed the trees and the leaves whispered in tongues. Without knowing why, without even consciously thinking about it, Gavin reached over and put his hand over Laurel's. He curled his fingers down and touched her palm. Her hand pulsed back and they both took a deep breath. It was the most intimate moment he had had with another human being since long before Chelsea had died. He realized that he missed touching. Maybe more than anything else.

"Are you okay?" Laurel asked from somewhere else.

He realized that there were tears in his eyes. He squeezed her hand a little tighter and closed his eyes. *Yeah*, he thought, *perfect. And goddamned lonely. And I'm glad you're here.* "I'm fine."

The roar of a car engine revving hard cut through the soft sounds of the afternoon and their hands slipped apart and it was suddenly as if they had never touched at all. Gavin stood up, dropped his empty beer bottle into the ice bucket, and headed up the steps. Laurel and Foots followed.

Gavin rounded the corner of the house to find Sheriff Xavier Pope standing on the front steps, his finger on the bell, his free hand resting on the rubber combat grip of his pistol. Gavin was tempted to sneak up on the man and whisper *Boo!* into his ear but didn't think it was worth a round in the spleen.

"Can I help you?" Gavin asked as he approached the big cop.

Pope flinched, then turned and tried to convert the reaction into a defensive stance. He gave Gavin the once-over, with his eyes resting on the cast a little too long. "You look pretty good for a man almost killed himself falling asleep at the wheel," Pope said insincerely.

"We've gone through this. Someone ran me off the road."

Pope sighed. "Mr. Corlie, there was no one out there. Dr. Paulson called it in and I came out. Paulson saw your lights go tumbling off into the ditch from his house. If he hadn't seen the accident, you'd probably have stayed there all night and died." Pope didn't sound too concerned one way or the other.

Gavin was suddenly fed up with talking to Pope. "Why are you here?"

"Look, there's been an accident on the lake and I am questioning everyone that I can. Hopefully someone saw something."

Gavin converted his body language into a *Well, I'm waiting* gesture. Laurel eased up beside him but stood a little away, almost between him and Pope. Gavin saw the cat circle around and sit in the shadow of Pope's cruiser, as if he, too, wanted to keep an ear to the conversation.

"A man was killed not far from here. I need to know if you've seen or heard anything unusual." Pope was getting irritated. "He was pulled apar—" He caught himself.

Gavin held up his hand. "What do you mean, pulled apart?"

"A pair of legs were found washed up on shore about a mile northeast of you." Then he added, "First we thought that they had been cut off. You know, someone trying to get rid of a body by chopping it up. But the ME's office said that there were no saw or knife marks on the wounds. Looked like they had been pulled off the body. Just pulled off," he repeated, as if this shit happened every day.

"When did this happen?" Gavin asked.

"Yesterday, probably. Won't know until the medical examiner's done with the case. Body was found this morning."

Gavin thought back to the day before when he and Finn had passed the afternoon working out a plan of attack for finding his monster. The monster that Gavin had still been unsure existed. A monster he had been using as a diversion: from sitting around with a bottle plugged into his liver and a pistol stuffed into his throat; from images of dead Chelsea fucking him to pieces; from the fact that he hadn't written a word in months; from the knowledge that his marriage had fallen apart long before Chelsea had died; from every destroyed aspect of his life that he was trying to forget.

Only now the sheriff was telling him that a man had been pulled apart. This was no longer a diversion. It was something a little more sinister and a lot more dangerous. Especially if people were getting torn apart. Ask anyone. Especially the local horror writer.

"I spent the day inside yesterday," Gavin said distantly.

"Most people did," Pope interjected. "Bad storm. Tore up a lot of property."

"I couldn't even see the lake through the rain." Gavin thought back to the staccato flashes of lightning that kept illuminating the living room, making strange shadows across the wall, the silhouette of Finn in his wheelchair looking like some huge biomechanical spider with a human torso. "Nothing unusual. Nothing usual. I wish I could help."

Pope's expression told Gavin that he didn't believe him one way or the other. And that he probably didn't really give a shit either. He was here because it was protocol. "Call if you think of anything or if anything washes up in your bay."

"You know who died?" Laurel asked from the sidelines.

Pope nodded, and the brim of his hat dipped down and covered his whole face. It was so dark in the bright sun that you couldn't even see his lips move. "Man by the name of Walter Pinkowski. Eel fisherman. We found his boat anchored between here and where we found his legs."

Gavin remembered something that Finn had said about the lake and the dam. "His legs were found upstream from where his boat was anchored? Does that make sense?"

Pope thought about it. "I don't know. Maybe. Maybe not. This is Lake Caldasac, the rules don't always work here. There was a lot of wind yesterday. Could have blown him upstream." Pope took one final look at Gavin and said, "You're a lucky man, Mr. Corlie. Could have ended up with your head screwed on backward and a skull full of tree roots." Pope's lips broke into a line of white teeth. "I'd count my lucky stars if I was you."

Then he walked over to his cruiser and got in. The cat got up and moved away, apparently not wanting to be too close to the cop. Pope looked over at Laurel one last time and the flat smile opened a little wider and he nodded a good-bye. Then he was gone, leaving a thin cloud of brown dust in the clearing.

Gavin stood staring after Pope for a few minutes.

"That guy makes me uncomfortable," Laurel said.

"That guy makes everyone uncomfortable, it's what he was made to do. Just look at that Eddie Munster haircut."

Laurel turned to the lake. "What do you think that was about?"

Gavin followed her vision and his thoughts of Pope were quickly washed aside as he saw the indifferent body of water beyond the trees. "I wish I knew."

# 39

"This the kind of unusual you were talking about?" Dr. Parks asked as he lifted the plastic sheet. He didn't sound angry, or suspicious, or accusatory. Simply puzzled once again.

As the sheet came away, a branch of black liquid dripped down a fold. The black line blossomed into red and fanned out, leaving a gritty trail, like old motor oil.

For all Gavin's mental preparation for this moment, his nerve left him and he felt light-headed. Nauseous. Seeing the sheet, being in that room, brought him back to the afternoon he had identified Chelsea's body. It was the before shot that came back and haunted him—the one he had seen after the doorman had come up to tell him that something bad had happened in front of the building. Gavin had gone downstairs. She was across the street. Under a blanket. Two cops stood over her remains while they waited for the meat wagon. Gavin had run straight through traffic, screaming at the top of his lungs. Torn the blanket off. One of the cops had pulled him away. But not before seeing that she was a bruised, broken bag of meat with her brains and hair matted into a clump, one of her eyes pushed flat against the splintered bones that used to be her skull. "Yeah," was all he could say with a weak little voice that was still raspy from the trach tube that had been plugged into his esophagus for a week.

"You have something to tell me?" Parks asked.

Gavin turned his head away from the metal table and took a deep breath through his mouth. "No."

Parks crossed his arms and leaned back against the middle of the table. Extending from his left side, behind his back, were Walter Pinkowski's legs. It looked like Walter was sleeping on the steel surface. Except the top part of Walter didn't extend out past Dr. Parks's right side. All that was there was an empty expanse of table with a neat hole in the center and a drainpipe underneath. In the old days, before Gavin had seen what a runaway Lincoln Continental could do to a body, he would have fought the urge to vomit. But that was before the new and improved Gavin. Way back when everything still felt safe.

"You come in here asking about any strange deaths on Lake Caldasac and fifteen minutes later we have the body of a man—correction—*body of half a man* found within a mile of your home. You believe in coincidences?" Parks looked serious, angry. "Because I sure don't."

"Meaning?" What the fuck could he say? *There's a monster in the lake*. Sure. That would go over well.

Parks shook his head, letting Gavin know that he wasn't buying the innocent act. "Look, Mr. Corlie—Gavin—what am I supposed to think? That you just happen to have an idea for a book and the questions you throw at me just happen to apply to the next body that comes across my table? If it was the previous body, there would be no conversation here. But it wasn't the previous one. It was the next one. *The very next one*. Fifteen minutes later!

"This may not be New York City but I know my work. And I do a good job. Right now that job is trying to figure out what the hell happened to this man here." Parks jerked a thumb over his shoulder. "You want to tell me what you know?"

Parks was right. On all counts. But how could he explain what this meant to Finn? Or himself? That it had him interested in living again? In writing again? If he told Parks what the kid had said, they would be dynamiting the lake in no time and every news team from all over the state would be out there with a reporter in a safari jacket, looking for whatever the fuck it was. And the story would go national, and some hack staff writer for *People* would do a weekend manuscript and that would be it—the inside scoop. No, he couldn't give it away. Not for Walter Pinkowski. Not for anyone. "Look, I can't talk about my work—I have a lawyer who specializes in intellectual property on staff. My own corporation forbids me from discussing my work. But I can tell you that it has nothing to do with what happened here in a concrete sense."

Parks shook his head. "You'll have to give me more than that or I'm talking to Pope. I have no choice here, Gavin."

He would have to give the medical examiner something. Even if it was small. The obvious response was a lie. "Sheriff Pope came by my house a few weeks back—wanted to ask me a few questions after a little boy had an accident out on the lake. To be honest, Pope and I didn't exactly hit it off. But it gave me an idea and I started going with it. It's the way my mind works. I'm a horror writer. I want to write about the lake. The place is giving me a story and I'm listening. And in my stories people get killed all the time. I'm doing research. And now you've got some guy on your table who was sawn in half and you think I know who did this. Sorry. Wrong. And you mention one more time that I know anything about this and I will have so many slander suits filed against you and this county that the whole fucking town will be filing Chapter Twelve before I'm done." Gavin took a step forward and looked straight into Parks's eyes. "Dr. Parks, an entire Park Avenue law firm exists to serve me—don't let the jeans and tattoos lull you into a false sense of security. I am a business and I could ruin this town and not even feel it in my grocery account."

The medical examiner's face went brittle.

"I'm not trying to be a prick here, I'm trying to protect myself. I've put a lot of hours into becoming the writer that I am and I will not let anyone come between me and my work." Gavin stopped and took a breath. He hated doing that to people but every now and then he was forced to dig that part of him up. "Understood?"

Parks looked down at his feet for a moment and did a fair job of looking all right with the wrath that had just been thrown at him. "I wasn't threatening you. You write. Entertaining people is what you do. I respect that. I'm a medical examiner. I try to figure out the cause of death—it's what *I* do. And I've got a case in front of me that I can't figure out. What would you do in my position?"

Gavin realized that he would have to give Parks a break or there would be no coming back into the man's office, and it looked like he could be a good source of information. "Dr. Parks, I'm not playing dumb here. I don't know shit, plain and simple. I saw a bird get eaten by a fish one of my first nights here and it got me thinking—"

"Yeah," Parks acknowledged, "muskies get 'em."

"So I've been told." Gavin didn't want to mention Finn's monster. "I'm a writer. I see things that no one else does. I see ghouls and serial killers and the ghost of Ichabod Crane. This case"—Gavin gestured to the legs on the steel table—"has *nothing* to do with what I was asking you but *everything* to do with what I was looking for. I hate to sound like an insensitive freak but this is the stuff that makes my work sell while some writers go straight to the remainder bin."

Parks nodded like it made sense, and when Gavin thought about it, it *did*. They were back on the field together.

"Okay," Parks said.

Gavin stretched out his shoulder, and the cast knocked against the door frame. He walked over to the table and leaned over what was left of the eel fisherman. The gritty blood had dried on the sheet and it looked like a negative of a lightning fork. Something about the caked drip was more disturbing than the unattached legs on the table. "So what can you tell me about Mr. Pinkowski here?"

In life it was obvious that Walter Pinkowski had not been a thin man. The limbs were thick and stumpy and had turned the color of antique candles, yellow and waxy, covered in weak little black hairs that looked almost prepubescent in their frailty. The bony balls of the two femoral heads were exposed, like two peeled hard-boiled eggs, neat, white, and shiny. The flesh where the legs had been attached to the body was swollen and pink, all the blood having seeped out into the lake. Gavin found the most disconcerting aspect to the whole thing to be the tag on the big toe of the left foot. The tag denoted a body—a corpse. But this was not a body. It was *part* of a body. A *fraction*. Less than. All that was left of Walter Pinkowski. The legs looked like they were ready to get up and walk away. If he closed his left eye while he was standing there, cutting off the vision of the upper thighs where the legs had been severed, they looked like they were still attached to a body. Only they weren't.

"There isn't much to tell. At least not much that *I* can tell. These were taken off of Mr. Pinkowski and I can't for the life of me figure out how." Parks looked honestly puzzled. "Right here." Parks indicated the edge of the flesh where the legs just stopped. "Murder? No saw I've ever seen can cut like this. And the femoral heads show no signs of damage—they aren't even scratched." Parks pointed at one of the white knobs.

Gavin leaned in and examined the big ball of bone. It didn't take a doctor to see that the thing was clean and whole.

"That should be badly serrated—maybe even splintered. But *nada*. Looks like it came in off a myocardial infarction death. The flesh around it is damaged with marks of some sort but they don't go past the epidermal layer. And they're too big to be animal teeth." Parks smiled eerily.

Gavin looked up at Parks. "It's got to look like something you've seen before."

"Once, years ago, I had a twelve-year-old boy come in— his brother had wrapped a bicycle chain around his arm and hooked it up to an impact drill. Just for kicks. Pinched his humerus off at the shoulder and the kid had bled out before his mother could get him to a doctor. The marks looked an awful lot like these. But they went all the way through. These stop."

"You're sure about this not being an animal?" Gavin prompted.

Parks nodded. "The only mammal that has the power necessary to do this is a bear. Maybe. And I stress the *maybe* part. Lot of pressure to cut through tissue like this. A bear just doesn't have the strength—it would have to do a lot of shaking and tearing with its paws to get a pair of legs off of a human body; this was done in one big snap. The pressure, force, and rending power required to do this isn't from any animal that I know."

"Let's assume for a second that the animal wasn't from around here. Let's say it was from someplace else," Gavin pushed. "I'm a horror writer, it's the way my mind works. If you say an animal didn't do this, then I believe you. I do. But humor me, okay?"

Parks nodded. "Go on."

"Assume that this *was* done by an animal. What would it take to make this happen? To make these wounds?"

Parks's eyes narrowed as he thought about it for a second. "Bite force would be tremendous. Ballpark would be in the eight-thousand-pound-per-inch category. Big teeth for hold-ing. And to get the legs off the body before connecting with the bones within? I'd say a very strong set of neck muscles to shake the legs loose. I would say a pair of hands to pull the legs off, but there is no evidence of bruising or tissue damage to give that any support." Parks looked at Gavin and the expression on his face said that there was no way an animal did this. "And whatever did this would have to live in the water." He smiled like someone explaining the birds and the bees to a small child. "You can't forget that."

"Any creature on earth fit that bill?" Gavin thought about Finn Horn alone out on the water with whatever did this to Walter Pinkowski and realized that things could have turned out different for the boy.

"You ever see the movie *Jaws*?" Parks asked.

Gavin nodded. "My favorite film."

"Remember the scene where the guy in the little rowboat is eaten and his leg floats to the bottom in a cloud of blood, the skin all tattered and torn?"

Gavin nodded.

"Well, for all the problems that film presented in a technical way, the FX guy got the wounds down right. That leg looked like it had been hacked off—which is how all animal attacks look. Animals go after human beings for one of three reasons. First off is hunger. The idea is to kill the prey then get as much of it into its stomach before something else comes along and challenges the kill, maybe even takes it away. It's not a style pageant. The second reason that an animal kills— at least in mammals—is to protect its young. Get between any animal and its baby and the thing is going to get mad. Three—it's wounded."

"You left out the fourth reason animals kill—pleasure."

Parks shook his head. "Animals don't kill for pleasure. Only men do that." Parks moved away from the table and went into his office, leaving Gavin with Walter's legs for a few quiet minutes. When he returned, Gavin noted that he felt a lot better. He didn't want to think about what it was like working down here at three in the a.m. with no one to keep you company but a dead guy's legs.

"Look at these," Parks said and handed over a pathology primer.

Gavin opened the flap and found a pile of eight-by-ten black-and-white photographs staring back at him. The first was bad: the body was laid out in a clearing, hair and clothing strewn about, the big muscles of the thighs chewed off, the bones in the femurs gnawed and splintered. Only part of the face was visible—the lower portion of the face—but there was no mistaking the blinding pain expressed in the open mouth.

The second photo was of a tent torn apart, human limbs and blood everywhere. Five big slashes hacked into every conceivable surface from the bodies to the tent to the trees—claw marks. Gavin thought back to Freddy Krueger and realized that this bear would chop that fucker up before he had a chance to get a lick in.

Gavin shook his head and closed the folder. Two photographs were enough. Parks was right: compared to animal attacks, Walter Pinkowski looked like he had been disassembled by a laser beam.

"See my point?" Parks asked.

Gavin tried to answer but his throat was dry and all he managed was a croak; he wanted to believe the trach scar had stolen his voice.

"When animals kill it's never neat. Not by a long shot. Comparing a shark attack to this is like comparing a car accident to Hannibal Lecter's work. For lack of a better word, I'd say this was almost *surgical*."

"So what on earth could do this?"

"Something with a mouthful of big pointy teeth and the neck of a bull elephant." Parks searched Gavin's features. "Still don't want to share?"

"There's nothing to share, Doc." Gavin thought about protesting, but what could he say? All he could do was lie. "I'm a horror writer, I make things up, create fantasies."

Parks turned to the pair of jaundiced legs, which now no more represented a human being than a bumper represented a car. They were just parts. "Tell that to Walter Pinkowski," he said.

# 40

Gavin and Finn sat on the dock at the boy's house, staring out at the lake. Finn was in his wheelchair and Gavin sat on the edge of the wood structure, his legs crossed under him in a conscious effort not to dangle them over the water. Between them, on a little plastic table, were some bologna-and-mustard sandwiches that Finn's mom had made. They both had Cokes in their hands but neither of them felt like eating the sandwiches. Probably something to do with the meat, Gavin imagined. Looked too much like cross-sections of Walter Pinkowski's legs.

Off in the distance thunderheads had started to form, like dust clouds kicked up by an advancing army. The weather was going to get ugly once again.

Gavin had filled Finn in on Pope's visit and Dr. Parks's unwitting analysis of whatever was out there. Finn was silent as a stone, staring out at the water, and for a while Gavin wondered if the kid had listened at all.

Finn opened his mouth to speak but said nothing, his lips pursed in a perfect O, as if he was about to start a hymn. After a moment of indecision his voice kicked in, and the sound was dry, unsteady. "At least I'm not crazy," he said, sounding a little disappointed. "Maybe it's a shark," the boy offered feebly.

Gavin had thought the same thing. A shark made sense. Sort of. How it got here, how it had stayed a secret—that was something else. Sharks lived in the water. Sharks ate people. It happened all the time. So a shark made sense. Sort of. But a shark didn't live in a freshwater lake in the mountains. After all, there were certain unbendable rules that applied to the natural world. Carl Sagan had nailed that one down. Be skeptical when presented with evidence, he had warned. So they were back at square one. *Monster.* It was all there was left. What would old Carl say about that?

That there was a scientific explanation. There always was.

Finn went on, his voice thin and dry. "You didn't tell him anything." The boy still wanted this to belong to them. Too many important things were at stake here. Forever kind of things.

"No, Finn, I didn't tell him a thing. You got the conversation from front to back. You should have seen the photographs he showed me. Unbelievable." Gavin thought back to the splattered chunks of bones that had been gnawed clean. "Whatever did this to Pinkowski was not something that makes any kind of sense."

"Not even the Loch Ness Monster?"

Gavin smiled. "Not even the Loch Ness Monster."

In the distance, across the lake, the clouds were solidifying into a pewter mass of angry weather.

Gavin watched a gull riding the wind about thirty yards offshore. The bird dipped and rose on the invisible current. Gavin spent a few minutes being absorbed in the bird's actions and listening to the wind that was picking up. There was no conversation.

He finally turned back to the boy. "Finn, I don't know shit about what we're doing here. This is serious. You could get hurt." A gust of wind flung one of the sandwiches into the water. "Hell, *I* could get hurt."

Finn slurped at his Coke, finished it, held out the can, squeezed it between his thumb and index, and crushed it straight down. Once again, Gavin was amazed at the strength the boy displayed.

"Well," Finn began, "I'm already hurt. And so are you. You got a busted wing and I got no drumsticks. Between the two of us, we've got a little more than a whole person. One extra arm and one extra brain." The kid smiled down at Gavin. "It's the brain that counts on this one. We got brains and we got know-how."

"Finn, I haven't got know-how. I've been here for a month and all I've learned is that a loon is about as lucky as a dodo and that if you spend a hundred grand on a truck it doesn't save your ass. That's it. I've got no know-how. None."

"Okay—correction—*I've* got know-how. And you've got imagination. Between the two of us, we've gotta come up with something. But it all depends."

The kid was starting to sound convincing. He wondered if Finn believed himself as much as he pretended to. "On?" Gavin asked.

"Our budget."

Gavin thought about Walter Pinkowski's legs lying on the autopsy table, yellow and stiff and dead. "Whatever it costs, Finn. As long as we do it right."

Finn rubbed his hands together like a rug merchant in the bazaars of Marrakesh. "Then we're in luck. I've got a shopping list a mile long! We can get everything we need from Fishin' Frank's Bait and Tackle in Florida. They're cool guys. There's a kid in a wheelchair on their website and as far as I'm concerned, that's all the recommendation I need! I found them on the Internet at school."

Gavin thought about that. A lot of Finn's fishing magazines were stolen from the waiting rooms of his doctors, and whatever he owned in the way of legitimate books had been gleaned from garage sales or hand-me-downs from friends. The kid didn't even have a computer at home. "My place is wired like MIT. You take care of all the research in the equipment department. I'll set up a laptop just for you. You make the orders and I'll pay for the gear. I don't want us wearing white tuxedos to a shit-sandwich-tossing contest."

"Or we end up like Walter, huh?" Finn was smiling again. He honestly didn't seem to feel any fear. This was exciting for him. Fun.

When he considered it, Gavin realized that he too was looking forward to this. "Yeah," he grumbled, "we end up like Walter."

"Only I got sexier legs."

Gavin turned to Finn. "What?" he asked.

"I said I got sexier legs than Walter. You said that they were big and lumpy, like mashed potatoes, right? Well, I got skinny white sexy legs. Chances are, something tears them off, I ain't gonna feel it anyways. So what the heck? Right?"

They really didn't make enough people like him. "Finn, you're all right."

"All right?" Finn asked. "I'm fantastic! You know why?"

Gavin picked up one of the bologna-and-mustard sandwiches. Ms. Horn had been nice enough to make them and he didn't want to hurt her feelings by not eating one. "No, Finn. Why?"

"Because I'm the guy that's going to catch the monster that's out there. I am going to catch it. I am going to kill it. And I am going to have my picture in the goddamned newspaper if it's the last thing that I ever goddamned do with my goddamned life. Now what do you have to say about that?"

"I think that you probably swore more in that one single sentence than you have in your whole life."

Finn looked up, smiled. "Goddamned right!"

# 41

It still felt like night. The air was cold and damp and even though the day was only an hour off, it felt like light would never touch the earth again. It was the between hour, when the wind had died and the birds were not yet singing, ushering in the new dawn. The planks of the dock were damp and Gavin stood at the water's edge, his hands in his pockets, staring out at the black expanse of the lake fading away before him. Right then it looked as big as the Atlantic. And just as unforgiving.

There was the squeak of Finn's wheelchair tires on the wet wood as the boy negotiated the dock toward him.

"We're gonna have a great day!" Finn's eternal optimism was the antithesis to the dark morning air and the black lake.

Gavin shuddered. "Cold," he said without turning around.

It was fifty degrees out. "We couldn't ask for better weather. You wear what I told you?"

Gavin nodded. "Yep." Finn had been specific in his directives. The idea, apparently, was to shed the layers as the day warmed up, then, once the tipping point was crossed (usually early evening) to start putting things back on. All of Gavin's clothing had been purchased from either Izzy's or Walmart—Finn's two favorite stores.

"Then you shouldn't be cold."

Gavin knew that it didn't have anything to do with the weather at all. "I'll be okay."

"That our bait?" Finn asked rhetorically, and thumped the coffin-sized hundred-quart cooler with his hand. Gavin had rolled it down from the truck with no small amount of swearing and considerable effort with his bad arm.

"Five fifteen-pound carp. Got them from the farm you recommended over near the Malone McDonald's. Ugly." Gavin had developed an instant dislike for the creatures— big brown bodies, bloated bellies, bulging eyes, and open suction-cup mouths that gave them a look straight out of the special-effects department of a low-budget science-fiction movie. They had been thrown into the cooler alive and had spent the evening dying slowly in the back of the truck. Finn opened the top and one of the fish flopped. Gavin jumped.

Finn got a good laugh out of that. "Harder to kill a carp than anything else that lives in the water. Tough little buggers." He grinned and his teeth flashed white in the dark, and for a second Gavin saw a sick little boy looking up at him. "Like me."

Gavin took his good hand out of his pockets and did a long cat stretch, pushing the cramps out of his body with a loud groan, the bad arm awkward and clumsy in the maneuver. His breath came out in wisps that quickly dissipated into the air. He stretched again, forcing the pain out of his back, and wondered just what the fuck he was doing out here. Finn had called an hour ago, his voice loud and determined, a miniature drill sergeant in training, shouting terms like *Up and at 'em!* and *Let's get this show on the road!*

"You okay?" Finn asked as he unstrapped his bent body from the wheelchair. "You look like a deer in the headlights."

"Just thinking about my arm. I wish it was better."

Finn reached up, grabbed hold of the galvanized pipes, and began his monkey-swing over to the new boat that was sitting in the water beside the dock. As he pulled himself up, his legs stretched out and Gavin realized that had the boy been able to stand, he probably would have been tall for his age. "Yeah," Finn said between breaths, "I wish my legs were better too. Don't waste your time wishing for something that ain't gonna happen. Start thinking about getting that friggin' cooler in the friggin' boat before the friggin' sun comes up and we're behind friggin' schedule!"

"You know what I think?" Gavin asked as Finn pulled himself out over the boat.

"No. But I have a sneaking suspicion that you're going to tell me."

"I think that you like ordering people around."

"Well." Finn came to a stop, his body swinging like a pendulum over the boat. "Someone's got to make the decisions around here. Who's it gonna be? You?" He was at the end of the grid and hovering over the boat. He did his *milking the cow* shimmy and dropped right into the seat at the stern.

"I suppose you have a point."

"Supposing ain't going to win us any medals either. My boat. I give the orders. What you gonna do about it? Tell my mom?" Finn buckled himself into the seat and snuggled comfortably into position. "Perfect!" he said proudly. He looked up at Gavin, who was struggling with the cooler. "Gavin, I love this boat. Best freaking present anyone ever gave me. Ever." He slapped the side. "And Izzy did a darn fine job modifying it!"

"Was that another swear word?" Gavin asked, arching an eyebrow, but Finn ignored him.

When he had replaced Finn's boat, his knowledge of fishing craft was nonexistent, so he had done a little research. What had recommended the Whaler was the fact that the craft was virtually indestructible; you could literally saw the thing in half and it would still float—the whole shell being

filled with an air-filled foam. Finn would never be at risk
of sinking again. The power was supplied by a big Mercury
175-horsepower inboard/outboard and the trolling motor
was a Johnson 9.9. CD player, GPS, and Fishfinder—all by
Lowrance—as well as an on-board live well, which, Gavin
had been informed, was a necessity for a serious fisherman.

Gavin had arranged the sale through Izzy's Sporting
Goods, and Izzy's guy had modified the seating to accommodate Finn's needs. The steering console was forward and
to the right and Izzy had put the seat on rails so that it could
be up front to steer the big 175 or, with the flip of a lever, slide
back to the transom to steer the little 9.9 trolling motor. It
hadn't been an expensive proposition but it had taken quite a
bit of creative thinking in the engineering sense.

Finn had been thrilled with the idea of coming up with
the perfect name for his boat and had attacked the process
with his usual vigor and enthusiasm. To help him in the
daunting task of getting the name *just right*, he had resorted to
complicated lists, charts, and word-association tables—none
of which had helped him to find a suitable moniker for his
new prized possession. In the uncomplicated way in which
things so often work themselves out, the name just came to
him one day while he was wheeling down the dock, humming his new favorite tune. The vessel was instantly dubbed
the *Low Rider*. Gavin had brought in a bearded, spectacled,
jean-clad monster of a man who specialized in custom paint
jobs on Harleys. The result was a wonderful Gothic script
intertwined with the skeleton of a fish, mouth agape, teeth
exaggerated into tusklike fangs. *The Low Rider*.

"Hey!" Gavin said, the early hour still making his voice
shaky and weak. "I almost forgot—I got you a gift."

Finn eyed him skeptically. "Water skis?"

"Ha, ha," Gavin said dryly and held up a compact disc.
"Hey, you finally joined the twentieth century!"

"It's the twenty-first century, kid." Gavin tossed the CD down into the boat.

Finn snapped it out of the air, shed the jewel case, and popped it into the console. The Latin rhythm of "Low Rider" echoed through the damp air. Finn's head bopped to the tune and he sang the first few lines. "Perfect. The rest of the doofuses on the lake better watch out for us!"

Gavin's eyebrows closed up as he frowned down on the kid. "Rest of the doofuses? Does that mean we're doofuses, too?"

Finn thought about it. "What do you think?"

"Well, we're out here at four in the a.m. with a hundred bucks' worth of bait in a cooler and a shitload of expensive gear listening to a song that made Cheech and Chong famous—all to hunt down a monster. It's kind of a rhetorical question."

"No, it's not. It's really simple. If we find the monster, we're heroes. If we don't, we're doofuses. Besides, no one but me fishes this lake, not since Frank Knechtel drowned anyway." Finn gestured to the boat. "You gonna get the bait in here or am I going to have to do it myself?"

Gavin slid the big cooler over to the edge of the dock and crawled down into the boat with a series of awkward steps that wiped out any doubt that he was a landlubber by birthright. Finn laughed so hard that he had to wipe the tears from his eyes. "Make sure you go pee. I don't want to have to watch you try to go over the side—I couldn't take it."

Gavin just snarled and wrestled the cooler over the lip of the dock and onto the boat. Finn started the engine.

As they headed out into Lake Caldasac all Gavin was aware of was the roar of the big 175, the cold early-morning air whipping around his head, and the smell of fuel. He turned back to the dock and house and saw the silhouette of Finn's mother in the big kitchen window, her hands in her housecoat pockets, her head tilted to one side. Gavin waved and the silhouette waved back. Then the dark stepped in between them and it was as if the shore didn't exist anymore.

"Finn!" he shouted over the roar of the engine.

Finn kept his eyes glued to the GPS and the instruments. "What?"

"You do know that I know shit about fishing, don't you? I mean, I couldn't find a lobster in a supermarket." He grabbed the back of Finn's seat as the boat lurched ahead into the dark.

Finn's face split into his grin again as he pushed the throttle up. "Don't worry. Whatever's out there is going to find us before we find it," the boy said, a little too cheerily.

# 42

It was earlier than the previous days they had hit the water, not quite four a.m. yet, and the air was just as cold and just as wet. Gavin walked down the dock toward the dark form of the boy in his wheelchair. Finn was spinning in small circles, his tires squeaking on the wet planks, his arms pumping furiously. Finn had explained that it warmed up his muscles and was one of the exercises that kept him as strong as he was.

"Gav!" he chortled amid the blur of motion. "You're late! It's almost four. You were supposed to be here at three forty-five!"

Gavin stopped rolling the cooler. "I'm four minutes late, Finn."

"Four minutes is a long freaking time!"

Gavin felt irritation bubbling up. Then he thought back to yesterday. And the day before. Watching Finn giving their endeavor everything he had. Fuck it, Gavin thought, the kid's right. I *am* late.

"How many carp you bring?" Finn asked as he reached up and grabbed the metal skeleton poised over the dock and began his complicated routine to get into the *Low Rider*.

"Five fresh with two more frozen."

"Good. Perfect. Today's the day!"

"That's what you said yesterday." Gavin liked Finn's optimism, but at four in the fucking morning it was hard to feel it. How the kid managed it was a complete mystery to him.

"And the day before," Finn responded. "And it's what I'll say tomorrow and the next and the next until that thing is caught and dead and my picture is in the paper!" Finn dropped into the seat, snapped the seatbelt home, and pulled himself up to the console.

Gavin was tired and cranky and was going to tell the kid to stuff it. All he came back with was, "Aye-aye, Captain!" in a very bad imitation of a pirate.

"So let's get out there and take care of business!"

"Jesus, first you're Captain Bligh, now you're Elvis." It really was hard to get into the mood this early.

"Who's Elvis?" Finn asked.

Gavin began his awkward descent into the boat, his bad arm doing little more than getting in the way. "You're kidding, right?"

"Nope. Never heard of him."

"He was a singer," was all that Gavin could muster. Between the broken arm, the still-bruised ribs, and the cooler of big rubbery carp, he was putting all of his concentration into not hurting himself more than he already was.

"Like Mantovani?"

"No. Not like Mantovani. Never mind. It's too early for this." By the time he dropped to the deck and untied the lines, Finn had brought the Johnson 175 to life with a deep roar that traveled through the soles of Gavin's feet right up his spine and into his brain. He wondered if Finn felt the vibrations in the same way. After all, it was an inner-ear issue, and even though Finn couldn't feel anything from the waist down, the vibrations would still reach his head, wouldn't they?

"Is he like Johnny Cash?"

"No, he's not like Johnny Cash. Not at all. Forget it. I can't explain it."

"Is he like John Kennedy?"

"Jesus, Finn, John Kennedy wasn't even a singer. He was president of the United States."

"Oh," was all Finn said. "I thought he sang with the Beatles."

"That's John Lennon. Doesn't your mother listen to any music?"

Finn thought about it. "Sure. Sure she does. She likes *West Side Story* a lot. I've seen it about a million times. 'When you're a Jet, you're a Jet all the way—from your first cigarette to your last dying day!'" The boy began to croon, moving his shoulders in a pretty good imitation of a 1950s dancer doing the tough-guy moves in a back alley. "But no Elvis Kennedy. Never even heard of the guy." Finn flipped the power switch on the CD player and jacked up the volume as Gavin untied the boat.

"There is no Elvis Kennedy, Finn. It's John Kennedy or Elvis Presley. They're both dead. It doesn't matter."

"It does to them." Finn's face lit up in his own special grin, the orange lights of the dashboard giving his face a jack-o'-lantern quality. "Trust me."

Gavin closed his eyes, shook his head, and eased back into the dew-covered vinyl seat, glad yet again that Finn had made him buy rain pants. They eased out into the dark lake and the boy turned back toward the house and waved to the silhouette standing in the kitchen window, big and bulky in a housecoat. The silhouette waved back and was almost immediately swallowed by the dark that once again stepped in between them. Finn turned back to the instrument cluster, dancing in his seat to what had become their theme song, like he did every morning.

"You're nuts." Gavin looked out over the bow at the black expanse of nothingness. Finn was running at about fifteen knots and using the global positioning system to navigate. They had made the same run every morning, and with the preplotted course on the GPS they didn't have to worry about running shallow or hitting a rock. Submerged flotsam or *something else* was another issue. It was the *something else* that they were concerned about. Because, as Finn had so eloquently put it, *something else* smashed the heck out of his last boat. And ate Walter Pinkowski.

Before their first trip out, Finn and Gavin had sat down with a map of Caldasac and the tattered copy of Finn's fishing record and divided the lake into roughly a hundred sections. They had cross-referenced Finn's map with the big map, marking the sections where Finn had caught a fish of note as a low likelihood of finding their monster—the reasoning being that their monster would consume all the food in any given area, thereby pushing out (or eating!) any other predators.

In the past week they had managed to troll twelve sections. They had lost a lot of rigged carp on structure. With the hundred-and-fifty-pound multibraid and the big saltwater rods, they had literally lifted two submerged trees and an old rusty swing set off the bottom of the lake. The only fish they had caught was a small pike—small in comparison to the lure at any rate—that had come in to sniff the carp out of curiosity; the fish had brushed against one of the big treble hooks and skewered itself. The fish had been bleeding so badly that Finn had said a prayer before returning it to the lake.

What Gavin had known about fishing before this week would not have been fit to print on a matchbook. Now, after eight days of hard fishing and a lot of late nights on the Internet, he had put more time into the sport than many seasoned anglers. When the gear had initially shown up from Fishin'

Frank's in Florida, Gavin had thought that Finn was a nut; the gear had seemed more suited to the trek of the Pequod than to their little freshwater lake. In way of a defense, Finn had nailed it when he had said that they weren't sportsmen— they were out there to catch something.

They were using big St. Croix boat rods, six-footers with a lot of backbone. For reels Finn had insisted on Van Staal 400s—they held six hundred and fifty yards of two-hundred-and-thirty-pound-test Powerpro and had a drag system that was unbeatable. In terminal tackle, they had used two-hundred-pound stainless-steel saltwater Sampo swivels hooked up to titanium six-hundred-pound leader wire. The leader was rigged with four chemically sharpened 8/0 treble hooks that were harnessed to the bait—providing enough hooking edge that Gavin had to lower the carp into the water using a Boga Grip to prevent being skewered; their lures basically looked like water-dwelling porcupines.

The song was not quite over when Finn switched off the sound and dropped their speed down to a few knots. Their wake sloshed along the hull, raising the stern and pushing the *Low Rider* forward a little, lifting the muffler out of the water. It coughed and gurgled noisily until the wave cleared the boat and the stern dropped back into the dark lake. "We're there," Finn said just above a whisper.

Gavin looked around, trying to place the *Low Rider* on the lake. He couldn't see the shore in any direction, the only evidence of land being a lone light winking off in the distance somewhere to their port side. "How do you know?"

"Science, Einstein." Finn flicked the screen of the GPS with his index finger. "Satellites and magic and stuff." He pulled the lever on his seat and pushed off the dashboard. His seat flew to the back of the boat and snapped into place. Gavin moved over behind the wheel and watched the boy at work.

Finn flipped on his LED headlamp and opened a cooler that looked big enough to house a body. After selecting a fish based on whatever criteria made it just right, he set about rigging it. The nearly dead fish twitched when Finn inserted the big barbed treble hook into its flesh just behind its skull, and Gavin winced in sympathy. The animal twitched once again when the second hook was inserted into its spine, near the tail; the third hook failed to illicit a response.

Gavin turned away. "Ouch."

"It's a reaction. Fish don't feel like we do. Their brains don't have enough space to handle pain receptors," Finn offered by way of a defense.

"Sure," Gavin hissed between clenched teeth. "I wonder if the carp would agree with you."

"Yeah, well, tough noogies. It's him or me on the end of this hook and since I'm making the decisions here…" Finn let the sentence trail off until he was done rigging the fish. When he was finished, he held it up, examining it with an expert eye. "Looks good to me."

"At ten bucks a crack, they better look fucking stupendous," Gavin said.

"Success is expensive!"

Gavin unceremoniously kicked the lid of the cooler closed. "So are these carp."

Finn winked and attached the harnessed carp to the leader, grabbed it by the lip with the Boga Grip, and eased it into the water. "Forward," he said, and Gavin pushed the throttle up and the boat eased into the wind. The kid released the fish and watched it slide away. The carp drifted back into the prop wash, where it was swallowed by Caldasac.

"Okay, punch it."

Gavin throttled up, and the zing of the line feeding out as the heavy bait dropped back into the lake rose above the sound of the engine. He heard Finn close down the drag and the *twang* as the rod picked up the weight of the big bait.

"About thirty yards out," Finn said and thrust the butt of the rod into the fighting belt he had strapped around his waist. "Keep it at eight knots."

"Aye-aye, Captain," Gavin snarled. "Arrrr." He was now awake, no longer grumpy, and as involved in the process as Finn. After a week of give-and-take they worked well together. Finn handled the bait and the rods, Gavin the boat.

Finn adjusted the big cork grip of the rod in his hand and turned to Gavin. "Time for a sandwich!"

"We've been out here for ten minutes."

"Exactly. This is hard work!"

Gavin reached into the soft-sided cooler bag and pulled out a sandwich—one of a dozen that Finn's mother had made for them. Experience taught him that they would be Wonder Bread, mustard, and bologna—a combination that he had grudgingly come to like. "Here." Gavin tossed the plastic-wrapped sandwich to the kid, followed by an ice-cold Coke; the week on the water had taught them more than simply how to work together—it had taught them how to live together as well.

They headed south-southeast. He glanced over to the left and saw the first traces of light creeping up into the eastern sky; it would be daylight in another half hour. He breathed in the cool damp air. Something about today felt different; the air was alive, as if something important was going to happen. Maybe Finn had been right; maybe today *was* going to be the day. The day they caught *it*. Whatever the fuck *it* was. If *it* was even out here.

Yet here he was. Moving at eight knots, dragging a carp wrapped in steel behind them. And Finn whistling the theme to *Gilligan's Island*. Things could be worse. A lot worse. Yeah, he could have been killed in the accident.

The accident.

He wasn't about to forget about it. Or the diffused silhouette that had stood over him. Somewhere in the shadow of the face he was sure he had seen a smile. Just before it had all faded away.

# 43

It was late afternoon and they had been raking the lake for the better part of twelve hours now. Twelve hours of bologna sandwiches, Coke, and Finn's eternal optimism. Twelve hours of broiling under the sun on a windless day. Twelve hours of steady trolling without so much as a single solitary fucking nibble. Twelve hours of the most relaxed fun that Gavin could remember having.

Ever.

It was Friday and their last full day of fishing until Sunday rolled around. Most lakes in the area were packed with weekend warriors and armchair fishermen stocked up with mail-order outfits and cases of beer, all intent on catching a trophy fish, which, for some, meant *any* fish. Caldasac, as usual, would be lifeless, but Finn couldn't fish on Saturdays because he and his mother had a standing date—it was the one day she didn't work and they used it to do the weekly shopping at Walmart, Mickey's Mercantile, and then off to Dunkin' Donuts over on 47E.

Finn was decked out in a white T-shirt, sneakers, and a pair of jeans that, like all his pants, were three sizes too big. Gavin wore a pair of heavy cotton shorts outfitted with too many pockets and an old concert T-shirt for the Cult's *Electric* tour.

"Hey, Gav, could you please pass me another Coke?"

"You diabetic?"

"It's the only disease I don't have."

Gavin reached into the food cooler and pulled out a frosted glass bottle. He popped the steel cap off and handed the drink to Finn. "Anyone ever call you Finnegan?"

"Anyone call you Idjit?"

Gavin thought about the question for a minute. "Only my mother and Chelsea." It was true.

Finn's response was a noseful of Coke sprayed over his lap. "Nice." *Cough. Cough.* "Real nice. You shou—"

Finn's rod bent violently toward the stern.

The boy dropped his Coke and grabbed the rod with both hands. "Suck on that!" he hollered, jerking back to set the hook.

Finn's shoulders were stitching back and forth like a sewing machine as he pumped the big anodized reel. "Cut the prop!" he yelled. "Now! Cut it now!"

Gavin yanked back the throttle and snapped the black gearshift into neutral. The whine of the engine dropped to a low rumble and he scrambled to the back of the boat.

The drag was humming as the sealed cork and asbestos washers did their best to keep the line from playing out. Finn was cranking hard, each revolution of the handle off center and bottom heavy, like a one-legged man riding a bicycle. The boy's jaw was set grimly and his eyes were angry, determined. "Who's the OBM now, huh?" he yelled. "Me!"

Gavin turned in circles for a second, trying to find something productive to contribute. "What do I do?" he asked.

"Stay at the wheel in case it starts running. Don't shut off the engine!" Finn pumped the rod and the thick graphite tip dipped as he spooled in line, then slowly rose up as he pulled back, gaining leverage to retrieve more line.

The rod jerked a few times and the line started to peel out. "Look at that!" the kid yelled. "It's running!"

Gavin watched the thick yellow braid dance to the left, cutting through the water. Whatever was on the end of the rig pulled a hundred yards inside a few seconds. "What the fuck is that?" Gavin asked no one in particular.

Finn's face cracked open into his smile. "That there is fame."

And then it broke the surface, all sleek, metallic green, and shine. It arrowed straight up, an easy ten feet, cartwheeling through the air and hitting the water nose-first in a picture-perfect dive. "Oh my God!" Finn yelled. "Did you see that?"

"It's a fish." Gavin felt deflated. "It's just a fish."

Finn shook his head and started reeling harder, his body bending with each jerk of the heavy boat rod. "That's not just a fish, City Boy! That is a fricking huge musky! Whoooo-eeee!" he chortled, and dug into the reel with all his energy. "That is the biggest gol-darned freaking sucker of a musky I have ever seen!" Finn hooted. "At least we get to have a little fun!"

Gavin focused on the point where the yellow line disappeared into the dark water, waiting for another glimpse of the fish. The line sawed through the smooth surface of the lake in a neat arc and the fish once again broke free of the water, spinning into an aerial pirouette.

Time slowed as if life were a film that had started to lag. Gavin had never seen a live musky before—his experience was limited to his weathervane, Googled photographs, and a stuffed specimen he had seen down at Izzy's Sporting Goods—but everything told him that this was a trophy fish. It had to be six feet long, and fat as a pig. It was silver with green stripes. Water shot off its back like blood off of a scalpel blade, spraying a thirty-foot line. There was no denying that it was beautiful. It rolled twice in the air, wrapping itself in leader. Then the airborne dance was over and the fish was back in the water, the atomic epicenter where it returned to its world rolling out in strong swells.

"It's getting tired," Finn observed. "It's coming in. No way it can compete with this rig. No way. Not in a million years." And Gavin saw that Finn was steadily picking up line with a lot less effort than he had been exerting just seconds before. The fish had worn itself down with the aerial acrobatics and Finn was winching it in.

Gavin turned back to the console and turned off the engine. The big 175 coughed one low burp and died quietly.

The only sound that Gavin heard was the *zing-zing-zing* of the sleeves of Finn's T-shirt as the kid pumped the big reel, pulling in the fish. Gavin squinted into the sun, trying to focus on the yellow line that disappeared into the glare.

"Gav, can you—" The sentence was cut short by the scream of the reel as line started peeling out. The rod bucked, then the tip snapped back, toward the water. Finn tightened up the drag and kept pumping the rod. "Start the boat!" The pitch of Finn's voice was almost as high as the whine of the drag screaming against the line being torn off the spool. "Follow my line!"

Gavin turned the key and the big Mercury growled awake.

Finn pulled back in hard jerks and cranked the handle. He kept losing line. "I'm down to a hundred feet! Go! Go!" Gavin swung the wheel of the boat as he throttled up and the *Low Rider* swung around in a tight arc. He spotted the yellow micro braid slicing through the water and headed after it at a thirty-degree cant so that Finn had a clear view.

"Where'd he get the energy?" Gavin asked as his eyes kept locked on the line.

"It ain't that fish!" Finn was cranking, trying to recover braid. "No way!"

They ran at roughly the same speed as the line peeling out; Finn neither lost nor gained line. Gavin checked the speed gauge: thirty-five knots.

There was a flash in the water off to the left, a hundred yards out, and a hump rose out of the black lake. The swell was smooth and long and—Gavin tried to estimate its length but had nothing to compare it to for scale—an easy ten, maybe fifteen feet was all he could guesstimate. It ran parallel to them for about five seconds, then zigged off to the far left and dove out of sight. It was gone. The line went limp.

"Stop the boat," Finn yelled over the engine.

Gavin dropped back the throttle and put the boat in neutral. "Sonofabitch," he said.

Finn was shaking his head and his shoulders were doing their samba as he reeled in the line. For the first time since he had known the boy, Finn was completely silent.

"What was that thing? What the fuck happened?" Gavin asked. Their wake caught up with them, sluiced by the transom, and the boat bobbed in the gentle swell.

Finn didn't answer. He reeled in the bright yellow line with a steady pulse of his muscles. Finally the big saltwater swivel rose out of the water and Gavin could see that something was dragging behind it, under the surface about ten feet back, dark and brown with a white patch. No doubt the carp. The way Finn rigged their bait it would take the charge of a rhinoceros to get it off the line.

"Get the net," Finn said flatly.

Gavin dipped the net into the water and swept it over the end of the fish. He hoisted it aboard and dropped it to the deck. Amid the black rubber netting, yellow line, and stainless-steel leader, the bright gleam of the anodized saltwater hooks stuck out. As did the blood that flowed out onto the white fiberglass deck in a widening pool of black.

Gavin kicked the mass of rubber and line over and the net opened up. Inside, neatly sitting upright, was the head of the musky that Finn had hooked. It had been cut neatly off just behind the gill openings. The mouth was still wrapped around what was left of the carp and the harness. Most of the carp was gone. As was half of the harness.

"What the hell did this?" Finn asked in a tone that came from a much older soul.

Gavin stared at the severed head of the fish and wondered what kind of creature could eat something that size and move at the speed of a car. "How big was this fish?" He nudged the severed head with the toe of his boot and the jaws reflexively snapped shut.

Finn shrugged. "Head's about ten inches across, maybe sixteen inches long. An easy fifty-five, maybe even sixty pounds. Record fish."

"Something ate a sixty-pound fish for a snack?"

Finn shook his head. "Something moved faster than the Batmobile, ate a fifteen-pound carp, bit through titanium leader, swallowed a hook that would choke a mule, *then* ate a sixty-pound fish for a snack." He looked up, the look of concern turning into his demented shit-eating grin.

"What are you smiling about?"

Finn turned in the direction where their monster had sunk out of sight. "I'm just gloating."

"Well, stop it."

"Why? Maybe now you'll believe me."

# 44

Gavin was in the passenger's seat of the ancient blue-and-rust-colored Ford F-150, breathing in gas fumes, farts, and the remnants of Hal's cigarette. Hal drove the area's one unofficial taxi, charging a flat rate of five bucks anywhere on the map. After the accident, and the demise of his gas-guzzling four-by-four, Gavin had hired the old man's services; the deal was seventy-five dollars a day (plus gas) whether he used Hal or not, until his arm was out of the cast. Besides, even if his arm had been okay, Gavin had no plans to replace the Hummer. And, with the exception of the farts and the fumes, Hal's beat-up truck had character and a big comfortable bench seat where he could stretch out without the arm getting caught up. He also liked the fact that the vehicle was invisible—no one noticed him in it. Meaning that no one was likely to run him off the road. Part of him felt guilty for using Hal as a hired human shield. Then he saw the cast and felt his ribs and realized that fear was useful in overcoming certain moral dilemmas.

Hal turned down the drive to Gavin's house. He eased over the road, the truck groaning in protest with each bump it hit. They emerged from the canopied drive to find Dr. Laurel sitting on the front steps, the big cat comatose in her lap. "Home sweet home," the old man said, opening a smile that wouldn't win him any beauty contests.

"Yes, it is."

When the truck rolled to a stop, Gavin got out and handed over the day's fare—plus a tip—and thanked Hal for his services. The old man pocketed the money, screwed a new Marlboro into his face, lit it off the dashboard lighter, and drove off in a cloud of blue smoke that could have come from either the truck or the cigarette.

Gavin turned around and Laurel was standing right there, the big beast in her arms dead to the world. "You could have let yourself in, you know," he said.

"I wouldn't want to intrude. It's your home. Besides, the cat wanted company."

"It's just a building. And you're always welcome in it."

Laurel smiled up at him, her eyes doing most of the work. "Good to know, Corlie. But there's a problem."

"Which is?"

"I would need a key."

Gavin's brow furrowed. "Don't they teach lock picking in med school?"

"Only in the good ones. I open doors the old-fashioned way. Call me a traditionalist."

"There's a key under the fountain." Gavin reached under the limestone lip of the basin and produced a key. "It's always here. Use it anytime you want. Also…" He went to the door and turned the knob. "The door's open. I was told that I don't have to lock the doors out here."

"I suppose I should have tried your knob." She stood up on her toes and gave him a kiss on the cheek. "Whew, you smell like fish!" Even the dead-to-the-world cat seemed to perk up to the smell.

"Carp."

"As in *carpe diem*?"

"No. Carp as in carp. I smell like carp. *Fish* is general. *Carp* is specific."

"Oh, I see. Specific. Well, in that case, I suppose the specific question to ask would be, Why do you smell like carp?"

The thought of lying to her felt wrong. "Finn and I are using carp as bait." Truth.

"Carp as bait?" Laurel shook her head. "I've seen carp, Gav. They're too big for bait. Unless you're fishing for the Loch Ness Monster."

Gavin's mind involuntarily dredged up images of Walt Pinkowski's legs on the medical examiner's table and something in his face changed, became brittle.

"Something you're not telling me?" she asked, suddenly serious.

"Not really, no." He opened the door and eased by her.

Laurel followed him into the house. "It's Finn, isn't it? What happened to him on the lake. And Walter Pinkowski."

The little movie projector in his head flashed another image of Walter's white waxy legs stretched out on the stainless-steel table, the only visible problem being that they were no longer attached to him. "Now you're reaching." He kept his back to her as he slipped off his jacket and dropped it onto an antique wing chair beside the door.

"Then why all the time on the water? You spend what? Sixteen hours a day on that boat? You two are up to something." Once inside she gingerly dropped Foots on the floor. He stretched, yawned, and moved off to the kitchen, presumably to have a can of anchovies. "How many fish you catch?"

"One." It was almost the truth. It sounded better than *Actually, just the head of a fish.* Less scary, too.

"In two weeks of beating that lake to death you've caught one fish. One. Singular. You're either the worst fisherman in the history of the sport or the best liar. And this sport has a lot of liars, mister."

He kicked off his boots. He had made a promise to Finn that this was to be their secret. "Look," he began, and headed into the kitchen after the cat, "this could be Finn's last season. We've only got another six weeks of fishable weather left. That boy has busted his ass to catch a record fish for the past three years and all he has to show for it is a wrecked boat, a near-death experience, and another stay in the hospital." Gavin pulled the canister of coffee out of the cupboard and started filling a filter. The heavy smell of the roasted beans offset the very real scent of carp. Laurel was right, he *did* stink.

Foots rubbed against his legs, the little fur-covered motor in his chest purring happily away. Gavin pulled a tin of cat food from the cupboard, peeled the lid off, and scooped a glob of the stinky paste onto a saucer. "Here, Foots. It's not anchovies but it's better for your kidneys." The cat went to work on the brown goop.

Laurel was leaning against the door, staring him down. Her arms were folded across her chest and he could see the compact muscles of her shoulders bunched up under the tight T-shirt she wore. Without knowing why or how, Gavin knew that stance, had seen her standing like that before. Déjà vu without the fogginess of uncertainty. And it suddenly hit him that he was falling in love with this woman. And there wasn't a fucking thing he could do about it. "I'm glad you came by. It makes the day worthwhile." It wasn't much in the way of a confession of love, but it was true.

Laurel smiled with her whole face. "That was a nice thing to say." There was an awkward pause before she continued. "And on behalf of Foots, the Sasquatch of the feline world, I thank you for taking him off of the anchovy diet."

Gavin was about to tell her that it had been Finn's idea but thought better of it—right now he wanted all the good-guy points he could scrape up. Besides, watching the cat eat seemed to have taken her mind off his streak of little white lies. He settled on, "He deserves it."

She suddenly seemed softer to him and her body language became more familiar, as if he hadn't really been looking at her before. Or she hadn't really been showing herself.

He dropped the empty cat food tin into the trash and walked over to her. He reached down and put his good arm around her, his bad one sticking awkwardly out like a radio antenna that a storm had mangled. She looked up at him, not sure what he was thinking. They stared at one another. Then their mouths moved together and they kissed. She smelled sweet and real.

"*Carpe diem*," she said softly.

# 45

Sheriff Xavier Pope popped the tab on his Pabst Blue Ribbon and dropped into the vinyl La-Z-Boy. He had spent ten minutes searching for the remote control for the TV and had decided that the effort required wasn't worth the payoff. What the fuck, a beer was better than the tube anytime. It was Wednesday night and Doris was out bowling. She wouldn't be back until after eleven. He checked his watch: six thirty. A solid four-plus hours of bitchless silence. Pope smiled and nodded to himself. It was going to be a good night.

He reached into his pocket and produced a folded piece of paper. He nodded a friendly hello to the packet, unfolded it, and rolled the two blue pills out onto the palm of his hand. He examined them for a minute, wondering rhetorically why the cockroaches loved them so much.

Pope took another swig of the cheap beer to clean out his mouth in preparation for the bitter familiarity of the Benzedrine. But the flavor of the ale brought an image of his wife to his mind. Why did she keep buying this watered-down piss when she knew that he was a Bud man? Because it was fifty cents cheaper for a sixer. And Doris loved to save money. Almost as much as she loved eating. *No no no no no*, Pope shook his head. Tonight was his night off. No Doris. Just him. And the cockroaches. He popped the pills into his mouth and rolled them to the back of his throat. Before they had time to start shedding, he washed them down with a mouthful of beer that for some strange reason suddenly tasted a fucking whole lot better. He tilted his head back, closed his eyes, and waited for the music to start.

While he was sitting there watching the inside of his head, he thought about G. Corlie, former resident of the Big City, lately of Lake Caldasac. Rich arrogant cocksucker who deserved to have his head go through a windshield while his body stayed in the seat.

Only it hadn't turned out like he had planned, had it? Pope had done his best, setting up the board of ten twenty-two-million-candle-power strobes on the last corner before Gavin had to drop his speed and turn onto Lake Road. Gavin's money machine had rolled in right on time and Pope had lit up his vision in one big flash of hate. The truck had gone off the road, Baryshnikoved through the trees, rolled, and almost killed the fucker. Almost. Guy had a horseshoe up his ass. Goddamned seatbelts.

If that chiropractor cocksucker hadn't seen headlights go tumbling off into the ditch and come running down the hill, Pope would have been able to put Corlie down. But the chiropractor had shown up just a little after Pope had managed to get the deer lights into his trunk. Fucking do-gooder idiots. Why couldn't people just mind their own business and leave well enough alone?

Pope shook his head. How the hell had he fucked that one up? Maybe he would have to fall back on his old favorite—break into the guy's house while he was sleeping and blow his brains all over the pillow. Make it look like a suicide. A guy like that kills himself and who's going to say different? Tattooed millionaire with nothing but booze and a crippled kid to keep him busy. No one would give a shit at all. Hell, Pope would probably be a secret hero. And there was always the hands-on satisfaction he would get from a job like that.

Pope remembered the schoolteacher who had drowned in her tub two years back. It had gone well. She had made some holier-than-thou accusations to the department after one of her grade-three students had said something that had implied that Pope had acted inappropriately toward the boy. After the kid's parents had made the intelligent—and only—decision to move away after dropping the ridiculous charges, Pope had paid her a visit.

She had been in the tub. He had simply walked into the bathroom and held her under the soapy water by her hair. The look on her face was priceless. Abso-fucking-lutely priceless. She had tried to fight but she had been a small woman and was no match for Pope's weight. He had got a kick out of the turd she had let go during the struggle and whenever he took a bath he always thought back on that one; one of his better moments.

The little insect entertainment troop started suiting up in their sequined outfits, snapping buttons and doing up zippers. The lights dimmed and they hit the stage, their little bloated bodies pulsing inside his skull. It almost sounded like ringing. And then he realized that it *was* ringing. Someone was at the goddamned door! He got up. Angry. The bugs sat down with a disappointed sigh.

Suzie Haggerty was standing on his porch, the little moron she called a son hanging off her side, his eyes rolled up in his head, mouth open. What was it they called that condition again? Some *syndrome* thing.

"Yeah?" Pope asked in his not too friendly voice. He and Suzie got along well enough but Pope was eager to get back to the Cockroach Capades.

"Hello, Xavier. I need a favor. Roger's stuck at the dam tonight and I have to go to the doctor with Alice."

Pope nodded. Alice was one of her kids. He had no idea *which* one, but he remembered the name. Maybe she was the one with the freckles.

"I'd take Toby here with me but he *hates* the doctor. You know that."

Pope nodded again. Why wouldn't the kid hate doctors? Born with most of his brain on vacation and his life spent with people who examined, poked, bled, shocked, medicated, and experimented on him all the time; it would make anyone hate doctors. Then his mind lost its train of thought and he looked into Haggerty's eyes. What was she doing here? Oh yeah, something about the kids. The one with the freckles. Or was it the one with the braces? All he wanted to do was go back and listen to the music.

"I was hoping that you could watch him. It would only be for about an hour and a half. I'll be as quick as I can." She let out a nervous little giggle.

Pope nodded again because it seemed to be the thing that she expected. Anything that would get her off of his porch and out of his life was a priority. So he nodded. "Can he watch TV?" Pope asked from his comfortable little seat in *I-don't-give-a-fuck-land*.

She let out a squeal of too much enthusiasm. "Oh, of course! Absolutely. Thank you so much. I know you've watched him before and whenever he comes back from your place he's so well behaved. I don't know what it is you *do* to him!" She blushed and that idiotic giggle squeezed out of her fat face again. "But he's as obedient as pie after he sees you." Pope stepped aside, letting Toby scramble past on his way to the 33-inch Trinitron. "Thank you so much, Xavier. I owe you one. I'll make you a nice cake."

Pope nodded for the last time and turned away from her, closing the door.

Toby was already installed on the floor in front of the television, the remote in his hand. How the hell had he found it? But them kids was like that: take away one set of senses, like brains, and they were usually good at other things. The boy was flipping through channels like a pinwheel.

"Hey, Toby, can you get me a beer?" Pope asked in the way of an experiment.

The boy nodded and ran over to the fridge, coming back with a can of soda. He sat down on the floor.

"Thanks, kid, thanks a lot." Fuck, this was just great. Pope went and got a second beer, putting the soda back in the fridge. Hell, he couldn't really blame the kid; after all, they did both come in cans. One was red, one was white, but then again, maybe color blindness was part of the way the condition went down. Down? *Down!* That was it—*Down syndrome!*

When Pope redeposited himself in the big chair, the kid was watching wrestling. Some guy in red satin shorts was kicking the ever-loving shit out of another guy in a yellow cape and some sort of a dog collar. Bunch of grown-up fags, Pope thought, but it seemed to keep the little retard quiet, so it couldn't be *all* bad.

Krupa Cockroach started up with a groovy little beat and a parade of scantily clad insects shimmied out onto the stage, doing a saucy little burlesque number that showed a lot of skin. He hummed along with the band.

Old Krupe was really letting loose, hammering away at the drums, a little six-armed maniac. Pope felt his head rattling and thought his teeth would shake loose. The insect broads in the G-strings were pulsing like a brown rotting heart, grinding away to the drumming. And his whole skull throbbed with the music.

On the TV, some guy in a cowboy hat got his teeth kicked out and they sprayed across the mat in a shower of blood and the kid chortled and clapped his hands together. The cockroach drummer started hammering in time to the wrestling, like the theme to *Hawaii Five-O*, big-band style. Toby bounced on the floor, his head snapping with the punches.

"Hey, Tobe," he said, reducing the boy's name to one syllable, "can you turn the volume down?" Pope tried to ease back into the place in his mind where the dancers were pulsing.

The kid snapped a few buttons on the remote and the volume dropped to half. Pope sank back into the vinyl and the Benzedrine show was in full swing now. Off in the distance he heard cheering. Oh yeah, the kid was watching the tube. Pope pried the corner of his eye open to see some broad get busted across the chops with a folding chair. She hit the canvas and one of her tits popped out. Jesus, the crap they let kids watch these days. Toby was bouncing up and down on the carpet, grinning, and enjoying every second of the show.

And that's when the roaches started chanting. They were in harmony, a wheezy little choir offset by the mad drumming. Pope twitched a few times, trying to shut them off, but it was no good. It never was. They would bug him—*ha, ha*—until he turned them off the old-fashioned way. Luckily, he and Toby had played this game before.

"Hey, Tobe," Pope said and stood up. "You and I are gonna play a little game. You remember the game I showed you, doncha, kid?"

Silence in his skull as the cockroaches held their collective breath, like orphans on visiting day.

The boy's big eyes darted around the room, searching for a place to hide.

Pope stood up and started unbuckling his pants. The boy scrambled backward into the corner. Pope just shook his head. "It's disco time, short bus," he said, and pulled out his cock to the sound of a thousand tiny cheers.

# 46

The moon shone through the big Palladian, laying out a checkerboard of light crisscrossing the linen duvet. The house was silent and the only sound was their breathing.

"Gavin?" she asked from a happy place nestled into his good shoulder.

"Hmm?" he mumbled into the common darkness above them. It was all he had the strength to say. His eyes were closed.

"You do know that I am older than you?"

He stiffened and there was an awkward pause. "At least tell me that you're a virgin!"

She laughed and bit his chest. "No, really. I *am* older than you. Older. The older woman. Does that bother you?"

"You mean, like, will I get annoyed having to climb over your walker when we take a shower together? That kind of stuff?"

She laughed again and in the dark it was a sweet sound that he knew he would never get tired of hearing. "No." Her laughter dragged the word out, adding a half-dozen syllables. "Not that kind of stuff." She paused, trying to find a way to phrase what she was thinking. "I mean that while you are entering into your Cary Grant phase, I am quickly approaching geezerdom."

Gavin weighed what she was saying. He'd be lying if he said that he hadn't thought about the age difference between them. And although it wasn't an average relationship, what was he supposed to do? He had been through all the stuff that Shannon had packed for him and he was pretty sure that there were no magic wands in the house. Besides, you couldn't control who you fell in love with any more than you could control who delivered your pizza. What mattered was how he had come to feel. "Why would it bother me? It's not like you're going to get older while I stand still. I don't know if you've noticed but I'm not exactly twelve. A lot of gray has moved into my hair—" He opened his eyes, looked over at her.

"I know," she said softly, "I love it."

"And it's not like I need your financial support. I happen to do all right for myself."

Her smile had migrated into a solid little giggle and her body pulsed with laughter. "Stop."

"And we seem to be pretty well-matched in the sex depart-ment. As long as you go easy on me, that is." Gavin stretched his good arm out behind her, the muscle tight and strong. "So why would I have a problem with you being older than me?"

"I don't know. Lots of reasons." There was something in her voice that Gavin had not heard before—insecurity, maybe.

"Like?"

"Like…well…um…it's…oh, Christ, I don't know! What would your friends say?"

"Considering that my best friend right now is thirteen, I can pretty much guarantee that it's not going to be much of an issue in the social circles I frequent."

"So you haven't thought about this? It doesn't bother you?" Her voice sounded serious.

"Sure I've thought about this. And no, it doesn't bother me. Not one little bit. I'm thirty-nine. What's the spread?" He knew that she was older but had no idea by how much exactly. He figured it would be around ten years, give or take.

"I'm fifty-six, Gavin."

Gavin smiled up into the empty space above them. "Fifty-six. I see. That *is* old." Then he laughed. And stopped because he felt his ribs light up. "Ou-uu-uch," he said in three syllables, between squeaks of laughter. "So you're fifty-six. I'm thirty-nine. Seventeen years. Nice spread. We have to worry about you getting pregnant?" And as soon as it was out, he winced, remembering Chelsea.

"Nope."

"Well," he said, coming back out of the past. "We're over the first hurdle. And you've got a better ass than most women half your age." He reached down and laid his hand over the tight muscles of her bum. Her backside was small and his hand, though not big, covered most of it. "What size are you? Seven?"

"Four," she said happily.

"I'll save a fortune in food. And you don't take up much space." He ran his hand up her back, the little bumps of her spine undulating under his fingers like the keys of a piano. "Except maybe in my heart."

She propped herself up on an elbow and stared down into his eyes. "You mean that?"

Gavin smiled at her, brushed a strand of hair off her forehead, and kissed her softly on the mouth. "Yeah, I mean that. When you're not around all I do is think about you." His smile broadened into a grin.

She grinned back. "That was a nice thing to say."

"It's your ass." His hand ran down her back again, settling on her bum. "An ass like this buys you a lot of points."

Laurel leaned forward and kissed him on the eyebrow that had been stitched back together. Her lips felt cool and warm at the same time and he felt a wave of energy run through his body. "Hmm," he moaned.

"It's the ass," she replied.

"Yes, it is." There was no denying the fact that she was beautiful; whenever he thought of her, it was her beauty that came to mind first. Followed by the way she looked at him. And the way he felt when he was around her. He was at ease with her, and it had been a long time since he had felt at ease with anyone. Even with Chelsea. Especially with Chelsea. "Look," he said, breaking their calm silence. "I've got to tell you something."

"What?" She looked into his eyes and he found himself back at the beginning, feeling like he was looking into his future.

"Chelsea—things with Chelsea—before she died…they were…"

She held his face in her hands and her eyes told him that whatever it was, it was going to be okay again.

"Things with Chelsea were broken, not right. We were getting a divorce." This was the first time he said it out loud.

Laurel's face took on a puzzled look, as if she hadn't quite heard him. "I don't understand. I thought that things with you two were, well, good. Perfect, even. You haven't said much, but you made your marriage sound so full. Idyllic."

Gavin shook his head. "No. Not for a while. I've been lying to you." His face went rigid and all the expression bled out of it. "And I've been lying to myself. The morning she died we had been yelling at each other for hours. She wanted a divorce. It had been coming for months. She wanted kids, I didn't, and eventually we had the Big Talk. Being the stubborn sonofabitch that I am, I refused to listen to what she was telling me and the conversation very quickly descended into self-parody. She told me off and went out to get some fresh flowers but she was really just trying to get away from me. She gave me this sad little smile as the elevator doors closed and I thought about all the real smiles she had given me and about how all of that had somehow come apart at the seams." He thought about Ernie, the crocodile he had thrown to his death, the final punctuation mark to all his self-blame.

"You're not being fair to yourself."

Gavin just lay there staring up into the moonlit darkness. It was true, he *knew* it was true, but he was having a hard time *feeling* it, *living* it. "I just wanted you to know that my life is real, it's not some beautiful bubble."

"This was nice." She nuzzled farther into his shoulder, willing herself into his body, an obvious ploy to change the subject.

He softened, accepting her into him. "Yes, it was." She was warm and kind and comforting and he felt himself slipping back into the calm. "Very," he added, and then, after a pause: "Do you ever wish that I was older?"

There was silence between them for a few seconds. "I would never wish your life away," was all she said.

With that sentence she had him. For good. Gavin closed his eyes and concentrated on the warmth of her cheek against his chest, the smooth muscle of her leg overlapping his, and the smell of her hair. He felt himself easing back into the warm waves of their synchronized breathing and found himself smiling. It was dark out now and the only light was a gentle twilight that bounced off the water. "How about a fire?" he asked.

"And a drink," she added. "I would love something cold."

He slid out from under her and instantly missed the warmth of her body. "Back in a minute."

She spoke into the pillow that was now substituting for his chest. The sound was somewhere between a moan and a yawn. He thought that he heard the word *ice* come through the feathers.

Gavin moved slowly down the steps, enjoying the tender spots that popped up in his body as he negotiated the old oak planks. His legs hurt a little and each step brought out a burning in muscles he hadn't used in a long time. The full moon hung in the center of the big Palladian that opened the steps onto the blustery night. Out in the yard leaves swirled by and shadows mingled with reality. Foots was spread out at the top of the stairs and Gavin had to step over him. As he walked past the cat, his peripheral vision picked out a form near the tree line. He turned his head, focused, and the form was gone. A branch quivered out of time with the wind that was washing through the foliage. Someone had just walked into the forest, someone who had been standing on the lawn. His imagination? But the branch was still vibrating, disynchronous even in the windy environment. Someone *had* been standing there.

Gavin stood staring out of the window until the soft tread of Laurel's feet pulled his attention away from the yard. He turned and saw her standing at the top of the stairs, nude.

"Everything okay?" she asked tentatively.

"Yeah, sorry. I thought I saw someone outside and just wanted to make sure they weren't trying to steal your car."

The light from the bedroom window spilled through the door and across the floor, bathing her silhouette in gauze. Gavin smiled up at her.

"What?" she asked.

"You look beautiful."

She came down and wrapped her arms around him. Her body was still warm from the bed and the sensation started flipping switches in his head. "Keep this up and you'll have a hard time getting rid of me."

He kissed her again. "Go back to bed. I'll get something to drink and we'll sit up and watch the fire until we doze off."

She shook her head. "No dozing, not yet. I still have needs to be met."

He kissed her and moved away. "Go. Go. Back to bed before you freeze."

She ran back to the bed and jumped in, the echo of her feet slapping the floor resonating loudly in the dark.

"And bring some food!" she hollered from the bed.

Ten minutes later they were propped up in the bed munching on another of Gavin's gastronomically sacrilegious snacks. Anchovies yet again, a wheel of soft cheese, a handful of crackers, Häagen-Dazs, and a plate of cold macaroni and cheese, all washed down by some ice-cold old-fashioned root beer in glass bottles. The fire was roaring, accentuating their faces with sharp chiaroscuro. Foots was curled up at their feet and was so comfortable that even the smell of the anchovies didn't rouse him from his catatonic state.

Laurel downed a slice of anchovy and washed it back with a big swig of soda, punctuating the whole affair with a stellar burp.

Gavin laughed and instantly regretted it when his cracked ribs let him know that they were still not willing to cooperate with him. "Real nice."

"Sorry." Laurel smiled sheepishly. "Root beer makes me burp."

"I see that."

"And the anchovies call for lots of root beer. It's a vicious circle. And it's all your fault. Who *eats* like this?"

"Hey, it's not my fault that there's nowhere in the neighborhood where I can order a good pizza!"

"Or Chinese, Japanese, Thai, Mexican, Lebanese, Indian, French, hot dogs, submarines, or souvlaki. I know, it's not New York."

Gavin stared at her. "I didn't mean it in a bad way. I'm not the one complaining about the food. I was just offering an explanation about this culinary massacre that I prepared. I usually put out a better spread than cold macaroni and cheese and Doritos."

Her head snapped up. "You have Doritos? Don't ever joke about Doritos."

Gavin reached down beside the bed and pulled out a bag. "I joke about overpopulation and nuclear war and such shit, but I never joke about Doritos."

"You're forgiven the mac and cheese. Forever."

"You eat Doritos? I have a hard time believing that."

She snatched the bag out of his hand. "My *only* weakness is Doritos." She smiled and this particular one lit up her eyes in the yellow glow of the fire. "And you."

"You amaze me."

"Because I eat Doritos? You're easy to please, Corlie."

He thought about what she had just said and shook his head. "Only when I'm with you."

She produced a chip from the bag and held it up. "Dorito?"

"Stop it. I'm being serious here." He covered her little hand with his.

"Me too." Her expression had changed from that of a mischievous child to that of a serious adult. "I'm in love with you."

"You can't say that."

"Why?" She was troubled.

"Because I wanted to say it first."

A slow smile worked its way across her lips. "You know something? For the first time in my life—my very *long* life," she added, "I believe those words."

Gavin leaned back in the bed and pulled her in close. "I'm not saying that I'm not going to fuck it up. Maybe I will. But whatever happens with us, happens with me loving you."

They lay quietly for a while, with nothing but the crackling of the fire and the purr of the cat to mar the silence. Then that too began to fade and the gentle waves of sleep rolled in and washed over him. In the background, beyond the reaches of his mind, part of his brain registered the gentle snapping of the fire competing with the nearby crunch of Doritos.

For the first time in nearly a year, Gavin slept a dreamless sleep while outside, in the driveway, a man with a head full of cockroaches stumbled around the property.

# 47

Pope trudged up the gravel driveway in the dark, angry with himself. Angry because this asshole was under his skin; angry that this asshole was fucking the doctor from the hospital; angry that this asshole was still alive; angry because he had left his gloves back in the car. No gloves, no sneaking into the house and painting the pillowcase with brains. Not that Pope thought he'd make a mistake. No, he was pretty sure that he'd get it right the first time around. But it was the little unknowns that got you smoked. That Son of Sam psycho had been nabbed on a parking infraction. The BTK pussy had been turned in by his own daughter. Hell, even Oswald had been short-listed based on the company he kept. But they had been criminals. Pope was the law. And he had buried enough hitchhikers in the woods out here to know that the badge made the difference. It made things right. The fun was just a bonus.

The gravel crunching under his feet sounded like eardrums exploding and the wind was doing a pretty good job at laughing at him. The Benzedrine was starting to wear off and the fluttering collapse of the high was pulling the world in toward him, like the eye of a storm, and he felt it all swirling into the drain. He shook his head, hoping that some of the static would lift. All he got was more. What he needed was a shot of vodka to calm him down. And vodka was back in the trunk of the cruiser. He picked up his pace.

Pope emerged from the dark tunnel of trees a few minutes later. He crossed Lake Road, popped the trunk of his cruiser, and yanked the bottle of Stoli out of his gear bag. Three gulps later and he felt a helluva lot better. Almost perfect. Except he still had the flutters in his brain. He pulled out the tight leather driving gloves and slid them over his fingers. Another few good swigs and the bottle was back in the trunk.

Pope stared down the drive for a minute, unsure of what to do. Killing this fucker would be a lot more fun with the knife-edge of Benzedrine scraping through his synaptic PC. Then he looked back at the car. Then at Corlie's drive. Why was this so goddamned hard? He really did need more speed. And he was out. Which left the booze. But booze would only take the edge off, not crank him up. And he needed to be cranked up for this one.

What to do?

What to do?

# 48

Laurel was poking him in the arm. "Get up!"

"Hmm? What? Jesus, it's early." Gavin forced one eye open. "It's not even daylight."

"Someone's at the door. And I'm naked." Her voice was a husky whisper.

"So if you whisper they won't know that you don't have clothes on?" he asked full volume. "Jesus, what is it about me that attracts the nutty ones?"

She punched him in the arm. "Get the door."

He stood up and fought his jeans on in the dark. "That's it, no more Doritos for you. It's back to bread and water." The fire was dead but he could smell the thick smoke of burned hardwood as he moved to the door. Foots was gone. The bell rang again.

He looked out the window as he crept down the steps. Other than Laurel's ancient gas-guzzler parked off near the trees, the yard was empty; whoever was here came on foot. Maybe it was one of the loons—they had smelled the Doritos and wanted a snack.

At the door he paused, then reached into the planter, removing the stainless-steel .357 he had stashed there— how long ago now? Years, it felt like. The combat grip was comfortable in his hand and he eased the hammer back just before he inched the door open. And—

"Good morning!" Finn bellowed.

Gavin jumped and for an instant felt a jolt of anger—he could have shot the kid. "Where the hell did you come from? What time is it? Are you nuts?"

"My house. Three forty-five. And no," he answered, all in order. "Now can I come in?"

Gavin shook some of the fuzziness out of his brain. Maybe he should have shot him. Then he realized that he wasn't even that tired anymore. He stepped aside and waved the boy through like a matador playing a bull. "Why not?"

Finn wheeled up the ramp Mr. Johannus had built for him then through the wide doorway. As he rolled into the house, he flipped on the lights and headed for the kitchen. "Got any Coke left?"

Gavin closed the door and took a deep breath, consciously fighting back the urge to yell at the kid. "Mickey's grandson delivered four cases this evening—last night—um—before. Christ, it's early." He unloaded the heavy revolver, pocketed the single bullet, and dropped the empty gun back in the planter.

"Which grandson? She has two."

"I don't know. The one who likes to honk the horn."

Finn nodded knowingly. "That's Early. Early's a nut."

Some of the dust started to clear out of his brain. "Finn, it's our day off," he protested to the minidictator. Then, by way of a more logical response to having a kid in a wheelchair show up at his front step in the wee hours of the morning, he asked, "How the fuck did you get here?"

Finn pulled the door of the fridge open and rattled around for a Coke. "Hal drove me. He works for you and we work together so I figured that kinda made him my driver too."

"Where is Hal?"

"Oh, he left me off at the road and I wheeled down here."

"It's a half a mile of ruts and potholes to get here from the road." The storms of the past month had undone a lot of the good that grading the drive had done. It was again reduced to a series of teeth-jarring dips and washboard gravel. "Are you out of your mind? Why didn't you just have Hal bring you to the front door? And how did you get him to drive you here at this hour? I'm surprised he didn't shoot you."

"I called him at Black Eyed Susie's—he's there all the time. I didn't have him come down the driveway because he was pretty liquored up and I didn't want him to crack up his truck on your crappy little road. Besides, I didn't want to wake you up; his truck makes a lot of noise."

"So do you, banging on the door at quarter to four on my day off."

Finn considered what Gavin had said for a second. "Good point." His face twisted into his smile again. "I see Dr. Laurel's car is here. You two having the S-E-K-S?" the kid said in a very good impression of Groucho Marx, complete with bouncing eyebrows and a leer.

Gavin couldn't help but laugh. Nonetheless, he managed to dodge the boy's prying. "What is so important that you paid Hal to drive you out here?"

"I didn't pay him, you did. I put it on your tab." Finn wheeled by Gavin, two glass bottles of Coke on his lap.

"Of course you did. How come I didn't know that?"

"Not thinking, I guess. It is early, you know."

Gavin smiled weakly; there was no beating out Finn's eternal one-upmanship. "It was a rhetorical question. And yeah, I know it's early. Which brings me back to the obvious—what are you doing here?"

"If you don't keep getting up early, your biological clock is going to reset itself and I'll be back to waiting on the dock for you every morning. I don't have the time to break you in. *Again.*"

"You know what, Finn? I wish I had your work ethic. Hell, I wish I had *half* your work ethic. I'd be dictator of my own country by now." Gavin dropped down into the overstuffed sofa and threw his feet up on the coffee table. "So this is merely a courtesy call so that *I* don't throw off *your* schedule. You're a very considerate human being."

"Actually, I *do* have something to show—" The boy slammed to a halt as Laurel appeared.

She was dressed in her jeans and Gavin's shirt. She had a pretty thorough case of bed head but looked awake and lively, her natural beauty accentuated by the fact that she wore no makeup and was grinning broadly. "Good morning, Finn," she said as she walked in, plopping down onto the sofa beside Gavin.

Finn smiled and said hello. "Your shirt is buttoned lopsided," he offered matter-of-factly.

"Everything's lopsided at four in the morning, Finn. You boys want some breakfast? I'm up now."

Finn nodded. "Sure."

Gavin weighed his options. "Why not?"

"Anything you don't eat, Finn?"

Gavin thought about Finn's horrifying diet. "Don't worry about him. This kid could eat a rat ass sandwich. Raw."

"Bacon and eggs it is."

Finn lit up. "Can I have my eggs runny? With ketchup? And burn the toast. I like black toast. And not too much ketchup. And don't forget to make the toast black. Really black. And lots of butter, too. And I like my bacon chewy. But not too chewy. So don't cook it too long. But the eggs have to be runny, like I said. The most important thing is the ketchup, and the black toast—"

Laurel stopped and slowly pivoted with the body language of someone who had better places to be. "I know how to make bacon and eggs one way. That's the way you get it.

Ketchup I can do, but you're out of luck on the snotty eggs and the rubbery bacon, okay?"

Finn was grinning so bad Gavin thought that his mandible was going to dislocate. "No runny eggs?" He looked at Laurel, trying to stare her down. He held his own for a few seconds but was no match for her—after all, a pediatric doctor is used to kids tightening the emotional screws. "What about the burned toast? Even *you* can cook that!"

Laurel nodded. "Deal." And disappeared into the kitchen, followed by the sound of Gavin laughing.

"So, what was worth Super-Dave-Osborneing down my driveway at this hour?" Gavin asked the boy. "Besides your schedule."

Finn glanced over his shoulder to make sure that Laurel was out of earshot. "This," he whispered, producing a map from inside his fleece pullover. "I know where it lives."

Gavin leaned forward, his attention nailed to the laminated map that Finn was unfolding on the coffee table. "*It*? Our *it*?"

The boy grinned like he was on nitrous oxide. "Here"— he pointed out a position between Kintner Island and Gavin's bay—"is where I got hit. Walter and his legs were separated somewhere near here, about a half mile upstream and close to shore—otherwise they never would have washed up so quickly. Walt was an eel fisherman, so he was in the shallow water where there is a strong current. And yesterday, where that musky got munched, was right here"—Finn ground his index finger into the map as if it were a cigarette—"which is also fast water. It's the trough between Kintner and Gardner's Island where all the water gets flushed through on the way to the dam. This thing likes fast water. Cold too. Baitfish get washed through there with the current and the bigger fish come there to feed. Like our musky yesterday."

"Why cold?" Gavin asked.

"The eel nets are right on top of one of the freshwater springs that feed the lake. One of the little ones. Izzy's always talking about it. I remember hearing about how it was one of the main reasons they put the dam in here. Those springs pump a lot of water into this lake. The big one is more like an underground river that comes in from a cave system that cuts under the mountains. That's why the lake is so cold all the time. Where else can you die of hypothermia in August? You have a pen?"

Gavin reached over and pulled one out of a notebook lying amid a pile of unopened mail.

"Look here—" Finn drew a line from where he believed Pinkowski had been killed to where his own boat was attacked, to where their trophy musky had been chewed up. "This is almost a straight line. And look at the numbers."

Gavin leaned over the hydrographic map and examined the black line of ink that neatly dissected Lake Caldasac. The path that Finn had drawn started out at the spring and ran straight through the trench of deep water that slashed through the middle of the lake like a wound. Finn was right; whatever it was had been encountered in deep water. "So what do we do?"

Finn pushed up his sleeves. "We roll up our sleeves and come up with a trolling system for the deep water."

Gavin's eyes were drawn away from the map to bright splashes of color all over Finn's arm. "Finn?" he asked.

"Yeah?"

"What the hell is that?"

Finn held up his arm and modeled it for Gavin. "My tattoo."

Gavin leaned forward and took the boy's arm in his hands, turning it over as if he were a museum curator examining a valuable artifact. The tattoo was an exact copy of Gavin's, from the broad image of a bearded Poseidon wrestling a sea monster, right down to the green waves and purple sky encircling his bicep. "This is perfect. Who did this?"

Finn smiled proudly. "Me."

"You?"

"Not bad, huh? It's auto detailing paint. Won't come off for a month of Sundays. I was going to clear-coat it but I thought that it might be bad for my skin. Then again, what's the worst that can happen? I get skin cancer. Big deal."

"This is car paint?"

Finn nodded, grinning.

"You painted your arm with car paint?"

Finn kept nodding and grinning.

Laurel entered the room, carrying two plates of steaming food. Foots was following close behind, obviously entranced by the smell of bacon. "Laurel, you have to see this," Gavin said, shaking his head and laughing.

Her eyebrows stitched together and she leaned over Finn's arm with the scientific scrutiny of her profession. As she did, Finn reached up with his free hand and relieved her of the plate he assumed was for him. As she examined his candy-colored artwork, he scooped up a piece of the charcoal-based toast and snapped a chunk off between his teeth.

"Nice work," she said.

"You, too! This toast is great!" Finn's smile was peppered with creosote and he chewed the burned bread with obvious relish.

Gavin folded up Finn's map and put it away under the table. "Thanks, baby."

Finn's mouth stopped in midchew. "Woo woo woo. I like sexy talk."

"Yeah, well, with a mouthful of charcoal you can keep it to yourself," she said, headed back to the kitchen to get the coffee.

"So, Mr. Horn, what brings you out at four in the morning?" Laurel asked as she came back in, two mugs of steaming coffee in her hands. She redeposited herself on the sofa beside Gavin.

"It's almost five!" Finn popped the bottle top off on the arm of his wheelchair and gulped down a good half in an obvious effort to avoid answering the question.

Gavin filled his mouth with a forkful of eggs and nodded appreciatively.

Laurel's eyes switched back and forth between the two of them. "I am going to sit here, and so are you, until someone tells me the truth. Who wants to start?" The cat jumped up on her lap and started the first of about fifty circles before finally lying down. "I'll know if someone is lying to me."

Finn looked at his watch, and Laurel shook her head. "No way, kid. If I have to, I'll let the air out of your tires and nail the rims to the floor."

Finn looked at Gavin and shrugged his shoulders. "She's *your* girlfriend. *You* tell her."

Laurel's jaw tightened and her head swiveled around to face Gavin. "So there *is* something going on. Thanks for the vote of confidence."

"Thanks, kid," Gavin grumbled. He wanted to add, *Always deny everything*, but thought better of it. He could give Finn life lessons after they were clear of this one. He just shrugged.

"That's it?" She stood up. "Are you sure?"

Gavin had spent enough of his life in a relationship to know when he was being given an ultimatum. He looked at Finn, who was just sitting in his chair, pretending to examine his new tattoo. "Okay. Fine. Sit down," he said in defeat.

"I want to know exactly what you two are up to. You start with some idiotic excuse, and I'm leaving." Laurel remained standing. She crossed her arms and cocked her head.

Finn brightened up. "I thought you said that you were going to sit here until someone told you the truth?"

"Can it, kid." She faced Gavin head-on. "So?"

"Finn didn't hit a submerged log or a rock or some other water hazard." Gavin took a breath and thought about how to word the next sentence that was going to come out of his mouth. All the options sounded idiotic.

"And?"

Finn stepped in. "And it was a goddamned monster that attacked my boat and tried to get me."

Laurel turned to the little boy, her mouth open in a perfect O to protest, and saw Finn's face. It was as serious as an oil portrait; all that was missing were the cracks in the pigment. She turned back to Gavin.

"He's telling the truth," he said.

Laurel sat down.

Gavin was silent for a moment, trying to figure out a way to tell her. He remembered the old adage about the truth being the simplest version of any story. Only problem was, the truth was nowhere near believable. "Finn was attacked by something in the lake. Walt Pinkowski was bitten in half by the same something. We caught a sixty-pound musky yesterday and something swallowed it, tearing off four hundred yards of line and biting through wire leader in the process."

"Can you be more specific than...*something*?" Laurel's expression was the one she reserved for crazy people.

"Isn't *monster* specific enough?" Finn asked, flexing his new tattoo. "How about flesh-eating, limb-munching, boat-smashing, fast-swimming, goddamned monster?"

Laurel sank back into the sofa. "This is for one of your novels, isn't it? It's role-playing or something. Right?"

Gavin scraped at the eggs on his plate. For some reason, he had lost his appetite. "No."

"That's all you can say?" She turned to Finn. "And you had better watch your language, young man! Gavin may have a case of Tourette's syndrome and tattoos, but that doesn't mean that you have to be just like him." Her head swiveled around and her eyes locked on Gavin. "I'm waiting."

Gavin put his plate down on the coffee table. "You know Dr. Parks?"

"We've been friends for years."

"Ask him about Walt Pinkowski's death. Ask him if there was anything unusual about it." Gavin was doing his best not to sound like a lunatic. "You were here when that fuckstick Pope came by—he said that Pinkowski had been torn in half. Hong Kong Phooey didn't come up with that diagnosis himself."

"I thought that Pinkowski had been in some sort of boating accident."

Finn stepped in, his mouth looking black and oily with the burned toast particles floating around on his teeth. "What kind of a boat accident rips a man in half? Think about it. Boats don't rip people in half. Monsters, on the other hand…"

Laurel was trying to digest what they were telling her. "How can you say that it's a monster?"

"Because the thing destroyed my boat and tried to eat me. Got Pinkowski. Turned a trophy musky into a Happy Meal without the fries." Finn was starting to get annoyed that she didn't see the logic.

"What are you two talking about? You're not making any sense."

"That's because you're thinking too hard. I'm thinking with what I've seen, not what I've been told. Hell, if Einstein would have listened to what people told him he never would have invented the lightbulb."

Gavin raised his hand to correct the kid, but realized that it really didn't matter—the point had been made. "Look,"

Gavin offered, "I was there, Laurel. I'm a lot of things but I'm not a liar and I'm not crazy. Finn had a sixty-pound musky on the line and he was reeling it in. All of a sudden, out of I-don't-know-where, something grabbed the fish and ran with it. We chased it for a mile before it bit through a metal leader and dove out of sight. The thing left a wake forty feet long when it surfaced and moved at close to forty miles an hour. We saw it. Sort of. We had trouble keeping up with it. But if you can offer up an explanation that makes any more sense than what we've come up with, knock yourself out."

Finn dropped an empty Coke bottle onto the coffee table with a thud. "And this is a secret."

Laurel stared at the boy for a few seconds. "You think that there is something out on the lake killing people and you're keeping it a secret?" Her voice was icy, distant. "That's not right, Finn. Hell, it's worse than not right, it's criminal."

Finn straightened out in his chair. "If we tell anyone about this, what do you think will happen? They'll send some doofus here who'll dump fifty million gallons of organic pesticide into Caldasac and kill every fish in the goddamned lake! And maybe the monster." Finn slammed his fist into his lap. "*Maybe.*" His face had taken on an expression that Gavin had never seen there before—anger. Tears rimmed Finn's eyes. "This is my goddamned monster and I am going to be the guy that gets it. I am going to get it and I am going to be in the paper and I am going to be famous and when I die no one is going to goddamned forget my name for a long goddamned time!" The tears shook loose and made their way down his cheeks. "People are going to remember that Finn Horn was here and he did something. Something important." His voice trailed off and dropped into a whisper. "Something extraordinary."

Laurel crouched down in front of the boy and took his hands in hers. Finn's eyes stayed locked on his lap and he made no attempt to wipe the tears away. "Finn?" Laurel's voice was soft and maternal. "No one is ever going to forget you."

Finn looked up at her and smiled the saddest smile that Gavin had ever seen. Except for maybe that last one that Chelsea had given him. "Yes, they are." He pushed the back of his hand across his cheek. "Because I'm nobody."

Laurel shook her head. "No, you're not. You're somebody. Somebody important." She paused and Gavin could see her struggling with what she was supposed to say. After a second it came out. "People are going to remember you because you are going to find this monster." She glanced over at Gavin and her tone hardened. "And Gavin is going to be right beside you." There was another pause, this time for a few seconds. "And this is going to be our secret."

Finn looked up and his smile opened up, still black with munched toast. "No shit?" He accentuated his question with a loud sniffle.

"No shit." Laurel smiled back at the boy. "Now blow your nose."

# 49

It was early morning and the lake was sealed in under a thick veil of fog that even the rain was having a hard time penetrating. It was windless and damp and Gavin thought that cataracts might not be all that different than trying to see through the heavy gauze of mist. Finn predicted that by midmorning the fog would burn off and they would be left with the rain. But midmorning was still five hours off, and for now visibility was limited to less than fifteen feet.

Laurel and Gavin stood at the water's edge, her shoulder leaning into his arm, their fingers intertwined. The only sound was the gentle tick of the water lapping at the dock pilings.

"Can you keep this a secret?" Gavin knew that her official capacity as Finn's doctor might bind her to some sort of ethical code.

Her grip on his hand tightened. "I can always plead ignorance or disbelief if this turns sour. I can say that I simply didn't believe you. Besides, I'll call Parks today and the last thing he'll blame Pinkowski's death on would be a monster. I'm covered from that point on. Unless—"

"Unless someone else gets hurt," Gavin finished.

"Yeah." She let out a sigh and leaned her head on his shoulder.

"Thank you for what you did just now. It was…" Gavin searched his vocabulary for the right word.

"Stupid?" Laurel let out.

"I was going for *kind*, but under the circumstances I guess *stupid* works too."

"Yeah, it does. What was I thinking?"

"That this could be the one shot Finn will have to define himself."

"You really think that there's a monster out there, Gavin?"

It was an honest question. "I don't know." He thought about what he had seen. "*Something's* out there. Something that can outrun a boat and has teeth like tungsten carbide razor blades."

Laurel unclasped her fingers and moved away from Gavin, stepping up to the edge of the dock.

"Careful," he said.

"Think I'll get eaten?" She grinned at him over her shoulder, her smile made all the more beautiful by the little extra zing her eyes threw into the mixture.

"No. I don't want you falling through a rotten plank."

"You mean a yunky yoist."

"Yeah, that's what I meant. A yunky yoist."

She balanced on one foot and leaned forward, spread her arms, and stuck her leg out behind her. "Look, perfect balance."

"Nothing scares you, does it?"

She didn't even think about the question. "Not a thing." She stood motionless for a moment, her torso balanced over the water, her leg pointing back at Gavin.

"Nice ass," he said in earnest. Laurel laughed and it cost her the pose and she stumbled sideways. Somehow she landed with her feet firmly planted on the dock. "Thanks a lot, Corlie."

"For what? Ruining your Atlantic City act or for scoping out your behind with immoral intentions?"

"Since you put it that way—" She came back and kissed him on the mouth, the kiss comfortable but still new. "I find your attraction to my ass charming."

"Good. Then stop fucking around or you are going to fall through this dock and you'll break your ass." Gavin touched his toe to a rotten board. "And that wouldn't be good."

"You forget, Corlie, I'm a doctor. As such, I can personally guarantee that it is physically impossible to break you're ass becau—"

There was a loud crack as the board beneath her gave way. She fell forward, grabbing on to Gavin. In an instant they were both off the dock, back on the stone boardwalk.

"That was, um, I, oh boy—" she stammered. "I almost broke my ass."

"Give me a second, I think I had a stroke." He could feel his heart pounding in his chest. "Okay. Okay. First thing Monday Mr. Johannus fixes this thing."

"Honest Injun?"

"Scout's honor."

"Were you ever a Scout?

"Were you ever an Indian?"

"Seriously, I can't picture you as a Scout." She smiled up at him.

"I bought something from them once. Cookies, maybe," he said through a squint.

"Scouts don't sell cookies. Girl Scouts sell cookies. Scouts sell firewood."

"I knew they didn't taste very good. So if I can't say Scout's honor?"

"You can say anything. It's a question of whether or not people will believe you."

"People never believe me. Never. Unless I'm telling them about liposuction fat congealing in the sewer and turning the rats into an army of human-hungry predators. It's the truth that they have trouble with from me. Stuff like the fact that I don't cheat on my taxes. I've only slept with four women in my life. I never—"

"*Four*? Are you kidding me? *Four*?"

Gavin smiled as they ascended the steps. "Sorry. It's five. I was thinking in terms of the old me."

Laurel stopped and stared at him, her mouth open.

Gavin glanced around nervously. "The bugs are out—you better close that thing."

"Five? But you're so...so...I don't know, cavalier about sex. I would have sworn that you've slept with loads of women."

Gavin shook his head. "Sorry to disappoint you, Doc. I'm a romantic at heart. Never slept with a woman I didn't love. Can't. Doesn't interest me."

"Where do they make men like you?" She was shaking her head in disbelief. "I wanna buy stock. Handsome, funny, talented, selective when it comes to sex. Hell, you should come with your own manual."

"I have one. You left out Chapter Fifteen, paragraph three—Monster Hunter."

"No, I didn't. Find that thing first. That'll impress me enough." She squeezed his hand. "You going after *it* today?" She paused, shook her head. "Jesus, listen to me."

Gavin ignored the self-flagellation—he had been through it himself and knew that there was no cure except the sight of a forty-foot wake and a piece of titanium cable cut clean through. "Today's our day off," he repeated with Finn-like enthusiasm.

"Good. Then let's go to bed." She let go of his hand and ran up the steps. "Last one in the sack has to be on the bottom."

Gavin thought about the ballistic possibilities involving her muscular little backside. "I happen to like the bottom." He slowed down.

Out on the lake the fog was starting to lift. In an hour it would be raining again and one of summer's final days would be saying farewell. In other parts of the Adirondacks the cottage crowd, owners and renters who had a year's worth of indoor living in the city crammed into three months of weekend outdoor living in the country, would be packing up their patio lanterns, Adirondack chairs, and canoes and heading back to the city for another nine months of fluorescent lighting, Nautilus machines, and Maalox. But here on Caldasac, there was no weekend crowd, and the leaves would turn from lively greens to bloody reds and bright yellows without much of an audience. Finally, the leaves would say good-bye in one last sigh of brown and then fall to earth to await snow. Old Man Winter would dillydally around his agenda for a while, intermittently sending the mercury down into the thirties before opening up his bag of goodies in earnest, and the big freeze would roll in. Winter would stop everything on Caldasac, even time, and nothing would move for months, the cracking of the trees in the thirty-degree-below-zero weather the only dependable tic of Mother Nature's clock.

Until then, when all of the residents of Caldasac were forced into cryogenic suspended animation, there were things to be done, preparations to be made. Feeding to do.

# 50

Gavin stood at the wheel and squinted into the rain, watching the other boat approach at a head-on bearing. Both were going slow, at trolling speed, and a collision was nearly impossible, but weather like this made people nuts—just look at the Donner party, he thought—and he kept his eyes on the approaching craft. After all, it was the little mistakes that got you killed—things like looking the other way when some cracked-out junkie in a Lincoln Continental decided to jump the curb and roll 3,628 pounds of Detroit iron over your wife when she was on the way back from buying a fistful of daisies.

The vessel was about their size, maybe a ten-foot beam, and blue. There was no cabin but the crisp hump of the Bimini top was decorated with a chrome rod rack, like spikes on a reptile's back. The boat rocked gently as it approached, the captain in no hurry. Gavin checked their bearing and nodded at the sonar. The other boat was trolling the edge of the weed bed where the bottom dropped off as well, in exactly the opposite direction that they were. And he was skirting the deep water.

"What do I do?" he asked Finn.

"Good manners say that you turn to the right. And so does he. Of course you could fire a couple of rounds through his windshield and he'd probably get out of our way. Your call."

Gavin turned the wheel slightly and the boat tacked off by a few degrees, enough that they would miss the oncoming vessel by fifty feet by the time they were parallel.

Gavin watched the craft approach. He had spent a lot of time on the lake and had come to realize that besides their little crazy team of two, not many people fished Caldasac. Finn had mentioned that there had been one man, Frank Knechtel, who had attacked the lake with a vengeance. But Frank was dead now and for some unspoken reason, few people went out on the water here. But the boat chugging toward them had been modified with only one purpose in mind—fishing.

"Finn"—he glanced back at the kid—"check this out."

As the boat drew past, the pilot came out from under the Bimini top and nodded a salute. He was wrapped in a dark green raincoat and matching pants with high orange boots. He lifted his head and a little light managed to dig into the hood and illuminate a pair of perfectly round tinted glasses and a big handlebar mustache befitting a nineteenth-century London dandy. Even under the loose rain gear Gavin could tell that he was a small man, not much bigger than Finn, and visibly wiry. He looked like he belonged behind a bar.

Finn's voice was aimed at a pitch that Gavin would hear but hopefully wouldn't travel across the water. "Check out the Canon downriggers," he said as softly as possible. "Loaded with lead-core line. And look at the pitch of the line into the water. He's deep with those downriggers. Hundred feet no problem. Way too heavy for this lake."

Or not heavy enough, Gavin thought. He nodded at the captain of the other boat and the man nodded back and raised a tall dark beer can in a salute.

The man leaned forward and yelled something that at first Gavin thought had been garbled by the wind and rain. It took a few seconds for his brain to sort out the sound and place the words.

Finn nodded like he understood and waved back, asking under his breath, "What the heck did he say?"

"'Hast seen the white whale?'" Gavin slowly repeated.

"Is he drunk? What does he mean?" Finn scrunched his face up.

Gavin watched the stern of the other craft as it headed away and was soon swallowed by the ugly weather. As the boat slipped out of sight, the line from Melville's opus brought a knot to his stomach.

"It means that he knows."

# 51

Pope rolled the car to a stop in front of Finn Horn's house, put it into Park, and took a swig of vodka to wash down the new blue pills he had picked up from his friend, Dr. Harper, at the hospital. Actually, maybe the word *friend* was a little strong. An acquaintance with a healthy belief in keeping Pope jacked into the zone was closer to the truth. At their first meeting Pope had informed Dr. Harper that he wanted a lifetime prescription for his uppers. After a little gentle persuasion, the doc had agreed to help make the world a brighter place. It was amazing what threatening to put a grandchild's eyes out with a hunting knife could get you. What was it they said? *God is in the details.*

He got out of the car and approached the house. If the planets were smiling down on him, Mary Horn would be alone. He walked up the wheelchair ramp and pressed the buzzer.

The first jolt of the Bennies hit him in the brain and he blinked. One of the cockroaches started to hum up there and his nerves suddenly felt a whole lot more in touch with the world. When he opened them, Mary Horn was staring at him through the screen.

"Mary," he said courteously.

"What can I do for you, Xavier?"

"Am I interrupting you?" Pope wasn't sure if it had been him or the cockroach who had asked. He shook his head.

"Nope. Just got back from work and was going to have a cup of coffee."

"I'm not busting up any sort of a party, am I?" A second insect joined the first, this one right behind his eyes. It started up on a kazoo. "Finn here?"

She pushed the door open and gestured for him to come in. "Nope. Just little old me."

The bugs crawled out of all the corners of his psyche, dragging their instruments with them. As he stepped through the door, the insects started up, belting out chords that were shaking his teeth.

Beautiful.

Badass.

Music.

He followed Finn's mother into the kitchen, the cockroaches belting out a throbbing, pulsing melody that racked his nervous system with ten million watts of power.

He felt like he could destroy the universe.

## 52

The bar was tiny and filthy in a way that the proprietors of establishments in the New York meatpacking district used to pay five-hundred-dollar-an-hour designers a fortune to imitate. But the look wasn't contrived; it was the natural result of fifty years of drunk-sponsored detritus piling up.

The actual bar was a series of fifty-gallon drums that had been welded into a counter. Susie, the barmaid-cum-proprietor, pumped the beer taps as if she were arming crossbows in the midst of battle, the fat of her arms and the meat of her big breasts jiggling with each pull of the lever. Tonight she wore an unusually witty T-shirt that said *Yes, I Swallow* across the front. The fact that the bar was called Black Eyed Susie's had little to do with the fact that the owner was, in fact, named Susan. She was its ninth owner and had changed neither her name nor the bar's—it was simply the happenstance of coincidence that had brought her a bar bearing her name. The original Susie of the establishment hung over the bar—a long, mean musky caught in the 1930s. The fish was frozen in pose, suspended over the dusty bottles of Kahlua and Grand Marnier, her ancient skin tobacco-stained the color of old pennies, straw sticking out of a hole in her side. A New York Yankees cap was perched on the fish's head and a Scotch-taped broken cigar was clamped between needle teeth, yellow but still threatening after nearly eighty years of time served overseeing drunken brawls and jokes punctuated with fart noises.

The dance floor was small and occupied by a woman in a pair of overalls dancing with a black Lab mutt. A few drunks hollered at each other over Lucky Lagers and no one paid any attention to the nine-year-old who was smoking Pall Malls and playing pool, each shot taken from a stool he dragged around the table so he could reach the felt.

A dense weather system of tobacco smoke hung in the air, making it hard to see without squinting. The success of the establishment was directly dependent on the three famous rules of real estate: location, location, location. It was the only bar within thirty miles in any direction, and it couldn't go bankrupt even if Susie had made a concerted effort.

Gavin sat at one of the tables, a few empty beer bottles laid out in front of him. He was waiting for Finn and had stopped worrying about how the boy was going to get into the place when he saw the other kid playing pool. Evidently the drinking age had been lowered since he had moved up here. Why Finn had suggested they have a late supper here was still a mystery.

On the small space designated a stage, a skinny guy with long hair and a Flock of Seagulls T-shirt with a guitar was doing a very poor rendition of BTO's "You Ain't Seen Nothing Yet" to a backup band that came out of a karaoke machine. He sounded like someone who had had music explained to him but had never actually heard any. The homemade banner over his head declared the singer to be Dan the Music Man. Gavin leaned back in his chair and tried not to grimace.

Gavin looked around and saw lenses from a pair of wire-rimmed glasses flash under a neon Pabst Blue Ribbon sign. The lenses were clear, not green, but there was no mistaking the face behind them. It was the fisherman from the other boat—the other monster hunter—staring straight at Gavin.

Gavin found himself marveling at Finn's skill at manipulating the situation. He wondered how much of the golly-gosh-golly routine was practiced and how much was honest.

Gavin lifted his beer in a salute and the other man responded in kind, and this time Gavin recognized the tall black can in his hand as Guinness. The man left his perch against the wall and headed over. For some reason Gavin wished that Finn were already there.

Guinness Man moved like a feral being, his shoulders and hips undulating with the ease of a cat. As he moved, people got out of his way, and Gavin wondered if it was because of the presence he conveyed or the history he had.

Gavin stood to greet Guinness Man, extending his good hand. Guinness Man smiled and his mustache tilted up. As expected, he had a grip that belonged in a circus tent. "How are ya?" he asked, pronouncing it all with a heavy British accent.

Gavin tilted his head to one side. "Liverpool?" he asked.

Guinness Man smiled again and this time his teeth showed through the hedgerow of hair. "I'm impreesed, lad! Yanks think we all sound the same."

Gavin shook his head. "Not me. I've lived in London, the city of neighborhoods." He squinted through the cigarette smoke. "I'm Gavin Corlie."

"Yes, I know. Our resident celebrity. People have been talking about you behind your back since you moved in. I'm Dave Duffy," he said with a big grin, pronouncing it *Doofy*.

Gavin gestured to a chair. "Have a seat."

"Don't mind if I do." Duffy popped into the chair and Gavin noted that the cat comparison was not inaccurate. He took a heavy draft off the can of Guinness then held the can up. "A leftover habit from my misspent youth, nights passed in the poob getting snockered and ending up in right big poonch-ups. Good English beer was thirty P a pint, this Irish

309

slag was twenty-five. It was a decision based on economics and now I can't break the habit." Duffy was closing in on sixty but the visible feline quickness about him was impossible to miss. He smacked his lips in relish. "Some things you never grow tired of." Beneath the loose-fitting white shirt was a sinewy strength. He had probably knocked out more than a few teeth in his time.

Gavin remembered the strong Irish ale that Mickey imported for one client. "You own the antique shop."

Duffy nodded. "'Tis me."

Gavin imagined the man in front of him would be more at home at a soccer game than in a room filled with brown furniture and silver candlesticks. Then again, Gavin had been told that he didn't fit the classic stereotype of a writer.

"You bought the old German place?" Duffy said. It wasn't really a question.

"Isn't everything around here an old German place?"

Duffy's mustache lifted up at the corners, showing a very expressive smile. "Sausage-eaters the lot."

"Ah, the English." Gavin raised his glass again. "At least you didn't call them Jerries."

"Before my time, lad. But this place—" He glanced furtively around the room. "Really is a little Wehrmacht enclave. The town that time passed by." He took another mouthful of the dark ale. "You like living on the old coont-kitty Caldasac?" The open Liverpudlian vowels and heavy consonants added a comedic tinge to his language.

"Great fishing." Gavin examined the man's face, searching for…what the hell *was* he searching for?

There was a commotion by the door and an electric murmur spread through the room. Gavin watched the crowd split and weld back together in the wake of a disturbance that cut through its midst. After a few seconds of peering into the jumble of bodies he spotted the familiar figure of Finn negotiating his way through the bar. The space had not been designed with wheelchairs in mind and the resulting collisions between Finn's chair and the legs, shins, and feet of a dozen drunks was accentuated by a series of curses, which were cut short when they saw who was running into them; even the crowd at Black Eyed Susie's had trouble swearing at a handicapped kid.

"Mr. Duffy"—Gavin leaned forward, his face inches from Duffy's ear—"you are about to meet a very *unusual* person."

Duffy's head swiveled around and even though Gavin couldn't see the expression on his face, he could see by the way his head cocked to one side that the man was taken aback.

Finn wheeled up to the table and dumped a bag of batteries onto the Formica top. "Get me a frigging beer!" the kid hollered at Susan.

Duffy smiled and Gavin laughed. "Hey, Hemingway, aren't you a little young for this place?"

Finn jolted a finger at the nine-year-old playing pool. "I'm old enough to be his father." And for some reason, Gavin noted that he looked it. "Now where's my beer?" Finn yelled at Susan again.

The barmaid nodded back. "Give me a minute, Pops." Evidently this wasn't Finn's first trip to the place.

"Sorry I'm late. I went by Izzy's to make sure he's got the new marine batteries I ordered. Me and Hal will pick them up tonight, I'll leave them in the back, and we'll bring them aboard tomorrow morning." He poked the Ziploc of D-cells with his finger. "Got these for the Maglites on board."

"Whatever you say, Captain." Then Gavin nodded toward Duffy. "I'd like you to meet Mr. Duffy."

Duffy's smile curled his mustache up and he stuck out his hand. "Nice to meet you, lad. Seen you around town before."

Finn eyed Duffy skeptically. "Lad? What the heck is a lad?"

As their palms met, Finn's sleeve pulled up a little.

"Can I see your tats?" Duffy asked.

"Tits? What the he—" Finn straightened up and pulled his arm back for a punch.

"No! No!" Gavin inserted. "Tats. Ink. Tattoos. He wants to see your tattoos. Christ." Gavin buried his face in his hand.

"So why didn't he say that?" Finn turned to Duffy. "Are you from Sweden or something?" He yanked up the loose sweatshirt sleeve, exposing the brightly colored paint on his arm. It had dulled a little and sweat and body oils had built up, giving it a natural look; to the average person, it really did look like a tattoo. "I did it myself," he stated proudly.

"Nice work." Duffy nodded appreciatively.

Just then, Dan the Music Man went into his rendition of Ace Frehley's "Shock Me." Gavin's face went sour and Finn stuck his tongue out. "This music sucks farts."

"Maybe he's having a bad night."

"Actually he's having a pretty good night. You should hear his version of 'Knocking on Heaven's Door.' Whew, stinker city!"

Susan showed up with Finn's drink. "Here's your beer," she said humorlessly, placing a can of Coke on the table. "Shall I put it on your tab?"

Finn stretched his head over the tabletop and slurped loudly through the straw, waving her away. "Yeah, put it on my tab. Thanks."

"Can we put our drinks on your tab?" Duffy asked, winking at Gavin.

Finn shook his head. "I'm the guy who supplies her Wednesday-night perch platters. Six perch and fries for eight bucks. She deducts what I drink off of what I bring in. I average twenty-five cents a perch—gutted and skinned."

"Perch?" Gavin asked over his beer.

"A perch is a fish. Very tasty little fish. I catch them by the dozens and skin them. My mom freezes them in milk cartons and Susie buys them from me for three bucks a container. You wanna try some?" Before Gavin had time to decline, Finn called to Susie. "Can we have two perch platters? My friend here is paying."

Susan nodded unenthusiastically but a little smile crept out. It was obvious that she liked Finn but didn't want anyone to see it; her general disdain for the customers helped her fight off the drunks that wanted to see if her shirt spoke the truth. Thing was, everyone in town knew her husband, Frankie, and steered clear of him. In the old days he had been a cage-fighting champion and he had a reputation for still knowing how to bust it up.

Dan the Music Man was in full swing with "Shock Me." Gavin couldn't decide which was worse, his guitar playing or his singing. The three fishermen lapsed into silence, every now and then one of them casting a sideways glance at one of their tablemates.

"You come here a lot?" Gavin asked Duffy. He was thinking about the big Canon outriggers. There were no fish in Caldasac that needed outriggers.

"When I'm not out fishing." Duffy smiled his big smile while Dan went into a very unsteady solo.

The screech of Dan's guitar had all eyes in the bar swivel in his direction, mostly out of morbid curiosity. For a full minute they watched him, amazed, and when he was done, the bar erupted in cheers and clapping that it was over. Dan, misinterpreting their reaction, bowed. Someone threw an empty beer can that bounced off of his head. More cheers.

Susan came out from behind the bar with two plates piled high with what looked like deep-fried tongues. "Your food's ready," she said with the same bluntness that she had laid on him earlier. Duffy downed the contents of his Guinness and raised it to Susan, who took the empty can away with the understanding that he wanted another.

Finn leaned in. "Saw you fishing on the lake. Heavy gear for perch." Finn held up one of the deep-fried perch fillets and wiggled it as if it were swimming. "Very heavy." He popped the yellow breaded piece of fish into his mouth and munched with exaggerated relish.

"You lads are using heavy trolling reels and tuna sticks. Too big for perch too." Duffy leaned over the table and the feeble light of the red bar candle gave his craggy face the texture of bark. "I believe that this is what one refers to as a Mexican Standoff."

"Is that where you're from?" Finn asked, then opened his hands in a well-I'm-waiting gesture.

Gavin marveled at Finn's natural penchant for salesmanship; the kid was doing a great job of playing it cool. If Gavin squinted through the smoke just right, he was staring at Gene Hackman in *The French Connection*; all that was missing was the crushed porkpie and five o'clock shadow.

Duffy's eyes did a little dance before they settled on the kid's face. His features suddenly softened, became almost childlike as a grin spread across the hard lines. "Finn, you're all right. Sitting here in this dodgy poob, secondhand smoking enoof fags to kill a horse, peeling perch bones, and drinking Coke with high style. You know why I'm out there. Just as I fookin' know why you're out there!" Duffy raised his fresh Guinness and offered up his response as a toast. "Death to the Leviathan!"

**53**

"The bitch ate me doag." Duffy downed his heavy Irish ale in three long drafts that left his mustache skinned with foam.

Finn stiffened. "Doug?"

"Not Doug. *Doag*. Woof. Me doag, lad."

Finn's expression went from confused to sympathy when his brain caught up to his ears. "That's terrible."

"I was thinking the same thing." Duffy ran his tongue over his mustache and the foam disappeared. "He was a good doag."

Gavin and Finn exchanged glances. Gavin turned down the corners of his mouth and nodded. It was time to do a little sharing.

"It tried to kill me." Finn jabbed a greasy finger into his chest. "And now we're after it." He picked up a piece of perch. "You see it?"

Duffy shook his head. "No. I just saw Pete get pulled under. He was wearing a life vest and it took him down."

Finn slapped the table. "Of course. Petey the boxer. Walks around in boots and a coat in the winter. I seen him in the window of your shop! You sell the broken old lamps and junk, right?"

"It's an antique shop, lad. Fine period furnishings and decorative objects. Nothing broken about it."

Finn held up his hand. "Last winter I saw a chair in your window had no fabric on it. No seat. Nothing. Couldn't even sit in it."

Duffy smiled. "That was a George the Third period wing chair. Perfect form, lovely carved Irish feet. Sold it for twenty-two grand to a very nice lady from New York."

"She sounds like a very stupid lady," Finn offered matter-of-factly. "You should talk to Gavin here." Finn jerked a thumb at him. "He spends money like it's on fire. Has a radio that cost as much as a house and it takes fifteen minutes to warm up. I guess you can't buy brains, huh?" Finn lowered his voice conspiratorially. "What's your cut of the heist?"

Duffy raised an eyebrow and glanced at Gavin, who said, "He watches a lot of old movies."

Duffy leaned forward and lowered his voice as Finn had done. "It's simple, little man. I want to kill the fooker that ate me best friend."

Gavin looked around the table at their crew of madmen. The lost tribe of Queequeg was now a going concern. Praise the Lord and pass the ammunition.

He held up his hand for another beer.

# 54

Gavin was halfway between the lucid and the unconscious, slowly slipping under the waves of sleep. He faintly heard the soft rustle of wind through the trees outside and the gentle thrum of the rain on the windowpanes but his mind no longer registered these as individual, distinct sounds, they simply joined the background hum of random almost-sleeping thoughts that were washing through his brain. The cat was snuggled up against his feet, purring loudly. Gavin was aware that he was warm and that he wanted for nothing. To all else, he was oblivious. He finally slipped over the edge into sleep and—

The shrill chirp of the phone jolted him from the embryonic comfort and he snapped up. He picked the cordless receiver up off the cardboard box that was still doing service as a night table and squinted into the dark, trying to make an educated guess at the time. Ten. Maybe ten thirty.

"Yeah?" he asked, a little more hostile than he had intended.

"Gavin, it's Laurel. Mary Horn is dead."

"What?"

"Finn's mother is dead."

Suddenly he was awake, lucid. "What happened?"

"I don't know yet. She was DOA when they checked her body in a few minutes ago. Looks like massive head trauma."

For a second the clinical speech of the doctor overshadowed the person. "The death certificate was signed by the attending physician and we're just waiting for the ME's people to pick up the body."

Gavin stood up in the gloomy near-dark of the room. "Where can I find you?" He looked around for his pants. There was a pair of black leather jeans hanging over the back of the big wing chair by the door. He fumbled into them while cradling the phone between his shoulder and his ear.

"I'm downstairs. Near the ER."

"And Finn?"

"He's in my office. Child Services will be sending someone up."

Gavin wrestled on a flannel shirt Finn had talked him into when they had gone to Walmart. "Keep him there. Do not let anyone take him away!"

"I don't know if I can—"

"Keep him there, goddamnit! Tell them he's in shock. Tell them that he's sick. Tell them that he needs his medication. Tell them he needs to see a doctor. You keep that fucking kid there until I show up, do you understand me?"

"I'll do what I can."

"Keep him there!" Gavin snapped and hung up the phone.

Gavin bounded down the stairs and ran into the kitchen. Hal's number was taped to the fridge and he dialed it as he ran by, heading into the living room. The old man picked up on the first ring, his greeting made up of a loud cough, the sound of spitting, and a "Yep?"

"Hal, it's Gavin Corlie. I need you here right now! It's an emergency." And he hung up before the old man could offer any sort of a protest.

*Okay, calm down*, he told himself. *What do I do?*

There only seemed to be one answer. *Call Harold.*

The curt professional voice of the call-service reception-ist came on the line. "Harold Lexman's Service. How may I help you." Gavin didn't recognize her voice—new girl.

"I need to speak to Harold Lexman right now. This is an emergency."

"I'm sorry, Mr. Lexman is away until the third and—"

"What's your name?"

"This is Suki. I'd be—"

"Suki, this is Gavin Corlie. This is an emergency. I need to speak to Harold right now. I don't care where he is, what he's doing, or how angry you think he's going to be. Please find him."

"Mr. Corlie, I apologize. Please give me a minute. Don't hang up." There was a click and the soulful strains of Schubert piped over the line from New York.

Gavin stopped in the living room and concentrated on breathing. After what felt like an hour but probably clocked in at under two minutes, his lawyer's voice snapped on. "Gavin, Harold, what do you need?" Harold Lexman had been Gavin's main lawyer for the past twenty years, his firm handling every last piece of paperwork that publishers, studios, publicists, and merchandising companies pushed across the table. Virtually owning his own law firm meant that Gavin handed a small fortune over to Lexman, Grizwacs, and Steiner every quarter.

"I need a lawyer here now, Harold."

"Take a breath and tell me what's going on." Harold's voice, always even and deliberate, instantly calmed Gavin.

"Okay. I need someone to hold off Child Services and represent the interests of a thirteen-year-old boy."

There was a second of hesitation. Obviously, Harold had not been expecting this line of approach. "Tell me what's going on."

"A friend of mine—a kid I've been fishing with—he's thir-teen. Name is Finn Horn."

"Aha," Harold said and Gavin knew that he was taking down some of the conversation with his signature monstrous gold fountain pen. "F-I-N-N...H-O-R-N?"

"Yes. The kid's father is dead and his mother died tonight. I don't want the state getting their hands on him and slapping him under some social worker's wing. I don't—"

"That's their job, Gavin. They—"

"I don't give a fuck!" he snapped into the phone and instantly regretted it. "Harold..." Gavin paused and collected himself. "I'm sorry about that. This boy is a friend of mine. If there's a relative that has a claim on him, fine, but Finn has a say-so before he's handed over to anyone. He's sick. Cancer. I don't want him ending up someplace..." He searched his mind for the right word. "Bad, I guess."

Harold would not care about Gavin's motive in a professional sense, all he wanted was to obtain desirable results for his client. In a personal sense, however, Harold very much cared about his well-being. Gavin had come to him when he and Max Steiner had first opened their two-man firm on Flatbush Avenue in Brooklyn. Gavin had just received an offer from Blacktree Books and he needed advice. Having Gavin as a client was one of the reasons they had gone from a third-floor walk-up in Brooklyn to glorious digs on Park Avenue. "Max Steiner and Carl Bergman would be the people for this. Do you have the name of someone we can contact?"

"Like who?"

"Where is the boy now?" Harold asked.

"He's at the hospital with a doctor I know. Dr. Jennifer Laurel. Malone General Hospital, Malone, New York."

"Got it. What town does the boy live in?"

"New Mannheim. Lake Road."

"Any siblings?" Harold asked, his furious writing an audible scratching in the background.

"No, I don't think so."

"Same cell number?" Harold asked.

"I got rid of my cell."

"You're kidding."

"Nope. Wouldn't work most of the places up here anyway."

"Jesus. Okay, call my BlackBerry every fifteen minutes to let me know where you are and to answer any questions I might have. Are you on the way to the hospital now?"

"Yes. Dr. Laurel has an office there—tell them to page her no matter what. I don't have the number."

"I do. How important is this?"

"Do whatever you have to. Anything. Understood?" Gavin asked.

"Go. I'll take care of this right now. Call me as soon as you get any more information."

"Thanks, Harold."

Harold had already hung up.

Outside, the rain was coming down. Gavin thought about Finn, about his mother, and the comfortable old feel of sadness warmed up his stomach. What was wrong out here? His eyes swept the lake and the water looked as if it were alive, black and unhappy about something.

And growing fatter with the people it consumed.

The screech of Hal's ancient truck careening down the driveway momentarily pulled Gavin's thoughts away from the monster. As the word sounded off in his mind, he shook his head. *Monster*. There was no such thing as a monster.

Only that wasn't entirely true now, was it? Not by a country-fucking-mile. There were plenty of things out here in gross exception to the norms of the ecosystem, weren't there? Monsters all over the fucking place.

You only had to look in the right places to find them.

# 55

Gavin blew through the hospital entrance and saw Laurel sitting in a bank of vinyl-covered chairs that matched the sci-fi look of the information console. Her back was straight, her legs out from her hips at a perfect ninety-degree angle thanks to the lift of her heels. Her head was back, resting on the custard wall, and her eyes were closed, jagged black hair brushed back from her face. She stroked Finn's shock of dark hair as he lay with his head in her lap, his body up on the chairs at an awkward angle. He was under a lavender hospital blanket, belly rising with the deep breaths of sleep. He was tethered to his wheelchair by his catheter, the surgical tubing hanging limp and full between the boy and his substitute legs. When Gavin approached, Laurel opened her eyes and lifted her head.

She had spent some time crying and her mascara had been reduced to a thin black line beneath her lashes. Her lipstick and eye shadow were long gone. Tears welled up in her eyes as Gavin sat down quietly beside her.

"What happened?" he whispered.

She shook her head and put her palm over Finn's ear. "He found her at home. It looks like she fell in the kitchen and hit her head on the counter. It was horrible." Laurel looked away and the movement pulled her tears to the corners of her eyes where they spilled out and slid down her cheeks. She wiped them away with a sleeve.

"How's Finn doing?"

She shrugged. "I don't know."

"Fuck."

"Yeah," Laurel sighed. "Double fuck."

"What now?" Gavin stared down at the rubber tube connecting Finn to his wheelchair.

"From what I can gather, Child Services will be sending someone over to collect him."

Collect? This wasn't a stray dog, it was a child.

They didn't talk. They just sat staring at the ugly linoleum and listening to Finn's breathing.

After what could have been an hour or a day or a week, the shadow of a flying saucer blanked out their laps and Gavin looked up to see the specter of Sheriff Pope towering over them, his big Stetson darkening his face.

"Mr. Corlie, Dr. Laurel." He nodded. "I thought you should know that I'll be watching little Finn here for a while. I spoke to Child Services and they seem fine with the idea. It'll only be for a few days and—"

Gavin stood up and stared the big cop down. "No fucking way. Finn's staying with me."

With the elevated volume in the conversation, Finn's eyes fluttered open and he started to hoist himself up on his arms.

Pope took a step back and pulled out the creepy sneer he used as a smile. "Mr. Corlie, I don't think that you understand what's going on here."

Gavin stepped toward Pope. "Pope, I understand *exactly* what's going on here. You, on the other hand, seem to be a little foggy. Finn is not going anywhere with you. You need to be appointed by the court and as far as I know, that hasn't happened yet."

Finn lifted the arm on his wheelchair and transferred himself, making sure that the catheter tube didn't get pinched in the process.

Pope's smirk widened. "Actually, I've got the authority to appoint myself in a situation like this. I personally spoke to Martin Lafferty at Child Services and he had no problem with the idea. I've got the fax right here." He reached into his black leather jacket and extracted a paper from the inside pocket. "Well, looky here." He held it up. "This is a faxed writ of custody. The original is sitting in the county courthouse and you can view it on Monday morning. Until then, you'll have to take my word that this document is valid."

Gavin was having trouble seeing anything but Pope's mouth sneering at him. "No. Sorry. That's not gonna happen."

By now Finn had strapped himself into the chair. "Gavin, don't get in trouble because of me."

A small crowd had gathered at the end of the hall, near the entrance, and were intently watching the exchange between the sheriff and the angry man.

Gavin shook his head. "The only one getting in trouble here is Sheriff Pope."

Pope backed up again and theatrically put his hand on the holster of his sidearm. "Mr. Corlie, I have a legal writ in my hand granting me temporary custody of this boy. I am also an officer of the law. Should this situation get out of control, I have the authority to end it in the most expedient manner possible." He opened the snap on his holster. "Do you get me?"

The muscles in Gavin's jaw shone through his skin like live wires as he felt the rage rise. Something flashed behind the big cop's eyes, like an insect crawling over a lightbulb. Then it was gone. Gavin opened his mouth to speak just as two men raced into the lobby and split the crowd near the revolving door. They headed straight for Gavin and Pope.

They looked like corporate clones from the head office of a big corporation. One was maybe fifty-five and well over six feet, five inches in height. He had a thick swatch of red hair that was combed perfectly. The other one, although an easy six feet himself, looked small beside his companion and was probably fifteen years younger. In direct contrast to his companion's thick head of hair, he was finishing up the tail end of a relationship with male pattern baldness. Both men carried briefcases.

"Sheriff Pope?" the younger one asked, approaching the conversation.

Pope's eyes swiveled in their sockets. His hand stayed on his pistol. "That's me." It was said with authority.

"I'm Vladimir Evanof and this is Frank Woolner."

"Well, Mr. Woolner and Mr. Vladinof, I'm a little busy at present. If you'd like to have a seat, I'll be with you shortly." Pope's eyes went back to Gavin and his smirk spread a little wider.

"It's Evanof, not Vladinof," the big redhead said.

"Whatever."

The big guy let out a sigh. "Sheriff Pope, I'm afraid that I haven't been clear. It's *Special Agents* Evanof and Woolner. We're with the FBI. May we have a word with you in private?"

Pope stared silently at Gavin.

"I'm not asking," Evanof said firmly.

The machinery behind Pope's eyes was telling him that he was outranked. He snapped the clip over the .45 and turned to the two men. "What the fuck do you two want?"

"Would you like to step over here?"

"No, but I *would* like you to tell me what the fuck you two want."

With the appearance of the two FBI men the crowd seemed to bulge, as if everyone in the hospital were bottlenecking at the entrance, like kids gathering around a schoolyard fight.

Evanof held out a sheaf of paper. "This is not our regular duty, we did this as a personal favor to the governor. This is a writ granting temporary custody of one Finnegan Cornelius Horn to Gavin Whitaker Corlie."

"What!" Pope's mouth actually fell open with the word.

"It's Finn!" the boy said from his chair.

"As I said, this is not what we do. We were the only two agents in the nearby area—we were on our way to Massena on unrelated business and were rerouted here as a special favor to Governor Marlowe. Apparently the court for this jurisdiction is unreachable after regular business hours." He pushed the paper into Pope's hand. "For some reason we were asked to give that paper directly to you. Before you get all bent out of shape and start calling Judge Kneutzel over in Malone, let me explain, in detail, how this writ works. It supersedes the writ that Martin Lafferty at Child Services granted you. It supersedes any order you may get from a judge in this area. It supersedes any writ you could possibly get from *any* official in *any* jurisdiction in the United States of America. That writ is signed by the president of the United States and would need an act of the Supreme Court to be lifted. We also have a copy of Mr. Lafferty's orders to rescind the writ he granted you as no challenge to our writ." Evanof pulled another paper out of his pocket. "This," he said, handing a second sheet of paper over to Pope. "Would be that document."

Pope read both papers, his eyes doing a nervous dance across the words. The angry machinery behind his eyes was burning orange and his hands started to shake. Every muscle in his body tensed and for a brief instant he looked as if he were going to rupture.

And then.

As if a switch were flipped.

He smiled.

The big mean dope-fueled cop smiled a smile that was supposed to make everyone relax. It was kind. It was understanding. It was warm.

And everyone knew that it was fake.

"I'm sorry, Special Agents Evanof and Woolner. Little Finn's mother here was a good woman and I'm just not feeling all that great right now. I suppose my instinct to protect little Finn here was making me a bit touchy. I think that Mr. Corlie might be more up to the job than me right now." Sheriff Pope filed the papers into his pocket and nodded a good-bye to everyone present. "Take care. If any of you need anything, let me know."

Pope turned and walked out of the hospital, the crowd splitting before his prow.

Evanof turned to Gavin. "Mr. Corlie?"

Gavin nodded. "Yeah."

"Here are your copies of the writ."

Gavin stared at them in disbelief. "How the hell did Harold manage this?"

"We were about ten minutes from here when we got a call from the bureau directing us to act on behalf of the Office of the President. They faxed the writ to our car and we headed here. The writ is actually signed by the president and authorized by Chief Justice Alan Schwartzman of the Supreme Court as both legal and constitutional."

Laurel slapped him on the arm. "The president? You know the president?"

Gavin smiled uncomfortably. "A little."

Evanof and Woolner smiled as if they were both running off the same CPU. "We're off, Mr. Corlie. We hope this turns out for you, sir. I'm glad we were able to help out."

The two agents left as quickly as they had come, easily slipping through the gash in the crowd left in Pope's wake.

Gavin looked down at Finn. "Cornelius?" he asked.

"Oh shut up!" the boy snapped.

# 56

"After eating at Black Eyed Susie's with you and Mr. Sweden, Hal dropped me off at home about eight thirty, and Mom didn't open the door. I thought maybe she—um—went to the Price Chopper. It's Friday and she gets me Pop-Tarts on Fridays and I know that we didn't have any last night so I thought that maybe—um—maybe she went to get them 'cause we didn't have any and I, I, I—"

Finn sagged in his chair, his black hair glowing blue in the light of the fire. His shoulders jolted as he cried, and no sound left his body.

"Come here, Finn," Gavin said, and picked the boy up out of his wheelchair, being careful not to snag the catheter tube. "Crying works for me, too."

Gavin sank into the sofa with Finn in his lap. Gavin stared at the fire, cradling the crying boy, and for the first time in a very long while felt like he understood a little about what was going on inside someone else.

The rain had come back now and was beating into the glass wall of windows that looked out at the lake. The forecast said that things were going to get worse before they got better, and that high winds were a definite. The big fire was roaring orange and the room danced with the usual eerie shadows of a nocturnal fall storm. The background noise was the clinking of pots and the sliding of plates that Laurel was producing in the kitchen. Foots, for whatever reason, was conspicuously absent, no doubt farting up one of the other rooms in the house.

After a solid half hour the boy's crying stopped. Eventually, and with great effort, he pushed himself up and fought into a sitting position, the big plaid throw Gavin had lain over him twisted and knotted around his legs.

"I'm hungry."

"Good." *Ah*, he thought, *progress*. "What would you like? I've got all kinds of gross combinations in the kitchen. How about a nice juicy aardvark snout with marmalade on burned rye." It was the best version of humor he could do right now.

Finn actually smiled, and he laughed, snot bursting from his nose. "Sobby," he said, burying his nose in his sleeve. Somewhere outside lightning cracked and the room fired white with the flash.

Gavin handed over a Kleenex. "So?"

"I'd love a bologna and mustard on burnt white bread with bananas and mayo. You got onions?"

Gavin did a quick mental inventory of the delivery from Mickey's Mercantile the day before. "Yeah. Sure. Big Spanish suckers."

"The kind that make you cry when you slice 'em? I love those! You get 'em from Mickey's? She grows her own— they're great. The Price Chopper's got the Chinese onions and I don't eat nothing Chinese. They don't care about pesticide in baby food, they ain't getting my business."

"You've got to stop with the lazy language. *Ain't*s and *them*s don't work."

"Ah." Finn nodded with finality. "The rules have started."

"Look, I don't know if this is the best time to talk about this or the worst time. We're friends, Finn. Hell, we're *best* friends. At least, you're the best friend I've ever been lucky enough to have. And best friends don't make rules for one another. They don't need to. Because they love and respect each other. The only rule here is that you decide how to behave according to how you think you should. If you're not sure about something, ask. Otherwise, this is as much your home as it is mine. All right?"

Finn pursed his lips and nodded, somehow managing to look like a sixty-five-year-old man. "You don't know much about kids, do you?"

"To paraphrase Charlton Heston: *You're no kid, you're a three-hundred-year-old midget.*" Gavin handed Finn another Kleenex. "I'll be in the kitchen if you need me."

"How's he doing?" Laurel asked as Gavin came into the kitchen.

"I don't know. In shock, I guess. He seems fine. And like he's got a broken heart all at the same time." *Or are we talking about us?* the little inside voice asked.

"I can't believe this happened. Or that he's here." Laurel peeked out the kitchen door and watched Finn for a few seconds. "How does this stuff happen, Gav?"

He shook his head. "You're the doctor, you tell me." He took in a deep breath, pushed it down into his stomach, and let it out in a long groan. "Let's talk about something else. *Anything* else."

Laurel stared at him for a moment, then asked, "Okay. Tell me how you know the president?" She came back and leaned against the counter on her elbows. The white cotton T-shirt pulled taut across her chest and the dark architecture of her nipples interrupted the clean line of her body.

"It's not very interesting."

Laurel crossed her arms. "I don't care."

"I've had an unlisted number for years but somehow the nuts always manage to find it. Well, one Friday afternoon I'm sitting at home, playing Return to Castle Wolfenstein or one of the other nine hundred games I play when I don't feel like writing but don't want to leave the Mac in case I have an idea, and the phone rings. Guy on the other end says that he's the president. I tell him to go fuck himself and hang up. He *did* sound like the president, but to be fair, so does that guy on SNL. A minute later he calls back and says that he really *is* the president so I recommend that he *really* go fuck himself. Ten minutes later my apartment is littered with a platoon of Secret Service agents flashing their badges and being just as nice as pie to get my attention. Turns out that the president's daughter, Jenny, is a big fan of my work. He wanted to know if I would like to join them at the Plaza for a private dinner. As a party favor, I sat down and wrote a short story for his daughter—just a quick little ten-pager that I didn't even have time to edit. He was a gracious and interested host. We stayed up late talking and when I was about three grand into two-hundred-bucks-a-snifter Louis Treize he told me that he thought the story I had written for his daughter was a thoughtful thing to do. He said if I ever need a legal favor that he could do, to just let him know."

"So you called him tonight after we spoke?"

Gavin shook his head. "Actually, I had forgotten that I had ever met the president until the J. Edgar Hoover brothers pulled out that writ tonight. After you called me, I called my lawyer. I've learned that most arguments are won by the guy who throws the first punch—and you have to let it fly while the other guy is still stammering *Oh, yeah!* I called Harold and *he* doesn't forget *anything.* I'm still a little in shock myself." He opened the fridge and pulled out the ingredients for Finn's sandwich. "Onions?"

She pointed, her index finger a divining rod for onion seekers. "On top of the fridge—big bowl."

Gavin dropped two slices of bread into the toaster. "Where's the eleven button on this thing? Four hundred bucks and it won't do what I…ah, here we go. Carbonite.

Perfect." After setting the toaster to cinder mode, he reached up and fumbled one of the onions off of the fridge. "Nice bowl," he said.

"It was in your cupboard. It's probably for nuts." She paused and a frown darkened her features. "Speaking of nuts."

Gavin knew what she was thinking before she said it. "Pope?" he asked.

"I thought he was going to shoot you right there in the hospital."

"Well, if there's one place I wouldn't mind being shot, it's in the hospital." He took a big butcher's knife and lopped a quarter-inch slice off the onion. Outside the wind shifted direction and the rain hammered against the kitchen window.

"Did you see that about-face of his? Gavin, I've seen some troubling people in my life, but he takes it to a whole new level."

He wondered what would have happened if the two agents hadn't shown up when they did. He felt like he had been someone else. A character in one of his novels, maybe. But he didn't want Laurel to know how much Pope worried him. "The guy has a tough job to do. Half the time he's doing the night shift and pulling over drunk drivers on the country roads. And most of the people he tickets are locals, people he has to shop with and eat with and say hello to on the street. Talk about negative interaction with the community. He doesn't have an easy job."

"I thought you hated the guy."

Gavin shrugged. "He's of a type. I can't stomach anyone who wakes up in the morning with the philosophy of *Who can I catch today?* It's antithetical to who I am. But someone has to do what he does, why not him?"

"Gavin Corlie, not only are you talented, you're logical as well. I love that."

"Talented? You haven't read anything I've ever written." There was a flash and the nearby rumble of thunder rolled over the house, rattling the dishes in the cupboards.

"Wrong!" she spurted, and reached into the battered leather US Mail bag she used as a purse. The noise she made as she dug through the contents sounded like she traveled with a hubcap collection. After more fiddling than could possibly be called for, her hand came out with a paperback of *Ironmonger*. "I got this at Mickey's."

Gavin saw it and smiled, remembering Mickey's take on the book. "You like it?"

"I wasn't able to put it down." Laurel said with a huge grin. "You really are talented. Don't you know that?"

Gavin thought about it for a second. Chelsea had been his biggest fan when all they had to talk about was his writing. Once *Ironmonger* had sold, and money was no longer an issue for them, they had started talking about other things; things like jewelry and vacations and clothes. And kids. Once there was a paycheck to prop him up instead of her lonely cheering, she wanted children. She thought it was time to have a family. Gavin didn't. Eventually, like sand running out of a hole in a bag, her enthusiasm had waned and she had just slipped away. "I make money. But so does Paris Hilton. The two have nothing to do with one another." As soon as he said it he knew that it was a load of crap. He believed in his work. He always had. This was defeatist dialogue—the kind that came from a writer who was afraid to do what he had been built to do.

"Where do you come from?"

"Brooklyn."

"Were you born in a pod or do you have parents like the rest of us?"

"Ah, the biography portion of the program." Gavin thought about the Internet, thought about how it had taken whatever privacy he had managed to keep and blown it all to bits. Better she got the truth than Wikipedia's fan-driven fantasy version. "I grew up in a poor Irish neighborhood where the guys still have red hair and wear green overalls and you see kids playing outside in their diapers and the women have black eyes they don't bother covering with makeup. My dad worked in a bank, drank a little too much. So did my mom. Good people and I don't have horror stories about being beaten when I was a kid unless I deserved it. And I deserved it more than I got.

"Sold my first magazine article to *Vinyl Magazine* when I was sixteen and haven't stopped since. Nineteen novels as Gavin Corlie, America's heir-apparent to the horror genre, seven film adaptations—all bad, three children's books as Thelonious Helonious, and a five-part sci-fi series called *Black Earth* as—"

"Jonathan Carlyle! You wrote that? It was fabulous. Only time in my life I was able to force myself to spend money on hardcovers."

"I'm glad the book-buying public at large doesn't think like you."

Laurel's grin spread wider. "I can't believe you wrote *Black Earth*. Wow. Who was the guy on the dust jacket?"

The toast popped. Gavin held a piece up and was reminded of a smoking tire. Perfect. He squeezed out the mustard and laid down the bologna. "His name's Mike Dimchuck. I met him at a chess club up in Harlem. Private guy and he liked the idea. I think the books help him get laid."

"Chess club? You play chess?"

Gavin shrugged. "A little." The storm had picked up in earnest and the earth itself seemed to be under attack. "I hope a tree doesn't fall on the place."

"This place?" Laurel asked. "You couldn't hurt this place with dynamite. They don't build them like this anymore." As if to illustrate her point, a branch bounced off the window and she jumped. "You play chess a lot?"

Gavin went to work slicing a banana. "I used to," he said, wanting to add the word *before*. "Not so much now. I used to go to the Harlem club every Wednesday night. I liked the uptown trek on the subway, and there's a great little Jamaican place on the corner of St. Nicholas and Hundred and Forty-Fifth that make the best goat rotis I've ever had. I usually walk from there. It's open-table night on Wednesday so the hardcore players stay away. You'd be surprised how much time a writer spends locked up with his own thoughts. I have to schedule activities for myself or I just sit in my office in front of the computer until I realize that it's a different season or I've run out of food or I have a three-foot beard." He smeared a dollop of mayonnaise on the charcoal bread, laid down the banana slices, pressed on the cross-section of onion, and flipped the bologna-and-mustard half. He pressed down and a brittle corner snapped but stayed glued in place by the ooze of condiments. He held up the creation. "What do you think?"

"I think that you and Finn were made for one another."

Gavin put the sandwich on a plate, grabbed a Coke from the fridge, and headed out into the living room. "Come join me trying to act all normal. I don't know what to say to the kid."

"And I do?" she asked.

Finn was still watching the fire. "It's really coming down out there," he said to no one in particular.

Gavin handed him the sandwich and flopped onto the sofa. "Why is the weather always like this here?"

Finn absentmindedly took a big bite out of the sandwich. "We're in the mountains. The storms get stuck between the peaks and get funneled through here. It'll be like this until March." Finn drifted off into his thoughts for a few seconds.

"We'll have to get some of my things. I don't have any underwear or anything."

"Tomorrow morning, Finn. I'll have Hal drive us out to your place."

The boy shook his head. "Tomorrow *night*. In the morning we're fishing."

"Agreed."

Laurel came in with a tray piled with some canned smoked oysters, crackers, a few hard cheeses, and two steaming cups of coffee. "Mind if I join you two?"

Gavin patted the seat beside him. "Plenty of space, Doc."

She sat down, handing a coffee to Gavin. "Somebody tell me a story," she said, and all eyes turned to Gavin.

His gaze shifted from her, to Finn, then back. "Why me?"

"All my stories are about fishing," Finn pointed out.

"I can barely write a grocery list," Laurel said defensively.

"Yeah, and no one else can read it, either," Finn asserted. "Besides, aren't *you* supposed to be some kind of an expert?" he asked Gavin.

Gavin took a sip of the coffee and nestled back into the sofa. "All right. Let's go old-school here." He took a breath and began. "It was a night not dissimilar to this one. In fact, it was a night *exactly* like this one. The rain was coming down like a screaming beast on a mission from hell…"

\*\*\*

Outside, Sheriff Xavier Pope watched the warm domestic setting as the storm raged around him. The rattle of rain that thrummed down on the protective plastic cover on his hat offset the screeching of the angry cockroaches that filled his mind. He was furiously masturbating as the insects cheered him on. He closed his eyes and focused on the theater inside his mind, the seats filled with chattering bugs.

# SAVE $0.50 Off any Nestlé Aero® Big Bubble Bar (95g–105g)

**Expiry Date: December 31, 2014**
**Date limite : le 31 décembre 2014**

# ÉCONOMISEZ 0.50 $ à l'achat de toute grande barre aux bulles Nestlé Aero® (de 95 g à 105 g)

**TO THE CONSUMER:** Coupon void if altered, transferred, copied or reproduced without the consent of Nestlé Canada Inc.

**TO THE DEALER:** Upon presentation of this coupon by your customer towards the purchase of the specified product, we will reimburse the face value of coupon plus regular handling fee. Application for redemption on any other basis may constitute fraud. Invoices showing purchases of sufficient stock (in the previous 90 days) to cover all coupons submitted for redemption must be presented on request. Failure to do so will, at our option, void those coupons. Coupons will not be honoured and will be void if presented through outside agencies, brokers and others who are not retail distributors of our merchandise unless specifically authorized by us to present coupons for redemption. No reproductions or photocopies of original coupon will be accepted. When submitted for redemption, this coupon becomes our property. Cash value 1/10¢. A reduction in any applicable taxes payable is included in the coupon face value. For redemption, mail to Nestlé, P.O. Box 3000, Saint John, New Brunswick E2L 4L3. Trademarks used under license by Nestlé Canada Inc. **Valid only in Canada. Not valid with any other offer. Limit one (1) coupon per customer. Good only on product sizes and varieties indicated.**

**AU CONSOMMATEUR :** Ce coupon sera nul s'il est modifié, transféré, copié ou reproduit sans le consentement de Nestlé Canada Inc.

**AU DÉTAILLANT :** Si votre client présente ce coupon à l'achat du produit spécifié, nous vous rembourserons la valeur nominale du coupon plus l'allocation de manutention habituelle. Toute demande de remboursement non conforme peut constituer une fraude. Vous devez être en mesure de fournir, sur demande, des factures prouvant l'achat (dans les 90 jours précédents) d'une quantité de marchandise suffisante pour couvrir tous les coupons soumis pour remboursement. L'impossibilité de fournir ces factures nous donnera le droit d'annuler ces coupons. Les coupons sont nuls et non avenus s'ils sont présentés par l'intermédiaire d'agences extérieures, de courtiers ou d'autres personnes qui ne sont pas des distributeurs au détail de nos produits, à moins que nous ne les ayons dûment autorisés à présenter des coupons pour remboursement. Aucune reproduction ou photocopie du coupon original ne sera acceptée. Chaque coupon soumis devient notre propriété. Valeur de rachat 1/10 ¢. Une réduction sur toutes les taxes applicables est comprise dans la valeur nominale du coupon. Pour remboursement, postez à Nestlé, C.P. 3000, Saint John (Nouveau-Brunswick) E2L 4L3. Les marques de commerce sont utilisées sous licence par Nestlé Canada Inc. **Offre valable au Canada seulement. Ne peut être combiné avec aucune autre offre. Limite de un (1) coupon par client. Valable seulement pour les formats et variétés indiqués.**

715C-1401E-02AE

1 0 0 3 8 6 4 8

On the screen, playing in an endless loop, was the film of him hammering Mary Horn's skull against the counter and the top of her head popping off, brains puking out in a placenta of pinkish-gray cantaloupe seeds. The cockroaches let out a whoop each time the gelatinous glob of her mind spurted across the Formica. This was the best thing they had ever seen. They hollered. They danced in the aisles. Hell, some of them even threw popcorn. This was just the best old time any of those little fuckers could remember.

His orgasm ruptured and he shot into the wet grass with a loud groan.

The cockroaches gasped along with him.

Then blinked out.

# 57

It was in between evening and night and they were slowly making their way back to shore. Finn piloted while Gavin leaned against the console, watching the sky above their bow fade from a marmalade orange to dark eggplant.

They were talking aimlessly, letting the conversation drift back and forth from one meaningless topic to the next. Finn seemed to be handling his mother's death a lot better than Gavin would have guessed; when he compared the boy's acceptance of tragedy to his own, he found the difference almost embarrassing. Finn had insisted on coming out, on sticking to their routine, but Gavin could see the sadness in his eyes. He found himself making too much of a conscious effort to keep their topics light and lively and every now and then the conversation lulled into dead air and Gavin realized that they were both trying not to talk about the same elephant in the room.

Finn's face scrunched into that special look he took on whenever he was trying to be social. "You're a writer. Let me ask you, what's your favorite book? I don't mean one you *had* to read. I mean one you *wanted* to read."

Gavin smiled, looked at the boy. "Easy. *Huckleberry Finn.*"

"If it's such a great book, how come they haven't made a movie out of it?"

"They did. Quite a few."

"Well, I certainly never heard of one. Probably some old movie so crappy even I wouldn't watch it. Black-and-white. No special effects. No CGI robots. Does it have dragons? I love dragons. No?"

"No."

"Then forget it."

"Finn, that book is everything writing is supposed to be about. It's the modern *Iliad*. Our time's *Odyssey*. If you get to read one book before you die, make it *Huckleberry Finn*."

"Stupid title."

"Would you like it better if it was called Finnegan Cornelius?"

"Shut up."

"Okay, so what's *your* favorite book?"

"*Fishing Secrets of the Expe—*"

"Fishing books don't count."

"Says you," Finn said, and squinted into the halo of the sun that was dropping behind the trees to the east. He snapped his fingers. "*The Zombie Survival Guide*."

"*The Zombie Survival Guide*?" Gavin shook his head sadly, unable to hide his grin of approval. "I have to know—what's rule number one in *The Zombie Survival Guide*?"

"No rules. *Tips*! It's full of useful zombie-fighting *tips*. Like did you know that a crowbar makes a much better weapon in a pinch because it doesn't need reloading? And it helps with B-and-Es when you're searching for spam and candy bars in abandoned towns. What's wrong with you, don't you read your own stuff?" He took a loud slurp off the top of his Coke and smacked his lips in relish. "The geezer who invented this stuff should get the Nobel Prize for greatness."

"He sold the idea for less than a thousand dollars."

Finn's face twisted into a vision of horror. "But it's so good!"

"Coming up with a viable product and having the brains to market it are—" Gavin stopped in midsentence and pointed astern. "What the hell is *that*?"

Finn swiveled around, one of his hands still on the wheel. Two hundred yards off the back of the boat, the water boiled with black shadows. The shadows advanced.

"Fish running," Finn said, and his eyes narrowed. "Big fish."

The school was moving fast, coming right for them, the water alive with their frantic plight.

"I've seen baitfish do this in the shallows. Shiners, shad, even suckers if they get spooked by a big fish. But this—"

The roiling patch of water was a hundred yards across and had closed in on them. Both Gavin and Finn stared as hundreds of fish, long flashing spears of green and black, rolled out of the water, obviously to get somewhere in a hurry. Or maybe away from something.

"Garpike!" Finn said, awestruck. "Look at them! Some of these have to be in the twenty-pound class."

The swarming tempest of water moved right by them and for an instant *The Low Rider* was in the midst of a boiling, frothing sea of jumping, running fish.

A ten-pounder cleared the transom and landed in the boat. It hit the side of the cooler with a thud and thrashed around on the floor.

And for an instant the sides of the boat were pounded with frantic fish slamming into it, their meteor shower of noise jarring the fiberglass with each thud.

"Holy shit!" Finn yelled above the din of the impacts. "They're terrified of something!"

Another garpike bounced off the railing and cartwheeled into Finn's lap. Finn scooped the fish up and chucked it overboard. "It's raining fish!"

To Gavin the whole thing had a taste of the Old Testament about it. He stared, waiting for the sky to open up and fire to start raining down on their heads.

The staccato of noise was almost deafening and neither one of them said anything—they just stared as the frantic fish pounded by, bouncing off the boat, jumping clear of the water, splashing all around them.

Then it was over. The churning school of garpike had vanished and all that was left to mark their passing was the lone fish thrashing around on the deck.

"Kick that thing overboard," Finn said, his voice wobbly.

"A fish stampede. Now I've seen everything." Gavin took the safety oar and flipped the creature over the side. "You ever see anything like that?" he asked the boy.

"Nobody's ever seen anything like that," he said quietly.

# 58

There was a break in the harsh weather of the past week and for a little while the world looked like a place you wouldn't mind living in again. Pope pulled into the dirt driveway and threw the shift into Park. He got out and automatically put on the big Stetson. He walked up to the house, opened the door with a key he had taken the day before, and stepped into the Horn home.

As on his first visit, he was both surprised and grateful that the place didn't smell like piss. He closed the door, set his hat on the hook by the closet, and went into the kitchen to see how it looked. Things were pretty much as he had left them yesterday except that someone had cleaned Mary Horn's brains off of the counter and cabinet doors. The vision of her head exploding like psychedelic popcorn blinked on in his head and his smile came on, crooked and pure.

Pope poked aimlessly around the place, peeking in drawers, opening cupboards, checking closets. In the living room he paused in front of Finn's wall of books and scanned the titles. Pope wasn't much of a fisherman, especially not on Lake Caldasac, but the kid sure was. There had to be five hundred books on the subject taking up the wall that flanked the TV. Then again, what's someone who's stuck in a wheelchair gonna do all day? He looked around the living room. No game console. No satellite receiver. No computer. If the kid had read all of those books and remembered 10 percent of what he had read, there were enough useless facts about fishing floating around in his head to bore your average jerk-off to death. A fishing Rain Man. A single insect voice screamed out *B-O-R-I-N-G!*

The sheriff pulled the curtains in the room and it dropped into a cryptlike gloom. Pope smiled into the dark. This was perfect. He walked on down the hall.

Pope found the master bedroom as depressing as the rest of the house and wondered just how many times Mary Horn had got it good here. With the boy sleeping right next to her, probably not all that much—a crippled kid was like a scarecrow for most men on the prowl. Then again, pussy was pussy, and some guys didn't have very high standards. Even still, it would take one determined motherfucker to get it up in this room, with the three hundred photos of the grinning kid plastered all over the place. Kill a hard-on faster'n a fire hose.

He ran through the drawers in the bureau and flipped through the clothing in the closet, noting that the woman hadn't owned much in the way of finery. The basics were her two waitress outfits with shitty brown trim, about fifty pairs of sweatpants from Walmart, and half a dozen pairs of cheap sneakers in different colors that she had probably bought on sale a thousand years ago. Nothing in the nightstand of interest.

Finn's room didn't look like the room of any thirteen-year-old he had ever seen. The furniture was typical big-box store fugly but the walls weren't covered with the usual posters of cars, girls, wrestlers, or any of the other shit that captivated every kid Pope had tried to fuck. No, little Finn's fetish was fish, and Pope knew enough to recognize that the kid's prey of choice was musky. Most of the photos were pages torn from magazines: guys grinning idiotically, each holding what to Pope could have been the same fish, the only differentiating characteristic between them being their choice of baseball caps. Mixed in with the patchwork quilt of magazine pages were a few eight-by-ten glossies hand-signed by whatever asshole happened to be posing, annotated with a slogan like *Tight Lines, Finn!* or *Fish Ambassadeur Reels, Finn, and you'll catch a trophy like mine!* The kid must have spent the winter writing letters asking for autographed photos. Who'd say no to a kid in a wheelchair? Always an angle, Pope thought, and lay down on the empty bed.

The mattress was small for the big cop and his ankles hung over the footboard. After a few minutes he drifted off to sleep.

He was still asleep in the boy's bed when Hal's Jurassic F-150 pulled into the driveway with Finn in the passenger seat.

# 59

Hal's ancient pile of rust holding hands, as Finn now called it, coughed to a stop and seemed to burp its death rattle. Hal got out, lit up another smoke, and pulled Finn's wheelchair out of the bed. He opened it up and the boy nimbly deposited himself in the seat.

"Thanks, Hal. You have your smoke and I'll go get my stuff together. I can get most of it out myself—I ain't taking too much stuff until the court thing is over—but I'm gonna need some clothes and books and maybe my shampoo because I don't like that peach cobbler farty-tarty stuff that Gavin has at his place." As usual, Finn's words came out all at once. "I'll be back in a few minutes. Besides"—the little boy jerked a thumb at the police cruiser in the drive—"the cops are here."

Hal nodded a no-problemo and climbed in behind the wheel, put his head back, and closed his eyes.

Finn maneuvered the chair up the ramp and had the door open in one swipe of his key. He rolled in and it closed behind him.

Back in the truck, the old man drifted off to sleep.

# 60

The room was dim except for the bright white rectangle that bathed the stainless-steel autopsy table, illuminating the architecture of death in bloodless white. Her sternum had already been closed, the large Y that started at the pelvic bone and terminated at each collarbone sealed with broad red baseball stitches. The block—in-house nomenclature for the bundle of internal organs housed in the main body cavity—had been removed and separated for various tests. The top of the skull, usually sawn open in a neat oval, was a jagged ring of broken bone and hair. Chunks of gray matter sat in a nearby collection trough.

Dr. Parks stared down at Case 2309432, Horn, Mary Elizabeth. Massive head trauma was always a tricky call. He stared at the purplish tinge of dead lining in the skull and made some notes on the clipboard balancing precariously on the corner of the table. Cause of death had been massive penetrating trauma to the brain; Mary Horn's head had hit something, as opposed to something having hit her head. Had he been looking at a depressed skull fracture, he'd hand the file over to the police. Even a blunt head trauma could be the result of being struck (although not always) by an object. Unless head trauma was the result of a vehicular accident, the ME always approached the case with more than a modicum of suspicion.

Parks scanned the file again, flipped through the death-scene photos, and shook his head. Mary Horn must have slipped while running; there was no other way a five-foot-six woman weighing a hundred and sixty pounds could generate enough force to open her head like that with a straight fall. Parks examined the wound, checked the thickness of the skull edge with a caliper, and did a few rough calculations. Impact necessary to cause this kind of damage would have to measure around sixteen hundred pounds per square inch. With her height and weight, and allowing for instinctive (nonfocused reaction) rotational movement, her skull would have had to have been traveling at about twenty-eight miles an hour, body-mass pressure as well as the arc of the swing included. Easily done when falling while running.

Parks peeled off the gloves and slingshotted them into the wastebasket in the corner. He grabbed the clipboard, turned off the lights, and headed to his office, where he would list the cause of death as a massive penetrating skull trauma caused by an accidental fall in the home.

*Case closed.*

# 61

"Hey, kid." The voice sounded like gravel rolling down a drainpipe.

Finn halted and peered into the dim living room. Pope's shadow was a little darker than the rest of the space and Finn directed his voice at it. "Hello, Sheriff Pope." For a second he wondered what the sheriff was doing in his house, then guessed that it probably had something do with his mom's death. He glanced toward the kitchen and saw that the blinds had been pulled shut in there too.

"Where's Corlie?" The big shadow shifted. It shrunk, became wider, as the cop folded himself into the La-Z-Boy that had been his father's.

"He's at his house."

"Don't you mean *your* house?" the sheriff asked.

Finn thought about his mom on the floor, her skull the fountainhead of a big black lake on the floor. "*This* is my house."

The shadow in the chair shifted and for an instant Finn saw teeth flash in the dark. "What do you do out there all the time, you and that guy?" the darkness asked.

Finn shrugged. "Not that much. Listen to music. Sit by the fire and talk. Eat sandwiches. The usual stuff." And Finn realized that it wasn't much of a lie; all he had left out was the monster hunting.

"You know, kid, people aren't always what they seem." The shadow paused, took in a breath. When he let it out it sounded like hundreds of tiny voices crying out. "You ever need any—I don't know—*help*, I guess, you call me, okay? I knew your mom."

"And my dad," Finn added softly. "He was a police officer too. I remember him. Mostly, I think. My mom, um, said that you worked together."

The shadow seemed to nod. "We had a difference of opinion on, well, *politics*, I guess you could say. But I don't hold no grudges. Hell, I was the guy who found your dad. Where he went off the road there, on that little slate cliff, no one would have noticed for days. His car went straight down about fifty feet and smashed into solid rock. For some reason I pulled over right there and found his car only minutes after he had taken his last ride. I'll never forget walking up to the edge, just to stare out at the lake, and seeing his cruiser plastered all over the rocks." Finn saw the head on the shadow twitch.

"I ran down that hill like a billy goat. He died in my arms, your dad." The dark form of the sheriff inflated a little, and his already big shoulders squared off even more. "I was the last person to see him alive. I'm glad I was able to be there." There was another pause filled with that same sad rasp. "He deserved that."

"Thanks," Finn said. "I didn't know you found him." In reality, his memories of his father had already faded, but like all little boys, he idolized the man, even if he was just imaginary.

"Yeah, well, you ever need a friend like me—even just to talk—you call. Okay? I'm a good guy to spend time with."

Finn smiled, nodded, appreciating the offer. "Thank you, Sheriff. I will." For a second the dark door of the kitchen caught his eye and he froze.

"You guys play any games out there?" The shadow vibrated a little and Finn wondered if Pope was feeling okay. His shadow looked like it was shivering.

"Not really. I'm a little old for games."

"I know a game you'd like," the shadow said. There was a pause and Finn wondered if maybe he was supposed to say something here.

Then the shadow stood up and came toward him. It reached out. A dark arm materialized and took the big round police hat off of the hook above Finn's head. "I'll be seeing you, kid."

The shadow slid past the boy and opened the door. A bright spear of light bisected the room, then flashed dark as the cop filled the frame, and blinked out in the slam of oak.

The little boy listened to the cruiser start up then drive off before he rolled down the hall, consciously keeping his face turned away from the kitchen door. After all, he was only here for some underwear.

**62**

The rain had been replaced by a stinging drizzle that the wind drove sideways. Umbrellas, hats, and raincoats offered little in the way of protection and for the first time in months, the citizens of New Mannheim were aware that fall was once again coming to their little corner of the world.

The hole in the ground could not be mistaken for anything other than what it was—a grave. The edges were crisp, chopped from the earth by a professional in such matters. The nearby mound that waited to be piled on top of the coffin was also neat and proportional, the surface glazed to a soft wet skin by the constant spitting of Mother Nature. The bottom of the hole was filled with water and every now and then a chunk of dirt would be washed off the wall and plop, loudly, six feet under the coffin lying in its sling.

The minister had been professional and, Gavin thought, properly brief. After he had finished a sermon narrated by rote, he stepped forward and committed Mary Horn to the earth. The box they had put her in slowly started to sink into the wet, dark hole.

Finn sat beside Gavin, silently holding his hand. He was dressed in a suit that he had asked Gavin to buy. He said he'd be okay if they went to Walmart but if he had a choice he'd rather get something really fancy at Morton's. The best suit in the place, complete with an extra pair of pants, imitation leather shoes and a matching belt, a shirt, tie, pocket square, and socks, came to fifty-seven bucks even—wrapping included. Finn had tied the tie himself, something he said he had learned to do from looking at his dad's old police portrait. He had done a good job too.

Finn's sticker-covered wheelchair was at odds with the gray clothing. He wore no raincoat and had refused an umbrella. For some reason the boy had insisted on going to his house alone yesterday, going so far as to yell when Gavin had offered to sit in the car. If he was going to sit in the car, what would be the point of him coming? the boy had asked. *Just in case.* In case what? It's my house and I'm going by myself! And Gavin had deferred, citing Hal as pinch-hitter on the gig.

Gavin, as a brother-in-arms, had left his umbrella back in the car and realized that he was too numb to feel much of anything. And he needed his one good hand for Finn. Laurel stood beside him, in black, trying to fend off the drizzle with her umbrella and not really succeeding.

Gavin recognized random faces here and there but few people had decided to go out on a day like today, not even for a funeral. Dave Duffy was there, his face wearing that resigned mask some people have after seeing death enough times. Mickey from the general store had come. Nurse Groucho had shown up, as had two waitresses and the owner of the diner where Mary Horn had worked. There were no blood relatives there and Finn had pointed out that he knew of no living relatives on either side since his maternal grandfather had died last year. The lack of attendance was bolstered by plenty of unhappiness.

Gavin thought back to Chelsea's funeral, the photographers perched at the church fence like one-eyed crows, single black eyes hoping to snap a telephoto image of grief. Fans had lined up at the church's gate, some dressed in black, some wearing black armbands, people who felt like they were supposed to mourn because they had read some words he had written. Other than those few vivid memories, though, Chelsea's funeral was a drunken dream of semiconnected images that still came and went. But the sight of Chelsea's urn, sitting benignly on the marble column under the life-sized effigy of Christ at Saint Francis's in Brooklyn, was still crystal clear in his mind's eye.

Gavin blinked and water fell off of his lashes. He looked off into the distance, to the road that passed the cemetery beyond the spiderweb shadow of the rusted wrought-iron fence. A car sat dead in the rain, the incongruous line of the double lights and siren atop the police cruiser the only discernible detail in the awkward light of the cold, foggy day. Gavin could see no shadow behind its wheel, no signs of life at all. But he knew Pope was there, watching. He wondered if Laurel had bought his monologue about *someone's got to do Pope's job*; he had tried to sound sincere but he wasn't sure that it had stuck. The logic had been that he didn't think it made sense for both of them to be worried about the cop.

Gavin turned back to the casket floating in the muck at the bottom. For a second it stayed buoyant, then one corner tilted down into the storm waters. Then another. It sunk, its volume pushing the water up, until it spilled over the lid and swallowed the coffin whole.

Gavin noted, with more than a modicum of worry, that a boy who was normally incapable of being quiet had uttered not a single word since he had come back from picking up some things at his house yesterday.

# 63

They now fished with two boats. Duffy fished the deep water, his heavy Canons combined with the four-hundred-plus horses of his inboard Mercury dropping Finn's ingenious carp rig down into sixty-plus-foot water. Where *it* lived. Gavin and Finn stuck with their heavy boat rod, trolling closer to the surface at the edge of the weed bed, clinging to thirty-foot depths. This was their third day working in tandem and they had an effective routine, their boats crossing paths four, maybe five times a day, each pass met with long-distance smiles, waves, and one of Duffy's jokes delivered over the small two-way radios that they all wore clipped to their belts. Finn had started calling Duffy *Mr. Sweden* because he had a hard time understanding Duffy's vernacular, especially after the man had a few pints in him and reverted to hardcore Liverpudlian. Gavin had tried to explain that Liverpool was nowhere near Sweden, but Finn had already made up his mind.

Gavin liked Dave Duffy. He was a feisty, intelligent man who openly enjoyed four things in life: period English furniture, cooking, fishing, and strong Irish ale. Duffy always had a can of Guinness plugged into his face. Gavin had quickly learned to wonder just how many cases Mickey's Mercantile had to truck in each week to keep Duffy topped up; the man filled a five-gallon pail with empties each and every day.

With Duffy riding shotgun, Finn used a newfound energy to plan both angles of attack. Duffy, a seasoned fisherman, quickly grew to respect and trust the boy's knowledge. And the teamwork bolstered Finn's confidence and helped him fight the mean reds he had been staving off since his mother's death.

Every night after sawing up their designated section of the lake they would hook up at Gavin's to go over water covered and plan their routes for the next day. By the time Duffy pulled in to tie up at the dock, the boat would be littered with dented cans rolling around on the fiberglass deck like empty shell casings.

Besides Duffy's vernacular taste in beer, he was hilarious, trustworthy, and kind. It was his loyalty that had armed him with a shotgun, a pair of outriggers, and a dose of vengeance to hand out. Loyalty to a dog named Petey.

Like Finn, Petey had met the creature while out fishing. It had been July, hotter than piss in a shot glass on the driveway, as Duffy had put it. The temperature was in the high nineties. Petey had been roasting, his pink and blue tongue lapping at the puddles of Guinness that Duffy's empties had lost in drops on the deck. Like he had done a hundred times before, Duffy had told the dog to go for a swim. The dog climbed the gunwale, teetered for a second, then went overboard. Petey swam around the boat for a few minutes while Duffy popped the top on another Guinness. It was in that split second when his attention was turned away that *it* hit.

Petey let out a high-pitched cry that Duffy still heard when he least wanted to. Something dragged his dog under the water, then smacked him against the bottom of the boat. Duffy had heard Petey's yelp through the hull of his boat. Duffy watched the trail of bubbles that left Petey's lungs as he was dragged into the deep and eaten.

Duffy swore vengeance.

So he hadn't flinched when Gavin had told him that when they got it—whatever the fuck *it* was—the credit would go to Finn. Finn would talk to the papers, Finn would be in the magazines. Any financial earnings would be split ninety-ten, the lion's share going to Finn. And Duffy had laughed at that. They were out here *to kill sommit, lad. Sommit that ate me doag.* Besides, he argued over a Guinness, they didn't know what the *coont* they were looking for. Maybe no one would give a *shite*, let alone financial earnings. *But sure, lad, if it makes you happy, then it makes me happy. As long as we get this fooker.*

So here they were, bulked up by another man and another boat, dealing with twice the water they used to be able to cover in a day, and all they were was three days closer to the end of the season. Three days closer to a winter that Finn might never see the end of. Three days closer to death.

Gavin tried not to think about it but it was always there, perched over their shoulders like a withered old bird. It wasn't just Finn's health—although that was the exclamation point to their efforts—that bothered him. What worried him was the idea that Finn wouldn't be able to accomplish the one defining goal he had set for himself. Even his mother's death had not slowed him down—if anything, it had fortified the boy's resolve. The boy had talked about it only once, the morning after the incident at the hospital with Pope. The one thing he had said that stuck in Gavin's mind had been that maybe his mother's death was supposed to happen so she wouldn't have to watch him die. Gavin was still reeling from that one. And ever since then, the boy had not talked about his mother once. But he saw Finn's sadness, recognized it with the intimacy of experience. To the outside world Finn looked like he was forging forward, the happy little boy that everyone knew. But Gavin, his friend, saw the cracks in the armor.

The kid worked endlessly out here, checking their line for nicks, going over their terminal tackle to make sure nothing was showing strain, and if it was, he changed it immediately. Every night he knocked twenty yards off the end of the spool because he knew that there was a slim chance that it had stretched, maybe snagged, and had some hidden weakness. Finn didn't want anything to fail—not their equipment, not them—because of weakness. If you took the weakness out of the equation, you took out the failure. And Finn's weakness was that old capricious bitch called Time.

The voice of the wind was overridden by the squawk of the radio at Gavin's hip—the familiar sound of Duffy's slurred, "Hey, lads, how are we doin'?"

"Roger that, Mr. Sweden!" Finn snapped into the walkie-talkie; his perceived professionalism that the radios added to their operation was directly proportionate to Gavin's desire to roll his eyes every time Duffy's voice cracked over the speaker.

"I'm doon with areas forty-three through forty-five. I'm going in. You two gonna join me for a beer?"

Gavin checked their position on the GPS, then looked at the map they had secured to the dash; they were almost done with the day's work. He looked up, examined the sky. There was still a good hour of daylight left. Gavin could see that the long hours on the water without rest were starting to affect the boy's health. Every now and then Gavin would look back to see Finn sitting in his chair, his head hung forward, his hand on his chest. Although he never asked him what he was doing, something told him that the boy was checking to see if his heart was still beating. "We're finished with thirty-seven now, Finn. You want to head in?"

Gavin watched the boy's hand stop and rest on his chest. "Not tonight. I want to work this water until my hands bleed." He turned back to the little radio. "Negatory, Mr. Sweden.

We're gonna beat these weeds a little longer. Wind's good, air's warm, and we ain't been drinking all day long like some people." Finn took his finger off the mike button and let out a snort of laughter, then pressed the button again. "Tomorrow morning. Usual time and don't be late!" Since Finn had started staying with Gavin, they had moved the *Low Rider* to Gavin's bay.

Duffy's voice boomed back. "All right, Cap'n. Tomorrow in the a.m."

Finn smiled and dropped the radio back into his pocket. "Look at us out here," Finn said, his face beaming in the waning light. "Three morons hunting for a monster. We're like some kind of bad religion."

"Yeah," Gavin agreed. "The father, the son, and the holy idiot."

Finn looked up and smiled. "I know who I am. Which one are you?"

Gavin looked off in the direction where he knew Duffy's boat was. "I'll let you know when I figure it out."

# 64

Unlike other lakes, the sparkle of lights on the shores of Caldasac was conspicuously absent. Gavin checked the GPS, powered in with the Zoom button, and saw that they were moving in almost on top of yesterday's course, deviating by maybe ten feet. He felt a twinge of pride and realized that not only was he enjoying being on the water, but he was getting good at it as well.

With the induction of Duffy into their little clan of madmen, the routine had changed; instead of meeting at Finn's before first light, they hooked up at Gavin's. The little bay was secluded and both their boats could dock without being seen from the water—not that there was much of a chance of anyone figuring out what was going on, but they didn't want people asking questions.

It was night now and Finn was leaning back in his chair, the butt of the big boat rod jammed into the gimble of his leather fighting belt. Every day as they headed in, Finn insisted on trolling all the way back to the dock on the off chance they crossed paths with the Leviathan. Gavin looked at his little body, wrapped with the thick leather belt, and tried not to let pity creep into his thoughts. The belt had been so big that Gavin had had to punch another five holes in it to accommodate Finn's tiny waist. Gavin was sure that the kid was losing weight. He had asked Laurel about it a few times but she had always come back with the standard response of "Ask Finn." But the kid said everything was fine, super even. Tip-top. So he let it go.

Gavin checked the sonar. "Finn?"

The kid's head swiveled around, annoyed that his attention was taken off the line that fed out into the darkness like some electrical conduit plugged into his monster.

"Bottom's rising. We're at sixteen feet. You're going to get snagged up."

Finn's mouth played around with a frown before he nodded in acceptance. "Slow it down."

Gavin dropped the throttle back and pulled the transmission into neutral. The boat drifted forward a few feet before the drag of the hull slowed it to a stop. It bobbed on the surface in the swells of its own wake before settling into a gentle roll. Finn went to work reeling in the carp and Gavin could see that the kid was still in strong form—his arms never slowed in towing in what amounted to a bucket of cement on the end of his line. The rod bent, the reel creaked a few times, but Finn never faltered.

Ten feet behind the boat the carp finally bobbed up, cutting a V in the dark, oily water. "Okay." Finn swung the bait aboard. "You can punch it."

The dark wall of the forest loomed up in front of them, the hill where Gavin's house was perched now obscured by the dark trees. Gavin tilted the wheel to starboard and skirted the shore, heading for the inlet to his bay. Little pins of light flicked through the trees and by their position, Gavin knew that the lights in the living room and kitchen were on. And all at once he felt glad, knowing that Laurel was there, waiting for him.

"Your girlfriend is here." Finn topped this off with a series of smooching sounds.

Gavin looked around for something to throw, but all that was at hand was a pair of saltwater cutters. He settled for a gruff, "Oh, shut up."

The forest was totally silent, even the soft hiss of wind through the trees strangely absent. The only noise was the low thrum of the motor. The mouth of the inlet opened up and they nosed into the bay. It would be another hundred yards before he would see the dock, and the house on the hill looming up behind it.

The silence was cut open by the howl of a loon somewhere ahead of them, the echo bouncing around in the forest.

For a second, the boy's face clouded over, and for no reason that he could put his finger on, Gavin knew that he was thinking of his mother. What was it about those birds? They seemed to be sadness personified.

They rounded the last bend in the dark shoreline and his house formed in the space above them. The eyes of the windows stared down, the French doors silhouetting Laurel against the light. Gavin watched her for a minute, saw her hip pushed out, her shoulder against the doorjamb, and he could imagine what she smelled like, felt like, and he found himself upstairs, in bed with her, their limbs intertwined, their bodies melded, fused together, their heat so close that there was no telling where his body ended and hers began. He thought of her mouth, her breath, her scent.

"Hey, bonehead!" Finn's voice came out of nowhere. "Slow down or you'll crack us up!"

Gavin eased back on the throttle and pulled the boat up to the jury-rigged dock. Mr. Johannus had started working on the structure and until it was done, the Finnish carpenter had made interim repairs using plywood and bracing. As the boat rolled in, Gavin saw that half the dock had either been taken down or fallen down that day. As usual, Duffy's boat was parked at the boathouse, tied to the big bronze cleats on the porch that overhung the water. He hoped Duffy had called Hal to get home. More often than not he sped home in his ancient Toyota minivan, dashboard awash in popcorn, cigar bands, and parking tickets.

Finn tied off the stern, Gavin the bow, his one good hand working by rote after weeks of practice. He looked up and Laurel was coming down the ramp pushing Finn's wheelchair, the big cat stretched out comfortably on the seat. "And?" was all she asked.

Gavin shook his head.

"Not a frigging thing!" Finn said disgustedly and spat over the side. "But we've got a new theory."

Laurel stroked the cat. "That makes what? Six?"

"You know, for a lady of science, your lack of vision astounds me," Finn said flatly.

"Hey, when it comes to cancer, heart disease, and emphysema I'm very forward thinking. When it comes to Bigfoot traveling via astral projection, I'm a little skeptical, okay?"

Gavin crawled up onto the dock and swung the boom arm of the boat sling over Finn's chair. What the hell could he offer the argument? The whole premise of debate was that the side that could offer up more facts and present them in an intelligent manner would win. Simple. Logical. But what did he have in the way of logical facts? Sweet fuck-all in a heart-shaped box.

Finn reached up and directed the web sling down around his body—they had adapted a hospital sling to the boom arm and had come up with a system that helped them get Finn in and out of the boat with very little trouble. Finn buckled the straps under his legs and cinched the last one around his waist. "Okay," he said and gave Gavin the thumbs-up.

Gavin began cranking the ancient bronze ratchet that dated from before World War II. The straps tightened around Finn's body and he began his ascent. Off in the bay the loon howled its lonely cry. Finn was rising when there was a wet *whump* and something came out of the lake off in the darkness. The big Maine coon tore free. The loon's wail was cut short in a loud bone-crunching snap. There was a second of silence, then another huge splash. The night was once again still.

Gavin's hand froze on the crank.

Finn started to scream. "It's him! It's him! Get me up! Get me up!"

Gavin started to wind the handle but the strain was too much for one-handed operation. Laurel leaned into the job with him, her well-muscled arms doing most of the work. Finn swung quickly up. Gavin fanned the boom arm in over the stone bank. Finn sat there in silence for a second, his body swinging back and forth in time with Gavin's breathing. Laurel had stopped cranking and was hunched forward, her hands on her knees, trying to catch her breath. The waves striking the retaining wall were dying out and in a few minutes they had all regained their composure.

"Jesus, what the hell was that?" Laurel asked.

Finn, his body no longer swinging, looked her in the eyes. "Bigfoot, smarty-pants."

# 65

Dave Duffy answered the door with a dish towel over his shoulder, a tall glass of wine in his hand, and a smile on his face. He wore a pair of black jeans, red velvet slippers, and a pressed white shirt that wasn't tucked in. A big platinum Art Deco watch and an Italian intaglio ring were his only jewelry. He was also fairly drunk.

"Lads! You found it! Excellent. Coom in, coom in!" The only thing more enticing than Duffy's broad smile was his body language; he waved them in with flourish and poise. His usual fast, wiry movements were gone and in their stead one could see the polished actions of a man with well-groomed social skills.

Gavin managed Finn's wheelchair over the threshold with a little jostling.

Laurel closed up the rear, a bottle of wine in each hand.

"Ah, Dr. Laurel, nice to see you on a nonprofessional basis. You look loovely tonight." Duffy took the bottles of wine and kissed her on both cheeks. "And you smell right pretty as well."

Gavin arched an eyebrow. "I thought you were in pediatrics."

Duffy shook his head. "In *my* professional capacity, not *hers*."

"I bought a few pieces from him over the years," Laurel said proudly.

"And I always thought you were a married lass. Had I known..." Duffy let the sentence trail off into a leer.

Gavin, Laurel, and Finn crossed through the foyer and took in Duffy's house.

"This isn't a home, David, this is a movie set," Laurel gasped.

The apartment above the shop was tastefully decorated with the finest in period furnishings. Persian carpets covered the hardwood floors in shades of deep maroon, chalk, and eggplant. The living room was furnished entirely in Georgian period pieces, the focus of which was a Chinese Chippendale secretary bookcase. Two big wing chairs flanked the fireplace, above which a portrait of an English general in full regalia stared down over the room, something about his face familiar. The furniture was of the finest quality and the handsomest proportions. It wasn't hard to guess that the best items that arrived at Duffy's shop came in the front door and went straight out the back to his home.

Gavin, who up to this point had fancied himself an antiques connoisseur, stood dumbfounded. "Dave, this is amazing."

Duffy was at the bar, pouring another two glasses of wine and opening a bottle of Coke for Finn. "I do all right for meself," he said with a smile.

"You afford this with the little shop downstairs?" Gavin asked, not able to see the numbers adding up.

Duffy laughed. "Hardly, mate. I had a shop on Madison and Seventy-Fourth for twenty years."

"You're from New York?" Gavin sounded surprised.

"Sort of. When I was a lad in Liverpool, there was a sign on the old coal bridge that I could see from me window. Big blue and red letters I'll never forget. *Liverpool to New York, One Hundred Pounds.* New York might as well been…" He let the sentence trail off, searching for the right word.

"The moon?" Laurel tried.

"Fook, no! I could *see* the moon, lass. New York was as unattainable as being the King of Sweden." He smiled down on Finn, who nodded approvingly. "Eventually I made me way to London and did all right. One day I got drunk and bought a ticket to New York."

"And when you got there you liked it so much you couldn't leave, right?" Finn added.

"I was so bloody petrified the whole time we were over the Atlantic I swore I'd never get back on a plane as long as I lived. So New York instantly became home. Opened up a small shop and the rest is history. A lot of my New York clients coom up here just to see me. It's the old *build it and they will come* philosophy. It's worked so far."

Finn swept his eyes around the room, finally settling on a Mr. Potato Head doll sitting on the bookcase. "What's with the Mr. Potato Head?" the boy asked.

"Got it when I was your age, young Finn. Me folks didn't have very much mooney. For Christmas I usually got a pair of socks, maybe some noots," he said, which Gavin translated in his mind as *nuts*. "One year I got Mr. Potato Head and I thought that the sky had opened up and the angels had visited. He's been with me ever since."

It suddenly dawned on Gavin that Duffy was a lot more complex than the ale-guzzling comedian he liked to portray. The man was fleshing out into another pleasant surprise in his new life. Gavin walked over to the secretary bookcase. "This is astounding. It's in Chippendale's *Director*, right? I've got a 1938 edition."

"Good eye, Gavin." Duffy handed out the drinks and went to the library, where he extracted a large folio-sized book. "This is the original 1754 edition. My piece was the first one ordered based on plate 114." Duffy opened the large tome and ran his finger over one of the engravings that had ensured Matthias Darly's place in history—an illustration of Duffy's secretary. There were several fingerprints on the page and Gavin wondered just how many people had run their hands over the paper. "It was purchased by the Earl of Northumberland in 1755. Now it's here."

Finn slapped his hand to his forehead. "Great. Another one. I bet you can't use it, either."

Duffy turned to the boy. "Lad, if a man can get past the point in life when he has all the things he needs and can afford some things that feed his soul, then he's looky. You have anything that feeds your soul, lad?"

Finn waved it away as obvious. "Fishing."

"But what, exactly, about fishing do you love?" Duffy asked and led them over to the fireplace.

Gavin saw the plaid cushion in front of the hearth that had no doubt belonged to Petey. The man also had his monuments to grief.

Finn thought about it for a second. "Every time I hook a musky and feel the rod flex and the line start to zing out and my shoulders tighten up, Mr. Sweden, my soul is on top of the world."

"What about the days when you catch noothin'? Are they bad days?"

Finn shook his head. "Are you noots?" the boy squawked, imitating Duffy's Midlands accent. "The water is beautiful. Rain or shine, as long as I got the right clothes on it's great out there. The wind sounds…I don't know, just *different*. And if it's sunny, man, it's like heaven! No one asking me to tell them the capital of Des Moines, or figure out the circumference of a rhomboid, or any of that useless stuff that is supposed to be so important."

Duffy nodded like he understood. "That piece of foorniture over there, lad, was built over two hundred and fifty years ago by a man that invented the way we look at things. It was put together by a master cabinetmaker. By hand. He had no power tools. Every single piece was designed, then cut, then fitted and finished by hand. The man who built that piece probably worked six months on nothing else, and he probably had to wait another six months to get paid by his client because that's the way the rich were and, to a large degree, still are with their tradesmen. And he probably died poor with nothing to show for his life's work except for a handful of pieces of foorniture that he put his mind and heart and soul into. And one of those pieces was this bureau bookcase. And it has survived two plagues, nine minor wars, and two world wars; managed to cross the Atlantic; and remained unmolested. This piece, young Finn, has lived through more than you or I ever shall. And it will be here a long time after we are gone. Like your fishless days on the water, it is a thing of beauty that not everyone understands but everyone should try to."

Finn, who had been staring at Duffy, absorbed in what the man was saying, turned his head to the piece of furniture and examined it. He looked at it for a moment, as if waiting for it to speak. He finally turned to Duffy and said, "It's just a piece of furniture, Mr. Sweden. It ain't *fishing.*"

Duffy shook his head and took a sip of wine. "From the mouths of babes…"

"No Guinness?" Gavin asked curiously.

"I may look like an alcohoolic but I am not a plebeian. Wine befoor dinner. Port after. A good scotch thrown somewhere into the mix. Guinness is not a dinner drink unless you're at the poob."

Finn sniffed the air like a cat. "Supper smells good. What we having?"

"Well, I know about Dr. Laurel's penchant for red meat, so I have Angus prime rib au jus, asparagus with a lemon-honey dressing, broiled tomatoes, and french fries. The appetizer will be lobster bisque, and for dessert I've concocted a right decent crème brûlée."

Laurel's face cracked into her monstrous grin. "Why aren't you married?" she asked.

"I was. Twice. Both ended badly. Lots of dish throwing and name calling and barrister's fees. Let's just say that I am a demanding sort of bloke. Drink too much. Work long hours. Now I spend too much time fishing. I am a singular type of man and have decided that the illusion of one woman differing from another is a fantasy that I simply cannot afford—in time *or* finances."

Finn turned to Laurel. "He always talks like that."

"But we *are* different, Dave."

Duffy smiled like he knew something that she didn't. "How I wish that were true."

"Men are different. All of them," she said, by way of defense.

"Not really, lass. Show up naked. Bring food. Or better yet—bring liquor. Very *un*complicated, actually. Women? You creatures are so complicated that you end up making us nooty along with you. Men? We are all pretty mooch the same. Different packaging, boot the same." He took a sip of his wine. "And there's a rule in life. Each man gets a shot at one perfect woman. I had mine."

Finn nodded knowingly. "Me, too."

Duffy stopped and stared at the boy. "A toast to your mum, young Finn. We only get one of those. And the good ones take care of us forever."

Finn froze for a second and it looked as if he was going to cry. But he stopped the reaction in its tracks and raised his Coke proudly. "To my mom."

"Bottoms up!" Duffy toasted.

Gavin raised his glass. "To your mom."

"And to killing the Leviathan," Finn proposed, and all the men lifted their drinks.

When the toasting was done, Laurel smiled over at Duffy, trying not to sound judgmental. "How did you get roped into all this?" she asked. "You don't strike me as a man prone to wild goose chases."

Duffy eased back into the big wing chair. "Quite the opposite," he said. "I am in the mad quest business by profession. I hunt treasure for my shop all the time. You two haven't told her the story?" he asked Finn and Gavin.

Finn nodded. "She believes us now. The Leviathan almost ate me tonight."

"Any professional opinions?" Duffy asked. "As a scientist, I mean."

Laurel shook her head. "It could have been a fish."

Finn slapped the coffee table, causing a small collection of antique boxes to jump. "Lady, did you hear that thing hit the water? Gavin's ex-Hummer would make less noise if you dropped it from a crane into a swimming pool. That thing sounded like ten tons of meat smacking the water." Finn slapped his hands together for effect.

Gavin nodded. "He's right, Laurel. Whatever hit the water was enormous."

"Yeah, I've been meaning to thank you for leaving me hanging over the water like a tasty treat for the monster. I really appreciate that. Next time just sprinkle me with a little salt and pepper. Maybe some shredded cheese."

"Sorry, Finn, I just…I don't know. Froze for a second. You *were* over the boat," Gavin tried by way of an explanation.

"Sure. Fine. Next time we switch places and you see how you like being left out there like a Snickers bar on a string."

"Sorry," Gavin said quietly.

"If it's not a fish, what is it?" Laurel asked, her fingers unconsciously stroking the stem of her wineglass. "Maybe you can't kill it."

Finn cocked an eyebrow and his mouth became a flat, serious line. "It bled. If it bleeds, it can be killed."

# 66

Laurel's work was spread out on the huge expanse of mahogany that served as Gavin's dining table. She had never seen a table this large in a private home and working at it made her feel like a captain of industry. Somewhere off in the basement the steam engine rhythm of Mr. Johannus's hammer connected with offending yoists.

Even though many of her previous acquaintances thought of her move as a step backward, she considered the change to be very much in a forward direction. She made five times as much money in Boston but her cost of living had easily been twelvefold. Not to mention the time she spent locked in her car, sucking in pollution and listening to talk-radio hosts complain about gridlock and pollution. No, leaving the city had been the best decision she had ever made other than deciding to get a divorce—that one had been a winner too. Not that her marriage had been all bad, it hadn't, but her husband had been a disorganized, key-losing, forget-to-take-out-the-garbage academic who thought about one thing in life—himself. For a man so poorly organized, he was narcissistic to a fault. He could forget to put gas in the car, lose a plane ticket on the way to the airport, and not come home for days, but God forbid she forget to pick up his dry cleaning. No, leaving Robert and moving out to the country had been just what her life needed.

And now there was Gavin. Younger-than-her, crazy, completely-nonsensical-any-way-you-looked-at-it Gavin. All she knew was that this very much felt like the one defining relationship she would ever get. She knew that the thought was naive, maybe even a little foolish, but the way she felt when she was with him—and the way she knew he felt when he was with her—made this bigger than the sum of its parts. This was huge. For both of them. And she was going to ride it out.

She was going over the itinerary for a lecture she had to attend in Phoenix when Mr. Johannus and Foots came up from the basement, sounding like a herd of cattle. The carpenter knocked on the frame of the open archway and walked into the room. "Dr. Laurel, you got a minute?" he asked.

Laurel took off her glasses and leaned back in the chair, stretching. She saw the old carpenter's eyes focus on her chest and she stopped the stretch before it had done any good. She crossed her arms and looked at the man. "Sure, Mr. Johannus, what is it?"

"I was in the basement sistering a cracked yoist—"

*Ah*, she thought, *the yoists!*

"And I found something that I think you should see."

She got up and followed the old carpenter, wondering what new nuttiness had come to visit.

# 67

Once down the stairs, the narrow beam of Gavin's flashlight illuminated a string hanging from the ceiling and he pulled it, lighting up an ancient bare bulb. The walls were stone, three of the four empty, the fourth covered with floor-to-ceiling shelving piled high with a hundred years' worth of rusty tools, tobacco tins of odd screws and nails, machine parts, scraps of wood that were too big to just throw out and too small to put to any practical use, and the usual detritus one finds in any basement. The rest of the room held enough garden tools, crates, old bicycles, dented milk pails, and odd pieces of furniture to have a very good garage sale.

"Did you know all this stuff was down here?" Laurel asked.

"Never been to the basement." Gavin shone the beam of his flashlight around the room, taking in the junk piled up everywhere. There were more bare bulbs fixed to the ceiling, and he found an old two-button light switch near the stairs. He popped it on and the room lit up, thanks to the new caged bulbs Mr. Johannus had installed.

Laurel pointed at what Mr. Johannus had shown her. "There, behind the shelving—you almost have to know it's there."

Gavin moved a few cobweb-covered pieces aside and shone the bright beam of the flashlight into the void behind the shelves. Behind the structure was a door.

"What do I do with all this crap?" he asked.

"Sell it on eBay!" Finn hollered from the top of the stairs. "I heard a guy sold his belly button on eBay. He stapled it to a piece of wood and dried it out in the microwave. Got eighty-four bucks for it! You can sell *anything* on eBay!"

"That kid has only one speed—fast-forward," Gavin said.

"Yeah, well, it ain't gonna help me get down these stairs. You gonna come help or what?" Finn's complaining was punctuated by the sound of his wheelchair fighting through the door frame at the top of the stairs. "Maybe I should just roll down the steps and hope I don't break something valuable—like my neck!"

"That would be a shame," Gavin whispered.

"I heard that!" the boy yelled.

Gavin and Laurel headed up the steps.

Twenty minutes later Gavin and Laurel stepped back into the pile of odds and ends that had been created by clearing the shelving. Centered in the wall, flush with the masonry, was an arched oak door. Around the edges, pounded into the jambs, were hundreds of big hand-forged framing nails.

"Someone went to a lot of trouble to keep us out," Laurel said, and pulled a section of the shelving away from the wall. It groaned across the stone floor. Finn rolled forward and ran his fingers over the nail heads that stitched the perimeter, over the hammer marks and splintered dents. "Maybe not," he said softly. "Maybe they wanted to keep something in."

# 68

Roy and Karin Perkins were out for their morning swim. For a change, Roy was in the lead and the achievement had his adrenaline pumping. He was in good form today and the water slid by as if he were a seal. They were both moving fast but Roy was really hitting his zone. It was a small lead but it gave him an immense sense of satisfaction; Roy's wife was twenty-three years his junior and he liked beating her at anything physical.

He had been doing a lot of swimming lately—in fact, he did a lot of swimming at the end of every summer. Out here, on Caldasac, he never had to worry about boats or Sea-Doos; the water was almost always deserted. Of course, once the cold weather set in and he was bound up in his office back in Syracuse, he promised himself that he would start earlier next year, maybe even with the ice out. But it never happened. Spring rolled around and he found himself working too much, making up for the slow winter. Then, by the time the busy season at his plumbing-supply business waned, he was back at the lake and out of shape from three-quarters of a year in front of the flat-panel and too many hot dogs from the wagon on the corner. So it took him a few weeks to talk himself back into the water. Then he hurt so much from the initial swim that it took him a week to get back in the water a second time. So he usually didn't hit any sort of a routine until August. A month later the weather went to shit and he was back behind his desk promising himself that next year was going to be the year. Next year he would start earlier. Always next year.

His first wife, Susan, had left nine years ago. Within a few months he was dating Karin, a smart, sexy redhead who also happened to be a hotshot oral-maxilla surgeon—which bought her a lot of points with the first wives of his friends who had managed to stay married. The fact that she was younger and smarter than him yet still wanted to be with him made him very proud; besides, the only people who seemed to be pissed off about it were his kids. Life was good now, remarkably so, and for the first time in his sixty-eight years he felt like things were working out all around.

He pulled in a long stroke and lifted his head to take in air, glancing over his shoulder to see if Karin was gaining on him. He had ten yards on her. Roy plowed ahead. In another hundred yards he touched the rusted red surface of the channel marker and turned to wait for her.

He pulled off his goggles and rubbed his eyes; they were uncomfortable but prescription and he couldn't see his hand in front of his face without them. He just wished that they came a little bigger so they wouldn't jam into his sockets. He heard Karin approach and felt himself smile as he lifted his head; when they got back to the cottage they would have a nice long hot shower, make love, then spend the remainder of the morning listening to Wes Montgomery and reading the papers. Not bad for a weekday. He was pulling on his goggles when he heard her miss a stroke and her hand slap the water a little too loudly.

He looked up.

Karin was—

—gone.

She must have dove under the water.

He waited.

After thirty seconds he started to wonder just what was going on.

At a full minute he felt the flutter of panic in his stomach.

Roy upended and pushed off the buoy with his feet. He felt the rust dig in and knew that he had cut his foot. He headed down into the lake, his eyes open, searching the murky water. His strokes were strong and his legs helped him gain depth. He saw nothing but a green that got denser the farther down he went. Back up to the world, his lungs said. He rose.

Roy broke the surface and took three heavy breaths. "Karin!" he screamed, then headed back down into the lake.

He had just gone under when he felt the pressure wave gently push him to one side, a surge that went against the current. Roy spun, expecting one of Karin's practical jokes. No Karin. No anything. Whatever it was had disappeared. Gone. He peered off into the water. There was blood in the water. Jesus, he thought, I *really* cut my foot.

Then he saw the black vapor trail through the water, like air bubbles from a sinking ship. It wasn't Karin.

It brushed by him again, this time touching his leg, and he felt the surge of water it brought with it. He reeled. Nothing. Blackness. Whatever it was, it was *big*. He stared off into the murky green.

Roy felt the shock wave of pressure wash over him as it brushed his back. He spun. Turned. Peered into the gloom. More blood. Fear opened its voice in his head. Get out of here, it squawked. *Get the hell out! Up! Up!*

Out of the corner of his eye he saw something coming toward him. A flash of white. Karin's bathing suit? Yes, it was! He recognized the shape of her bra. And an arm. It came closer.

And then he saw it. As well as what was left of his wife in its jaws.

Roy screamed and bubbles exploded from his mouth. He fought for the surface, for air. Up! Up!

It moved in.

Roy no longer thought about Karin. Or the surface. All that filled his mind was the sight of the beast coming for him.

# 69

The old fire bucket was full of nails, rotten teeth pulled from the jaws of an ancient crocodile. Gavin pried the last one out, dropped it into the old leather container, and stood back to admire their handiwork. Armed with pry bars and hammers, it had taken them almost two hours. The door would never be pretty again.

"Looks like a family of woodchucks got to it," Finn said.

Gavin held up the cast. "I can barely move the fingers on this hand now."

"Stop whining," Finn said, rolling his eyes.

Laurel's white T-shirt was plastered to her body with sweat, once again the only anomaly in the chestful of ribs being her nipples. "Nice nipples," Gavin whispered and leaned over and kissed her through her smile.

"What? What was that?" Finn rolled forward now that he didn't have to duck the swinging hammers and flying nails. "Did I hear the word *nipple*?"

"Nice try, kid," Laurel said and dropped the old oak-handled hammer onto a shelf beside an aquarium with a cracked glass. "Now, before we open Pandora's box, I need a drink. Beer?"

"Yes, please!" Finn said through a honking big grin.

Laurel ignored him. "Gav?"

"What? Sure." He squinted at the door and ran his hand over the rough surface.

"Most people go into all the rooms in their house, Gav. At least once." Laurel disappeared up the stairs.

Gavin stared at the door and he was quickly lost in the make-believe world behind it where he'd find some ancient wine cellar. Or something else.

Out of nowhere a voice whispered in his ear. "Here's your beer."

Gavin jumped.

"Sorry," Laurel's mouth played around with a smile. "I didn't mean to scare you." She rolled her eyes. "Being the tough horror writer and all."

Gavin took the beer from her hand, embarrassed. "Sorry. Writer's imagination." He popped the cap and took a drink.

The handle was a recessed pull in the old oak and had rusted in place. It took a lot of prodding with one of the pry bars to get it to move. Once up, Gavin wrapped his fingers around it and twisted. It gave way easily, and the bolt clicked. He pulled. Laurel helped.

The door didn't move.

"There's gotta be a way to open this thing."

"Dynamite!" Finn hollered.

Gavin began to nod when Laurel cut the kid off. "Don't be an idiot. We'd blow the whole house up." She turned to Gavin, cutting short the obituary he had been working on in his head. "You got any chain?"

"Chain? What do you mean, chain?"

Finn rolled forward and maneuvered between them. "If you ain't got any dynamite for taking out stumps, the next best thing is chain. You tie one end of the chain to the stump and the other to a tractor. Then you pull like a motherfu—"

Laurel shot the kid a glance that froze the curse in his throat.

Gavin looked skeptical.

"Did you have a better plan?" Finn asked.

Gavin thought about bringing up dynamite again. "Not really."

\*\*\*

They found a chain in the boathouse—a hundred-foot section with links as thick as Gavin's thumb—and it took them fifteen minutes of cursing to get it up to the house in the wheelbarrow.

They used a clevis from the boat to attach one end of the chain to Laurel's tow hook under her bumper, then they had run the chain through the basement window straight back to the door. When they were done, their hands were rusty and rough and they knew thc door was coming out.

Finn sat under a tree around the corner of the house, the cat in his lap, fuming over being benched just when the action was getting good. OBM, sure. Sitting out here with Farts the Cat like a little old lady.

He heard Gavin's voice from the basement. "Okay, slowly."

Finn eased forward to the corner of the house where he would get to see a little of the action.

Laurel shifted into reverse and gently stepped on the gas. Once the chain was taut the car stopped. She put a little more muscle into the engine and the chain clinked as the links shifted and all of a sudden the old Benz rocketed back about ten feet and slammed to a stop. Dust billowed out from the basement window as if a mineshaft had collapsed.

Finn beat Laurel to the top of the stairs. "Help me down."

"First let me see if Gavin's all right."

"I'm fine!" Gavin's voice came up from the basement between violent spasms of coughing.

"Did it work?" Laurel asked as she backed down the stairs with Finn's wheelchair held out above her. "Is the door open?"

There was more coughing. "I guess…you could…say… that."

Laurel eased backward down the stairs while managing Finn's chair. Dust floated in the air, made all the more eerie by the sunlight cutting in through the open window. The door had not opened—the ancient lock had held. But the whole thing, frame and all, had come right out of the wall, slammed through the basement, and stopped about a foot from the window.

Finn whistled. "Holy crap."

"Good thing I stopped," Laurel said.

Gavin smiled, and his teeth were outlined with gray dust. "I think we wasted our time taking the nails out." He pointed at the big iron bar that lay across the back of the door—it had been locked from the inside.

"We'll know for next time," Finn said happily.

The hole in the wall was jagged and irregular and dust still hung in the air, obscuring anything beyond. "I think Mr. Johannus is going to be a little pissed at you," Laurel said.

Gavin held up three big Maglites.

"Let's roll." Finn snatched a flashlight and wheeled toward the opening. "Who's first?"

"It's my house, I go first," Gavin said, and slipped through the opening. He was swallowed by the dark for an instant before his flashlight came to life.

Hundreds of eyes, glowing like cigarette ashes, stared out of the dark.

# 70

"What do you mean, drowned?" Pope asked wearily into the phone. "How do you know?" The sheriff had his feet propped up on the coffee table and the game was on the tube. He had a beer in his hand, Doris was out for the day, and the last fucking thing he needed was to drive out to the south side of Caldasac to check out a drowning.

"They went out for a swim this morning and haven't come back."

"Maybe it was a long swim," Pope offered.

"They went out six hours ago."

*Maybe it was a really long swim,* he wanted to add. "I'll be there in half an hour. Who was it?"

"Roy and Karin Perkins. They're city people who have—" the dispatcher started.

Pope cut her off. "I know them." Roy was about seventy and wore yellow and pink sweaters over his shoulders like the tennis-playing preppie faggots did in the movies. Married to a high-strung woman half his age that reminded Pope of a Pomeranian. She had probably cried herself to sleep the night Viagra had hit the shelves. "Who reported it?"

"Cleaning lady said that they went out before breakfast and said they'd be back in half an hour."

"All right. I'll go down to the house, check things out. Get a boat out on the water." Pope hung up.

The sheriff stood up, downed the last of the Bud, and crushed the can. He grabbed two more cold ones from the fridge to tide him over on his drive out to the lake, and walked out of the house to look for two people he knew they'd never find.

# 71

"Can you believe this?" Laurel asked no one in particular.

Gavin shook his head.

Finn wheeled forward, the flashlight balanced on his lap. He stopped in the middle of the room and shone his light around the walls. "What is this?"

"An obsessive-compulsive's dream," Laurel whispered.

The room was huge, almost as large as the house above. Fifteen hundred square feet easy. The walls were the same hand-hewn limestone blocks that made up the rest of the house, laid here almost two hundred years ago. But the walls were hard to see; hundreds of mounted animal heads stared down on the room from their backboards, suspended in the stiff body language of taxidermy.

Gavin's beam crawled over the walls, intermittently stopping on this or that particular creature.

There were a pair of moose heads that flanked the portal they had just ripped in the wall. Finn whistled. "Look at those, they must be seven feet across, eighteen, maybe twenty points. I ain't ever seen one that big!"

Gavin's light kept moving, illuminating every kind of game imaginable. In one corner, overlooking a huge snooker table, a double-horned white rhinoceros observed the dusty felt surface with one eyebrow lifted condescendingly. Two elephant heads competed for attention, poised directly across from one another—one Indian, one African. Tiger-, leopard-, lion-, cheetah-, and zebra-skin rugs covered the floor, long since moth-eaten and dry-rotted. Gavin's beam locked on a sleek silver fish eight feet long with a hinged mouth that unfolded into a toothless bucket, twisted in mock flight, scales as big as guitar picks. "Tarpon," Finn offered. "A freaking huge sumbitch tarpon."

One after another, every popular species of sport fish and big game leapt out of the shadows. The head of a hippopotamus yawned silently, teeth as large as carrots. Elephant-foot coffee table. A mahogany desk with antler pulls. And countless skulls and sets of jaws.

"It's like the Jumanji-Jurassic funeral parlor in here. This guy killed everything!" Finn hissed as he rolled silently through the room, his wheels kicking up twin vapor trails of dust. His light froze and his voice clawed out of the dark. "Gavin?"

"Yeah?"

"You better come here."

Gavin followed the bright glow of Finn's flashlight beam, carefully picking his way over the rugs on the floor, decorated with heads, paws, and tails.

Laurel's flashlight beam bounced up and down the walls, her voice eerie and distended in the cryptlike chamber. She shone her beam at the ceiling, where dozens of electrical fixtures hung down, like bats in a cave. "There's lighting."

"Hopefully it works," Gavin said, aware that no one had spoken in here for eighty-plus years. He stopped beside the boy and stared at what he had found.

The nickel-plated parts were pitted and dust-laden and they looked eerie, almost alien, as a draft whispered over them, undulating the cobwebs that had been undisturbed for decades. Even half hidden by time, Gavin recognized four heavy saltwater fishing rods fitted with massive trolling reels.

# 72

A garishly painted concrete Little Black Sambo holding a weather-beaten fishing rod sat on the dock. His legs were missing from the knees down and Pope wondered why the fuck anyone would want one of those things unless it came alive at night like some kid's story and did all kinds of magical shit like clean the car and bake cornbread. Then again, what good would a little black cornbread-baking and car-washing fairy be without legs? He wished he was back at home watching the game but knew that wishing didn't make it so. He had left the house in a hurry so that he could make it back for the end of the game and in his rush he had forgotten to bring along any pharmaceutical entertainment. He was stone-cold straight, the beers he had on the way over reduced to a memory, and the only thing he could taste with any clarity was resentment.

Pope looked out at the water and waved to the Department of Fish and Game boat just beyond his ability to make out the print on the side. The distant form of Pete McGibbon waved—some kind of signal.

Pope keyed his mike. "Whacha think, Pete?"

McGibbon's voice started with a burst of squelch that made Pope flinch. He almost pitched the fucking thing in the lake. "Don't see a thing. I've covered the water they had to have gone through. *Nada*. Maybe they went right out to the channel marker. Maybe they're in the current," McGibbon said.

Pope sucked the cool air through his teeth and wished he had some Benzedrine with him. He looked down at the cripp—uh—handicapped concrete fisherman. "All right," he said. "I'll get a boat out into the channel. You get a diver in the water."

# 73

Finn ran his finger over the row of rods and let his finger linger on each. "These are saltwater trolling reels—early Fin-Nor twelve-oughts. Hemingway used one of these. Best in the world besides the ones that Kovalovsky made. These are the nonanodized aluminum ones. Before World War II. Must have cost a fortune, even back then." The reels were almost the diameter of gallon paint cans, and three-quarters as wide. The rods, although only six feet in length, tapered from a one-and-a-quarter-inch diameter near the handle down to three-eighths at the tip.

Laurel shrugged her shoulders. "So? You two have equipment almost as big as this on board the *Low Rider.*"

The boy smiled. "Yeah, we do."

"You mean to tell me that this thing has been out there for decades and no one has ever seen it?"

Gavin shrugged. "Is there enough food in this ecosystem?"

"Maybe it's a coincidence," Laurel said weakly.

Finn flicked one of the rods with his finger and dust showered off in a fine mist. "These rods on this lake is like hunting groundhogs with a Panzer. These are for something huge." He turned the handle of one and it clicked loudly. "Really huge."

Finn wiped dust off of one of the rods. A small silver tag was attached to the handle, long since tarnished and gray. He leveled the beam of his flashlight at it and leaned in to see what it said. After he rubbed the dark surface with the fleshy part of his thumb, the words became legible. The name *M. Koestler* had been neatly hand-engraved in a bold Gothic script. "These are custom-order rods, built to the owner's specifications; Loomis and St. Croix do this kind of work but the magical stuff gets built by little old guys in their garages over the winter months. You pay two grand for a rod and they write your name on it. These"—Finn flicked the rod again and more dust flaked off—"were more expensive than the reels."

"M. Koestler," Gavin read aloud.

Finn's eyes narrowed. "I know that name." He snapped his fingers. "Koestler. Koestler," he repeated, pronouncing it *Kessler* as Gavin had done. "No. Wait! Koestler!" He pronounced it with three syllables, the word coming out Ko-est-ler. He pounded his fist into his hand. "The musky at Black Eyed Susie's—the one with the cigar in its mouth! This guy's name is on it!"

"When were you in Black Eyed Susie's?" Laurel asked.

"I go all the time," Finn said defensively. "I had a beer there the other night with Gavin and Mr. Sweden."

Laurel looked at Gavin and he shrugged. "It seemed like a good idea at the time."

"I've got my eye on you, pal."

# 74

Mike Shawchuck crawled up onto the diving platform, pulled off his mask, and fumbled the big flippers off. He dropped the diving harness to the fiberglass floor. "Man, that water is cold ten feet down. I hate this lake. Nobody ever swims here, why would these two clowns?"

Ten yards off their port side a big metal channel marker bobbed up and down in the roll of the waves, its surface scabbed with red paint, rust, and bird shit.

McGibbon climbed down from the deck of the boat. "Any luck?"

Shawchuck looked up and nodded, water dripping from his blue lips. "Found this," he said and pulled a piece of dirty white fabric out of his mesh dive bag.

McGibbon took the piece of material and turned it over in his hands. It didn't take a genius to see that it was half a bikini top, half a tit shy of a full load, as his daddy would have said. It was torn and punctured and looked like it had been in a blender. "Christ," McGibbon said. "This is not good."

Shawchuck, toweling off his hair, shrugged at the obvious.

"Them folks got into a heap of trouble out here." McGibbon sat down on the console and keyed the mike. "Sheriff?"

"Yep."

"Looks like the Perkinses got run down by a boat. Propeller chopped the shit out of Mrs. Perkins at least. If they were swimming in line…" He let the sentence trail off. "Over."

"Christ," Pope growled. "I'll see if I can run down who was out here in a boat this morning. Now I have to miss the end of the fucking game. Why'd they have to get killed today? This is the shits."

McGibbon examined the fabric in his hand. "I'm sure that Mrs. Perkins would agree."

# 75

Finn wheeled through the room, his tires carving tracks into the dust-covered floor. Up to about thirty-six inches, the entire perimeter of the room was crammed with books. All of the titles had to do with hunting or fishing in one capacity or another. Finn rolled along the shelves, ignoring the mounts that grew up into the dark above him, running his finger over the dust-covered spines, leaving a trail in the sediment of time. He began to recognize titles he had either read about or actually owned. He pulled a volume out of the shelf and turned it over in his hands. "Hoch…hoch…see…is this word *fish*?" Finn fumbled with the translation.

Laurel was only a few steps away, following in his dusty wake, and she took the book out of the boy's hands. She wiped the spine clean. "*Hochseefischeri*," she read in perfect German. "*See* is 'sea' and *fischeri* is 'fishing.' *Hoch* is…'elevated,' I think."

"Elevated sea fishing?" Finn asked. "What the crap is that?"

"Sorry. Invert it. Deep-sea fishing," Laurel corrected. "It has to be."

"That's better."

"Not really," Gavin offered from somewhere off in the dark.

Finn and Laurel turned to him with *Why Not?* written across their features in bold relief.

"Because it means that we're hunting down something that has managed to stay undiscovered in our lake out there for the better part of a century."

## 76

The old Mercedes wagon crested the hill and went airborne, the tires free of the earth for an instant, and all sound stopped except for the growl of the engine and Finn's high-pitched "Yee-haw!" Laurel drove with the fury and punch of a rally driver, continually up- and down-shifting, her feet double-clutching and braking with the precision of a Swiss watch. Gavin sat in the passenger's seat, his good hand wrapped in a death grip around the *holy shit* handle and his eyes ratcheting over to the speedometer. He had never seen anyone drive like this. Not even on television.

"Man, I wish my mom had driven like this!" Finn said from his position buckled into the middle of the big bench seat in the back. The words were sparkly, bright, but Gavin could hear the sadness under them. "We could have got all the shopping done in ten minutes flat!"

"Your mother was a sensible woman," Gavin hissed from between clenched teeth.

Laurel took her foot off the gas and downshifted into third. "Okay, Mr. Scaredy-Pants, I'll slow down." The big German engine compressed and their speed dropped down to the high spectrum of Gavin's comfort zone. "Mr. Big-Time Horror Writer afraid of a little ride in the country."

Finn flicked Gavin in the ear with his finger. "Thanks a lot."

"Y*ou* asked *me* to drive, remember?" Laurel offered by way of her own defense.

"To town, not to the ER. You get some kind of gift for sending people there? Stock options or free jam or such shit?"

Ten minutes later they rolled into the parking lot at Black Eyed Susie's. Gavin jumped out, grateful for the solid feeling of the earth beneath his feet. For all of Laurel's efforts at keeping him comfortable, her speed kept creeping up until they were back at their white-knuckled pace. After the third attempt to get her to slow down he gave up and lapsed into frightened silence.

Finn, an expert at getting in and out of cars with the wheelchair, talked Laurel through the process with his usual enthusiasm.

Inside, the lunch crowd consisted of three people spread out at tables, morosely poking at their plates. "Busy today," Finn said and waved at Susie.

"Hey, Pops," Susie said dryly, and tried to hide the smile that played with her eyes.

"Hey yourself!" he said. "Nice shirt." Today she sported a T-shirt with the slogan *I Like Animals—They Taste Good* across the front in red letters. "We're here to look at the fish." Finn pointed at the old smoke-stained musky sporting the baseball cap. "My friends here were asking about muskies and I thought that I'd show them a nice one."

Susie gave them a quick once-over and Laurel realized that standing there, covered in dust from the basement, they looked like a group of half-assed anthropologists—all they were missing were pith helmets and shovels.

Susie gave them a *please yourself* shrug. "Try not to break anything."

By default, Laurel was nominated to take the fish down off the wall. Surprisingly, it weighed a lot less than she thought.

"Not too heavy," she said as she lifted it off the wall behind the bar.

"Filled with straw and sawdust, not fiberglass and plastic like the newer mounts," Finn dictated. "This is a real skin mount. The newer ones are painted plastic toys. This has bones in it and everything."

Laurel brought it to the pool table and laid it under the lights. She gently removed the baseball cap from its head. The once vibrantly colored skin had turned to a light brown, and the fins and tail, coated with shellac well before the advent of plastic varnishes, were chipped and broken, giving the fish an ancient look. The musky was mounted in a straight pose, as if darting forward, and even though it lacked the dynamic of newer mounts, there was no mistaking the beauty it had possessed in life. The fish took up a good part of the table, and once down, illuminated in the harsh light of the billiard lamp, the big yellow teeth made them all realize just how much of a threat this thing could be in the water. The largest of the teeth were comparable to the tip of a well-sharpened pencil, the rest close in length and diameter to roofing nails. Gavin thought back to the loon that had disappeared in his bay; a musky half this size would have no trouble swallowing a gaggle as a snack.

Laurel leaned in, examining the mouth. "Look at these things," she whispered, and reached out, touching the tip of a tooth. "They're huge."

"Over four hundred teeth in the upper jaw alone," Finn said, demonstrating that his library of fishing books had been put to good use. "Old Snaggletooth here is the big bad granddaddy of the genus *Esox*, the most widely distributed freshwater fish genus in the Northern Hemisphere."

Gavin brushed the dust off of the engraved brass plaque that had been screwed to the heavy oak backboard. Oxidation had bled out around the screw heads and the plaque had turned a dark brown. He had to squint to read the engraving. "Caught by M. Koestler, October thirteenth, 1931, Lake Caldasac, New York. Weight: sixty-one pounds. Length: fifty-nine inches. Mounted by Alfred Kuntzel and Sons, 1267 Main St., New Mannheim, NY."

"Told you I knew that name." Finn smiled with victory. "And this guy was one helluva fisherman. Look at this thing! It's close to a world record, especially on the lousy tackle they had back then. Why it's hanging in this place beats the crap out of me. I told Susie a gazillion freaking times that this thing is a national treasure. It should be in the IGFA museum or the Freshwater Fishing Hall of Fame in Wisconsin!" Finn stared into the bony jaws facing him and lowered his voice to a whisper. "Did this guy come here to catch *it*?"

Gavin shrugged. "This fish was caught before the dam was opened in December of '32." He ran a hand over the scales on the taxidermy fish. "The early part of the twentieth century was still the Dark Ages when it comes to natural history and sciences. The world was still full of the unknown back then; the mountain gorilla wasn't discovered until 1901; the lost Incan city of Machu Picchu was found in 1911; Carter discovered King Tut's tomb in 1923; the *London Daily Mail* actually hired a big-game hunter to hunt down the Loch Ness Monster in 1935. The early twentieth century really was the age of discovery and myth."

"Are you saying that there is a lost species of animal on our lake? Something undiscovered?" Laurel was shaking her head. "Do you really believe that?"

"It's not a question of belief, it's a question of evidence. No, I don't. But what I *am* saying is that Koestler, who apparently killed everything on the planet that walked, crawled, or swam, was a trophy hunter who was after a trophy. Either he came here to kill *it*, or he came here fishing for a trophy musky and came across *it*. Nothing would turn a man like

Koestler on more than hunting down a monster. Like Finn here, Koestler was a sportsman. And he was here hunting something."

Susie came over. "Like the fish? 'Cause it ain't for sale."

"How about some lunch then?" Finn asked. "Can he buy lunch?"

Gavin smiled. "Hungry?"

"Duh!"

"Lunch would be great. Get us a couple of beers, two Cokes, some cheeseburgers, and two perch platters."

"You know the menu?" Laurel said, impressed. "City Boy is learning his way around here."

"Him and Pops were here the other night with Dave Duffy. Ran up a nice long tab," Susie said and walked away.

"I thought you were joking about drinking here." Laurel looked at Gavin disapprovingly. "Finn is underage, you know."

"And you sound like a broken record," Finn shot back. "See? Everybody has their problems! Now what about our guy Koestler? What happened to him?"

"I say we go to the town hall. They'll have records." Gavin straightened up and looked at the dark space on the wall where the musky had spent the better part of a century looking down on the bar.

"Meaning what?" Laurel asked.

Gavin turned back to the ancient fish stretched out on the stained felt surface. He reached out, running his finger over the bank of teeth that glistened under the bright lights. "Maybe he didn't drown at all."

### 77

### NY State Form 21223-54.LD.NY.GOV
### Record of Death

**Name:** Koestler, Maximillian Agustus.

**Birthdate:** October 8, 1887. (According to passport issued in Germany.)

**Date of death:** August 23, 1933/August 23, 1938.

**Place of death:** New Mannheim township.

**Address of death:** Lake Caldasac, exact location unknown.

**Cause of death:** Suspected drowning. (Deceased lived alone on a lake. House had been locked and the body was not inside, suggesting that deceased locked the doors from the outside. His boat was also missing, further establishing drowning as probable COD.)

**Declared missing by:** Town Clerk, Helga Schneider, August 23, 1933.

**Declared deceased by:** Karl Dusseldorf, MD, Office of ME, New Mannheim, New York, August 23, 1938.

**Approved by:** Judge Rufus Clarence, August 23, 1938.

**Relatives:** No known relatives.

**Comments:** Foul play not suspected.

# 78

Laurel stood on her tiptoes, overreaching to screw the bulb into the last socket. When she was done, she climbed off the ladder and took off the safety glasses. "Go ahead!" she yelled.

There was a loud *crack!* when Gavin threw the breaker at the other end of the basement and the room lit up. The light spilled over the taxidermied denizens of the long-forgotten room, etching the gloom with jagged shadows.

She looked around and the only word to come to mind was, "Wow!"

Gavin stepped through the haphazard opening that a hundred feet of chain, Laurel's Mercedes, and Finn's stump-pulling philosophy had produced. Dave Duffy and Finn closed up the rear.

"Knock yourself out, Mr. Sweden," Finn offered, waving the antique dealer-cum-monster-hunter into the library.

Duffy spent ten minutes walking through the room, taking in the details as if he were casing a home. He made no noise other than the occasional clicking of his tongue in surprise. When he finally spoke, his voice echoed in the dark expanse. "Fooking daft," were his first words.

He stood in a narrow pool of light that accentuated the shadows of his face, setting his eyes in dark sockets. "I'd hate to be drunk down here," he said. A thin crescent of light bounced off the top of the Guinness can in his hand, a bright

Cyclops happy face in aluminum. "That being said—" He raised the can and took a sip.

"Cool, huh?" Finn poked.

"That it is, lad." Duffy walked among the dead animals. "This man killed everything there was to kill," he said as he paused under the yawning hippopotamus. "I don't know a fooking thing about animal mounts, but I'll write you a check for a hundred grand right now for the contents of this room. And I'd make money," he said, pronouncing it *mooney*, the shadowed sockets enlarging with the movement. "Fooking loads, I suspect."

"We don't care what this stuff is worth," Finn snapped. "Why are they here?"

Duffy's mustache curled up in a smile. "As one mental patient to another?" He finished his beer in a monumental slurp, as if insight was to be found at the bottom of the can.

"Something like that, yes."

"I think you've got the original butterfly collector here."

Gavin held up the photocopies taken from the ancient microfilm files at the town hall. "Koestler simply disappeared one day. Poof." Gavin snapped his fingers. "His bills stopped getting paid. He didn't show up in town. Finally, someone realized that he had gone missing and reported it. The house got closed up and the whole thing slipped into the collective amnesia of New Mannheim."

"Like David Kenyon Webster," Finn interjected.

"Who?" Duffy's mustache curled down with the question.

"David Kenyon Webster," Finn snapped. "David Kenyon Webster for chrissake! How can you call yourself a fisherman?" He faced empty stares. "Wrote *Shark: Myth and Maneater*?" Still nothing. "You guys are a disgrace to fishermen everywhere. Greatest book on sharks ever! Never got finished. Went out fishing in California and never came back. They found half his boat and one oar."

Gavin and Duffy nodded in unison, letting Finn know that they were both thinking the same thing.

It was Duffy who spoke. "Not a comforting comparison."

In the dark, the room had been gloomy and ethereal; in the light, it was organized and frightening. Laurel stopped at the elephant-foot coffee table that was nestled in between two crocodile-hide-covered club chairs that sprouted springs and tufts of horse hair. On the table was an empty sardine tin with a fork resting on the edge, the contents long since turned to dust. Beside it, sitting on a saucer, was a dust-covered teacup. "Looks like someone's lunch is still here." She smiled. "Incidentally, they ate like you do."

Gavin and Finn followed Duffy to one of the walls of shelving. The desk with the stag antler hardware sat in the middle of an alcove among the books. Finn passed a mounted fish skeleton, the ribs covered in a skin of spiderwebs that rippled as he rolled by, giving breath to a creature long dead. He smiled at it and said, "Pike. Thirty, maybe thirty-five pounder. Big, big fish."

Sitting in the middle of the desk were two books. Gavin picked up the first, a large leather-bound volume that seemed to be crammed with extra sheaves of paper; the spine was close to bursting. It was a journal of sorts, the kind that Peter Beard would eventually make famous. Inside, folded in among the endless photos of the same man standing over dead trophies, invariably cradling a rifle in his arms, Gavin found random souvenirs from faded feathers to long-dried swatches of snake skin. The hunter had a blond flattop and a jaw that belonged on the front end of a bulldozer. From his forehead the deep line of a scar traveled over his left eye and terminated just over the flat line of his humorless mouth. Probably a fencing scar, Gavin mused—his type *always* had a fencing scar. In the different photos he wore the same outfit: a pair of breeches, high boots laced to just below his knee, and a light shirt with the elbows rolled up. Around his neck he wore a necklace that had been crafted out of claws of some sort. Gavin put the journal back onto the desk.

The second book was much older than anything else they had seen in the library, having been printed on a hand press. Duffy whistled. "Almost certainly fifteenth century—early German Gothic script. A book like this belongs in an archive, not in some lost room buried under a house on a haunted lake." None of the others shared his smile. "It was a joke," he said.

Duffy squatted down on his haunches so that Finn could share in the discovery. He gently opened the relic, keeping the pages at no more than a ninety-degree angle from each other to prevent it from disintegrating in his hand. True to early books, the pages were filled with weighted-down text and there was very little in the way of empty space on the page, a nod to the expense of paper when the book had been produced. What illustrations there were all dealt with sea monsters, devils, and distorted denizens of the oceans—most were detailed studies of the creatures in situ, going about their business. In keeping with all art of the period, they looked slightly askew, heads too big or bodies too fat, their creator relying on the artistic style of the times.

As Duffy leafed through the volume, the book fell open to an illustration, as if the book was used to being opened to this page. It was an etching of an enormous creature pulled from a river that ran by a stone wall dotted with a row of medieval archer's windows. It was being hoisted out of a canal by a horse and tackle—the creature was fishlike but the twisted features and sheer size of the beast lent it an unmistakably malicious aspect—evil embodied for the God-fearing audience of the time.

"Right out of Hieronymus Bosch," Gavin said aloud, not really meaning to.

"It's spooky, too," Finn added, his eyes drawn into the ancient engraving.

"Medieval morality lesson: the monster is an allegorical representation of God's wrath," Duffy said. "Typical of the period."

They all squinted at the heavy lines of the five-hundred-year-old stone etching. Even in its simplicity, there was no denying that the artist had wanted to inflict a sense of fear in his public. Half a millennium later he was still succeeding.

"Scare the shite out of me, it would." Duffy moved the book into a bright cone of light so they could all better examine the page. The sharp contrast between the yellowed paper and the harsh, jagged lines of the engraving was absolute, no use of shadow hinted at. Like good and evil of the period's literature, there was no middle ground in the artist's technique.

"I'd love to catch that thing," Finn said through a big grin.

Duffy lifted his eyes from the image and focused on the wall. For a few moments he stared blankly, trying to absorb what they had found here. After a few moments his mustache broke into a broad furry smile.

"What you staring at?" Finn asked.

"You don't see it?"

Finn looked up at the vast expanse of wall over the desk. It was the only wall space in the room that wasn't occupied by a trophy. "There's nothing there," Finn said condescendingly.

"Exactly." Duffy looked down at the boy. "He was saving this space."

"For what?" Finn asked.

Duffy glanced around a room filled with the dead stares of Koestler's trophies. "That, my dear lad," he said slowly, "is the sixty-four-thousand-dollar question."

# 79

Dr. Duncan Parks stood over the autopsy table, staring down at what few chunks were left of Roy and Karin Perkins. Mrs. Perkins was represented by her used-to-be-white bikini top and the slashes of violence that had ended her life. Mr. Perkins provided a little more in the way of remains. But not much. There was the left lens of a pair of diving goggles and a patch of scalp with his ear still attached—the whole thing not much larger than a dollar bill and looking like a chunk of retread lying by the side of 47E. They had been lucky with the ear— Mr. Perkins had been a little on the chubby side and the subcutaneous fat had added buoyancy; they had found it floating near one of the big channel markers.

Parks stood over the table with his arms crossed, magnifying glasses pushed up onto his forehead like a miniature welder's mask, his personal version of a frown straightening his mouth into a line. Even though the subterranean room was air-conditioned, the layer of fat from the hairy bookmark had melted a little and it looked like a smear of margarine on the stainless-steel table.

This time the thing throwing him off was the lens of the diving goggles; there was a neat pressure hole on the right, approximately where Mr. Perkins's tear duct would have been, as if someone had fired a .22 round through the plastic. Parks had done a series of pressure tests and the force required would have to have been greater than 130 foot-pounds, nearly 26 percent stronger than a .22 slug (the redneck round of choice out here). No, that hole had not come from a .22. Parks had run through everything he could think of that might have caused the hole, from a crossbow bolt with a round target head to a ball bearing from a Claymore mine, and in every case the puncture hole would have been inconsistent with the type of damage that had been inflicted on the lens. Even a .222 or a .223 slug was incapable of producing this kind of damage. Parks was at a loss.

The bikini top was another story. The slashes and holes were consistent with the type of damage that a boat prop would cause. No problem there.

Except that he still had the flap of scalp to explain; it looked like it had just been peeled off of Mr. Perkins's skull. The flesh was ripe and plump and for all intents and purposes looked like a medical model. Except that this was an autopsy lab, not a classroom. What had happened to these people?

He was going on the assumption that the piece of hair and skin belonged to Mr. Perkins. It wouldn't officially belong to the man until a swab was sent off to the lab in Albany and it was confirmed by a DNA match. Same with the bathing suit top. Although with that one, chances were it would come back inconclusive.

The shrill chirp of the phone startled him. "Parks."

"Dr. Parks, Sheriff Pope. You get the reports for that boating accident finished yet? I need to file them with the state troopers before the end of the day."

Parks could picture Pope, big boots propped up on his desk, smelling like vodka and mouthwash, eyes that looked hijacked off of a rabid animal doing a little jig as he talked. "Not yet, there are a few things—"

"Good. I'll be by in fifteen to pick them up. Make sure that you cross the T's and dot the I's, 'kay?" And Pope hung up.

Parks glanced at the wall of filing cabinets, his focus locking on the pending cases drawer. "Two more," he said, and touched his pen to the first autopsy form. He paused, wondering if he had been keeping Caldasac's secrets for so long that he had become part of the problem. But what could he do? Who would listen to him? And what about the past? Someone would be blamed. And that someone would be him.

He scrawled two words into the box reserved for cause of death. He repeated the same two words on the second form.

*Boating accident.*

# 80

"I don't want Gavin to know." Finn's eyes looked like they belonged to a much older, much harder man.

Laurel put the four-inch-thick file down on the potential paper avalanche of her desk and came around to the boy. She squatted down and looked into his eyes. "Finn, I am your physician before I am Gavin's friend, but Gavin is your legal guardian right now. If I withhold this from him, I could lose my license."

Finn's eyes filled with tears. "Is there any way we can keep this a secret?"

Laurel shook her head. "I don't have a choice here. This isn't something I can ignore. As your physician *or* as your friend." She stood up and leaned against the desk, arms crossed, professional composure back.

Finn pounded the arm of his wheelchair. "Friends keep secrets for each other all the time. That's what they do. That's like the number-one golden rule in the handbook!" He looked at the thick file perched on her desk, three years' worth of operations, hospital visits, checkups, blood tests, and myriad other pokings and proddings. "I ain't gonna die tomorrow, am I?"

"Finn, your kidneys aren't working like they're supposed to." She tapped the thick file. "You've been seeing blood in your urine for a few days now. If things keep on sliding, you could be facing renal failure. And I'm worried about other things. Things that need to be checked out."

Finn shook his head. "That means no more fishing."

She just stared down at the boy.

"Look, lady, you're supposed to be some sort of hotshot genius. If you were me, what would you do?"

Laurel leaned over. "I'm not going to lie to you—this is serious. Very serious. But there's something else that's in the handbook—friends look out for each other. Sometimes they buy one another time. We could do some more tests."

Finn's eyes narrowed. "What kind of tests?"

"Well"—she looked up, accessing the information—"I have to order a second battery of blood tests to make sure that these are accurate."

"You mean it could be a mistake?"

Laurel shook her head. "I don't think so, Finn. But we can order more tests. More tests take time." She raised her eyebrows in inquiry. "I wouldn't have to inform Gavin of the results until we've confirmed these," she said, tapping the thick file. "That could take a while. It's lying a little, and I don't like it. But it will buy you some more time."

Finn's face slowly spread into a decent smile, not huge but genuine, which, under the circumstances, was a small miracle in its own right. "Two weeks?"

Laurel shook her head again. "Three days. They'll go out today and I'll get them back Monday."

"At the beginning of Monday or the end of Monday?"

Laurel shrugged. "I don't know."

"So I don't need to come in before Tuesday, right?"

Laurel pursed her lips, stared at the boy, shifted her eyes to the file sitting on the desk, then zeroed back in on Finn. After a few seconds of cost-benefit analysis, she said, "I could do Tuesday. *Early* Tuesday."

"Make it three o'clock."

Laurel threw up her arms. "Why not? But you feel anything change—anything at all—you let me know. No matter what. If you promise, we have a deal."

"Only if you don't tell Gavin. I know how people act when they get all smoochie. They start sharing sandwiches and toothbrushes and secrets. It's disgusting." He stuck out his tongue in revulsion.

"Finn, you should be a lawyer."

"Nah." Finn waved his hand dismissively. "Lawyers don't fish."

# 81

After adjusting the wire-rimmed glasses on his nose, Dave Duffy squinted into the wake his boat carved through Caldasac. With a hundred yards of line out and the big lead-weighted daisy chain of carp down to sixty feet, there were constant problems: structure, weeds, submerged rock piles, sunken logs and trees. The only way to make sure things ran like they were supposed to was by feel, and everything felt fine. The rod tip was vibrating perfectly, the drag on the daisy chain creating a steady thrum. He spent as much time paying attention to the feel of the line and the vibration of the rod as he did to piloting the boat. More, maybe.

With the heavy load on the outrigger, he only had one rod mounted. Even though he had a three-dimensional sonar, any unexpected structure, either topographical or other, would create hours of work if both Canons tangled. So he kept it simple.

He was running the edge of deep water—an underwater shelf that went from thirty feet straight down to ninety in a nearly vertical drop.

Duffy popped another Guinness and trimmed his direction by a hair. He had converted the live well to a cooler, and every morning before heading out onto the lake he stocked it with fresh ice and as many four-packs as he could molecularly pack into the confines of the space, making sure to rotate yesterday's ice-cold remains in front of today's lukewarm offerings. The frigid ale almost cracked his teeth whenever he opened a fresh can and it was this sensation that he loved. He pulled off a long draw and the bitter beer went down like mother's milk, and that warm haze that had been building up with the previous four-pack washed over him and he felt the world get a little softer. Three massive gulps later and he tossed the empty into a five-gallon bucket.

The rod started to twitch erratically; the big daisy chain had fouled and risen to the surface and the unbalanced tension on the outrigger caused the hum. He snapped his head back and saw the bait dragging on the surface, like a water skier unable to lift out. It skipped ungracefully for a few seconds then cut into the water, bobbing up a few seconds later in a series of clumsy flips. Duffy throttled down and there was a zing followed by a snap as the downrigger clip released and line started disappearing off the big spool of his reel with the high-pitched scream of a jet engine shaking apart.

The bait was gone. Line was tearing off to the starboard side. Duffy yanked the heavy rod out of the holder and tightened up the drag as much as he could. The high-pitched wail of the reel went up an octave but kept peeling out. He looked back at the water; whatever had taken the carp rig was running.

Holy shite, was it running!

# 82

It was dusk and Finn and Gavin had just finished trolling the same underwater ledge—about two miles upstream from Duffy—when the call came in over the handheld. Finn had just taken his carp rig out of the water when the radio on his hip squealed a blast of static. Duffy's voice boomed across the dead air.

"I've fookin' got the bugger! The daisy chain fouled and came up. He hit it on the surface. Gotta go, lads—" And the signal went dead.

Gavin started up the engine and Finn pulled his seatbelt tight. The prop kicked up a white wake fifteen feet long and the Boston Whaler lurched forward into the setting sun.

# 83

Duffy worked the big reel hard and he was getting nowhere. He had tightened the drag up to the point that it had nothing left to give and the asbestos washers were squealing like a stuck pig. He was losing line faster than he thought possible.

At first the run was straight aft, heading away from the boat. Moving fast. Moving very fast. When he was almost down to the spool, the line slowed, then stopped, and Duffy saw that whatever had taken the bait had turned and was circling back. He needed to regain some of the line he had lost. Line was what kept the fight going. It was also the weakest point—which is where the drag on the reel and the flex of the rod came in.

The rod tip slowly came up and lost its set. Then the line started to slacken and bow. Whatever was coming toward him was doing so at a speed greater than he could recoup line. He pumped harder and the muscles in his wiry arm knotted and burned. He kept pumping, hoping to gain leverage by bringing the line back to a tension-on state.

But it was coming at him too fast.

There was an instant when he realized that it was coming straight for the boat and he felt glad. Glad for himself and glad for a dead dog named Petey. If it came alongside, he would put a deer slug into it from the sawed-off shotgun he kept on board. If he had to, he'd kill the bloody thing with a fire axe! All he had to do was get it close enough. You could kill anything if you got it close enough.

And then it surfaced.

Duffy saw it.

The massive snout broke first, creating a wave that washed up and over its misshapen skull, a natural lens that magnified its jaws. Its back moved and pulsed, propelling it forward with the steady speed of a Le Mans car. Its path bent the water out and away from it and it rode in a trough, its massive scaled body virtually hydroplaning on top of the water. It screamed in on Duffy.

"Fook me," he whispered as he reached for the shotgun.

It was thirty feet from the boat when its body left the water, stabbing skyward, arcing through the dusk. It exploded into the darkening sky, a ton of water shattering into the air. Duffy had time to duck but there was nowhere to go. He was on the deck. Naked. Vulnerable.

He had time to bring the barrel up but not to aim.

He saw the snout, open and skewered with hundreds of hooks, the remnants of his daisy chain hanging off to one side. Teeth everywhere. As far as he could see. The beast pounded into him.

Duffy was sure that he had squeezed the trigger. At least the last impulse that the nerves in his hand had received had demanded that action. But he never heard the shot or felt the kick of the gun. He was gone and all that was left of him was half of his right hand, the index finger repeatedly scratching at the fiberglass gunwale where it had plopped, trying to squeeze a trigger that no longer mattered.

## 84

Gavin saw Duffy's boat from a half a mile off. It was drifting with the current, the engines idling on low and the blue-gray smog of the exhaust dissipating in the light breeze. He knew immediately that something was terribly wrong.

"There it is," Finn said a second later. "Mr. Sweden, you there?" He spoke tentatively into the radio, the false bravado of pseudomilitary jargon gone. "Hello?"

"Turn it off," Gavin said. "He's not there."

When they were a hundred yards off, Gavin saw that the line on one of the outriggers was knotted into a bird's nest that twisted in the wind. The windshield was simply not there anymore. What was left of the Bimini top was a single bent pole and a scrap of fabric—the rest was just gone. If Duffy was still on board, he had to be lying down.

"David!" Gavin yelled, cupping his mouth in his hands. "Hey, David!"

Finn slid his chair forward on the rail system, craning his neck, trying to see into Duffy's boat. "You see him?" he asked, not really expecting an answer.

"You stay put. You don't move. You don't breathe. And you don't make any fucking noise. Keep your eyes peeled."

"For what?"

"For anything." Gavin looked around for their bearings. They were in the middle of the widest part of the reservoir, and shore was an easy mile off on either side. Without binoculars no one would have seen a thing, especially in the gray twilight.

Gavin eased the *Low Rider* up against Duffy's boat and tied off. "Okay," he said. "Pay attention and keep your wits about you." Gavin eased over the side and stepped onto Duffy's deck.

The scene was offset by a mournful wail that was coming from somewhere on board. A noise that sounded human but wasn't human at all.

"What's that sound?" Finn whispered.

Gavin held up his hand while he looked around the boat.

Everything above the gunwale was destroyed, splintered, twisted forward as if the boat had been dragged down a mountainside on its roof. The Bimini top and windshield were gone— just gone. The mounting brackets and screws ripped violently out. The railings, rod holders, and flagpole were mangled and bent. The engine cover was scratched in a three-foot swatch right down the middle, chunks of fiberglass flecking the deck in flakes of white and blue. The steering wheel shaft was bent, and the wheel sat off to one side, lopsided and goofy. Duffy's shotgun was on the floor, covered in shards of fiberglass, windshield, and metal. The boat looked like a dog's chew toy. Only the dog would have to weigh in at the size of a small house.

Gavin found the source of the eerie cry that moaned through the humid air: a Guinness can was sitting on what was left of the console, somehow miraculously untouched by whatever had plowed through Duffy. As the boat slid in the easy swells the wind licked across the mouth of the container and drew out a sad howl. Gavin picked it up and, after looking around for a place to put it, simply dropped it to the deck, where it bled beer from its mouth. "Fuck." The thought that Duffy had somehow managed to survive wasn't even in the wings of Gavin's mind.

Then he spotted something on the gunwale. White and bloodless and waxy. It was part of a hand—a thumb and two fingers.

"Oh no," was all he said, and closed his eyes.

"What? What!" Finn half yelled, half whispered. "What is it?"

"Duffy's dead, Finn. The thing got him. Smashed his boat." Gavin sat down heavily on Duffy's chair. "It's over. Done."

"Why? How do you know he's dead?" Finn was craning his neck like a turtle, trying to see on board.

Gavin pointed at the three fingers on the gunwale. There was no mess, no globules of blood, no tendons, just a neat little row of three digits and part of a palm, ready and waiting for someone to pick them up and yell, Gotcha!

"What is that?" the kid asked. "Ohmygod, ohmygod, ohmygod—are those fingers? Ohmygod."

Gavin stepped across the deck and over the side, back onto the *Low Rider*. He turned on the radio and spun the knob to the emergency channel.

"What are you doing?" Finn asked, turning the radio off with a snap.

"I'm calling the police, Finn. Duffy is dead. This thing is fucking dangerous. We have to tell someone."

"We don't have to tell anyone anything!" the boy pleaded. "Not a soul. We can still find it ourselves. We can still get it!"

"Finn, look at Duffy's boat! It's torn to ratshit! The thing killed him, Finn. Duffy got chewed to bits and all that is left is a few fingers and Duffy was one tough little fucker! If he couldn't find a way out of this, we certainly aren't going to get anywhere. What are we? Two cripples. You got no legs and my fucking arm is busted. No. It's over. I am calling the police."

Tears rimmed Finn's sparse eyelashes. "Maybe he drowned. No one has to know!"

"Have you looked around, kid? His fingers are right there! Did he chop them off before he went for a swim?" Gavin turned away from the boy and powered up the radio again. He didn't see any options, not anymore.

Without a word and with a move so precise that it looked as if he had practiced it, Finn snatched up his fishing rod and struck out with it as if it were a fencing sword, flinging Duffy's fingers off into the water. He dropped the rod to the deck and crossed his arms. "It's my word against yours."

Gavin exploded. "Are you nuts? Are you completely out of your fucking mind!" He wanted to hit the boy, to knock some sense into him. Instead he smashed his hand into the steering console. "Fuck!" He dropped into the pilot's chair, defeated, and closed his eyes.

After a few moments reprieve, Finn's voice started chattering. At first it was slow, almost imperceptible, but it steadily grew into a noise that Gavin couldn't ignore.

"Look, Gav, we don't have to tell anyone. We can keep this a secret. We can. It's easy. All we do is say nothing. We let the boat drift, someone finds it, and they think that he drowned. There's no evidence. We can do it. It's okay. It's—"

"No," Gavin shook his head. "It's not okay, Finn. It's not. Not by a fucking miracle mile it's not. Walt Pinkowski was killed. Duffy was killed. That's two people who are dead because I kept my mouth shut. I knew that something was out here. I fucked up."

"Wait a second! You knew? What did you know?" Finn crossed his arms over his chest, the homemade tattoo bright against his threadbare T-shirt. "What did you really know for sure? You didn't know shit."

"I knew that Walter Pinkowski had been killed by whatever the fuck this thing is. That's what I knew."

"No! No, you didn't! You suspected, but you couldn't have known. Not until now—not until you saw those fingers!"

The kid was right. He had had his doubts. He had never really known anything. It had all been about belief. And he hadn't really believed. Not the way he should have—not in his bones. But that wasn't the point. The point was that Duffy was dead and this thing wasn't about to stop. "Finn, look at this." Gavin swept his arm over Duffy's boat. "Look at what happened here. Something came aboard and fucking ate Duffy. He had a shotgun in his hand and the fucking thing ate him before he could get off a round!"

"That's not true. Maybe he got off a few rounds. You can't know! Not for sure!"

"I know that he's fucking dead!" Gavin screamed. He ran his hands through his hair and tried to stop shaking. "If he had pumped a shell into the thing there would be blood. You said yourself that the thing bled. I don't see any blood. I don't see any empty shells. And I certainly don't fucking see Duffy!" Gavin closed his eyes and tried to consciously push the adrenaline down with a series of deep breaths. *In with the good, out with the bad.* Over and over and over again. But the bad wasn't listening, it was having too much fun staying right where it was. Gavin flipped the breech lock and popped the sawed-off twelve open. Two unfired big blue shells were in the side-by-side chambers. Duffy hadn't got a round off. "He's dead."

"Yeah? So what!" Finn suddenly screamed, his face bursting red. "So fucking what! My mom's dead! My dad's dead! People die. It happens all the time! You wanna let it make you scared? Go ahead! Hide and be afraid! But I'm no coward. You'd be surprised what I can do! I'm going to find this thing and I am going to kill it and you can sit at home and watch television and miss your wife and be a big baby all by yourself!" His voice ripped out in ragged gasps. "You wanna die on your sofa listening to your stupid records like an old man? Good. But count me out! I ain't dying like that. Not me. No

way. No way in hell! I got a half a week left and I'm gonna—"
He stopped abruptly.

"Half a week, Finn? What half a week?"

Finn's eyes dropped to his lap and his face grew old, haggard. He shook his head. "Nothing."

Gavin squatted down in front of the boy, looked up into his face. "Finn, what's going on? We're supposed to be friends. You're supposed to tell me things."

Finn lifted his too-big skull and smiled weakly. "I have to go back to the hospital on Tuesday and I don't know what's going to happen to me. I'm getting sicker." He reached down and lifted his trouser leg. The urine bag around his calf, secured in place by elastics, was clouded with blood. "I can feel stuff not working inside. I have headaches all day long and it hurts when I breathe and I taste plastic and sour eggs all the time. It's like I'm rotting inside or something. I'm glad my mom ain't here to see this. I don't have no more time."

Gavin stood up and looked around. Duffy's splintered boat was ready for the dump. "Finn, you could get killed." *I could get killed*, he wanted to add.

"I'm already dead, Gavin. This is it for me. This is my last autumn. Maybe my last few days. I'd rather die doing this than rot away in the hospital with Russel Sprouts the fart machine to keep me company. This"—Finn waved his arm through the air—"is where I want to be."

Gavin felt his anger go through a fast chemical burn and convert into sadness. "Okay. Three days. And we find this fucking thing. No more being pussies. We're the Original Bad Motherfuckers, right?"

Finn nodded and tears plopped onto his lap. "Bad Motherfuckers. Sure."

Gavin took Duffy's shotgun and tucked it away under the console. "We have to sink his boat, Finn. Do you know how?"

Finn nodded and wiped his nose. "Sure. Easy."

"Anyone finds out about this and I'm off to jail. Do you understand that?"

Finn pulled the back of his hand across his face, wiping away the tears. "Sure. Striped clothes and bad chow."

"Don't do that. I don't want to hear any of your late-night movie analogies or bad jokes. This is a criminal offense. This ever ends up in front of the authorities and I am going to be in the cooker. It's possible that my money buys me a way out of this; possible but unlikely. Judges like to make examples of people like me."

"I understand what's going on." Finn's eyes narrowed to dark slits. "Really."

Gavin looked over at Duffy's boat and shook his head. Why was it that the people he liked ended up dying? "I hope so, kiddo," he said. "Now tell me how to sink this thing."

# 85

Laurel paced the retaining wall with the tired gait of someone who should have been in bed hours ago. Aside from the deep fatigue, she was angry and cold, the hot cup of coffee in her hand and the antique quilt doing little to stave off the evening frost. Sundown had been well over five hours ago and they should have been home shortly after that. She was well past angry and on her way to scared when she heard the irregular chug of the *Low Rider*'s engine.

As she waited for the boat to enter the little bay, she watched the water closely, looking for anything that might hint at a presence. Look at me, she thought, all of a sudden I believe in the Yeti. She shook her head and turned away from the water. *Presence. Monster. It. The Thing.* All of it sounded like bullshit to her. Complete stellar macho bullshit. It was thinking like this that turned wrestling and Hooters into American institutions.

She was a scientist and she believed—no, she *knew*—that the world operated on certain unbendable principles. Evolution was a fact. Gravity existed. And there were no angels dancing on the head of a pin. Following closely behind these was the biggest truism of all: *There are no monsters.* And up here, on a lost lake in northern New York, they weren't going to discover any new species—lost, forgotten, or otherwise. Mathematical probability proved that. Too many people here for too long. It was something logical. Something that made sense.

But here she was, Ahab's widow pacing the walk, waiting for her man to come home to his Karloffian house, anchovy-addicted, farting cat, and sex-crazed handyman. Oh, and she couldn't forget the personal assistant, all good boyfriends had one. Shannon had called earlier that night and when she found out that Gavin wasn't home, she insisted that he call her as soon as he came in, regardless of the hour. Who the hell lived like this? She shivered again and turned back to the sound of the approaching boat. All she knew was that some-one was going to get his ass kicked.

Gavin's face appeared in her thoughts, another in a count-less line of random images that had run through her mind while she had been pacing. There were a thousand reasons why they shouldn't work but the only thing that she could think of was how deliriously happy she was when she was with him. This man broke every rule she had about men. First off, she had been weaned on academia and, as such, had always gravitated to the hypereducated brainiacs in her field. And all of them had been complete and utter disasters. Not all disasters in a Pearl Harbor sense, although she had had her share of those, pyrotechnics and all, but failures nonethe-less. In retrospect, it was the fizzles that were even more dis-appointing than the ones that exploded. The slamming door, the thrown coffee mug, the kicked-over pot of flowers—all decreed a certain level of what? Passion, maybe. But the rela-tionships that just died were all so sad. So forgettable.

Then there was the fact that he was younger than her by a decade and change. A *lot* of change. Enough to make up almost another decade. She had been prom queen before he had even been born. She had been pounding her way through medical school when he was just learning the differ-ence between a dog and a log and a frog.

And what about the money? She made a good living by any standards; with the cost of living in New Mannheim what it was, she was considered well-off. But his income was simply not measurable in terms she knew. She had no idea what he made on a book but she had read somewhere that his average advance—and that didn't include paperback or foreign language rights—was now over ten million. Then again, she didn't want him to support her. So what did she want from him? And then it came to her.

She wanted to be with him.

Laurel thought about Gavin Corlie, his body, his face, and she felt twinges of desire on so many levels. He wasn't handsome in a classical sense. But there was something alluring about his face. The eyes were definitely a part of his charm. And his smile worked a million different ways. His hair was still thick—and he was right, it was starting to turn gray. When he took off his clothes, she liked his body. And he seemed to like hers. A lot. So what was the problem? When she thought about it like that—in the basic terms that did away with all the crap people keep telling themselves is so important—she couldn't find a thing wrong. Not a single solitary thing. Except he was five hours late. And had made up some bullshit lie about a monster on the lake that was eating people. Other than that, he was a good guy. Mostly.

Oh, and he had a secret underground crypt that housed a hundred-year-old shrine to Norman Bates. Couldn't forget that one; that was a biggie. Stick it up on the list taped to the fridge somewhere between *Forget dead wife* and *Kill monster*. Then everything would be all right, at least as all right as things were going to get with this one. This one. Again. *Christ*, she thought, *I'm getting too old for this.*

Finn's boat seemed to be limping into the bay, listing to one side, the engine thrumming erratically. Laurel peered into the dark. Gavin was driving and Finn was at the back, against the stern. When the boat was about twenty yards off, Gavin waved and then asked, "What are you doing up so late?" He looked beat.

The *Low Rider* eased into the boathouse, which was nearly finished except for the half-done shingles on the bright new plywood roof, like a skin graft in the early stages of reepithe-lialization. Laurel entered through the side door and flipped on the light. Gavin tied off to the bronze cleats. He smiled up at Laurel. "You look tired, baby."

All the anger and frustration washed away. "I am." Then that little voice in the back of her mind, the one that had been chattering away all night about what an inconsiderate bas-tard he was, started up. "Where the hell have you two been?" She looked at Finn, half asleep at the back, his hands filthy. "And what's wrong with your hands?"

Gavin climbed up the ladder, his bad arm left out of the equation, his good arm compensating for the deficiency. "Engine trouble," he offered.

Finn wiped his hands off on a rag. "Goddamned spark plugs gummed up. I had to take all of them out, clean them, and get them back in while Mr. Shakyhands here held the flashlight for me like a blind man. Hand me a wrench, I say. What's a wrench? he asks. Give me that caliper. What's a caliper? he asks. It's like dealing with a…a…city boy." Finn looked too tired to unbuckle his belts.

Gavin gave Laurel a hug and she winced at the strong smell of gasoline and oil that radiated from his clothes.

"The engine conked out, and if it wasn't for Finn's sur-geonlike approach to the motor, we'd still be out there float-ing around in circles."

Laurel stepped back and pulled the ancient quilt tighter around herself. "Your boat broke down? This smells fishy. No pun intended."

"Look, can you give me a hand getting Finn up? We're both pooped, and my arm's killing me."

"Where's Duffy?" she asked from the unhappy place that seemed to have her boxed in—*Bullshitville*, she liked to call it.

"I thought that he was back already. It's possible that he docked at Finn's place. I don't know. Why?" Gavin swung the boom arm over the boat, lining it up with Finn. Insects had started to swarm around the overhead light and Finn made a point of swatting the bigger ones that came near him.

"Because every night for the past eight days you boys have been coming in at dark, and tonight neither of you comes back on time and one of you doesn't come back at all. That's why. And now I'm supposed to believe that this Cadillac of fishing boats had engine failure. It all sounds like bullshit to me."

It was Finn that settled it. "Look, lady, I know that you're a famous doctor and that you like to tell everyone what to do all the goddamned time, but it's one in the morning, I haven't had anything to eat or drink in hours, my hands are covered in oil, I pulled off a fingernail trying to get a plug back in a hole, and I have a headache that I would trade for a broken arm. Can you crab at us tomorrow?"

Laurel looked down and was about to blast the kid but the expression on his face said, *Go ahead, it can't get any worse.*

"Why don't we get you out of that boat," Gavin said politely, as if he was afraid of the boy's wrath.

"And people your age run the world," Finn said with more than a hint of sarcasm. He threw his arms in the air. "What the hell do you think I've been trying to do?"

Laurel ignored Finn's ranting and poked Gavin in the arm. "I almost forgot, Shannon called. She said that you were to call her as soon as you got in."

Gavin glanced down at the big diver's watch strapped to his wrist.

"*As soon as you got in,*" Laurel repeated, stressing her point, and headed for the door. "I'll be up at the house making coffee."

"Thanks."

After she was gone, Gavin went to work on the winch. As Finn's body rose he kept swatting away the cloud of insects that hovered around him and for an instant he looked like he was flying. "You know what, Finn?"

"What?" he asked as he smacked a big moth that fell in widening circles into the water.

"You're a pretty good liar."

Finn stopped waving his arms and smiled. "Always let people underestimate you," he said.

# 86

Laurel was working on getting the fire going when Gavin came out of the bathroom toweling his hair. For the first time in what felt like a month he was clean, and the pungent stink of fish and diesel fuel had been replaced with the soapy smell of apricot, lemon, or some other chemically reproduced scent of fruit. While Laurel concentrated on the fire, Gavin pulled on a pair of jeans and a loose T-shirt with *The Clash* spray-painted across the chest and sat down on the edge of the bed. Laurel thought that he looked tired, but more than a bit of his trouble would have been attributed to the fact that Dave Duffy had died, and to appease a thirteen-year-old who had used guilt as a hammer, he had agreed to lie for another few days. In short, he felt like shit inside.

"You get Finn tucked in all right?" he asked, trying to forget what had happened out on the lake.

"He and Foots are snoring loudly."

Gavin hung the damp towel over one of the bed's mahogany posts. "I hate to break your bubble but that noise isn't snoring—that cat's got a serious problem."

Laurel tried not to laugh while she blew on the small fire she had managed to coax to life. "Finn's started calling him Farts instead of Foots, and I hate to admit it, but it fits."

"That it does." Gavin picked up the phone and held the handset to his chest for a few seconds. "You look beautiful," he said. And, as corny as it sounded, it was true.

Shannon answered on the first ring and from her tone, Gavin could tell that she had been awake. "What are you doing up?"

"Amy and I had a few friends over tonight and they just left." There was a slight slur to her voice.

Gavin looked at his watch. "I just got home."

"I told the doctor lady to tell you to call as soon as you got in. Incidentally, she's very nice. Am I allowed to say I like her?"

"Of course." Laurel was in front of the fire, watching the white flicker of flame. "I take it that you talked to McFee."

"Yes, I did. He wanted me to ask you where you dig up the stuff that you do. He also said that he wants a nice big present for his efforts, mentioned a new lawnmower—the kind you sit on. Apparently he feels that the FBI archives aren't there for your personal use. Go figure. You got a pad?"

"Give me a second." Gavin cupped his hand over the mouthpiece. "Baby?"

Laurel looked up from the fire, her eyes smiling.

"Do you feel like getting us something to drink? Something with a high alcohol content."

Laurel stood up and walked out of the room, her small hips swaying just enough to keep his attention until she was gone. He turned back to Shannon. "Sorry, Shannon, but I have had a very long day and I have a feeling that I'll be needing a drink after this."

"I e-mailed you the whole thing. You want a rundown or should I just say good night?"

Gavin took a notepad from the nightstand and unscrewed the cap on a fountain pen. "Give me what you can remember."

"I can do better than that, I've got my notes right here." There was the sound of pages being turned.

"Koestler, Maximillian Agustus. Born Vienna, Austria, 1887, to a wealthy industrialist—his family owned a series of foundries. Little Max spent his youth skiing the Alps, hunting tigers in India, and searching the lost continent with his father for monsters that time had forgotten. Real sporty type. Hunted big game, skiied, rode horses, and—"

"Fenced," Gavin interjected.

There was a pause on the other end. "How'd you know that?"

Gavin thought back to the photo he had seen in the journal. "A lucky guess."

"Sure." She paused and the silence was accompanied by the sound of her flipping through her notes. "Studied embryology at the University of Frankfurt. Did his thesis on Mendel's genetics—a branch of biology that focuses on hereditary traits, the basic way in which chromosomes are sorted. Graduated with honors 1908 and spent the next six years traveling the globe with his brother, Gunter, hunting. Made a name for himself in big-game circles, bagged three world records: one for a bull elephant in Kenya, 1911; the next for a hippopotamus in South Africa, 1912; then another for a twenty-one-foot Nile crocodile in Egypt—killed it with a spear after it attacked his boat. His brother and three guides were killed by the animal in the struggle."

"Impressive." Gavin thought back to the photo of the cinder-block-jawed man in the wool britches.

"When war broke out on the continent, he enlisted. Spent the entire war at the front lines. Distinguished combat record. Came back a hero. Emigrated to the US in 1918. Spent six months traveling the country before he had an address— your house. He buys it for cash and lists no occupation on his census registration form. Takes two dozen recorded trips out of the country in the thirteen years he lives in your house, from February twenty-first, 1919, until his supposed death on August twenty-third, 1933."

"Supposed?"

"Same as the New Mannheim town records you dug up. Simply disappeared. The body was never discovered. He never turned up anywhere else and his family's fortune went to a distant cousin so it's a safe bet that he did die."

Laurel walked back into the room carrying a bottle of Jim Beam and a pair of tumblers filled with ice. She moved silently past the bed, her hips doing what they had been doing before, and sat down on the rug in front of the now very healthy fire. Gavin imagined Koestler sleeping under the same roof where he and Laurel were now enjoying a fire and thinking about making love and he wondered what had happened to the man.

"The date of death is listed as August twenty-third, 1933, but he wasn't declared dead until August twenty-third, 1938. The five-year spread denotes that there was no body and the state had to wait to legally declare him dead." Shannon sounded sober now. "You want to tell me what's going on, Gav?"

"When the rough draft is done, you'll be up to speed. Now kiss Amy good night for me and I'll see you soon." He hung up before she had time to protest.

Laurel looked up from the fire. "Sounded ominous."

"A little." Gavin came over and sat down on the carpet.

She held up a tumbler. "See, half the ice melted and now we have Jim Beam and water on the rocks. Smart system, huh?" She smiled a little chipmunk smile and Gavin was glad that she was there to help him stop thinking about what had happened to Duffy. How much time had their little stunt bought? A day? Two? Someone would notice that Duffy was gone. And that someone was likely to be Laurel. Then what? Doghouse time. And with a woman like Laurel, certain things would be irrevocably broken. This wasn't good any way he looked at it.

"You have little systems for everything, don't you?"

"Oh, absolutely," she said as she poured the whiskey. "Without little systems, life is boring. I don't ask for much, but what I do ask for, I want to be perfect."

"Good philosophy."

"Oh, it's more than a philosophy, it's the code I live by. Well, that and *eat no fat*."

Gavin smiled. "Except for Doritos."

Her mouth did yet another version of a beautiful smile and she nodded. "Except for Doritos, yes." She handed him his drink and they clinked their glasses together in a silent toast to what they knew they had. "Now what did your lovely assistant have to tell you?"

"First off, she said that you were exceedingly nasty on the phone earlier this evening."

Laurel's smile broke into a laugh that animated her whole face. "Actually we had a very nice conversation about you."

Gavin took another sip of the Jim Beam and the warmth spread up from his stomach. "This doesn't sound good."

"Actually, it was *very* good. Shannon told me that you are truly a unique person, one of the honestly nice people of the world, and that I had better treat you well or she was going to stomp my head into the dust."

Gavin's mouth hung open for a minute. "No, she didn't. I can't see Shannon saying that she'd stomp anyone's anything into anywhere."

"I believe the phrase was *I'll kill you if you hurt him*. Yep. That's it. *Kill*. Exact words."

Gavin smiled. "It's nice to have people feel that way about me."

Laurel leaned in to him. "And why wouldn't they? You are a phenomenal man, Corlie. I told her that any hurting to be done would be coming from your side of the court. I love this man of mine."

Life was back to one of the good moments. He leaned over and kissed her and her lips tasted of bourbon.

"So tell me about Koestler," she said.

Gavin gave her the broad strokes then downed the rest of the whiskey. "Killing twenty-one-foot crocodiles is not high on my to-do list. Guy must have been a real badass."

"Biologist and big-game hunter, the perfect symbiotic hobby–profession equation. The best way to catch something is to know what makes it tick on a genetic level." Laurel took the antique brass poker and moved one of the hardwood logs into the center of the grate. Sparks snowed off and bounced onto the tile surround and she blew them back into the hearth. "Someone who kills a twenty-one-foot crocodile with a spear doesn't sound like the kind of man who spent time relaxing in the woods with nothing to do. And he certainly doesn't disappear into thin air."

Gavin was staring into the fire, but his mind was out on the lake. "Finn's monster," he said quietly. "The trophy room. The journal. That antique book. The fishing rods. He was here to kill it."

Laurel pulled her knees up to her chest, a movement that made her appear very small. "Then why is it still out there?"

"Because it got him first." He downed the contents of his glass. "Now get undressed and get into my bed."

"All these orders," she whispered through her lopsided grin, and began to undo her buttons.

**87**

*Nature is usually wrong.*
～ JAMES McNEILL WHISTLER

The morning was truly cold and Gavin had to concentrate to keep his teeth from chattering. Fall had finally arrived. The usual excitement that they had felt each morning had been replaced with a much more serious focus—a deadline.

Finn went about the usual preparations and Gavin found himself making a concerted effort not to frown. After all, they had been at their diluvian task for a month and had nothing to show for it except the chewed-off head of a musky and Duffy's death. Of course, if he thought about it, Walter Pinkowski's legs were part of all this. And probably the two city people the paper said had been in a boating accident.

"You ready?" Finn asked.

Gavin pulled the plastic zipper of his fleece jacket up to just under his chin, adjusted his cap, and nodded. "As ready as I'll ever be."

The old enthusiasm was in the boy's voice. "Let's get this show on the road!"

Gavin turned the engine over and the big Mercury bubbled to life. The sound was clear and loud in the small confines of the boathouse, and the smell of diesel fumes filled the space. "Bad motherfuckers," Gavin said, and backed the boat out into the dark waters.

They had gone over their plan of attack during a home-cooked breakfast that Laurel had insisted on getting up and preparing for them. They had pieced together the "incidents" involving their monster. The one consistent factor was depth. The two swimmers who had disappeared had obviously been near the surface; Duffy's daisy chain had been on top of the water when it had been hit; their musky had been attacked when it was running shallow; Finn's boat had been rammed on the surface; and Walter Pinkowski had been fishing for eels, also found in shallow water. Whatever it was hit its food on the surface.

"I don't know why I didn't see it before." Finn was angry with himself. "It makes sense, just think about the ecosystem on this lake. Now that this thing has graduated to eating people-sized snacks, where is it going to find them? Swimmers? Boaters? Dogs? On top of the water! How could I have been so stupid?" He had whacked himself in the forehead loud enough that Laurel had winced over the rim of her coffee cup.

So their new approach was surface presentation with the bait. Same area of the lake—right above the deep trough that ran beside the weed bed. Same speed. But Finn would no longer weigh down the carp with lead. It would float neutral and rise as it was towed, creating a wake and vibrations on the surface of the water. They would also be moving much faster, therefore covering more water in a day.

As they eased out into the bay, Finn reached over and pulled Duffy's shotgun out from under the console where Gavin had stashed it. "What do we do with this?" The boy drew a bead on a bird that was riding the wind at their port side, hoping for a scrap of bait to be thrown its way.

Gavin snatched the sawed-off twelve out of his hand and jammed it back under the console. "Rule number one: Never point a firearm at anything you don't intend to shoot. Period."

"What's rule number two?"

"There is no rule number two. Just number one."

"So, really, when you say rule number one, it's wrong. What you mean is that there's only one rule. Period. Rule number one implies that there's a rule number two. Which there isn't. So what you really mean—"

"Finn?" Gavin interrupted.

"Yeah?"

"Shut the fuck up."

"Okay." Finn nodded thoughtfully. "Now how about you pick up our speed before I die of old age."

"Kid, you make me crazy."

Finn crossed his eyes and stuck out his tongue. "You're not the first person to say that."

Gavin pushed the throttle up and the boat lurched out into the dark fall morning, the first tint of daylight starting to bleed into the eastern sky. "Let's hope I'm not the last, either."

"Keep our speed at ten knots," Finn said over the purr of the engine. He fed the carp rig out into the wake and the bait skimmed along on the surface. "This is a good trolling speed—it will keep the bait up but not be too fast for our friend."

"I don't think that we have to worry about it keeping up with us," Gavin said dryly, remembering the almost forty-knot speed when it had taken the big musky.

Finn had explained his theory in detail. If they trolled too fast the carp would barely touch the water and skim across the surface. They wanted it to drag on the surface and vibrate. Since *it* lived in the water, Finn figured that *it* hunted with vibration like a fish. "Perfect," Finn said as he watched the carp rig pulling a wide V. The carp dipped and darted from side to side and looked very much like a live creature out for a swim. "Kind of looks like Flipper, don't it?"

Gavin checked the GPS and sonar, then looked back at the carp. "Kind of, yeah."

Finn tuned to Gavin. "I miss my mom today. Is that all right?"

Gavin recognized something in the boy's eyes, something he saw in his own every time he looked in the mirror—loss. "When people die, sometimes we miss them forever."

Finn nodded thoughtfully and adjusted the knurled drag on the big Van Staal reel they were now using. It was an empty gesture to keep himself from crying, and Gavin recognized that as well.

"I don't really talk about it. I can't."

"Finn, remember that handbook you talked about?"

"*The Zombie Survival Guide*?"

Gavin smiled. "No. The other one. The friend handbook."

"Oh, that."

"Well, there's a chapter in there that says friends let each other deal with shit in any way they want."

"I can live with that."

Finn brought the rod tip up, adding a little action to the bait, and let it drop back again. He did this three or four times and watched the carp dive and pop to the surface. The bait really did look alive. "I just don't want you to think that I don't miss her or anything. I just try not to think about it because if I did, all I'd do is cry all the time."

And that's when Gavin saw it rise out of the water about fifteen feet behind the carp. Finn saw it too. A thick hump that zigzagged back and forth as it moved in on the bait. It hitched to one side in two rapid jerks, then dove, disappearing in a swirl that was big enough to swallow a Volkswagen.

Slowly, ever so slowly, Finn dropped the rod tip back to give him the leverage he would need for a good hook-set.

He loosened the drag a hair. There was a tense second and a half as nothing happened. Then the water around the carp exploded and line started screaming out like an air raid siren. Finn yanked back five solid times, intent on driving the big saltwater hook into the monster's mouth.

*One!*

*Two!*

*Three!*

*Four!*

*Five!*

The rod tip bent and the reel shuddered with the force.

"Who's a baddy now?" Finn asked.

Gavin kept his eyes on Finn's rod tip, watching where the line was going, and he followed it with the boat. They had to keep as much line on Finn's reel as possible.

"Man, this sumbitch is strong," Finn squealed as the rod tip jerked a half dozen times as the creature sounded, heading straight down. "What's our depth?"

Gavin glanced at the sonar. "Sixty-one feet."

"Structure?"

He examined the pixelated bottom on the color LCD screen. "Sand and some gravel."

"Logs? Rocks?" Finn worked the reel, fighting for every inch of line. The drag was set to a hair under the breaking point for two-hundred-and-thirty-pound Powerpro and the boy cranked steadily.

Gavin kept his eyes on the sonar. "Flat flat flat," he said. Then the picture of the bottom disappeared and all he saw was the irregular form of static. "It's blocking the sonar," Gavin said loudly. "It's fucking blocking out the—"

"I heard you the first time," Finn snapped. He fought the rod tip up as the beast headed straight down into the core of the earth. "Not this time!" he yelled and yanked back on the rod, the graphite pole dancing.

The big open-water rod was bent almost double, the strands of carbon somehow managing to hold together. Finn gained a few yards of line. Then a few more. "It's tiring!" he said and he leaned into the work. "It can't compete with this gear." In the heat of battle, Finn's manners had been wiped away and he was the man he would never grow up to be, all at once.

It ran and Finn pulled back, keeping the tension on. "No you don't!" The boy's chair swiveled with the rod and was facing port as Finn fought with his quarry. It sounded again, heading into the bottom of Caldasac. "It's right under the boat!"

Gavin turned the wheel and throttled up. The boat chugged forward.

Suddenly Finn was gaining line. "It's coming up! It's coming up!"

It broke straight off starboard, directly behind Finn, and the boy tried to swivel around. The line ran under the boat and there was no getting the rod tip over in time.

They saw it, huge and twisted and evil, plucked from some primitive point in hell where the only rule was the one with the biggest teeth gets to stay alive. A nightmare large enough to swallow a cow.

"Holy fuck!" Finn screamed.

It rose straight out of the water and twisted in the air, wrapping itself in the black titanium leader. Its muscles twitched as it leaped, and it arced over the boat, showering them with water and blood that gushed from its mouth and gills.

The form registered in some primitive corner of their brains and they both knew what it was. But it was the size that clouded their judgment, stopped their software from recognizing the leviathan above. All they saw was the beast that they had been hunting. A twisted scaly terror out of Revelation.

Gavin ducked and Finn pulled back on the rod, hoping to stop its aerial pitch skyward and somehow fight it back into the water. But the boat was between him and a clean line to the creature. The line ran down one side of the boat and it had come up on the other side. There was no structure on the bottom for it to wrap around, so it had used the boat.

The line pulled tight and the tackle reached its limit.

The rod exploded into fragments and the reel vanished over the side.

It hung in the air over them. It snapped its jaws to throw the hook and the sound was primal and frightening. Then headed back into Caldasac.

The lake exploded as it hit the water.

It was gone.

The boat rocked in the heavy swells generated from its reentry. They sat there, unmoving. The wind had died and the engine had somehow gone silent and the only sound was the dripping of water off their clothes and the lap of waves against the hull. Finn's mouth was open and Gavin's hand was still glued to the steering wheel as if they had both been frozen in time. A good six inches of water sloshed around the deck. An empty Coke can and a half-eaten bologna sandwich floated at their feet.

"Sonofabitch," Gavin said, not really believing what he had just seen.

Finn closed his mouth, licked the water off his lips, and held up the three-foot cork handle that was still clamped in his hands, as if to prove to himself that what just happened was not a hallucination. "I can't believe—" he said, but didn't finish because there was no need to.

Gavin wiped the water out of his eyes. All of a sudden, it made sense. All of it. Finn had been right all along. It *was* a monster.

# 89

*A credulous mind...finds most delight in believing strange things, and the stranger they are, the easier they pass with him; but never regards those that are plain and feasible, for every man can believe such.*

~ SAMUEL BUTLER

Mr. Johannus was on the roof of the boathouse nailing down the final row of shingles when the *Low Rider* entered the bay. The Finnish carpenter looked up to wave but the boat was moving too fast for him to believe that Mr. Corlie was paying much attention to anything, otherwise he'd be going a lot slower. He studied the craft for a minute, and watched it speed straight into the boathouse, that crazy writer jamming it into reverse just as the nose entered the door. If he kept driving like that he was going to crack up his boat just like the overpriced truck he had wrecked.

Almost instantly, Gavin was on the grass beside the structure, yelling up. "Mr. Johannus, you said that your wife was German. Could you please call her and ask her to come over here immediately. I need her help. I'll be happy to pay whatever she wants. It's important." The man was obviously in a rush. Probably drunk as usual. Or maybe smoking that stinky shit that he plugged into his face.

"Good morning, Mr. Corlie. Yes, my wife is German. I think that today is shopping day. She might not be at home."

"It's eight thirty—the stores aren't open. Does she read German?"

Mr. Johannus slid his framing hammer into his tool belt and started for the ladder. "Yes, she reads German. And you're right, she might still be at home. You want her to read something for you?"

Gavin was hopping back and forth on the ground as if he had to pee. "Yes, I do."

"What, exactly, is it?" he asked as he took off his tool belt and hung it on the boathouse door.

"I don't know. It's in German."

"So you said. But you don't know what it is?" The carpenter tilted his head toward Gavin, waiting for a better explanation than he had received so far. After all, if he wanted her to read something, he had to know what that something was, correct?

"It's a book. I found it. Look, I hate to rush you, I know that you have a schedule and…"

"You gonna help me out of the boat?" Finn hollered from inside the boathouse.

"Yes, I have my schedule." He looked down at his watch. "And I was hoping to get to the kitchen cabinets this morning. If I call my wife I will lose some time and it will cost you more money and—"

"Mr. Johannus?" Gavin interrupted. "MR. JOHANNUS!"

"Yes?" the carpenter asked, doing his best to stay polite.

"Here's the deal: I pay you twenty thousand dollars per three-month season, right?"

The old man nodded slowly, doing the math in his head. "Yes, twenty thousand dollars per three months, half in advance, three thousand dollars at the end of every month."

"Okay, look. Get your wife over here and I'll pay her a thousand dollars just to read something for me."

The carpenter took a step back, eying Gavin skeptically. "I thought you liked women with little boobies."

"Jesus Christ! Would you please please *please* listen to me? I need her to read something for me. I'll pay her a grand. Yes or no? I haven't got time for this right now!" Gavin looked like his blood pressure was dangerously close to blowing a hole through the top of his skull.

"Me neither, there's the kitchen cabinets to start and the cold weather is coming and I have to—"

Mr. Corlie closed his eyes. "Okay, Mr. Johannus, listen to me...no...listen! If you don't get your wife over here, I am going to sell the house and move away. Okay? Are we clear?"

"But I'd have no work to do and all of this would—"

"Exactly. So call her, okay?"

"Why didn't you just say that from the beginning. It's past eight thirty and I have the kitchen cabinets to start and—"

# 90

Gavin and Finn were on the porch off the kitchen, Finn working on his sixth Coke in an hour and Gavin nursing a coffee that had passed cold a while ago. The slow strains of the Rolling Stones' album *Sticky Fingers* filtered in and out of their respective conscious worlds; they hadn't shared a full sentence in the past hour. Both their attentions were drawn out to Caldasac, where a dark sheet of white-capped swells had reared up, sweeping in with one of the storms that Gavin was starting to understand were a constant up here. The sky over the lake had grown dark with clouds, the flat top of an anvil head looming over the horizon. It was going to rain soon.

When the screen door opened they both snapped out of their respective thoughts, which, had they been in a sharing mood, were remarkably similar. Mr. Johannus's wife, Gretta, stepped out onto the porch. She was of medium build, not unbeautiful, but stern looking. When he thought about it, Gavin realized that the carpenter had been apt in his description of her—she *did* have very big breasts. Her salt-and-pepper hair was pulled into a tight bun and her mouth seemed to have a few too many teeth. Regardless of these seeming contradictions, she was not unpleasing to look at. Gavin had a hard time not imagining her beating Mr. Johannus with birch branches in a steam-filled sauna while the old carpenter drank beer and talked dirty to himself. In her hand she carried a few pages of notes and the fifteenth-century book that Gavin had given her to translate. Several pastel-colored Post-its stuck out from the hand-cut pages.

"So, Gretta, what can you tell us?" Gavin stood up and offered her a chair at the table between him and Finn. When she sat down, he noticed her husband watching them suspiciously from the roof of the boathouse.

"You have to understand," she began, tapping her finger on the old calfskin binding, "that this is old German. *Very* old German. And some of the words I just didn't understand."

"But generally it wasn't a problem?" Gavin asked.

She shook her head. "Once I got used to the type it was fairly, well, *easy.*" By the way she accentuated the last word, Gavin could tell that she didn't understand what was so important about the book.

She turned to the notes and her voice took on a mechanical tone as she scanned her handwriting. "The book dates from 1498. It was printed in Dalberg, which I think no longer exists." She read a note in the margin. "It was written by Johann Reuchlin—Reuchlin was the Baron of Dalberg at the time. He was also a close confidante of the Elector of Heidelberg. He plays a central role in this story and his involvement was the reason for him to write this…this…*journal,* I suppose. A journal of the discovery of a monster at the imperial castle at Lautern near Mannheim."

"What kind of monster?" Finn asked.

Gretta picked up the antique book. She found the Post-it she was looking for and opened the yellowed pages. She checked the illustration, then turned the book for Gavin and Finn to see. "This," she said.

The line drawing was uncluttered and bordered on crude, but its naive simplicity conveyed the unmistakable image of the creature they had seen that morning. Both Gavin and Finn instantly recognized the subject and neither could take his eyes from the illustration. Twelve men were walking out of the water, their arms held overhead cradling a beast—an enormous malformed fish with a long snout and an evil grin full of knives. Its body was wrapped in weeds and black blood dripped from its gills. One of the men, the fourth from the front, had his face turned toward the artist, his mouth spread into a Stan Laurel smile that gave the line drawing a candid effect, like a fifth-grader flipping the bird in a class photo, lending it a sense of realism that was almost as jarring as that which they carried.

The fish was huge, enormous, and there was no mistaking the genus for anything other than what it was: *Esox.*

"What's this?" Finn asked, pointing to a line that ran around the creature's neck.

"According to the book, it's a copper ring that was put there when the fish was first placed in the fishpond that surrounded the castle at Mannheim. Apparently the ring came from the hand of Frederick the Second."

Finn's mouth was open as he stared at the picture, his eye crawling over the details, the proportions. "Tell me this story."

Gretta shrugged. "It's not very interesting. It's an old-world fairy tale. Germans have always used fables as a way to teach lessons on morality, shame, good, and evil. This is a very silly story. It doesn't even have a very interesting ending."

"Oh, yes, it does." Finn took the book from Gretta's hand and brought it up to his face, his nose inches from the antique illustration. Then he looked at Gavin and nodded. It was *him.* The monster that had smashed his boat, eaten Walter Pinkowski, and killed Duffy. It was out there, on Finn's lake. And now Finn knew how he was going to catch him. Original Bad Motherfucker time. "It has a very interesting ending," he said.

# 91

*In the year of our Lord, 1230, at the great castle at Lautern, the Emperor Frederick the Second, the Enlightened Monarch and Kaiser to the people of Prussia, did, during a festival to celebrate the vernal equinox, place into the royal pool a large pyke. Before depositing this fish—a veritable giant among its kind—he took from his own hand the royal ring, forged in copper and bearing his seal, and had the smith bind it to the fish's gill with a chain of copper, knowing that copper would not rust. When this fish was deposited into the pool, it immediately sank out of sight and was gone.*

*Over the next two hundred and sixty-seven years the fish faded from memory, not even surviving in legend. Every now and again some farmer, stooping at the pool for drink, would disappear. Mules, cattle, and children that wandered into the shallows were swallowed whole, onlookers believing that they had been taken by a monster that lived in the royal moat. The castle at Lautern—now known as Kaiserslautern—became known as a haunted place.*

*It was not until the 6th of November, in the year 1497, that a fisherman managed to hook and miraculously land an enormous pyke. The size of this fish was so large that it required a horse and tackle to remove it from the pond. Once ashore it was measured and found to be nineteen feet long and weighed more than 350 pounds. In its gill was a copper ring that bore—in Greek—the inscription:*

"*I am the first fish of all, put into this lake by the handes of Frederick the Second, ruler of the world. The fifth day of October, in the yere of our lord 1230.*"

The fish was butchered and brought to the Royal table in Heidelberg, to grace the table of the Elector Phillip, where it fed two hundred guests during a three-day celebration.

The animal's skeleton was preserved and hung at Mannheim Cathedral, so all could witness the greatness of both Frederick the Second and his pyke, which many had believed was a devil.

For years afterwards, people still stayed away from the moat at Mannheim Castle, believing it to be inhabited by monsters.

# 92

The rain came down in fits, rattling off the slate roof and bathing the house in harsh echoes. Gavin and Finn sat in the basement trophy room by the big fire, and even down here, ten feet below the earth, the hissing of the rain beating the house sounded like snakes trying to chew their way through the walls. Gavin only had to sweep a little dust out of the trap where this basement fireplace joined the main chute of the house to make it operational. They sat amid the grinning, growling, glowing faces of long-dead beasts. Sparks danced and popped in the grate and whenever an errant raindrop found its way down the chimney and hit the fire it sputtered around in its death throes and added a new instrument to the white noise of the burning hardwood. Foots was spread out on the floor, rolling around in the warm dust only inches from the hearth, purring happily.

Finn had the remains of a sandwich in his lap on a plate, and a Coke in the cup holder on the armrest. Gavin had found a bottle of ancient scotch in one of the drawers of the desk and he was enjoying a glass, albeit not guilt-free; his father had taught him that drinking another man's booze was like fooling around with another man's wife—it was something that *just wasn't done*.

"Koestler was a big-game hunter," Gavin said in classic understatement, waving his arm around the room. "He came here to fish for musky and found our fish out there. Our monster." Gavin took a swig of the whiskey in his hand.

Finn's demonic grin came back; for him, this was a fantasy come true. "You think that it's been in the lake since 1933?"

Gavin shrugged. "If it was here when Koestler was here, it's been here a lot longer than that. How would it survive all these years without being discovered? Someone would have seen it."

"Not many people go out on that lake," Finn offered weakly.

The orange fire rippled and everything in the room seemed to be alive. Gavin looked around the dark room and wondered if this were all some elaborate joke. *Let's get the horror writer real good!* "The Mannheim fish was a pike and the closest relative to the pike is the musky," Gavin recalled from Finn's endless narration of facts about the fish.

Finn nodded.

"European pike record is what?"

Finn dipped into his memory banks. "Current IGFA all-around world's largest northern pike on record was caught in Germany. Sucker weighed fifty-five pounds. Year 1980 or '81—I forget which. Apparently there's a sixty-five-pounder coming out of Italy but it hasn't been accepted yet."

"The musky record was sixty-nine-plus pounds, right?"

Finn nodded. "Sixty-nine pounds, eleven ounces. But there have been reports of hundred-pound muskies netted in the Saint Lawrence." Finn's eyes crawled up the wall again and his face took on a stern look as he pulled the stats from his head. "The *unofficial* world-record musky taken on traditional gear was at Intermediate Lake in Michigan, 1919. The fish was seven feet, four inches long and weighed in at a hundred and ten pounds."

Gavin looked at the boy. "Why is it unofficial?"

"They don't have the name of the guy who caught it. There's a picture of it in *The Expert's Book of Freshwater Fishing* by Steve Netherby. Thing is ginormous. Fish-zilla!"

"Every species produces anomalies. World's tallest man, or longest crocodile, that kind of thing. Why not with fish?" Gavin mulled it over for a few seconds, wishing he had paid more attention in high-school statistics. "Even if I forget the story of the pike that hung in the Mannheim Cathedral, we saw an anomaly out on that lake. And I think that Koestler did, too."

"You think he came here to get that fish or do you think that he was here for regular fishing and got lucky?"

"I don't know. But those reels," Gavin said, tilting his head to the corner where the big Fin-Nors had slept away the better part of a century, "were for *that* fish, nothing else." Gavin pointed through the wall.

"The lake's that way," Finn contradicted, and pointed in the opposite direction.

"I was making a point." He took another sip of Koestler's whisky and the glass was empty. The scotch warmed his throat and he was glad for the rest from working the lake. "What's the best sport fish in North America?"

"You get the *pound-for-pound it's the gamest fish that swims* crap from the bass guys. The trout guys are like some weird little cult that get all giddy when someone comes up with a brooky over a pound. Tarpon is supposed to be *the* saltwater species. But the musky is king, man." Finn punched his fist into his palm. "All other fish are just bait," he said in way of a mantra—no doubt taken from a magazine ad.

"I think that Koestler found the emperor of all sport fishes here in New Mannheim." Gavin swiveled his head around and focused on the empty stretch of wall over the desk. "An *Über*-fish."

Gavin poured himself another glass of the dusty scotch and took a slug of the liquor and the burn radiated down his throat.

"Gavin?" Finn asked tentatively.

Gavin looked up from his glass.

"How long was that fish this morning?"

Gavin thought about it, comparing the fish to the boat for scale. "Shit, I don't know. Fifteen feet. Thick as a forty-gallon drum around the middle."

"And the fish in that book?"

Gavin leaned forward and picked Gretta's notes up off the floor. "Okay, let's see…" He scanned the pages. "Nineteen feet long and weighed three hundred and fifty pounds."

Finn did the math and shook his head. "Doesn't make sense. A nineteen-foot pike would weigh ten times that. Maybe four thousand pounds. Not three-fifty."

"The numbers could have been screwed up. Maybe it was thirty-five hundred as opposed to three hundred and fifty. When Plato translated the legend of Atlantis from Egyptian into Greek, he made a mistake with a zero and all his calculations were completely off. Don't forget, that copper ring was inscribed in Greek. Maybe the original text of this book was written in Greek and later translated to German."

"Atlantis? Are you listening to yourself? No one's going to believe us."

Gavin looked over at the boy and saw that he was tired. Even after the weeks out on the water, his skin was gray and waxy and you didn't need a medical degree to see that the kid was getting sicker by the day. "They will when we come up with that fish."

"Which we are going to do how? It's only a matter of time until someone in town realizes that Duffy hasn't been opening his junk shop and starts to ask questions. And this"—Finn picked up the *New Mannheim News*, folded up into kindling—"this was not a boating acident. You know it. I know it. They knew it when our fish grabbed them."

Gavin leaned forward and tossed another split maple log onto the fire, not sure if the heat he felt prickling his skin was from the alcohol or the flames. Maybe it was stress. "What do we do?"

The new log started crackling and popping like breakfast cereal and Finn began to speak. "You go into town and get us a gaff—something with a barbed hook and an eyelet on the end that we can fasten to a chain and then to one of the cleats on the boat. We are going to have to slow this thing down if we want to kill it."

"The boat's still running bad, I noticed it when we came in this morning. Something's not firing right. Should we take it to Izzy's?"

Finn shook his head. "No. When I took the plug out the other night so we could feed that story to Dr. Laurel, I didn't put it back in right. It's misfiring and I should take the time to clean all of them plugs before we end up sitting out there like one giant musky lure." Finn smiled, and this time it looked genuine. Then it faded and his eyes took on the thousand-yard stare that Gavin had seen creep in and out of the boy's face since his mother had died. "I wish my mom could be here to see this. She'd be proud of me."

Gavin reached over, put his hand on the boy's shoulder. "Kid, she'd pull you off that lake faster than you can say burned toast and llama lips."

"You're probably right." Finn looked up, his goofy grin a little sad. "Gavin, I've never had so much fun in my life."

"You're thirteen, what do you know?"

"You're what—eighty? Have you ever had more fun than this?"

Gavin looked around the dusty old shrine to a time gone by and thought back to the month of days passed on the lake, learning about fishing, putting endless hours into the mad quest for a ghost. A ghost that turned out to be real. He polished off the whisky and placed the solid tumbler down on the floor, beside a dust-covered crocodile-hide footstool that had real crocodile feet for legs. He realized that poor old Ernie would have loved it here. "No, Finn, I haven't."

"So there you go." The boy poked Gavin in the shoulder. "You're never too old to be surprised." He held his can up in a toast then took a loud slurp off the top.

Gavin studied the five-hundred-year-old engraving of the fish being carried out of the moat. The storm was still raging white upstairs. "That fish is a beast, Finn."

"The King of Mannheim," Finn offered. "King Esox."

"Mannheim Rex."

Finn finished his Coke. "So let's go kill the sumbitch." He threw the can into the fire and watched the flames lick over the red painted surface. "Before I die of old age."

# 93

Finn was doing a heartfelt rendition of the Rolling Stones song "Dead Flowers" at the top of his lungs as he worked on the engine, the CD player on the workbench providing a nice accompaniment to his yodeling. He had fallen in love with the album earlier that day while they had waited for Gretta Johannus to translate their book, and Finn had decided to listen to it again while he worked on the boat. He had programmed the one song to repeat for the past hour while he worked away on the plugs. Outside the rain was thumping down on the newly shingled roof and added a nice bit of white noise to his performance, like a crowd cheering.

Before he had gone into town with Hal, Gavin helped Finn get the cover off the engine and left him in the boathouse with his tools, the CD player, and enough Coke to crank Finn up for a month. Finn was in the boat without the aid of a chair, sitting with his back against the gunwale, his tools laid out on the dock above him where he could reach overhead and grab what he needed. The spark plugs were laid out on a rubber mat on the deck.

It was nice being able to afford new plugs. Back before that freakin' dumbass fish had smashed the heck out of his antique Johnson, he had cleaned the plugs every second day—that old puppy gummed up faster than a colostomy bag after a corn dinner. But it had been faithful. Until that damned fish had sent it to the afterlife, leaving him to freeze to death in the middle of July. If it hadn't been so damn scary, it would have been funny. Frozen to death in July. No one would believe that. No more than they would believe in a monster that ate people.

Finn bopped away to the music as he worked, the lyrics to "Dead Flowers" now burned into his memory banks. These Rolling Stones guys were pretty good and Finn wondered if anyone besides Gavin had heard of them. He'd have to ask.

He tightened the last plug a half turn past hand-tight and laid the ratchet on the dock behind him. The wire harness snapped back in place and he wrapped the engine cover over the motor with a lot of cursing and swearing. After all, the thing was designed for bigger people to handle. At least that's how Finn saw it. Bigger—not healthier.

After half a dozen tries at securing the cover, the first latch finally caught and it was smooth sailing after that. Flip… flip…flip…flip. Motor reassembled. Time to turn it over. Finn grabbed the seat back, hoisted his dead weight up, and clamped himself in. Once buckled into the chair, he flipped the lever and slid forward so that he was at the console. He stuck the key in the ignition and was about to turn it when a voice he recognized said, "Hello, kid."

Finn turned to see the dark silhouette of a big man in a uniform blocking the doorway. "Hello, Sheriff Pope."

# 94

Pope had parked the cruiser under the canopy of trees in a little clearing off Lake Road. After shutting the engine down he sat there for a few minutes, watching the rain wash over the windshield in one thick swatch of distortion and wondering what he was going to say to this asshole before he beat him to death.

Pope took his travel mug out of the cup holder, downed a swig of the vodka-laced coffee, popped a Tic-Tac into his mouth, and straightened his Stetson. After all, he didn't want to go in there looking slovenly—there had to be a professional edge to the uniform when you killed someone. Kind of like the Mexican wrestlers on TV the other day, their costumes inspiring a certain amount of awe in the retard that Pope had babysat. In this case, that Corlie asshole was the retard and Pope was the Mexican wrestler, only without the dumbass costume. He cracked his knuckles and opened the door. The lights went on and the cockroaches started to whisper expectantly.

He hated the plastic cover on his campaign hat—thought it looked like some faggot shower cap. After his first Stetson had become stained and unpresentable in the field, and he had been forced to personally pay for the next one, he had decided that the queer cover was the lesser of two evils.

Besides, experience had taught him that blood washed off of plastic a fuck of a lot easier than felt.

He walked up to the house and rang the bell. When G. Corlie opened the door, the cockroaches would get something new to watch.

Waited.

Rang the bell a second time.

Waited another minute.

Maybe the fucker was jerking off that cripple—oops—*handicapped* kid upstairs. Maybe it was his responsibility as an officer of the law to check out the premises. Make sure that no one was doing anything that they weren't supposed to. Hand out some justice.

Pope reached down, slowly wrapping his big hand around the knob. He turned it and to his surprise it opened. Guy moves out from the city and all of a sudden he thinks he's living in an episode of *Little House on the Prairie*. At least this way Pope didn't have to break in.

The house was as the sheriff had remembered, only the boxes that had been cluttering up the hallway were gone and the place looked a lot neater now. Pope kept to the carpets while he nosed around. If the guy was sleeping upstairs, he didn't want to wake him. Not just yet.

The first room he checked out was the living room. A fire was smoldering and the coffee table was piled up with papers and magazines. The sheriff was surprised to see a copy of a *Bass Pro Shops* catalog in the stack—he figured Corlie to be more of an *International Male* kind of guy.

When Pope turned away from the fire he found himself face to face with Adolph Hitler, sitting comfortably in an upholstered chair, casually reading a book. "What the fuck?" Pope asked aloud. Why would anyone have a picture of Hitler on their mantel? He picked it up, read the inscription, and shrugged. Some people were just plain fucking nuts. He put it back with a thud, not really caring anymore if he made noise or not. This sicko *deserved* what was coming to him.

Pope wandered through the dining room, then into the kitchen. On the floor was a bowl of dried cat food and on the counter there was an almost empty bottle of Jack Daniel's. Pets and booze too; the guy had gone domestic.

The hallway upstairs was clean and carpeted by a long Persian runner that curved a little to one side and gave Pope the impression that he was walking on a tilted floor. He walked into the master bedroom.

The ensuite bathroom was in the midst of being renovated and tiles were torn up everywhere. The tub and toilet had been replaced with new ones that the guy had probably paid a fortune for because they looked antique. Stuck to the wall was a convex mirror the size of a dinner plate, and when Pope leaned into it, his face doubled up and stared back at him with the veins on his nose being the only thing he saw. Why the hell would someone want to look at themselves in one of those things? Crazy fuckers.

He saw a razor on the counter, some shaving gel that looked like it was expensive because he couldn't pronounce the name, and a woman's toiletry bag full of little containers with G all over them. Pope wondered if G was the woman's initial or the logo of the company that made the stuff in the little jars. There were two big white terrycloth robes on the back of the door. Evidently Mr. Corlie was getting himself some on a regular basis.

Back in the bedroom, Pope looked over the dresser and poked his nose into the closet—mostly men's clothing, but the unmistakable scent of female was in the air. On the clothes. On the bed. He opened the bedside table drawer—the one that wasn't a cardboard box—and found a tube of KY staring back up at him. He smiled and picked up the tube, twisted off the cap, and smelled the contents. Smelled good. He bet the woman smelled good in person, too. Her smell was everywhere and Pope could picture Corlie having the time of his life here, banging away and not worrying about money in the slightest. Nice work if you could get it.

"Well, folks, there's some things that money can't buy," Pope said in his official tone, and placed the KY back in the drawer where he had found it. Beside it, wrapped in a plastic bag, were two joints. Pope unrolled the bag and dropped one into his hand. He inhaled elegantly, like a sommelier, and nodded appreciatively. Vintage Maui Wowi—four hundred bucks an ounce, and damn hard to find. Leaps and bounds above the forty-dollar-a-quarter shit he had to buy. He inhaled the fine scent of the best endorphin releasers he had seen in some time. He dropped them back into the drawer and had one of the cockroaches file it away in the archives; it might be useful in a warrant later on.

As he walked past the big Palladian window that faced the lake, Pope noticed the light on in the boathouse. He saw shadows bouncing around inside and realized that Corlie must be in there. The cockroaches started their sound check behind his eyes and he felt the membranes begin to vibrate.

The rain pounded into the earth in one big downpour but Pope barely noticed it as he moved down the stone steps toward the lit windows of the boathouse. Through the hiss of the rain he heard someone doing a shitty job of singing music that wasn't all that great to begin with. He walked slowly up to the little building and peeked in the window. The little cripple was fastening the last snaps on the engine cover and singing away like a bird. Pope watched him for a few seconds, gimping around on the floor of the boat like some sort of circus act, until he climbed into the captain's chair and started to buckle himself in. His wheelchair was in the back corner, empty and out of the way.

Pope moved to the doorway, where he watched the kid belt himself into the seat then slide forward so that he was at the wheel. He watched the boy's movements, the boy's actions, and was intrigued. There was something familiar about the way the boy moved, and Pope felt the little cockroach roadies inside his head start to plug in the patch cords and fire up the amps.

The lights in his head went out and the insect crowd went nuts, roaring as one. A single pinpoint of light lit up center stage. A lone cockroach, dressed in black leather pants, stood in the center of the spot, his flaming guitar slung low like an Apache warrior's rifle. Behind him, glistening in the eerie stage light, was a wall of Marshall amps, all set to eleven. The cockroach with the guitar smiled, looked around the auditorium. His hair hung in his eyes and he wore an oversize top hat decorated with Mexican silver conchos. The insect was shirtless and his naked chest was covered with chains and crucifixes that sparkled all the way to the cheap seats. The bug lifted one claw into the air above his head and the tattooed arm vibrated with energy. The crowd cheered and he hit a chord and the wall of amplifiers shrieked.

The stadium went absolutely apeshit.

Pope stepped into the little building and the overhead light poured over him. "Hello, kid."

\*\*\*

"Nice boat," the lawman said as he circled around the back of the craft and squatted down beside the transom. "Must be great for fishing."

Finn nodded, his grin shaking out in the process. "I love this thing."

Pope gave the boat a once-over. "Fiberglass decks don't give you any trouble? You know with your…condition."

Finn shook his head. "Not at all. And they're easy to clean. Mud and blood washes off in a snap."

Pope's smile came back. "You don't say?" The big man started to crawl down into the boat and the cockroaches leaped out of their seats, stormed the stage, and tore the arena to shreds.

# 95

Izzy's Sporting Goods was a throwback to the days before the Internet and large mail-order retailers had pushed most family-owned specialty shops out of business. Izzy was past the point of worrying, into what he called his *I-don't-give-a-shit* stage in life. It was a dusty little store with oak counters and rod racks that weren't made of plastic. The walls were adorned with at least one—often several—taxidermy examples of the local game, from a monstrous sixty-three-inch moose head right down to a chipmunk mounted on a birch log. Gavin wondered what old Izzy would say if he ever saw the trophy room in his basement. Probably shit his dusty old pants.

Izzy relied on a local clientele that wanted it fixed *now*. He wasn't at all concerned that Bass Pro Shops was selling the new Shimano baitcaster on their website for 12 percent less. *You want to wait two weeks, go ahead*, he would say. *Knock yourself out. Just don't bring it here when the bearings go and you need it in a hurry. Thanks so much. Don't let the door hit you in the ass on the way out.*

Izzy looked like one of the taxidermy denizens of his store. He was ancient and was fond of telling everyone *what didn't used to be way back when*, as he put it. He was a thin little man with skin the color of beef jerky and eyes that told you he didn't give a shit no matter how you put it. His head, too big in that skinny-little-old-guy way, was bald and splotchy from too many hours in the sun. There was an island of cancerous-looking skin on his forehead that he absentmindedly scratched every so often. He was dressed in wool pants, moccasins, and a faded plaid shirt with a Remington patch on the breast. One look at the man told you that he had caught, killed, and eaten every kind of creature the woods had to offer.

Izzy ushered Gavin behind the counter. "How about this?" the old man asked, holding up a serious-looking stainless-steel gaff. "It ain't got an eyelet on the end but the shaft is made of tempered steel. I could have Chuck drill a hole through it and you could hoist a truck with this thing." Outside the rain was still coming down and any cars going by were distorted by the waterfall that washed over the big display windows.

Gavin picked up the gaff and weighed it in his hand. The thing was solid and heavy and a deadly weapon in its own right. "Can you have him cut a barb into the hook?"

Izzy's eyes narrowed. "The biggest thing on that lake is musky, Mr. Corlie. And it ain't too sporting to snag a fish with a gaff, no how. A barbed gaff is even worse, if you ask me. It ain't like the old days when everyone pulled every fish out of the lake that they could. We got the conservation now."

Gavin ignored the dead bear over Izzy's shoulder. "First off, I *didn't* ask you. Besides that, I agree. However, I lost a very big fish the other day because of this—" Gavin nodded to the big cast that still encompassed his arm and a good part of his shoulder. "Between Finn and me, we aren't exactly batting a thousand. I kind of need that barb right now."

Izzy nodded like he was sorry for the oversight. "Sure. Forgot about little Finn. Where is he anyhow?"

Gavin wondered how Finn was doing with the gummy plugs back at the boathouse. "He's working on the boat."

Izzy's gaze shifted to the rain coming down outside. "I hope he's someplace out of harm's way."

# 96

Pope watched the tiny wheels grind slowly around in Finn's skull. For a second the boy smiled. Then the grin fell off his face as if it was made of sand, and the sheriff saw his old buddy, Fear, come out to play.

*Whoopee!* the cockroaches squealed, and the bulge of their communal voice went straight to his crotch. Pope converted the sensation to a smile. Outside the rain rattled down and the swells of the lake were bumping the pilings of the boathouse with loud slaps. Pope had waited for this a long time. His smile got bigger.

The boy's eyes shifted nervously in his sockets. Pope stepped forward, goaded on by the thousands of little bugs murmuring feverishly, twitching and shaking in their seats like a southern Baptist congregation witnessing an exorcism; they wanted the demons to come out and play.

"Hey, kid. Wazzup?" Pope said in a pretty good imitation of that idiotic cartoon raccoon that sold those purple cancer pellets to kids on TV.

The effect was beautiful. The boy's bottom lip started to tremble and the sheriff was sure he would have pissed himself if his body worked properly.

He could see Finn trying to figure a cute way out of this one but it was an empty gesture; in a little while Pope would be dropping him in different parts of the lake for fish food.

Maybe he'd put him through the dam and the boy's file would end up in that drawer where Parks buried the rest of his failures.

Pope stepped closer and he could hear the swish of the kid's clothing, like nervous bees.

"This ain't a good idea, Sheriff Pope." Finn did a pretty good job of keeping his voice level but his eyes were frightened and wide.

Pope nodded. Some of the cockroaches shook loose and went rattling around in his skull with the movement. "You're wrong about that. This is a *very* good idea." He reached down and started to undo his belt.

The boy bit his lip to stop himself from crying and his arms fell helplessly to his side.

By now the cockroaches were giggling like schoolgirls at a barn dance. A few made smooching noises on the backs of their hands.

"Get—get—get—" Finn stuttered like a busted snorkel. "G—get away from me. I'm warning you!" He was gripping the seat now, squeezing the vinyl covering so hard that Pope heard his fingers squeak across the rubber. The sound sent the cockroaches into a frenzy of catcalls and whistles. Some pumped their little fists up and down. *Go get 'im!* they whooped.

All he said was, "You're not gonna like this too much."

And then there was a whistling sound—an actual *swoosh* that filled the air—and Finn came up with Duffy's antique sawed-off shotgun gripped in his oily hands.

Pope's eyes mimicked the surprised double O of the twin barrels. The cockroaches scrambled for cover and the sheriff had time to begin a single word. "Do—"

Then Finn squeezed both triggers.

# 97

As Izzy, the grizzled tobacco-stained killer of moose and woodchuck alike, moved to the cash register, he passed by the wall of shotguns, cleaned and polished for the fall bird season. "One more thing," Gavin said. "Can I get some shells?"

"What gauge?" Izzy asked.

"Twelve. Something that would stop a bear in its tracks."

Izzy stopped and turned to Gavin. His eyes narrowed again. "How close you gonna be to this bear when you shoot him?" Izzy scratched the patch of skin on his forehead again and Gavin was worried that the old man was going to pick his way through to his brain.

"I don't know. Close, I suppose. Maybe ten feet."

Izzy eyed Gavin. "Well, up here we call those kinds of bears mother-in-laws!" The old man smiled, then laughed at his own joke in an attempt to get a reaction out of Gavin. When there was none he said, "That's a shitty joke anyhow."

The old man scanned the shelf of shells. "Ten feet, huh? I'd go with either SSGs or buckshot. SSGs are great if you're close in, got a big ball bearing load that will go through a four-by-four." He held up a dark red shell, heavy and clean, and Gavin thought back to the old blue ones that Duffy hadn't had time to fire; they were still in the breach of the sawed-off gun.

The old man went on, "Buckshot will chew flesh up pretty bad but it ain't got the same impact. If you're going for impact, take the SSGs." He tossed the red shell in the air and caught it in his open palm. "Go through a six-by-six like it was made of butter." Izzy's lumber references were getting more exaggerated by the minute; pretty soon they'd be shooting down telephone poles.

Gavin thought about the fish that had cartwheeled over the *Low Rider* that morning, all muscle and speed and teeth. "I'm going for impact," he said flatly.

"How many boxes? There's twenty-five per box."

Gavin remembered that Duffy hadn't managed to squeeze off a round. "One box will be more than enough."

"Only got one mother-in-law, huh?" He smiled but didn't let this one get away from him. "Okay, I'll ring this up." The old man punched the gaff and shells into the register and added five bucks for Chuck's work. "Fishing should be good this fall, the weather's nice and cold. Good musky weather. You and young Finn there are the only folks that fish Caldasac anymore. You got yourself the pick of the litter." He took his hand from the ancient NCR machine and worked at getting through to his brain again. "I hope you catch yourself a monster."

Gavin smiled. "Me too, Izzy," he said, meaning it.

# 98

Pope stared up at the night sky. He tried to shift his gaze but nothing seemed to be working. He realized that it was some sort of a minor miracle that he was even conscious. He watched the crystal sparkle of the rain coming down and was vaguely aware that the deck below him was thudding into waves as the boat raced across the choppy surface of the lake. He felt no pain or discomfort, only a mild sense of curiosity. The double hammer of buckshot had thrown him back into the engine cover, and when he had hit the floor he'd heard a liquid burst of parts glop out onto the deck. And he could no longer move anything, not even his eyes.

After what could have been seconds—or even years—his inner ear detected a shift in speed and the boat swung to a near stop in the water. He heard the engine gurgle and the Boston Whaler dropped down into the trough of a wave and Pope saw the concrete face of the Caldasac Dam come rising above the stern in one violent surge of motion.

*Sonofabitch*, he thought, and felt a jolt as his hearing kicked in. All he heard was the omnipotent roar of the dam as it fed on the outflow of the lake. Distantly, he felt the rumble of the turbines and saw the mist it produced rising in the rain.

There was the screech of unoiled metal when Finn snapped his seat lever and swung around to the back of the Whaler, riding on that crazy rail-device that he used. When the boy was beside the cop, he poked him with the shotgun. "You ain't gonna hurt me, are you?" he asked.

Pope couldn't even smile at that. He just stared up at the sky and wondered if he was even breathing at all anymore.

"I'm sorry about this, Sheriff Pope." The boy sounded weepy and Pope wished that he could see the little fucker's face; he still couldn't move a muscle, not even his eyes.

The raindrops shifted course as the shotgun poked him again and he heard the scrape of the barrel on his leather tactical jacket. Then the dark above was filled with Finn's face, blocking out the falling rain that Pope could no longer feel. The kid *did* look weepy.

*Faggot-ass*, Pope thought.

Still strapped in his chair, the boy began to hoist the big cop off the slippery deck.

As Finn shifted his weight, the sheriff heard the harsh gust of the wind interwoven with the roar of the dam all around him. The boat's engine chugged irregularly in the swells.

Pope watched the boy's face clench as he lifted his almost-dead weight, close enough that they could kiss. Then he was upright. Head back against the gunwale. Staring into Finn's eyes.

Finally, he had passed a little of himself on to another human being. Something good. It was at that moment that Pope felt a pang of pride slip from his grasp and go shambling off into the universe.

There was a sick sweeping roll to the world as Finn hoisted him up and wrestled his limp body atop the gunwale. "I really am sorry about this," the boy said. And for the first time he could remember, Pope actually believed someone. He tried to laugh but there wasn't even the sad little gurgling noise he had expected.

Finn grunted once and the sheriff went over the side.

The world spun out of control and he was blinded by a black flash of cold that filled his mouth and nose in one sharp jolt. The current spun him end over end. Then he was on the surface, bobbing lopsided, spinning toward the blare of the turbine. He could feel the lust of the dam pulling him in and he began to pick up speed.

It was then that the little insect congregation dusted off an old classic for their friend the sheriff, who had taken one on the chin for the team. They began their own special version of "My Way."

*And now, the end is near—*

And with a great sweeping sadness Pope realized that the little friends he had done so much for had never really loved him at all.

# 99

The ride back to the house was uneventful in that all Gavin and Hal talked about was the price of cigarettes. Not that Gavin cared all that much about the price of smokes, but Hal certainly seemed to. The recent increase by twenty cents a pack had almost sent the old man to the hospital with a *harty-tack*, as he put it. Of course, Gavin had replied, maybe it was the cigarettes that had almost sent him to the hospital with a *harty-tack* in the first place. Gavin's comment had pretty much killed any warm fuzzies that Hal may have felt toward him.

The rain was coming down in one steady stream and Hal had to continually fight the old pickup through potholes that had filled with water and countless streams that flowed over the dirt road. As usual, Gavin gripped the *holy shit* handle and tried to picture himself in a happy place.

After a few minutes of surly silence, Hal fired up another cancer stick. "What's the part you like best 'bout writin'?"

Gavin was surprised by the question; it was one he hadn't been asked often. "I like it when a character does something that I never saw coming."

The old man's face tightened up around the cigarette as he pulled in a lungful of Virginia tobacco. "But you're writin' it. Can't you just make 'em do what you want?"

In theory that sounded feasible. Only whenever he got down to the nuts and bolts of the process he was surprised by what usually happened. "When I start a story I have a pretty good idea of what I want. But it's like a road trip with a friend. You start out to, say, Plattsburg from here. You're going with your best friend, Darren."

Hal shook his head. "Best friend's Marv."

"Sorry. Marv." Gavin smiled. "So you and Marv know that you're going to go to Plattsburg. Pretty standard. How many miles?"

"Sixty-one."

"Okay, so the mileage, like the pages in a book, is the length of a journey. So you and Marv know you're going to Plattsburgh, you know it's sixty-one miles away, but you don't know exactly how it will play out. All kinds of weird shit can happen along the way. Maybe you get a flat tire along the way, you meet a guy at a gara—"

"Change it m'self. Or Marv'll change it."

"Okay. But if you hit a deer—"

"Bleed it. Throw it in the back. Take it home. Butcher it. Eat it."

Gavin tried to find a way around the mental roadblocks that Hal was throwing up. "But you didn't see it coming. You see, you can't always figure out exactly what's going to happen before it does. Writing is kind of like that. I'll be writing about a character walking into a grocery store, looking for an ice-cream bar for his pregnant wife who's waiting in the car. All of a sudden some guy with a knife stabs him and steals his car—with his wife inside. Hell, I thought the guy was going to hang around. Maybe even be my main character. Now he's dead on the floor of a 7-Eleven and I got a drunk with a knife barreling down the highway in a stolen minivan with a kidnapped pregnant woman whose water just broke in the seat beside him. What the fuck happened to the ice-cream sandwich? I wonder." Gavin watched the sweep of the wipers for a few seconds, pushing the water off the old, scratched windshield. "That's the shit I love about writing. The stuff I just don't see coming."

# 100

Pope was carried on by the hunger of the dam, inexorably forward toward the great grinding jaws of death. The water around him was a swirling surface of rough eddies that roiled and rocked and shot up angry foam. He was spun, sucked under, spit back up, dragged by the same unstoppable current that took Tom Stockman through here a month ago. Through it all, the cockroaches were giving it their best, doing Old Blue Eyes proud.

Pope saw the dam rising high above him in the stormy night sky, the concrete slick and shiny in the rain. The current roared forward and all of a sudden the sound of the turbine was a solid roar that almost drowned out the insect choir. But they somehow managed to keep singing.

The current flipped him around and for an instant he saw Finn sitting in the boat beyond the guard fence, a million light-years and a full lifetime away. The boy was saluting, his hand poised rigidly at the brim of his ball cap, still looking weepy.

The image of Finn was the last thing the sheriff saw before the current grabbed him by the legs and sucked him into its frothing belly, seventy-five feet below.

He lurched down, tumbling deeper into the frigid void that swallowed everything, even light. He hit the bottom of the concrete infeeds and scraped along, face-first, dredging up great mouthfuls of slimy silt and gravel and debris that rammed down his throat and burst his stomach in one rending concussion. Then he thudded into something hard that shattered his jaw, tearing it away. A few of the cockroaches flinched in mock sympathy but the rest kept singing their little hearts out.

There was a loud pop as the pressure imploded his eardrums and loosened his brain from its mooring. The determined body-politic of the cockroach traveling road show had just enough time to finish up in style.

*Yes, it was myyyyyyyyyy waaaaaaaaayyyyyyyyyyyyyyyyyyyyyyyy yyyyyyyyy!*

There wasn't a dry eye in the house, and with that final F-sharp still ringing in Pope's head, the cockroaches snapped on their seatbelts and braced for impact.

Sheriff Xavier Pope's brain had time to squeeze out one last thought before it was popped from his skull, extinguishing all the extraordinary things he had been.

That thought was: *Fucking pussies!*

The sound of the rain thumping into the roof lessened considerably now that they were under the trees. As they pulled into the yard, Hal opened his mouth and the usual, "Home sweet home," came out.

Laurel's car wasn't there. Gavin checked his watch; she'd be back in another hour.

"Thanks, Hal." Gavin got out of the truck.

"Hmph," was all that the man had to say, and the truck sped off, the usual cloud of blue smoke quickly dissipating in the rain.

Gavin ran for the door and threw it open. He jumped inside and the wind snapped the door shut behind him. He flipped on the lights and looked around. Off in the distance he thought he heard a boat engine. Or had it just been the rain? He dumped the new gaff and the box of shells down by the door.

The house was empty and Finn was nowhere to be seen. Could the kid still be working on the engine? He walked through the kitchen, out the back door, and headed for the steps.

As he walked down to the boathouse, the rain came off the lake horizontally, stinging his cheeks, and he had to squint to see. Water worked into his collar and dripped down his back. He moved over the flagstones as fast as he could, trying to ignore the bitter bite of the rain on his skin.

When he was almost at the boathouse door, he heard the muffled sounds of Mick Taylor's guitar playing and knew that Finn was still inside. Gavin opened the door and went in, a gust of rain following him.

Finn was at the transom of the boat, soaked to the bone, his jet-black hair plastered to his skull and face. He was scrubbing down an area of the gunwale with one of the shop towels he had finagled from one of the mechanics at the truck stop over on 47E. He worked furiously, without looking up. The interior of the boathouse was hazy with blue exhaust.

Gavin tried to fan the smoke away. He coughed. "You're lucky you don't have a carbon-monoxide buzz!"

Finn kept working with the rag. "Took it for a quick spin." He repeatedly reached over the side and wrung the rag out in the lake.

"Without rain gear?"

"Wanted to make sure it's running right." He was scrubbing furiously at the side of the boat, working on the wispy remnants of a stain.

"What are you doing?"

Finn finally looked up from the rag in his hands. "Got some oil on the fiberglass—got to clean it up or it'll stain."

"Well, Mr. Greenpeace, that's not exactly the thing to do if you care about the lake."

Finn's mouth scrunched up and he shrugged. "Forgot."

Gavin leaned up against the tool bench and crossed his arms. For a kid who insisted that every piece of fishing line—from two inches to two miles in length—ended up in the recycling bin, the flippant ecoterrorist attitude didn't ring true. But he was too tired to give the boy a speech. "You go far?"

Finn continued rinsing the rag, squeezing it clean again and again. "Just out into the big water, turned around, and headed straight back in." The oil that he was wringing out into the lake had a red tint to it. "But in this shit it don't take more than a minute to get soaked through." The worldly turn in his vocabulary seemed to be making headway.

"Who's always telling me to dress for the weather?" Gavin asked.

Finn laid the clean rag out on the floor just above the gunwale. He turned to Gavin. "Can you help me up to the house? I'm tired and hungry."

Gavin looked at the little boy and saw something distant, something new, in his face. For some reason, he looked older. "Sure," he said, and swung the winch arm over the stern of the Boston Whaler.

# 102

Gavin was in bed going over the fifteenth-century book when Laurel walked into the room. The German–English dictionary notwithstanding, he felt like he was reading a Klingon manifesto. He placed the book on the night table and gave her a big smile. Her hair was wet and her eyeliner had smudged and she looked like a very beautiful and very damp raccoon. She dropped her briefcase on the carpeted floor, where it landed with a deep thud; kicked off her wet shoes; and jumped on the bed.

"Hey, you," she said as she leaned in and kissed him.

"How is it that no matter when I smell you, it's always great?" Gavin asked and ran his mouth down her neck, cradling his face in her collarbone, taking in the smell of rain and perfume.

She laughed, shook her head. "Not always. There was this one time when I had come out of surgery after amputating a gangrenous leg and I was covered in…well…bits of rotting flesh. It was horrible. Even you—*Mr. Easy-to-Please*—would have agreed on that one."

"And I'm the horror writer." Gavin bit her neck. "We should switch places."

"Okay," she said through her big, beautiful smile. "I like the top." And she flipped him over, pinning him to the mattress.

"Ow...ow...ow! Watch the arm! Jesus. I thought you liked being on the bottom?"

She scrunched up her face. "Bottom. Top. Side. From behind. All good." She bent over and kissed him. "All good," she repeated, and rubbed her hips into him.

"Can I tell you something?"

"Sure." She pulled off her damp sweater and flung it over the back of the bench. The tight sleeveless T-shirt she wore did little to hide the great job that her nipples were doing in letting him know that they were there.

"I'm glad that you're older than I am."

She looked down, frowned. "Why?"

"Because I couldn't keep up with you if you were my age. You'd fucking kill me, lady."

Laurel seemed to honestly consider the question for a second. "You're right, I probably would." She grudgingly climbed off of him and headed for the bathroom. "Where's Finn?"

"Asleep. Tomorrow's the day we catch it."

"Mm-hm," she mumbled.

"We saw it today." He did his best to sound casual and bored. "We know what it is."

She stopped in her tracks and turned, the move somehow graceful. "You what?"

"We saw it today. *It*. Our monster. We hooked it and the thing leaped right over the boat." Gavin was smiling now, broad and proud.

"And?"

Gavin shook his head. "No *ands*. It's real, Laurel. Real and alive and out there."

Laurel came back and sat down on the bed. "I was going to shower then seduce you with this tiny ass you seem to like so much." She crossed her arms. "But that can wait."

"Doc, you are not going to believe what I tell you." He reached for the notes that Greta had made. "Not one little bit."

"Corlie." She leaned over and gave him a kiss that was more tongue than lips. "Tell me something I don't know."

**103**

*Blessed Virgin, pray for the death of this fish.*

~ ERNEST HEMINGWAY, THE OLD MAN AND THE SEA

Gavin and Finn trolled into the sunrise. Finn was bundled in layers that started out with fleece underwear, moved up to wool pants and a sweater, grew into breathable Gore-Tex pants and a jacket, and ended in a big red sombrero that Laurel had snagged out of a garbage can at the side of the road; it was beat up but a suitable replacement for the one he had lost. Gavin was bundled up in similar fashion, but instead of the goofy hat, his hair was clamped down by the hood of his parka to keep the rain out. In his pockets, rattling around like a rock collection, was a handful of shells for the shotgun.

The rain came down in a steady beat, and even in the right clothing they'd be soaked through and shivering in an hour if they weren't careful.

Finn's attention was nailed to the *Low Rider*'s wake, to the bait ripping across the dark surface of Caldasac. "After we catch this thing, I'll be in big demand as a guide."

"No doubt." Gavin wiped his hand across the GPS to see their coordinates; they were almost on top of where the fish had hit yesterday, as good a place to start as any. Finn had been very clear that the fish could very well be at the other side of the lake by now, chowing down on dam workers. "This is where we saw it," Gavin said over the throb of the rain bouncing off his hood. The sound was thin, metallic, and intimate, like someone shaking a can of pebbles inside his head.

"I know." Out here the boy was in his element, the high priest of angling. He was comfortable. At home.

For the next three hours they worked the corridor along the weed bed that flanked the deep trough. They barely spoke. Finn handled his reel like it was a crystal ball, continually massaging the aluminum mechanism as if his contact was needed to summon the great fish.

By noon Finn was tired. "Can I have another cup of that coffee, Gav?"

Gavin filled a stainless travel mug and handed it to Finn.

Gavin watched the bait skim along across the top of the water, cutting through the massive rolling swells. Today was the worst weather they had been out in. Period. If it didn't calm down just a little he'd be wiping his puke off the windshield in order to see. Heavy waves kept rolling over the bow and every now and then Gavin would get sprayed. If the weather got any worse, they would have to head in.

One of the waves behind the bait sped up, zigged to the right, then back. "Finn!" Gavin said, and the boy dropped his cup, snapped his head toward the bait, both hands wrapped around the cork handle of the rod, ready for a bone-penetrating hook-set.

"Come on, you fat fucker, come and get it," Finn said between clenched teeth. The rod tip was pointed back, toward the bait, ready to set the chemically sharpened hooks into the oversize bony jaw. He knew that at the best of times it was hard getting a hook set with a musky—with this thing it would be like hammering a roofing nail into concrete.

The fish followed the bait for about thirty seconds, moving left and right behind it, as if it couldn't decide whether or not it was hungry. "Okay," Finn said quietly, "keep it steady. Don't slow down no matter what. And watch my line."

Gavin kept his eyes glued on Finn, waiting for instructions.

"Come on come on come on come on come on…" Finn whispered over and over, his eyes locked on the bait cutting over the water behind the boat. "Come on come on come on come on come on…"

Finn's finger was on the spool, feeling for the fish.

He held his breath. Clenched his jaw. And waited.

The water erupted as the beast came barreling out of the lake, as if the earth had spit out a demon. It swallowed the carp rig as it came out, snapped its mouth shut, and soared straight into the air.

When it hit the water, it looked like half the lake emptied into the sky and the shock waves pitched the boat forward.

Then it began to run.

Finn's thumb came off the spool and he waited as line fed steadily out, the drag completely open.

"Hook him!" Gavin hissed.

"I want this in his stomach! He ain't gonna spit it out this time!" Finn yelled to the fishing gods. "Come on! Fifteen…sixteen…seventeen…eighteen…nineteen…and… TWEN-TEE!" The boy spun the drag knob and ripped back on the rod to set the hook deep in the animal's flesh and bone.

The fish headed down, a chariot rocketing toward hell.

"He's…going…down…just…like…before!" Finn cranked the reel handle as the fish pounded down into the lake. "Not this time! Not this time!" Finn fought back, his jaw set grimly, words hissing out through clenched teeth. "When he…realizes that he can't beat me, he's going…to…come…up. When he starts, you…pull…ahead so that he doesn't use the boat against us. I want to tire him out. If I can keep him busy, the lactic acid is going to build up in his muscles and it will kill him." Finn sounded sure, certain. "Maybe his heart will explode!"

"Yeah, maybe." Gavin remembered Walter Pinkowski's legs on the stainless-steel table in the morgue and Dave Duffy's fingers piled up on the gunwale of his destroyed boat. If this thing kept going, there'd soon be enough spare parts to build a whole new person, Dr. Frankenstein style. Fuck optimism, he thought, and reached under the console to pull out the sawed-off twelve.

Gavin took two cartridges out of his pocket and popped the breach on the gun. Duffy's old blue shells were gone and he placed the shiny red SSGs in the twin chambers. Then he snapped it closed. If that fish came near the boat it was going to die of lead poisoning.

Finn pulled hard, trying to tire the fish. "He's turning! Keep an eye on him."

The fish headed out and away from the *Low Rider*. Gavin and the heavy line cut into the swells, cleaving a neat slice through the waves.

He throttled up and headed after it, keeping the line at a shallow pitch so that the fish was away from the boat. The rain was coming down hard now and it would have been impossible to keep the line in sight if Finn hadn't opted for high-visibility yellow. They followed the monster for almost ten minutes, more than a solid mile according to the GPS. Finn kept cranking, not giving him the line he needed to go deep, back to the bottom, back to structure.

Gavin's eyes were glued to the line. When it tired—hell, *if* it tired—and if it got close to the boat, they would gaff it, blow its brains out with the shotgun, and drag it back to shore.

There was a ripple about eighty feet off the port side, just at the edge of their vision, and a tail the size of a wheelbarrow hissed out of the water and slapped down with a loud *smack*.

Finn yanked back and the line dug into the water again, the fish heading deep. He pulled hard, fighting the fish back up, and the line started to come back onto the reel. There was a ripple, a small whirlpool, then the fish burst through the surface into the gray sky, spinning in an attempt to throw the hook. He was huge.

"Not this time, motherfucker!" Finn chortled.

The fish hit the water and the lake exploded.

Line peeled off as the fish sounded, going down. Once again Finn hit into him with his shoulders, yanking back on the rod, and again the fish went airborne. This time he danced a good twenty feet into the air. He turned over, his belly flashing white, and hit in the water in a right-angle Immelmann. This time he was so close that the splash he set off rained down on *The Low Rider*.

The fish headed into the bottom again.

Again Finn hit back, this time tightening the drag with his thumb. "Not…this…time!" the boy yelled at the fish and cranked the handle with a vengeance.

Twenty feet off the port side the fish came up, resting on the surface, his anterior dorsal fin eight or ten feet ahead of his tail. The fish was huge. Big as a station wagon, it seemed.

"He's up! He's up!" yelled Finn. "Get the gaff ready!"

Gavin folded up his seat and jammed the shotgun in between the collapsed backrest and the seat bottom where it would be out of harm's way. He wiped the water out of his eyes and took the gaff out of the holder that Finn had screwed to the console.

Gavin kept the fish in sight in case he decided to wrap around the boat again but it didn't look like he had it in him. The fish looked beat.

Gavin eased the boat over to the fish as Finn retrieved line, keeping the rod tip up in case the fish started to run. When they were almost beside it, Gavin reached over the side with the gaff. The fish was a foot too far and Gavin extended himself, leaning out.

The fish flared his gills and Finn turned to Gavin. "No, wait…"

But it was too late. The fish thrashed and its tail hit the boat.

Sideswiped by the bulldozer of a fish, the *Low Rider* pitched sideways in the heavy swells. Gavin dropped the gaff and tried to grab hold of something—anything—to steady himself. His good hand shot out and he grabbed the railing. Then tumbled overboard, somersaulting into the cold, gray swells. He managed to keep his grip on the railing, but he was submerged from the chest down in the water. He hung there, dazed.

Finn's eyes flashed white in the rain and he fumbled for the chain that was attached to the gaff. He started pulling up with one hand, retrieving the gaff from the lake, his other hand firmly gripping the cork handle of the rod. If he could get the end of the gaff to Gavin, he could get him in. The fish thrashed again and the rod jumped out of his hand, bounced on the floor, and was dragged back where it got caught against the stern bulwark. Finn flipped the lever on his chair and shot to the console to reach Gavin.

The boy glanced back. The fish was moving slowly away from the boat, the acids in its muscles leaching back into its system. It was recovering. The rod quivered as line fed out and the resistance kept pulling the fish to one side.

"Gavin, grab the gaff!" Finn held it out.

Gavin tried with his bad arm but it was a no-go. He let go of the railing with his good hand and started to sink into the deep swells. "I can't." A wave washed over his face and he breathed in a mouthful of lake water and coughed. "Can't!"

Finn turned to see the fish turning back toward the boat. The pressure from the hook and line was bringing it back, like a chained dog circling a tree.

Gavin kicked his feet in an effort to get up the side and the fish seemed to come alive, to respond to the noise.

"Jesus, Gav, stop moving!"

Gavin thrashed again, trying to get up. Another swell dunked him and Finn heard him gasp for air, coughing violently.

The big tail swished and the fish shot forward, heading for the boat.

Finn was superextending himself, reaching for his friend. Gavin clung to the side of the boat. He gasped for air. Tried to scramble up. Finn unbuckled his seatbelt, reached with all his effort.

Out of the corner of his eye, Finn saw the fish moving in, coming straight for Gavin. The rod zinged overboard and was lost.

Finn looked down at his friend, then back at the fish. There was maybe ten feet between them. The fish's gill plates flared as it came in to hit Gavin, closing fast.

"Get away from MY FRIEND!" the boy screamed.

In one fluid motion Finn reached over the side and grabbed the monstrous head by the gill plate. The fingers of his other hand wrapped around the hand-carved grip of Duffy's shotgun. When his hand connected with the fish, the musky snapped its head and jerked away from the boat, pulling Finn overboard.

Gavin tried to reach out, to stop him, but he couldn't move more than a few inches. The fish moved off at a right angle from the boat, taking Finn with it.

As the fish dragged the boy away it shook its head, trying to get free.

The fish went under and popped up twenty feet away, Finn holding fast like a rodeo rider atop a supercharged bull, his sombrero hanging off his back like a pistolero in an old movie. The fish shook its massive neck, trying to rid itself of the parasite, but Finn held firm. "WHO'S A BAD MOTHER-FUCKER NOW?" the boy screamed, and brought his trailing arm, the one that ended with a shotgun, around. He jammed it into the fish's gill slit.

Finn pulled both triggers.

There was a muffled WHUMP! and the fish's head jerked violently upward, the top of its skull spiraling into the sky in a mist of black blood and bone.

Finn looked over at Gavin and smiled the biggest smile of his life.

Then the fish sank into the heaving autumn waters, taking the boy with it.

# 104

The clouds had been gone for days and everyone was saying that it was the most enchanting Indian summer they could remember. The leaves had all turned and the forest around Caldasac was dappled with as many shades of orange and red as could possibly be imagined. The temperature had been in the seventies all week and it felt as if autumn was never going to make it to the lake. But everyone knew better.

Gavin had been at the water's edge since before sunup, hugging the urn and staring out at Caldasac, thinking about the past year and what it had done to him. He had grown up, become the man he was supposed to be, here.

He sat down in the Adirondack chair and placed the urn between his legs. The marble was cool and bit through his jeans and he wondered if what he was about to do was right. After all, a person's last resting place should be of their own choosing.

But something about this place just seemed right, as if there was no other place for this ritual—this parting of friends.

He was thinking about the past week, about the reporters and the photographers, when he heard the soft tread on the steps behind him. He didn't have to turn to know it was Laurel; he knew her sounds now.

"Hey," she said. "I woke up and you were gone. I saw the Mac and your notebooks spread out on the dining table but no you. I got worried."

Gavin reached up and took her hand as she came and stood behind him. He dropped his head back and rested on her hips and the warmth of her body was in sharp contrast to the stone urn that was cold and harsh against his legs. "I came down here to say good-bye."

Foots the cat jumped up on the chair beside him and sat down as if he, too, felt a need to be there.

"I don't know if it's the thing to do."

Laurel squeezed his hand. There were a thousand things that she could say. "Yes, you do," was all she offered.

He stood up and opened the urn. A slight breeze whistled across the open container and pulled a wisp of dust out into the air that swirled and dissipated over the water. Gavin held the container steady for a few breaths before upending it. The gray ashes fell for a second before they were picked up by the wind and carried out over the lake.

Tears formed on his lashes. "Good-bye," he said, and the tears broke away and washed down his face.

He put the cap back on the urn and threw it out into the bay where it landed with a splash. It bobbed up and down in the gentle waves for a few seconds, then upended and sank out of sight.

Somewhere not too far off a loon seemed to respond with a cry.

"What the crap are you guys doing down here?" Finn bellowed as he moved the wheelchair down the ramp.

Gavin wiped the tears from his eyes and turned to the kid. "Hey, bwana."

They looked the boy over.

"Where did you get those clothes?" Laurel asked, hiding her smile behind her hand.

Finn rolled in a circle, modeling his new look. "You like?" He was outfitted like a billboard for an advertising firm. His cotton safari shirt was covered with so many fishing company patches that the color of the shirt could not be easily discerned without careful scrutiny. His beat-up sombrero was similarly adorned, the corporate patches contrasting with the gaudy gold braid that winked out from behind all the advertising. His jeans had been pressed, the crisp hard edge of a seam running down the front of each leg. On his feet he sported an expensive pair of deck shoes tied off with bright yellow laces. "Pretty snazzy, huh?"

Gavin laughed along with Laurel. "It pays to be famous, huh?"

Finn nodded like he was driving over speed bumps. "Does it ever. Thanks for the name of that lawyer—he's got me more money than I'll ever spend!"

Gavin turned toward the lake. "Then I'd buy some new clothes if I were you."

Laurel snickered into her sleeve.

"Are you kidding? Do you know what they pay me to wear this stuff?" Finn picked some imaginary lint off of his lap. "More than Randy Ketchum makes, I can tell you that! Shimano wants to issue a Finn Horn Musky Sombrero!"

Laurel laughed.

"You're just jealous that I'm famous," he said indignantly. "The company that made my CO2 life vest gives me five thousand bucks every time I tell some reporter how that thing saved my life. I mention it on TV and I get ten grand!" The kid giggled like he had been breathing nitrous oxide.

In the past week, Finn had been on the cover of absolutely every fishing magazine in the world, his fame even spreading to *Time Magazine* and a spot on *Good Morning America*. Shannon had taken over as his PR manager and the boy would be famous for quite a while, at least in fishing circles. But back behind it all, Gavin knew that this was just a temporary reprieve; Finn was still sick. And getting sicker. But he was here now and that's what Gavin thought about.

The surrogate adopted son he was somehow sharing his life with.

Finn's grin cut short. "Oh, forgot, there's a cop up at the house. Wants to talk to you," he said.

"Really?"

"Yeah. Says that Sheriff Pope's gone missing. They found his cruiser not far from here and thought that you might have seen him."

"Great," Gavin said flatly.

"I'll go put on some coffee," Laurel said and headed up the steps.

"Take out doughnuts!" Finn added. "Cops *love* doughnuts."

"I don't have any doughnuts," Laurel replied.

"Too bad. We could have made friends with the guy."

Gavin and Finn stayed at the water's edge, staring out at the bay. A little while after Laurel had disappeared into the house, Gavin turned to the boy. "I better go see what this guy wants. If I'm lucky he'll tell me that Pope's gone for good."

Finn smiled up at Gavin. "Don't worry. Sheriff Pope ain't coming back anytime soon."

"How can you be so sure?"

Finn held up a pair of empty blue shotgun shells. "Trust me," the little boy said, smiling.

Gavin left Finn at the water's edge, staring out at the bright day ahead. Mr. Johannus was coming down the stairs, his tool belt over his shoulder, mumbling to himself, no doubt about the yunky yoists.

"Morning, Mr. Johannus," Gavin said automatically. His thoughts were wrapped around the two empty shells Finn had just given him.

The old carpenter stopped and pushed up his hat, the movement showing that he expected Gavin to stop, too. So he did.

"Morning, Mr. Gavin. I'm off to install the last window on the boathouse. Got to glue the sash and we're off to the races."

Gavin figured that he was expected to nod, so he did. "What about the yoi—um, I mean joists?"

"Yoists? Yoists? Why the yoists are fine, Mr. Gavin. Great old big hemlock yoists are the best there is. And now that I've sistered the cracked ones and repaired the ones that had rotted out at the ends, the yoists don't need me anymore. I'm a sash man, now, Mr. Gavin." The man's warm blue eyes crinkled up with a smile and he examined Gavin's face for a few awkward seconds, as if he were trying to make a decision. Finally, he said, "I also wanted to thank you—it's about time somebody killed that fucking fish."

The old carpenter tipped his cap and continued off to the boathouse, in search of a sash to glue instead of a yoist to mend. *Progress*, Gavin thought, and turned back to the old house on the hill.

# 105

It was a little after three a.m. and the only noise was the sound of the trees shifting in the wind outside and the soft wheeze of the coffee maker. In between those two disynchronous noises, the world was silent and still. He leaned against the counter, watching the pot fill. He was aware that there were still things to do, amends to be made, and he had to get to them before it was too late. After filling a mug he walked through the dining room, nodding a hello to the cat on the stone hearth, absorbing latent warmth from last night's fire. In way of a response the cat farted and rolled over, stretching its wide paws toward the embers.

He stood in the doorway of his office for a minute and the old feeling came at him, the one he used to have way back when it had only been him and the night and the work. Before the deadlines and the specter of an audience over his shoulder had changed it all. He stood there for a few moments, sipping his coffee and wondering if he could be that version of himself again. Or if not that one, at least an acceptable replacement.

It took a minute for the MacBook to come to life, and when he logged in he was glad that Shannon had installed Word for him. He opened the program and formatted his document—double-spaced with no extra break between paragraphs, Times New Roman in a size twelve. Same old, same old.

And he began to write.

# 106

...a few hundred yards below the dam, a small bay—little more than an indent in the shore—swirled with flotsam and other debris that had pulsed through the gates of the dam. In this shallow fingerprint pressed into the shoreline, a dark shadow throbbed below the surface, undulating to the heartbeat of the water pushing by. It wasn't a solid mass, but a collection of tiny bits of darkness glued together, sucking in light. It had no form to speak of, just an amorphous outline that changed with the current.

A fox poked her head from the tree line at the edge of the small bay and sniffed at the damp air that washed down the roaring rapids that trailed the dam. Using whatever risk-assessment software she possessed, she decided that all was safe, and trotted out to the water's edge, her three yearling kits following lazily behind. The pups were almost as large as their mother, and would soon be finding their own dens for the winter, their summer of training over. The animals moved easily over the polished rocks of the shore, threading their way over old tires, dented and paint-worn beer cans, and chunks of other human detritus that the dam had spit out. Up-current the roar of the dam was an audible thrum, but it didn't frighten her—in fact, she barely heard it at all; she had lived here all her life and had become comfortable with the noise. She went to the water's edge, bent her front paws, and leaned in to drink.

The shadow below the surface deepened, sucked in light, and reflected it back in a rainbow of iridescent hues.

Then it exploded from the water, a solid body of interwoven particles that twitched and cracked. The fox lifted off her front feet, tried to turn. To run. The seething mass fastened onto her snout. She yelped and was yanked, headlong, into the roiling mass of wet darkness.

She howled and screeched as the cockroaches tore her to pieces. Flipped her. Spun her. Consumed her. Blood spurted, bathing the black crackling body, and it pulsed deeper, radiating color—radiating *joy*.

Her pups sat back on their haunches, dumb, hypnotized, and unable to move. When the last of her marrow was swallowed by the flurry of tiny gnashing jaws, the shadow throbbed and rose from the water, a clattering insect mass that ticked and twitched and jerked toward her puppies.

The body of cockroaches kicked stones aside as it lurched forward on shaky legs, stumbling drunkenly. Clumps of wet, matted hair hung off the almost-formed head, and a dark mouth opened below the obsidian eyes of the thing. It stretched in the morning sunlight, black arms sprouting out, formed of the whirling insects that moved as one being.

The thing stopped before the three cowering pups and the black face spread into a twisted version of a smile. The hole it used as a mouth opened and a wet gurgling scream bubbled out. Black water and blood and slop spilled down its chin.

It coughed, vomited more oil-like bile, cleared its throat. For a moment it stood there, seeming to assess its canine audience, its chest heaving with the heavy breaths it sucked in. Then, in a voice that sounded like a fish being squeezed in a vice, said, "It's disco time, fuckwits."

And a slimy cloud of insects spewed from the dark hole in its face.

# Author's Note

It should be noted that all of the details pertaining to the Mannheim Pike, or Emperor's Pike as he is also known, have been taken from documented sources that date back to the sixteenth century.

The tale first appeared in print in 1558 in *Historia animalium III* by Conrad Gesner and has been found in various forms in angling books ever since.

The narrative's first appearance in English that I am aware of was in William Samuel's *The Arte of Angling*, published in 1577 (of which only a single copy is known to exist). There are only two illustrations in *The Arte of Angling*—one a detailed line drawing of a copper ring that Frederick the Second placed on the famous fish of Mannheim when it was deposited in the moat in the year 1230. For centuries this story was taken seriously by both academics and laymen alike; it's the kind of story fishermen *want* to believe. All of the details in my novel, including the fish's age, weight, and length, were taken from this source.

The Natural History Museum in London has a painting from the seventeenth century depicting this same fish. In the top right corner of the canvas is the text:

"THIS IS THE BIGGNESS OF THE PIKE, WHICH THE EMPEROR FREDERICK THE SECOND WITH HIS OWN HAND, HATH PUT THE FIRST TIME INTO THE A POOLE AT LAUTERN; AND HATH

MARKED HIM WITH THIS RING IN THE YEARE 1230. AFTER-
WARDS HEE BROUGHT HIIM TO HYDELBERG THE 6 OF NOVEM-
BER 1497. WHEN HE HE'D BEENE IN THE POOLE 267 YEARES."

This painting is unsigned and there is no record of how it came to be in the museum's collection.

Anyone who has read more than a handful of angling books has come across this legend in one form or another.

All in all, I have tried to stay as true to musky fishing techniques as the limits of this story allowed. When musky fishermen find something lacking in my details I hope they afford me the use of artistic license.

Above all, I hope they enjoy this book for what it is—a story about finding friends in unlikely places.

And a tale of monsters.

～ RP

# About the Author

Robert Pobi is a former antiques dealer and an avid fisherman. Originally from Montreal, he now splits his time between a cabin in the mountains and the Florida Keys. Author of the international bestselling psychological thriller *Bloodman*, Pobi writes every day at a desk that once belonged to the enigmatic Italian banker Roberto Calvi.